First published in paperback in Great Britain

www.rhonawhitefordauthor.com

Text © Rhona Whiteford 2020

Rhona Whiteford asserts the moral right to be identified as the author of this work

Editor: Liz Harris

Cover design: Lucy McSpirit - Freelance Graphic Designer

Cover painting: Rhona Whiteford

ISBN   978-0-9957483-1-6

.

All rights reserved.
No part of this publication may be
reproduced, stored in a retrieval system or transmitted in
any form or by any means, electronic, mechanical,
photocopying, recording or otherwise without the prior
written permission of the publisher.

.

Printed and bound by

Flexipress Printing Ltd

Unit 1, Windmill Avenue, Ormskirk,

Lancashire L39 4QB

Rhona Whiteford lives in Lancashire, England with her family and their animals.

She has been writing professionally for 30 years.

ALSO BY THE AUTHOR

Breaking Points

And coming soon:

The Undertaker's Daughter

www.rhonawhitefordauthor.com

CHILDREN'S NOVELS

Mac

Stolen

Dave the donkey's diary

On a knife's edge

Coming to get you

The horror of Henley's Hole

Trouble in Transylvania

Ten minutes of terror

Time Lord trauma

The diamond and the bear

The haunting of Swallows' Hall

The sign of the snake

The secret of the tomb

The task of the Devourer

Valentina Seraphina

www.wildbooks4children.com

THE HOUSE BETWEEN TIME

Rhona Whiteford

For my mum, Nancy,

who taught me to read and was lovely.

Aberffraw, Anglesey

AD 1228

Beyond a common joy...

Gonzalo – The Tempest

WILD, RINGING CRIES filled the air; a flight of oystercatchers raced along the beach, chased by the spray of the rising tide. Nest stood at the end of the estuary with her face to the open sea, her skirts, her hair, her brychan stretched out behind her by the strength of the inshore wind. And she laughed aloud. She ran towards the waves, now holding her brychan aloft like a war banner, spun around and danced for pure joy of the bright Autumn day. Her feet took her under the cliffs where the sea left its flotsam and she stopped to gather a huge heap of driftwood for the fire; some she took with her and the rest she left for later. No one would take it, knowing it hers in this place.

She decided to make for home before the tide cut off the way round the cliffs; this time she was buffeted along, forced to skip several paces with each gust. But she hadn't gone far when she heard the sound of playful barking and yipping, and turning, she saw a pair of wolves racing towards her down the beach. As they came they carried on their game, leaping and snapping, feinting and ducking.

'Come on, my beauties! Well met!' Nest cried, and no sooner were the words from her mouth than they were on her, jumping up, a paw resting on her hip to lick her mouth, her ears, her face. They ran around her legs trapping themselves in her skirts, twirling and barking in an ecstasy of greeting.

'You have had a good hunt, I see,' she told them, catching one round the neck with her free arm and grimacing as the wolf rubbed its blood smeared mouth on her shoulder. 'Rub yourself on a rock. Be off!' she cried, pushing it away, laughing.

And after a little more of this happy reunion she said, 'Come,

All three continued their way along the beach, heading towards a small house that stood on a jutting rock. It was surrounded with a low wall made of stones, stones of all colours and shapes, all smooth and gifted by the sea. Further down the estuary stretched several cottages of similar style, but none made of stone like the house on the rock, which was hers. The others were made of wattle and daub, roofed with turf and they belonged to fishermen and their families. Every front yard was festooned with nets and crowded with baskets and children, hens and rope. Each dwelling had a low-walled fish trap and a boat moored by the wall yet resting on the hard sand, for soon the coming tide would swell the river to the width of a lake and the boats would be lifted, bouncing on the swell. Nest could hear the shouts of the men and their families as they loaded the boats ready to go with the tide. She waved a greeting and it was returned by those who saw her.

Not far from her own wall was a small island of rocks interrupting the smooth stretch of sand, and on the landward side of the rocks the swirling tides had carved a deep rock pool. Here the treasures of the sea hid until the water returned. Nest had often found unusual things in this pool, so she stopped to see what riches lay caught today.

'Will there be pearls this time, hid in their tight blue shells?' she murmured as she put her wood to one side and knelt to look.

In the lee of the rocks the air was still and the water glassy calm, crystalline too. She gazed into the depths and at first saw only her own reflection, then in turn, each of the wolves who came to see what she did, only to disappear again before she could blink. She looked past the surface into the depths, finding bright anemones, open and busy, clusters of tiny creamy clams, a strand of lime green sea grass and some rosy bladder wrack.

'But no oysters...'

She smiled, leaning down on her forearms to watch the tiny fry darting away from her shadow, then withdrew a little to use the smooth surface as a mirror. Her hair had been dragged from its plaits by the wind. But as she gazed, she realised that she could see a face in the water that was not her face. It was so like hers yet could not have been because the young woman's dark hair was long, loose and wild and behind her were lightning lit clouds that raced across a night sky. It poured with rain and the woman was drenched.

Nest craned forward. 'What is she…who?' she wondered aloud as she watched. Visions such as this, in the waters, were a familiar experience because she was gifted with the power to scry.

'What has happened to you?' she whispered to the face. 'What has frightened you?'

The woman moved and Nest saw that directly behind her was a wholly familiar rock on a beach, and on it stood a house that was surely Nest's own with a little wall surrounding it. The colossal storm raged all about and as Nest watched the woman closely she saw the moment she turned and recognized the house with relief and longing.

'You know it. You are thankful,' she gasped. 'But who are you?'

Chapter one

Aberffraw, Angelsey

AD 2020

Flight

Hell is empty and all the devils are here...

Ariel – The Tempest

BEA CHOKED as blood and seawater filled her mouth. She spat most of it out and tried to drag in a breath, but before she could manage that another deluge hit her. Blood poured from her nose and from a savage cut across her cheekbone. The dressing that had covered it hung on by a single corner and flapped wildly against her face. She snatched it off. The wind and the sea roared in concert, but she barely noticed because she was focusing on breathing and putting one foot after another. She fought her way along the beach path from the village, heading towards the wilderness of roaring darkness, the yawning mouth of the estuary and the open sea. Midnight and the worst storm in living memory, people said later.

What drove her on was fear – the fear of pursuit.

We'll be safe in the cottage, she told herself. *Can't even see it yet! You're a mess, Bea. God! What a mess.*

Wind tore over the water, ripping inland across the wide sands. The going was hard against the wind; sand and stones dragged at her feet, gorse bushes clawed at her coat. Huge waves grew into monumental ones, reaching up and up with arms of spray hurling their load inland with violent intent.

Bea's hair was turned into sodden ropes that slapped her savagely, but she didn't feel anything. She couldn't grab hold of the hair because one arm was injured, and the other was gripping a small dog cocooned under her coat. The long, padded coat was drenched; it sabotaged each movement, dragging her every which way with grasping hands and the backpack she carried bumped awkwardly against her bottom.

Ice coursed through her veins; the cold was intense and numbed physical sensations so that all she focused on was getting to the safest place she knew and far away from him. Need drove her on, but even out there on Aberffraw beach at midnight and in a storm, she looked behind constantly.

Yet she was jubilant, jubilant and terrified because she'd finally escaped – *they'd* finally escaped, she and her dog, Archie. She'd snatched at the first chance of escape, didn't know how she'd summoned up the energy or more importantly, the courage, but she had. And Archie, who was very old, had looked barely alive when she got him out of the cellar. Bea felt like screaming, finally letting go, there on the beach, and as it dawned on her that she could do just that, she stopped in her tracks. She threw back her head and screamed and screamed, only knowing what she did by the feel of her throat because the noise of the storm was immense.

Then she carried on walking.

Keep going, keep going, Bea told herself. *One day I'm going to kill him. He won't hurt me again and he won't touch Archie. Ever. I'm going to poison him or stab him or push him under a train. I'm pathetic...But I'm going to make sure he knows it's me - and that I'm all right and I hate him. I got away.*

Bea cried loudly as she struggled on. Tears, snot and blood ran unnoticed.

Earlier that day when she'd fled from Manchester, Jeremy, her husband, had left for the airport at four in the afternoon to catch a plane to Prague. He was going to speak at a conference on new developments in neurosurgery. He'd announced in the morning that someone had dropped out at the last minute and he'd been asked to step in, he'd be away all weekend. Would she be alright?

He'd chatted away as he packed his briefcase, as though the world were a bright and lovely place. She'd been astonished. She'd held herself rigid as he pottered round and thought that if he really did go, she would bite the bullet, snatch her handbag and passport and just walk out of the door, then get on a train to anywhere: Orkney, Oslo, Okinawa - anywhere. Perhaps she'd be safe in a war zone? Maybe she should join Médicins Sans Frontières; doctors were always needed. But there was Archie. So, they'd go to the Shetland Isles, Orkney or somewhere else remote and dog friendly.

In the end, before he left, he'd put down his overnight case and his sturdy leather briefcase and looked steadily at her. She waited at a little distance. He'd kept eye contact and took his leather gloves from his pocket, drew them on carefully, as though he were putting them on for surgery. Suddenly, he took a stride forward and drawing back his right arm he smashed his fist into her face. Much later she realised he'd only used enough force to shock and hurt her but not to damage his hands – his surgeon's hands. Nevertheless, the blow had thrown her off her feet, and she'd landed on her back on the hall floor, stunned and gasping. Her eyes blurred and through the singing mist of pain and shock she'd seen him carefully remove his gloves, which he put in his pocket, then gather up his bags and open the door. The last thing he'd said before he shut the front door carefully was:

'Stay here until I return. Understand?'

Then he'd left.

She'd heard someone whimpering and it was some minutes before she realised it was her own voice. She'd managed to sit up and gingerly examine her sore face, then she opened her eyes and looked around to make sure he'd really gone. She'd strained her ears for any tiny sound that would tell her he was in the house somewhere but heard nothing except a persistent and strangely familiar noise that had been going on for some time. It was somewhere in the background and it took several more minutes of painful concentration for her to recognise Archie's bark; it was faint, and she could tell, it was angry.

She'd hardly believed it. He was alive. Jeremy had taken him last night and told her she might have him returned, depending on her behaviour. She'd begged him not to take the dog, which was a mistake, she knew, because he liked her to beg.

She'd cried most of the night, fear for Archie's safety keeping her alert, then when she'd asked about him next morning, Jeremy had ignored her completely.

There was an echoing note to the sound and then once she understood this, she knew where it was coming from. It was the cellar, the cellar of their Victorian house. Jeremy had locked him in the cellar, and he was barking and clawing at the door to be let out.

Bea managed to crawl to the cellar door and reached the handle only to fall back sobbing because the key wasn't in the lock, so she pulled herself to her feet and with her head still swimming and her nose bleeding freely she made her way to the utility room and found a hammer. She pounded on the door handle until it broke, but it couldn't be opened so she smashed a hole in the wood panel above the lock and finally reach her hand in to turn the lock from the inside. In seconds, Archie was free. He staggered through and was on her lap trying to jump up and lick her face. He was filthy, thirsty and hungry, and terrified, but he was with her again.

Hours later she was struggling to reach the end of her journey. It was impossible to see any landmarks until lightning tore the sky apart. The first ragged bolt was followed by myriad others so close together that they seared the Earth with an eldritch light. When Bea tried to shield her eyes, the vision was instantly replaced inside her eyelids by fluorescent images of the same pebbles and sand, the same sea and cliff. The images pulsed sharply, hurt unbearably and blinded her briefly. And the lightning was partnered by thunder so loud and so long that it made the ground shake, the movement and sound becoming a single element.

A colossal storm raged. Bea understood then how wholly insignificant and vulnerable any human was in the face of such a force. The next crack of thunder and lightning knocked her off her feet. She stumbled over a rock and threw out an arm to break the fall, but it was her injured arm because the other was holding the dog and she twisted to avoid landing on him. She felt so sick with the pain that she slipped and her head bumped painfully on the rough path. She landed sprawled over her backpack.

'Bugger, bugger, bugger!' she screamed at the sky.

She still had hold of Archie, but he was squirming against her body and she had to let him go. He shook and looked about him, disorientated, his back hunched, his head down then he tried to shake off the rain off and get back inside Bea's coat. She lay on her back. Now there was sand and seaweed in her mouth, almost impossible to spit out. When she finally managed to lift her head, she saw the cottage was just ahead and felt overwhelmed by emotion, a feeling of pure relief that blotted out everything else for a short time. She scrambled up, retrieved Archie and looked ahead. Lightning flashed again, this time throwing the building into stark silhouette. As she struggled up the beach, she saw that the cottage had been hidden from view by a newly blown sand dune, but there it was, as always, up on its tiny promontory of rock where it had stood sentinel for almost eight hundred years.

Nest's Point, both the rock and the cottage were called now. It stood alone at the end of the long beach, facing the broad estuary and the open sea.

'It's there! God, it's there!' Bea said, as though she dreaded it might not be. Thunder filled her existence again and she stood dazed, trying to get her bearings. She ran a hand carefully down her face, trying to clear off the sand and water; a futile movement. Then she tried to tug her coat down from the position it had taken round her chest when she fell, but it was tight and plastered against her by the wind.

Bea struggled on towards the cottage. The sea roared into the estuary; a heaving wall of water hurling itself against the rocks until, a long minute later, it was sucked back, leaving a mass of flying foam. She stumbled the last ten metres towards the front door and collapsed into the wooden storm porch. It lived up to its name and was a welcome pocket of shelter.

She put Archie on the ground where he stood shaking. She had to fight with her soggy coat to release the key from the pocket, but the small triumph was short lived because when she finally stabbed the key into the lock and heard the satisfying click, finally managed to turn the handle with the uninjured wet hand, the door refused to move.

'Jammed! Of course it is!' she muttered. 'Why? Why won't it open?'

She tried a shoulder barge and only hurt the good shoulder. Her drenched coat clung onto the door.

'Bollocks! Oh, let me in, Auntie Nest!' Bea screamed, as the wind snatched the sound away. She rattled the handle in her annoyance, but then the door simply opened quietly, as though newly oiled. It swung gently inwards.

Well at least it's not creaking like a horror movie prop, she thought.

Archie walked unsteadily and yet determinedly indoors. He went ahead of her and shook himself, spattering everywhere with sea water and rain, then he disappeared into the darkness of main room. Bea took a step in and a deep, deep breath; there was still the scent of herbs, the scent of hot Summer and all the other homely smells of the place. No touch of damp, no dust-laden air, no staleness, no feeling of emptiness or neglect.

She heaved the door shut behind her and slammed the bolts in place, dumped the wet backpack on the floor.

'At last!' she told the air. She slid down the wall in a state of exhaustion, panting with relief, crying as she had done as a child, with open mouth and loud sobs. It was a full five minutes before she attempted to haul herself to her feet. Outside the door the sea breathed heavily.

The sea! You can always hear it even though the walls are so thick. So dark in here. Matches? Where Auntie Nest usually keeps them, of course. Where's Archie? 'Archie!'

She heard him sneeze and then begin a series of grunts and knew instantly that he was scraping up one of his favourite rugs to make a bed for himself. It made her smile inwardly; her face was too cold to manage the movement.

It was pitch dark in the cottage, there weren't even any moon shadows or flashes of lightning just then to show the way, but that wasn't a problem. She stumbled, exhausted, along the passage to the tiny back kitchen and felt the position of the drawer in the dresser with old familiarity. Bea knew to the pace the exact distance to any point in the little house. Then she flicked the light switch in the kitchen, but with no success. It was an automatic reaction, because the electricity usually went off in a storm. When the matches and candles were found, the old oil lamp was lit and as the warm glow began filling the room, Bea gazed around with a sudden and an overwhelming sense of loss and sadness.

Nest was gone. She was dead.

Even bringing this to the front of her mind gave Bea a stab of such anguish that a sob welled up inside her again. She forced it back, waiting for the more usual and comforting sense of belonging. She always felt it here, and she was suddenly wrapped in the old woman's arms, filled with her love and her mystery. It had to be said, Auntie Nest was enigmatic, fey. But Bea relished the sensation and hugged her own wet arms around herself; winced as one arm gave her a sharp reminder of the injury. That brought back the hate, the fear and the disgust that grabbed her throat every single day, and squeezed, squeezed just enough to keep her from losing consciousness, but squeezed until self-loathing and utter helplessness threatened to overwhelm her.

'Oooo, damn, that's sore. And what's more, I used to be able to get my arms right round! It's this stupid coat. I hate it,' she told the air, or whoever was listening. 'And it's you – you're fat, just fat,' she shouted. There seemed always to be someone listening in this cottage. 'He's done this to you, you stupid idiot,' she yelled. 'And you just *let him*, didn't you? You let him hit you too. You let him lock Archie up…'

She lurched from one emotion to another. So, she screamed out loud, not from the physical pain alone, but from the remembrance.

Her head was pounding. She wrestled with the fastening of her wet coat and snapped the long zip in frustration, finally dumping the garment behind the back door. Moving over to the sink, she turned on the cold tap, intending to hold her mouth under the water to drink but winced as the jet hit her nose. It was agony, her whole body hurt, so she turned the water to a trickle and, closing her eyes, she moved her face this way and that under the stream until it felt numb. Blood, streaks of mud and sand and even a piece of seaweed were left in the sink.

Bea patted her face cautiously with the tea towel, then as she reached over the sink to draw the curtains across the little window, a thought came to her. She closed her eyes. It was impossible to see anything out there on a night like this, instead she looked with her mind's eye at the long rock and the hillside sweeping away from the back yard. It had been hollowed from the bedrock centuries ago. She saw the late Summer flowers dancing in the meadow grasses: the cornflowers, cranesbill, purple thistles and dog daisies. She gazed at them inwardly, seeing the old metal tubs in the yard overflowing with herbs, especially the nasturtiums her auntie loved for their colour and cheeky scrambling habit.

Bet they seeded themselves, but this storm will've flattened everything. Mind you, Auntie Nest loved this time of year; tidying up after storms, getting ready for harvest.

Bea began wringing out her hair over the sink and tears ran down her face. She was soaked to the bone and beginning to shiver. Auntie Nest had loved her hair: 'It's your Welsh heritage, cariad; long, dark and wild like mine used to be,' she would say. 'Now I'm silvered as the moonlight, and twice as bright!'

I need to get dry, must get these things off. Where's my backpack?

It was where she dumped it, dripping quietly; it waited behind the front doorway which led straight from the sandy garden path on top of the rocks and directly into the living room. She carried the oil lamp to light her way into the living room and found Archie had done as she thought; he had scrabbled up a sheepskin rug into a rough mound and was curled up on the top of it.

'Little sausage!' she said, affectionately, and rubbed his head. She lifted the whole heap up, with him in place and put it on the settle by the fireplace, out of the draughts, then covered him with a woollen brychan.

'Your fur lets in the water, sausage. I'll get you a warm drink in a minute. You'll dry out now.'

She put a match to the fire, which was ready laid and told him, 'We're not going back, don't worry, Arch. You're going to retire here, in peace.'

He'd been her mum's dog, but was hers now, since she had died too. Archie was white, with brown patches over his ears and a tawny spot on his back, with irresistible rough fur one could bury one's fingers in. A Jack Russell terrier Auntie Nest had called 'nicely matured', being eighteen years old.

Bea watched him turning around in his new nest a few times until, finally satisfied, he laid his head down with a grunt and closed his eyes. Only then did she take the oil lamp and make her way slowly upstairs to the two bedrooms under the eaves. She stepped into each, the lamp held up, and saw, by the soft light, that everything was as it should be. She lingered a little longer, gazing at everything in the smaller room, ran a hand along the edge of the cupboard by the door, feeling the familiar texture, and finally set the lamp carefully on it. Only then did she go back downstairs to get her backpack.

Why didn't I leave it in the car? If it had been low tide, I could have driven the car up the beach, like I used to do, instead of flopping along like a stranded jelly fish. Damn. No one'll bother about it at the pub; they know it's mine. It's okay round the back.

She knelt to open the pack on the landing then paused, listening.

'Nothing,' she said aloud. 'Silence, silence.'

The pack was a testament to panic, things stuffed in haphazardly. There were a couple of Summer tops, a single shoe and a pair of grubby old jeans which were nostalgic remnants of long past student days and unworn since then.

Why are they here? What do I want them for? Stupid.

There were two of her favourite books, part of her life before she met him - Jeremy. The jeans were crumpled around an old portable typewriter that couldn't be left behind because it had belonged to her mum who'd been a novelist. The last of these treasures was her stethoscope, which every doctor needs but just then she couldn't face because it was part of the life she'd escaped from, so she rammed it under the books.

Bea had stopped on her journey down the coast to draw out money from her own private current account, one Jeremy didn't know of, and she'd bought a basic phone because he had taken her own from her. It was hidden in the house, the former home she'd escaped from six hours earlier. She couldn't believe she'd got this far.

But what did I expect? Will he follow me? No, he's in Prague. He loves being the centre of attention. He's there.

Her hands had been shaking as she paid for the new phone at a supermarket and the assistant at the check-out had eyed her strangely, asked if she was okay. Bea's hand had flown to her bruised cheek, sure that that was what the woman was curious about, so she tried to smile and explain that she'd fallen, but she knew she hadn't been believed when she saw the sceptical expression on the woman's face.

Now, in the cottage, she pushed the episode away, sighed deeply; the knot of terror inside her was tight but the idea that maybe things could be okay was growing. She craved safety – just that.

Safety, quiet, peace, ran through her mind, a mantra.

It was unusual for her to be physically alone, apart from Archie that is, with no one watching her every movement, restricting, demanding, and accusing. And it was odd to be able to decide what to do next, not to be waiting in fear for the next instruction or insult, or for the door to be unlocked in the morning. Worst of all was knowing she should have run away before now. Each day at work, she could have gone – escaped. What worried her more than anything was that she hadn't. She'd carried on, looking calm, competent, in control.

So, with that jewel-like feeling of owning her own actions for the present, and trying to ignore the pounding of her headache, she went down and lit the fire in the tiny kitchen range; the one in the living room was going nicely. Both had been made ready after the funeral by Bea herself.

She'd been quite alone in the cottage then, apart from Nest's good neighbours who dropped in for a while. Bea was her only surviving family member; she was Nest's great niece; her grandmother had been Nest's younger sister. Jeremy had allowed her to leave for three days, excusing himself because he had, 'Some very sick patients and life-saving neurosurgery can't be put on hold for quaint coastal funerals!'

That had been in the Spring and it had been a desperate Summer to follow. She shivered and with sudden decision clambered back upstairs and stripped off every item of wet clothing, dried herself slowly and dragged on a warm jumper and loose joggers that she'd left here in the bedroom cupboard. She used an old scarf as a sling for her sore wrist.

'At least *these* clothes aren't tight. I'm a wreck. And I'm weak. Would Mum or Auntie Nest recognise me - the person I've become?'

She spoke aloud, and her voice was flat. She stared at her reflexion in the little mirror on the chest of drawers. Her brown eyes were bloodshot, sitting expressionless in a sallow, fleshy face, made even more puffy now because of her injury. Her nose was badly swollen and dripped watery blood.

Doesn't feel broken, she reassured herself. *But what a mess.*

Both eyes and cheekbones were reddened and would show a spectacular bruise in a few hours, she knew. The cut on one cheekbone was livid and needed butterfly stitches. She promised herself to deal with that when she got downstairs.

Bea turned away from the ruthless honesty of the mirror. She knew well enough she was two stones overweight. Three years ago she had been a tall attractive brunette, an intelligent person, the witty one in any group, a bookworm, theatre goer, jazz lover, a besotted football fan, full of energy, someone who adored her job, relished its challenge; but now she looked as though her life was a torment.

It was.

So, Bea really didn't know the person in the mirror; she was shocked to see a strange image staring back at her. And it wasn't just the physical person she didn't recognise; she had no sense of herself, her uniqueness as a person, no sense of belonging in her usual everyday surroundings, no direction to go with her life – apart from away from Jeremy.

She raked her fingers through her damp hair which hung almost to her waist. Bea decided there and then that she would never again, as long as she lived, wear it smoothed back and captured in a heavy knot at the base of her neck. She had wrenched out of its fastenings in the car on the way down earlier. Jeremy, her husband, had liked it long and loose at first; he'd said she was the loveliest woman he'd ever met with eyes that had melted his heart, but for the past year or so he'd taken to instructing her to, 'Get it out of the way, get it tied back, get it styled. For God's sake cut it off; smarten yourself up, can't you?'

They'd been married three years and it had been wonderful for the first of them; he had cossetted her, adored her, told her that she had completed his life; she was his companion and soul mate, he was a better man because of her love. Then he'd started giving her advice, which in the beginning she'd listened to, and she'd tried to do what he suggested because he was twelve years older than her and so much wiser. In any case she'd been infatuated, blind to anything but his flattering attention, whatever flavour it took. And even when he'd started his insults, there were times when he said kind things, or, she wondered, had they sounded kind in contrast? But as she turned the painful reminiscences over in her mind, she found she couldn't remember the feelings of being in love.

It was one thirty in the morning. The clock in the living room chimed the half hour; it was a Victorian mantel clock given to Auntie Nest's father by a sea captain, one whose ship had foundered on the nearby rocks. He'd saved the man's life and he'd been grateful – a hundred years ago. Everything Bea's gaze touched in the cottage shouted out its place in her life, inspired one memory after another; a hand-carved wooden candlestick she'd helped make, an ancient pewter mug, a Welsh brychan that Nest herself had woven as a girl which Bea loved to wrap round her shoulders.

The water had boiled; she'd only put a cupful in a little pan on the kitchen range. She put a little warm water in a small bowl for Archie and he lapped it up and ate a couple of dog biscuits she got from the box she kept in the kitchen cupboard for him. Bea had a mug of black tea and a chocolate bar that she found squashed in the bottom of her bag and she began to feel a little better. She'd lit all the lamps and fires and the rooms warmed with more than light and heat, they warmed with life, because Bea had come home to Nest's Point to stay, as Nest had said she would – one day.

She was standing in the living room with another mug of tea, wondering if she should go up to bed or watch out the night in front of the fire until the storm had gone, when Archie growled. He pushed his head from under the brychan, stood up and began to bark, long outraged sequences. There was a hammering thump on the front door that made her slop the tea in fright.

God! Who is it? Is it him? He's followed me. How? How? He's at the airport...or should be in Prague by now.

The thumping came again, and this time a man's voice thundered. The porch managed to amplify and contain his voice so that the wind couldn't snatch it away.

'Who's in there? Come on out! Oy, come out here!' It was a bellow, a deep voice.

Archie leapt up and ran to the door, barking, jumping up at it.

Bea was suddenly filled with dread, cold, clammy dread. She hadn't recognised the voice. Most of the tea had been spilled and she could barely put the mug down on the floor for shaking. Archie continued to bark. She turned slowly to look at the door. The man hammered on it again and her heart began to pound inside her chest, knocking against her ribs. Blood thumped its way round her body leaving her lips bloodless and tight and she bit them as she tried to hold herself together. When the man banged on the glass of the front window, Bea shrieked, a thin feeble noise. She shut her eyes, clenched her hands, digging nails into palms without any sensation at all.

'Oy, you in there; come out! You're trespassing!' the voice yelled loudly. 'I can see you in there! And you've got a bloody dog in there!'

Bea swallowed. *It isn't Jeremy. Maybe he's sent someone? But he doesn't know I've gone, I hope. How could he, unless he's phoned the house?* She crept to the door, scooped up the still furious dog. *How can he see me?* she thought, frantically searching the blank walls near the door for a non-existent window.

Her tongue was glued to the roof of her mouth but with a huge effort she found her voice and screamed, 'Go away!' It was reedy, pathetic, inadequate. Archie continued to bark, his body lunging in her arms with each volley.

'I said open up!'

'Who is it?' It was almost a cry this time. Bea was shaking uncontrollably, her knees felt weak, there was a tight pain growing in her stomach. She thought she'd escaped.

'I said get out here! Can't you shut that animal up?' The voice shouted again, right by the door jamb as though he hadn't heard her, and he rattled the handle. She stared at it moving as if it were a live thing.

Bea looked quickly at the door bolts. *Thank God! Closed. Thank God I did that.*

She put the dog down and he began to scrabble at the bottom of the door, barking, growling, occasionally stopping to cough. Bea cleared her throat and picked up Auntie Nest's 'thumping stick' from the corner and hefted it in her good hand, at least she tried to hold it firmly, but her hand was weak with fear. Nest had named the stick so because it looked like a cudgel; it was an oak root she'd found on the beach.

'Who is it?'

'Open this door. Come on, you shouldn't be in there, whoever you are,' the man called. 'I'm the caretaker. Come on, open up!'

'Go away. I'm not opening the door to a stranger on a night like this. You must be mad!' she screamed back, finally stung into retaliation by the last remark, and feeling some protection behind the stout door and with the cudgel in her hand. 'And there is no caretaker! And I should know!'

'Why, who are you?' The voice was authoritative, demanding.

'I'm the owner' she called triumphantly, hoping that, having played her ace, he would apologise and go away. *Who walks about on a beach in a coastal storm?*

'Who are you? I said,' he yelled again. 'Shut the dog up. It's impossible to hear with all that racket!'

'I won't shut him up. He's guarding. Who are *you*? What are you doing here?' she shouted back. She felt furious now. If only she had been able to charge the new phone, get the police somehow.

'God! Look I'm Dr Roberts and I live at the end of the beach near the bridge,' he bawled. 'I saw a light. Thought it was a boat in trouble. Then I saw it was a light in the windows here and I'm checking the place out. I knew the old lady who lived here.'

She ignored that. 'Which cottage?'

'The bloody yellow one.' This time he was roaring. 'I moved in a month ago when the owner died – old Hywel Hughes. That enough for you? Now open the door! It's terrible out here!'

There was no letterbox and she knew she wouldn't be able to see through the keyhole.

'No! Go away! Go on. Leave me alone.'

He was silent for a short time, so she opened one of the curtains at the tiny front window and held the oil lamp at arm's length to try and see if he had gone, angling it so that she was in shadow. She almost dropped it when a disembodied face appeared on the other side. It was a man's face, as she expected, and soaking wet. His dark fringe was plastered across his forehead, his neck tucked down in his collar and the sea cap he wore shone with water. The rain was so ferocious that it drenched him as if he were under a hose pipe, and coursed down the glass, distorting the image into a melting waxwork. Ghastly, frightening, terrible. His expression was furious, which she hadn't expected. What right had a stranger to be furious with her?

'Can you let me in?' he shouted. 'I'm drenched out here.'

'No, I can't. Just go!' Bea's mouth was dry, the hand holding the lamp shook. She was sweating too. This was too terrifying after the day – the year she'd had. She managed to put the lamp back on its shelf without dropping it. Archie was jumping up at the window ledge, frantic to get at the intruder.

The man bellowed again. 'Y'know what? That's a bit bloody much. I'm only being a good neighbour. I didn't have to come out on a night like this y'know! Who the hell are you anyway?'

She decided that if by some chance he was there to frighten her on Jeremy's behalf, he'd know her name anyway.

But she said, 'I'm Nest's niece,' she shouted back and snapped the curtains closed and retreated to the back of the room, away from the window. *He could smash it of course, but it's too small for a man to get through, surely. And the two doors are oak, centuries old oak.*
Archie followed reluctantly but glared at the window from the edge of the fireplace. He kept up a low rumbling growl.

'Well she would have let me in, I'm telling you.'

She didn't answer.

'I'm only checking everything's okay, y'know!' he bawled again, this time, his voice near the little window.

She heard him bawling something else but couldn't make out the words. Through a crack somewhere in the old house, the wind began to scream a high pitch counterpoint to his voice. There was a dull thump at the door. It sounded as though he'd kicked it, pettish, and final. She assumed if he had gone, the storm would have hidden the noise of footsteps retreating in any case.

Bea scooped Archie up and climbed to the top of the stairs; sat down heavily against the wall. Archie wriggled round to the small of her back and settled there. She stayed where she was for over an hour, alternately shivering with fright and battling with righteous fury at the intrusion, the assault.

Who had she become that not only her husband, but some lunatic who strolled out in storms could treat her like this? And she knew very well what it felt like to be assaulted, abused with words, to have someone shouting, yelling, screaming or even criticising quietly and conversationally.

Chapter two

Imprisoned

This thing of darkness I acknowledge mine…

Prospero -The Tempest

BEA'S HUSBAND, Mr. Jeremy Fitzmartin, Jem to friends, was a consultant neurosurgeon at a Manchester hospital. He was adept at the fine dissection of a personality. He also specialised in the severing of all confidence from the soul, the delicate separation of courage from reason, the dismemberment of self-image into worthless components. However, he was generous with criticism, excelled at the classic put-down and had perfected expressions of disgust for the tiniest mistakes Bea ever made. She noticed that people found him witty as they come; he had everyone chortling whenever he was forced to cover up what he saw as her social incompetence and solecisms with a kindly correction, and a smile of course. That renegade blond fringe did it, of course; it was a charming accessory for a handsome consultant.

At the beginning she knew she wasn't rude or naïve in her conversation but felt, as a newly-qualified doctor amidst the consultants, lawyers and MPs of Jeremy's social circle, that perhaps she should try and be a little more sophisticated, now that she moved in this civilized and heady plane of existence. She was flattered to be included. Blind. The hilarity and bawdiness of the junior common room in the hospital or the pub at university were light years away from the grown-up parties Jeremy took her to. They were charged with challenge, frequented by people with power and money, all watching each other carefully as they guffawed and smiled and touched each other. Jeremy was very tall and thin and had a charming way of bending down to look into a person's eyes if he wanted to impress them with his sincerity, which he often did when he was speaking to a woman. At one time that woman had been Bea.

Jeremy's amusing corrections were always accompanied with an affectionate squeeze of her shoulders, a playful pat on the head once, and astoundingly, 'Never mind, darling, we all have to learn,' on another occasion. As time went on, he would sometimes ignore a remark by simply changing the subject bluntly and it would dawn on her that she'd been crass. People once used to look embarrassed by his treatment of her, but she'd noticed they gave him complicit smiles these days.

When Bea thought about it, she realised he'd been doing this all along, but she'd not noticed until earlier this year; someone they'd met at a party asked her whether she felt any benefit from having therapy because they were thinking of it for themselves. When she'd asked what they were talking about they told her they understood she'd been having psychotherapy for her severe depression for years, and that Jem was so worried about her. He thought the medication wasn't effective enough and he was wondering if she'd be tipped over the edge one day. It was his constant fear because she had people's lives in her hands. Bea had stammered a noncommittal reply and fled to the bathroom to be sick. He denied it when she asked him whether he'd said this about her, adding, 'But if you feel you would benefit, do tell me – I know a good man…'

She was stunned into nodding. Later she thought, *I'm a doctor. How is this happening to me? I'm not ill. I think I'd know. And why would he say this about me? But is he right? Why would he tell other people and not mention this to me?*

Rain lashed the tiny kitchen window as she walked slowly into the room. She boiled some more water for tea. She remembered she'd thrown a couple of sachets of cooked dog food in her backpack and went to get it. Archie was hungry.

The kitchen was what designers would call 'beautifully retro' and its shallow stone sink and 17th century pump would have been snatched away to Knightsbridge if one of them ever got their hands on the property. Bea knew that the tiny ebony cupboard was of the same period and very valuable, but Nest said it was handy for her tea caddy and refused to sell. For Bea, the little room and all its contents were simply treasured as part of her happy childhood.

The stone cottage had stood firmly since it was built in the 12th century and Nest's family had lived there continuously since it was built in the time of Llewelyn the Great. The roof had been changed a couple of times; an upstairs added in the 1890s. There was electricity, indoor plumbing and a tiny bathroom extension but there were items of furniture from many of the preceding centuries scattered in the five rooms, each piece with its own story related by Nest. The iron range in the kitchen was over a hundred years old, put in just before the Great War and as Bea ran her hands over the oven doors, she had sudden memories of baking with Auntie Nest as she grew up. It felt like that had been a century ago.

She made the tea, still reeling with mingled fury and fear after the stranger's visit, then her mind returned to Jeremy and she thought how, even here and now, he was still demanding her attention, forcing his way into her consciousness.

Not long after that party and her challenge, his behaviour towards her took a different turn. In private, although he began to criticise her openly, his tone was still pleasant. There were constant small oblique criticisms about a variety of things: 'Time keeping's essential for a junior doctor, darling.' 'You're wearing that I see?' '*Sure* you can manage?' '*Not* one of your strongest assets…' 'Stay within your skill range, darling.' 'Does that fit, I wonder?' 'Go and get yourself a beauty treatment or something…do something nice with the hair'.' Then, 'Sort yourself out, Beatrix.'

Bea had been frantic to please him. She tied her hair back, went to the gym, bought clothes, agreed with whatever he said but nothing seemed to make any difference; he continued to belittle her efforts, simply finding a tiny fault with everything she did or said, refusing to look at her unless it was to drive home a criticism. He stopped touching her even going to the lengths of backing away when they were forced into a tight space together. Once, when she'd tried to speak to him in his study, he'd slammed his laptop shut, almost guiltily and told her never to come in there again; it was private. Then one day he moved her things into one of the guest rooms. Eventually when she no longer had the confidence to decide which white coat to put on at work, he'd changed tactics to openly aggressive and unpleasant.

'Beatrix, you are such a slut these days.' 'Pile on the weight if you must, what difference can it make?' 'Working on dreadlocks? Not a look for a professional person, particularly a doctor. A prospective GP can't afford to look more in need of help than the patients. Mind you, do you think you'll manage to complete the training? Really?' 'I can't bear to touch you.' 'A complete turn off for any man.' 'What *is* that smell…?'

It was only around that time that she realised he actively disliked her.

But does he love me? Did he ever love me?

It was a shock that she felt she needed to consider this, and she saw that she'd been very slow on the uptake. She'd married him. She'd committed herself to him – for life. Eventually she knew he hated her but had no idea what she felt for him. Her mind was a blank. She'd gone against all her friends when she'd married him. They were all in awe of him or just plain scared. They were shocked when she said she was even going out with the great *Mr Evil*. When she turned up one day with an engagement ring – a big one, they had laughed. It was a joke, surely? But to go and marry him on a whim, at the Registry Office – secretly? They'd all backed off.

Three years later, here I am in Aberffraw, a wreck, she thought.

That afternoon in Manchester, after he'd left, it took her an hour to get herself and the dog together. She'd sobbed uncontrollably. Her nose was bleeding and her eyes ached; her entire head ached. Everything ached, including her heart. Archie trotted round after her, anxious, quiet.

Eventually she managed to find the medical supplies, plug her nose to stop the bleeding and to put a dressing on her cheek. It was cut. She took painkillers and made tea, some of which she got down before it spilt. Then she crept to the front door and stood listening intently for almost half an hour.

Finally, she made up her mind and packed a bag in a panic. She was barely able to breathe as she did it. She got the dog lead, a couple of packets of cooked dog food, the dog and his blanket. She got her old car out from the back of the garage. She'd found the spare key at the back of one of her drawers. The car was confined in the garage because Jeremy said she couldn't be trusted to drive; he insisted on taking her himself, every day, to the central Manchester hospital where they both worked. Of course, she could have walked out of the hospital any time during the day, but she never did. She had no idea why.

Faced with the car and no opposition, Bea's stomach felt full of cold dread and she was nauseous and drenched with sweat. Archie lay wrapped up in his blanket in the back, curled up, shivering with anxiety. It took her long fearful seconds to remember where the ignition was and then four tries to fire the engine up; she was clumsy with terror by the time it did. She almost forgot how to drive.

What frightened her particularly was that, up until that day, Jeremy hadn't left her alone at home. For the past fortnight he had locked her bedroom at night, 'for your own safety'. He said she'd been sleep-walking. And he told her he was having her watched at work. She needed to be watched there, he said, for everyone's safety.

She was puzzled too because whenever he caught her talking to any other man at work or socially, he would then refuse to speak to her for the rest of the day. She wondered why he had left her to her own devices, but her head was fairly vague and muzzy these days and she thought the sleeping pills he gave her were perhaps too strong. She ought to be able to sort that out herself, she knew. But as soon as the idea occurred to her, she forgot it.

Bea had no idea why he was so incensed when other men spoke to her. She gave him no cause for blame on that score. She hadn't the energy to look at another man. If the man he suspected were a patient he reminded her that it was unprofessional to lust after a person one treated; if it were another junior doctor he would mock her, saying she retained that student mentality and enquired if they all sniggered as they reminisced about their rotation on obs and gynae. If it were a man he judged to be above her status, he demanded curtly that she refrain from embarrassing him with his peers with her pathetic sexual advances. Did she feel she was a nymphomaniac? If she spoke to a hospital porter or electrician, he chuckled maliciously about lower class birds of a feather flocking together. That was another puzzle, because her parents were extremely middle-class academics; her mother was a famous literary novelist and her father had been a professor of chemistry.

So, she avoided speaking to Jeremy's friends at all and developed the habit of constantly looking over her shoulder if she had to speak to any other men on a routine matter at work, or anywhere. Even her old friend, Rob, charge nurse on one of the obs and gynae wards said, 'What's up with you? You used to be the life and soul! Are you feeling okay?' She hadn't had the courage to answer him.

Jeremy insisted her salary go into a joint account and calmly took her bank card from her when he became openly hostile. She was mystified as to why she allowed that and many other things he'd done. The one comfort was her secret bank account her mother opened for her before she died. She told her not to tell Jeremy, 'just keep it for a rainy day'. So she had. Her mum, Eleanor, hadn't liked him at all. Jeremy also took Bea's phone when she was off-duty and he hid her own laptop at home and somehow managed to monitor her email account at work. It seemed that his reach was everywhere at once.

For the past twelve months he refused to share a bed and had sent her to the guest room, the one with the door lock. He said she unmanned him, she disgusted him with her pathetic needs. He found her repulsive. He taunted her by saying, 'You know, I can be myself, be a man, a *real* man with other women.'

Bea then found herself speculating lamely if he were telling the truth and then wondering which women he was speaking about. What did he do with them? Were they at the hospital? Who were they?

Then he asked, 'Why is it you stay? Why are you here at all, sponging on me? Nowhere to go, Beatrix, now Auntie is dead and gone for good? How on Earth do you even exist if you are so very *unnecessary*?'

When she replied that she would go, he rounded on her, his eyes blazing triumph, and in a vicious whisper replied, 'Ah, so that is actually what you want. I thought so. I might have known you had no staying power. Ha! Easy for you to abandon me but I can't allow it. You would embarrass me unbearably; people would talk, and I can't have you tarnishing my reputation. No, Beatrix, you are going nowhere. I'm your husband and I'm going to look after you for as long as it takes.'

'As long as what takes?' she asked but he left the room, closing the door firmly. Then she worried about which of the statements had been true. Did he need her? Did she need him in some twisted way? The first time he'd locked her bedroom door she was so shocked that she tried to push past him. He simply took hold of a fistful of her hair, almost tearing it from her scalp and threw her in – then locked the door. She was stunned by the action itself and by his terrible and unexpected strength and she just lay where she landed for some time, just as she had when he punched her. That was the second incident of physical violence. Both shocked her more than his disdain because she had never seen such behaviour in him before. It seemed out of character, unexpected because of his profession and yet, and yet – a tiny admonishing voice told her she knew it was entirely him.

When he told her to go to her bedroom the next night, she walked in and allowed him to lock the door behind her without any objection at all. Then the night before she escaped, when he was about to lock the door, she surprised herself by whispering pathetically:

'Please don't, Jeremy. Please...'

His expression did not change; he pushed her further into the room with an outstretched arm and a single finger on her chest, then he smiled and closed it in her face, locking it with a jangling, metallic flourish.

Bea knew without doubt that she hated him, loathed, and much worse than that, she feared him, and for some time she'd recognised with growing panic that she had to get away. The problem was that she couldn't find the right opportunity or the will. The will. And she was so tired, so tired all the time.

Eventually she realised what had happened. He had diminished her. She couldn't even show a kindness to anyone or make a sympathetic remark without him staring at her accusingly and later commenting on her needy behaviour.

'D'you know, Beatrix, you're like a female Uriah Heap - just desperate for people to approve of you in any way. It's sickening.'

When he punched her in the face and coolly instructed her to stay, she found that was the very tiny chance she needed, and she fled into the night, a hundred and twenty miles to her Auntie Nest's home in the village of Aberffraw, Anglesey. It was hers now. He didn't know that, she was certain. And she'd taken with her the one living thing that loved her unconditionally, her dog.

So, the man who'd come shouting at her in the storm that night was nothing compared to Jeremy.

But all the same, this stranger in the night had unnerved her. Surely that was a normal reaction? She wandered anxiously between the kitchen and living room until she was certain the unwelcome neighbour had really gone. The repetitive action was soothing. Her hands shook unbearably as she made yet more tea to take back to the fire in the living room. Archie lay curled up in front of it now and she got down next to him and sat cross legged. The fire had burnt down but was revived with another log and some twigs and she crouched on a small stool right inside the nook. Auntie Nest had pushed bits of sea-glass into little gaps between the stones and it they glimmered in the light of the dancing flames.

The light caught her wedding ring and the huge solitaire diamond of her engagement ring. He'd given her that a week before they were married, saying he wanted everyone to know what she meant to him. Bea had been swept away. She put the mug on the hearth and spilled most of the tea in her haste to pull the rings off.

'Swollen. Damn. Come on, come on,' she muttered between gasps of pain, but it was no use and she gave up when she'd wrenched enough to make her finger bleed and swell even more. She leant against the stone hearth and cried silently.

Bea could feel, rather than consciously hear, the distant growl of the sea. It was ever present, a fixed point of nature which, although it could be terrifying, it was natural, its power unchanging and eternal. She found that comforting. The storm was rumbling in the far distance so that the sea's own voice was all she could hear.

She thought about the cottage, watched herself in her mind's eye as she had looked around earlier. It was as though Auntie Nest had just left for a walk on the beach and would be back any minute; everything seemed as normal, everything *clean*. In her bedroom, Nest's glasses were in the open case on the white bedside drawers. Her books were still in the usual piles of different subjects, some left open on the table by the window. Her bed, with its masses of pillows, was neatly made and the knitted blue counterpane hugged the bed and beamed invitingly as it always had done. She'd adjusted the earthenware flower jug on the wide sill, it was bursting with dried grasses and sea holly. Bea herself had filled it on the day of the funeral and that had been months ago. They weren't even dusty, nothing was. Everything was as normal and that's what she expected. Being related to Nest meant that you were surrounded by things that were sometimes weird and other-worldly and Bea accepted this. It was everyday magic.

The other bedroom had been hers ever since she was a small child.

Dry and clean and lovely. The sea-green stone jar, still there on the sill – all that lovely long, heaven-scented lavender. I adore it. The perfume just fills the air. Everything smells new and Summery in the whole house. And there was my lilac counterpane with all its little knobbles and knots. Those lovely twisted rope stitches and fringes where they're least expected. I love that, she thought.

The cottage was filled with Nest's presence and Bea hugged it to herself, felt the beginnings of being comforted.

As she sat and watched the fire her head nodded, but she felt herself jerk awake every few seconds, unable to relax properly. So, she leaned forward, hands outstretched to warm them, and as she stared into the fire, her eyes began to pick out shapes in the flames. She always did this as a child. Auntie Nest used to ask her what she saw, encouraged her to tell the story of what she imagined was there. Slowly she became aware that her eyes were focused sharply on the flames; she began to make out, not shapes, but figures moving.

Chapter three

Summons

While you here do snoring lie, open eyed conspiracy his time doth take, If of life you keep a care, shake off slumber and beware. Awake, awake...

Ariel – The Tempest

IT WAS ALMOST three o'clock in the morning. Bea rubbed her eyes and bent closer to the fire, saw that the figures moving there in the flames were walking stealthily abroad; they were outdoors. They were creeping around a cottage, *this very cottage*, and it seemed to be daytime because she saw high, wispy clouds and the sun. Every detail was clear; they were all strong young men in their prime, warriors, dressed alike in red woollen tunics, knee length cloaks with good leather boots. No marauders these. Their dark hair was trimmed to their shoulders and they were clean shaven for the most part but had long drooping moustaches. As they moved around, she couldn't help but notice each had a long knife, kept in its scabbard, not drawn, so it was possible their stealth was not intended for attack.

Bea could smell smoke, but not from the fire next to her in the hearth; it was outdoors, light and fragrant, pine she thought, swirling high in the bright air, part of the flame picture. There was no wind and the bluey plume came from a hole in the roof, not from the chimney, so she wondered sleepily if the chimney had been hit by lightning during last night's storm.

As she watched, a hesitant breeze nudged the column of smoke and sent it drifting across the turf roof to sweep groundward and wrap the men briefly with a diaphanous veil that was so starkly the opposite of their vital masculinity. She could hear them whispering to each other, saw clearly the glint of adventure in their eyes. They looked excited; they were anticipating some fun and after some laughing exchanges with each other; a decision seemed to be made and one of them stalked forward and beat on the cottage door with his fist - full of bravado.

'Ho, Nest! Come forth. Come on. We want you!' he called and glanced over his shoulder to share a grin with his companions.

Bea gasped. *Nest?* She could hear them clearly and as she stared, the images seemed to enlarge and take her into the scene so that it felt as if Bea were actually standing there close by them. Suddenly, as she watched, Bea saw Auntie Nest. The oak door was flung open and there she stood. Only it couldn't be her, Bea knew, because she looked no more than thirty as she appeared in these flame pictures and Auntie Nest had been in her nineties when she died. Bea remembered her with silver hair, not this vibrant dark crown. Was she dreaming about Nest when she was young? The clothes told her that couldn't be, but she remembered that Nest's mother had been named Nest too, and her grandmother, all the first-born girls had been so named for as long back as she could remember, centuries probably.

Bea found herself drawn into the events unfolding yet sensing that she was still separate.

This woman who Bea watched wore the clothes and style of a distant age: a long, olive green dress of fine woollen cloth with a deep russet border, caught at the waist by a braided leather sash with coloured beads threaded along its intricate weave. There was an embroidered design of interlaced leaves around the neckline worked with fine russet silks. Around her shoulders she wore a brychan of soft butter yellow wool and her dark hair was wound in a plait round her head. She was beautiful and fierce.

She spoke to the men.

'Ho, Yestyn. You are the bravest, is it? I see the others hiding behind you. Hywel, do you hide behind your big brother?' Her voice sounded like Auntie Nest's.

'What do the Prince's own guard want with me? Surely his favoured warriors, his Uchelwr, the flowers of his nobility, do not want anything from me?' She paused to laugh. 'Or perhaps you do? Is it a posy of sea pinks or a love potion? No, you must have no need of such favours!'

She smiled broadly, and her face was lit by teasing merriment, full rosy lips parting to show small even teeth like sea pearls, a dimple in the corner of her mouth that made the smile beyond enticing, and eyes that sparkled like gems. They were all held in thrall for long seconds but suddenly sensed her scorn and became uncomfortable in the face of this confidence. One or two of them sniggered weakly.

The leader, this Yestyn, swung round to look for his brother and their friends but they had stepped back. His mouth seemed dry because he licked his lips and began to swallow constantly, looking unnerved.

'My Lord Prince wants you – now. You are to come to the llys. We are to fetch you,' he called, and Bea realised that his voice not as confident as it had been.

'I see. You and four others were sent to *fetch* me? You were to protect me from the thieves and vagabonds I suppose?' she enquired lightly. 'A child would have brought a message. You are the prince's armed guard, his hand-picked knights, where are your spears, your horses? Are you alone? Where are the men of his Teula, the whole hundred and twenty household soldiers he keeps? Have you not brought them also? Is some enemy approaching that I need such a force?'

'They are in…' he began, but his voice trailed off.

Nest smiled. 'I have no need of you,' she said, her voice soft and calm, 'As you know. I have all the guardians I need.' She made a slight motion of her hand and on each side of her appeared a large beast; they were wolves, grey and glittering in the sun as they watched the men. Their pointed ears reached her waist, but then she was a petite figure.

'Oh, Yestyn, Madoc, Gwyn, Hywel, Gwian. I know you all, do I not?' she called the list. 'Why would you want to harm me? I saw you approach, did I not? I heard you plotting, laughing. I know you are afraid now,' she crooned, her voice hypnotic, soft, menacing.

'You are to come!' Yestyn croaked, taking a step back, his fingers crossed to ward off the evil eye. The others were melting away as he turned and then, seeing them flee, he pelted after them.

Nest laughed and stroked the head of each of her guardians.

'Well then, I shall see what my Lord Llewelyn ab Iorwerth, Prince of Gwynedd, Lord of Yr Wyddfa requires of me,' she said grandly to the two wolves. 'How very powerful he is become! But will he need me to take him a potion to sooth his stomach? Perhaps he needs me to look in the flames or the water to search for his English enemies - or his English friends?' She laughed softly. 'Will he simply want my singing to lull him to a magical slumber? Ah, but that would anger his bard, would it not?' She smiled broadly. 'And that would be a good reason to offer him one of my songs, I think. What say you, Mellt, Seren?'

Both wolves looked up at her, ears softly folded against their heads, submissive, loving. They each licked a hand.

'Mellt, my boy, you look up suddenly, keen to be moving perhaps?' she said, but both wolves sat down. 'Ah, you wait at my pleasure, I see. What boon friends you are, my loves. You,' she stroked the larger of the two, 'Seren Mellt, *Lightning Star,* for the shooting star I saw on the night the Prince brought you to me. You are magnificent.'

The wolf nudged her hand with his nose.

She turned to his sister and ran a gentle finger along her white muzzle. 'Beautiful Seren y Bore, *Morning Star,* the last star in the sky as morning pushes away the blanket of the night, and that's because you are always the last to appear from sleep each dawn. My lovely Seren.' She tapped the wolf gently on the nose with her finger and the animal bared her teeth in a grin and rubbed her head against Nest.

Bea thought they were perfection with their brindled grey pelts shading to white chests and white muzzles.

Amber eyes and coal black noses shining with health and how devoted they are to Nest she thought and felt envious and strangely lonely. *And they live with Nest in her stone cottage on the rocky promontory. Everyone knows this.*

Bea wondered how she knew this. It seemed to have been part of her own knowledge, her own understanding for ever. Nest in this dream (this *must* be a dream...) spoke of Llewelyn, the greatest

Prince that Wales had ever had. Llewelyn Fawr they called him, Llewelyn the Great, but that had been in the 12th or 13th Century, surely? Yr Wyddfa? That was Snowdon, of course. Bea struggled to focus and tried to drag her eyes away from the fire, but the scene before her, the scene she felt part of was wholly hypnotic and she felt herself lean forward a little to see deeper into the flames, to see Nest more clearly.

Nest drew her brychan closer round her shoulders.

'Ah, the wind at odds with the season and it bodes ill, I think. Mmmm, a sudden chill. It smells of snow, but it is far too early yet. I wonder…' she murmured. 'The Prince has called for us; they would not dare lie about that! So, we will go, and we will take him gifts, of course,' she told the wolves and the pair settled by the door to wait while she went inside.

The thick oak door stood open as she packed her leather scrip and aloud she itemised everything.

'A parcel of wild honeycomb wrapped in a comfrey leaf for his sweet tooth, a small earthenware pot of my soothing lanolin and calendula cream for the deep cut on his hand which will fester if I am not allowed to treat it, a small jar of sweet mead infused with poppy to help him sleep and my distillation of feverfew in honey for his headaches. He's such a sufferer.' She called over her shoulder to the wolves, 'I think I have everything, my loves.'

Then she closed the door to and set off to walk the half mile to his llys on the high ground inland. Mellt and Seren yawned and rose gracefully to lope after her, then, overtaking her they went in front. Nest smiled as she reminisced.

What a gift they were; the Prince himself finding them in their birth den, newly born and mewling beside their dead mother; she thin as a rake and starved. Ah, but many men starved too that Winter and into the Spring. My Lord thought the pack must have left her behind when she birthed, but they had been driven off by the poor people.

Bea heard Nest's voice but was puzzled because she didn't appear to be speaking aloud.

Am I hearing her thoughts? she wondered.

Nest walked on briskly.

And my Lord's hound, Gelert, one of that long line so named, was the one who nosed the cubs out. My Lord Prince put them both in his sleeve and fetched them to me to care for – and three years ago now! She smiled at the memory. *In that one act he gave me my guardians, my friends for life and the companions of my soul.*

Bea thought, *She had two wolves as companions! The people must have thought she was magical – or a witch or something – maybe mad?*

As if hearing their story, the wolves stopped and gazed back at Nest. It was a fine and shining day as she walked along the beach path inland, delighting in the crisp wind which rippled across a bared estuary as wide as the sky. The wet sands were split jaggedly by a stream that had made its journey from the hills. It grew into a goodly river which broadened when it spilled into the estuary, then picked a dainty way over the pebbles and shells to the sea. On one side of the estuary colossal sand dunes touched the sky themselves. Their tops were crowned with sea grasses that bent and tossed in the wind like hair on the heads of giant men who nodded sagely as they spoke together. On the other side of the estuary was a craggy outcrop with turfed headland.

A high, whistling cry pierced the air. Seren and Mellt stopped abruptly. They looked up, letting out a volley of short harsh barks and leapt forward in excitement to try and meet the bright swooping shapes that zipped past, just skimming their ears. The air was now filled with the high whistling notes of the oystercatchers soaring over Nest's head, racing for the open sea. She laughed aloud, and Bea felt the rush of joy with her.

Nest loved the oystercatchers' urgency, their flashing black and white plumage, their high, wild song. She would always stop to watch them skimming the ridged sands and the dancing water of the estuary, crying their exultation as they met the waves and wind. The wolves snapped playfully at them then cavorted ahead, rolling each other on the wet sand, chasing and leaping over rocks and tussocks of grass, their bodies coiled together in playful waves that mimicked the sea.

It took her ten minutes to make her way around the huddle of village huts, past the new stone church. St Beuno had founded a Christian church on that site centuries before, but the prince had recently given the people stone and timber to build a worthier and more substantial place of worship. The llys, with its own fine buildings of wood and stone, was a little further on.

As they neared the homes of men, the wolves moved to her side, not in fear but in the companionship of pack. Some people waved and smiled as she passed, a few hid themselves. And when she arrived at the entrance to the llys, the guards there just nodded as she passed through into the compound. It was enclosed within a stout palisade of thick tree trunks and commanded a view of the surrounding countryside and the sea. This was Llewelyn's court, his llys at Aberffraw, and he said it was his real home, a childhood home.

Bea found herself remembering his other palaces, his strongholds more castles than homes. He had his father's llys at Dolwyddelan, by the River Lledr, on the mainland of Wales, a well-fortified castle with a stone curtain wall. Also on the mainland was Aber, another favourite and more regal dwelling, and Caer yn Arfon lower down the coast, guarding the estuary there.

But at present Llewelyn, the Prince with all this power, had a headache and lay on a settle in a dark corner of his private chamber. It was a room used for meetings with his trusted men and visitors of importance; bright tapestries hung on the walls, A huge bearskin lay in front of the settle and there were soft rushes and herbs, verbena and rosemary, strewn over the main routes and by the fire. It was cold within the thick walls, and a brazier glowed at each end of the settle giving off the scent of charcoal. Llewelyn's body servant, Morgan, had lit a fire in the stone hearth, but the Prince said it made him feel like an old woman.

Although the upper part of the building was made of stout, warm timbers, the lower floor was stone, some newly quarried, some much older. The hearth and chimney of this chamber were built into one of the older walls which were the legacy of an ancient building that once stood high and powerful on the site. The Prince valued it greatly.

He directed his stone masons to leave the patch of once brightly coloured mosaic floor which abutted the wall because the colours were of the outdoors, where he truly belonged, he said. The design was of foliage from other, warmer lands; acanthus leaves and grape vine. They were once part of the patterned edging of a whole room and coloured birds had flown all the way across the floor. Only the tip of a beak and a single fine wing were left, and Llewelyn said it reminded him that this had been a place of rulers for centuries before and would continue for more to come. The permanency of power was very satisfying. So, he had the floor completed with fired clay tiles decorated with the same designs.

But that morning, the Prince was in no mood for architecture. He was prostrated in agony.

Chapter four

Rumour

*Let us not burthen our remembrance with
a heaviness that's gone...*

Prospero – The Tempest

FLASHING LIGHTS EXPLODED in Llewelyn's head. He often told Nest that the slightest noise made him want to scream in pain and rake his skin with his nails. So, he did not even raise his head when she arrived at his chamber door. Morgan, his body servant, waved her in and, using his thumb, he pointed to his Lord and then rubbed his own stomach. She nodded understanding; Llewelyn had been violently sick, but not in the sight of any save Morgan. He and Nest knew what to do for the Prince's ease. She helped him to finish hanging rugs over the windows to darken the room.

'A shame to cover the windows, my Lord, the holy pictures please me so,' Nest murmured as she and Morgan worked.

Llewelyn groaned, and Morgan flashed a grin at Nest. There was little draught from the windows as they were glazed and three of them were decorated with expensive stained glass. Some of this had been found near the old floor mosaics and the Prince had had the pieces incorporated into designs showing The Virgin Mary and the Infant Christ, The Crucifixion and The Ascension, all to please Joanna, his wife.

Indeed she was delighted, and caused a prie-dieu to be set under the windows so that Llewelyn could pray for guidance before his councils. There was a finely wrought gold crucifix hanging above the prie-dieu, on which lay an open bible, made and illuminated specially at the prince's orders by the monks at Penmon Priory. It had been his bridal gift to Joanna. Beside the prie-dieu, on the wall hung a small painting of the Virgin Mary and the Christ Child, done by an Italian painter. Llewelyn had been given this by a Norman lord who had been on pilgrimage to the Holy Land and had returned with overtures of friendship for the Prince. It was a comfortable and richly fitted chamber reflecting the character of a cultured and powerful prince.

But now this Prince had no thought for anything but his head and the moving light from the outdoors streamed through the coloured glass in dizzying patterns and it made it ache even more – therefore Nest and Morgan covered the windows.

Morgan brought iced water in a leather pitcher so that Nest could bathe his neck and then left to continue his work; the Prince's heavier cloaks and boots needed cleaning. Nest set to work. She gave Llewelyn some of her own tincture, the soothing mix of honey and feverfew and he lay back, ready to be comforted, feeling the promise of ease.

'How do you know what men go through, Nest? Are you a witch, my love? How does this magic of yours work?' he muttered, his voice tight and his eyes still pressed shut. He was a big man, well-muscled and heavy of face, his black hair greasy with sweat and hanging loosely just above his shoulders, his long moustache wilted over a bristled chin.

She made a wry face and tutted.

'My Lord, if putting myself in another person's shoes, imagining how it would feel for me to be sick with the pain, and feeling compassion enough to want to lessen the pain for that person, then I am as you accuse, though I would that you might keep this to yourself. It is no magic,' she whispered into his ear as she smiled.

'You've tamed the wild wolves, bewitched them, Nest,' he said, opening one eye to glimpse her reaction. His eyes were the colour of periwinkles and her own sparkled to see him peeping at her.

She sighed loudly, hands on hips. 'Llewellyn, Lord, I fed them their first milk – *goat's milk*. They think I am their mother. I think they are my boon companions, my soul mates, and so they are. We are pack,' she said as she stroked his hair from his eyes.

Mellt and Seren snuffled in the herbs and rushes strewn on the floor and lay down preparing to doze at her feet. The Prince's hound, Gelert, the fourth of that name, lay stretched before the blaze and greeted the wolves with a single wag of his tail then lay his head back on the rushes near the fire. It had been he that found them as cubs.

'Men would kill them for their pelts,' Llewelyn muttered.

'And I would kill those who even *try* to take their pelts, my Lord.' Her voice was composed, casual even, but the prince knew a true word when it was spoken. He reached out and grabbed her wrist, drawing her to his side.

'Would you be as fierce to those who threaten me, Nest? Would you kill to protect me, like one of my Uchelwr?' He was wholly serious. She put her own hand over his on her wrist and bent down to kiss him lightly on the lips.

'Always and forever, my Lord. Why ask when you know the answer?' She held his eyes with hers as she stroked his brow.

'I do know it and I value that knowledge beyond price, cariad.' He managed a smile and moved a little to get comfortable, then, lifting his hand in a gesture of thanks he allowed her to step back. She soaked her cloth once more to cool his neck.

'And you also know that my loyalty and love is far greater than all of your household knights, Llewelyn – *Lord*.'

He grunted and patted her on the arm. 'The pain is beginning to go. You are a witch indeed and I value your magic. But I've been told of whisperings, some say the wolves are your familiars.' His voice held a teasing note; he raised his eyebrows.

Nest was full of scorn. 'But you know that is nonsense, children's prattle, my Lord. Surely people have better things to do. I give my healing simples to any who ask, for themselves and their animals; I always will.'

'And you are right. I have real troubles aplenty of this only too real world, never mind letting people imagine witches and goblins. But when are you not right?' He reached up and patted her cheek. 'We'll nip this in the bud. If my head stops cracking in twain you will stay for the meal. You will bring your hairy family, *your pack* here to the hall, girl, and all shall see that the Prince of Gwynydd welcomes these guardians - *your* guardians to his table. Ha! God's Blood. Oooo,' he winced, 'that felt as though I'd an axe in my skull, an English one at that – blunt, cariad, blunt as my boot toe!'

'Lie back! Patience…You are like a boar shut in a pen, banging your head to no effect. Pig-headed, it is,' she murmured and began to bathe his forehead and neck with the water. She sang to him as she worked; softly, slowly, a lullaby and he soon fell into a gentle doze. Nest sprinkled some dry lavender stems on the braziers to perfume the air with soothing vapours.

She stayed with the Prince until, after an hour, he woke gently and felt his head was better. It was late afternoon and approaching the time for the main meal in the hall. He swung his legs over the edge of his couch and took a mouthful from a cup of camomile tea she had made, but suddenly thrust it back at her.

'Oh, yeuch! A foul brew. Very disappointing that! Get me wine, would you? I'Faith, I've something to talk over with you, Nest.'

He bent to fondle Mellt's ears as he lay on the rushes between the Prince and the fire. The great wolf opened his amber eyes a little and licked his lips when he saw who touched him then he let his head sink comfortably onto the rushes and fell back to dozing.

'Mmmm?'

'It is my wife, the Princess Joanna, Nest. I've heard rumours that she is unfaithful – again. What am I to do this time? By the Virgin, is this to last my whole life?' he said. He moved his face close to hers, stretched out a hand and took her own. 'This time it cannot be Will de Braose.'

'He died for the crime, yes,' she answered and waited.

'And the people continue to condemn her simply for being the daughter of John of England. But God knows, there are many who love her still. She is a good woman, Nest, and a princess by birth – alright – from the wrong side of the blanket but that changes nothing for us in Wales; we have ever acknowledged our bastards, as did her father. But Joanna, she is twice royal, beloved child of King John and *my own* Princess.'

'Still, she is Norman, *English,* I suppose we should say; although those who are Saxon, would argue allegiance as much as any.'

'Why can't her critics see how important the alliance has been for

Gwynedd? God's Wounds, their malicious tongues a-wagging would invent gossip enough to hang her simply because of her birth. Damn them. John's dead and she remains my Lady wife and a good wife of over twenty-four years. No one has said with whom she is supposed to have sinned - this time.'

He stopped suddenly, gasped and clutched his head in his hands as a new paroxysm of pain swept over him.

'By the Blessed Virgin, my head cleaves in twain. I thought it'd gone.'

Nest pressed her hands to his neck and kneaded until he groaned with pleasure.

'You're getting upset, which is why the pain stabs,' she told him. 'Think it over calmly. The Princess Joanna is your wife, my Lord; you love her as your wife, and you've been faithful, never seeking other women – I hope? And we know many who are bedding those they should not. But you're afraid because of her past, I know, and it's only natural.'

He nodded and dropped his head into his hands, scrubbing his hair. She could hear his hands rasp over the stubble on his chin.

Nest considered before she spoke. 'She was seduced by William de Braose, yes. That's what she told you. But this was in the past, years ago. You and she were a little estranged at the time, were you not? It may be that she was lonely.'

He nodded. 'Ah! Could she not control her appetites?'

'As many men do, I suppose?'

'Well, no. Oh, but it rankles still after all this time. To think he was my hostage, become friend – *good* friend I thought. 'Twas a formality to wait for the ransom to be paid by John, after all; a recognised part of financing one's warfare; the higher the rank, the greater the ransom. He and I got on well, despite the decades of struggle between us Welsh and the Normans.'

'Let it go, my love, let it go. It was years ago.' Her voice was soothing.

He shook his head. 'I cannot. We hunted together, feasted, talked; how we talked! I thought he was of my mind. It was the worst blow of my life when I actually discovered de Braose and Joanna in bed together; and in my own bed too, my marriage bed at Aber! God!' His huge body shook with fury to recall the outrage. He was on his feet in a second and strode the length of the room with the contained movements of a powerful man full of righteous anger.

Bea saw that Llewelyn was a man of great personal authority, a man who knew the extent of his power and was proud of it. He wasn't handsome, in the way she would have described it, but his face was full of wisdom, intelligence and determination, and there was humour too and violence. His dark hair was thick and would be shiny, if it were clean, and his eyes, under the beetling brows were piercing. He was big boned, strong and healthy; hard sinew and muscle with no soft edges blurred by easy living. Bea thought he was interesting, charismatic, vital, even with a headache.

Nest looked at Llewelyn. 'She was in the bed and he was in the room, I think, and fully clothed? He had forced his way in, wasn't that the case?' she reminded him.

'No matter; he was with her in that situation – the whoreson, and they had been lovers; she admitted it to me, later.' His voice rose as the humiliating memory surged back into his mind. 'Alright it was a while before that incident, but you cannot excuse her, and God knows she didn't try to excuse herself.' He stopped his pacing and stood hands on hips, breathed deeply and steadily. 'I have forgiven her now, you know that. I could not live without her, nor she without me. I believe her. Deep in my heart I do, so why am I suspicious now, Nest? Why? Is it just an old man's fancy?'

'No, no, Llewelyn, love. And you are not old, never say it.' She smiled, shook her head. 'If only I had been here to be a friend to you. A prince can have so few real friends. And I was away in the hills by Yr Wyddfa. Everyone knew about them but you, my Lord.'

'Everyone knew.' His voice was flat.

'You acted rightly; you know it. You took revenge very publicly with the hanging of de Braose. A deserved punishment. And he died bravely, thus a worthy revenge. The Princess Joanna was two years secluded at Llanfaes, by your order. When you showed mercy to her it was a princely act,' she said and laid a hand on his shoulder, leaned over the shoulder to put her cheek against his.

'It wasn't mercy, Nest, it was *need.* I wanted her near me, at least across the Straits from me, or if I were here, then just down the coast, not locked away in some distant priory cell. She was my beloved wife, still is; as you are my beloved friend.'

He and Nest had been close since childhood. An intimacy such as this was the comfort of long friendship and of the loving they shared as young people before his royal marriage.

He nodded again, rubbing his face.

'I'Truth, she was frustrated by the politics, desperate for Dafydd's safety as Gruffydd's hostility towards his brother became so blatantly open. Ah, Nest, both of them my beloved sons, and God knows, so different. Both lords of Wales, yet my Gruffydd - so warlike; he cannot understand that this world is oiled by talk and later, maybe by battle, if need be. Aye and gold too. Men's lives should not be used so cheap. Dafydd is more like John, his grandfather; wily and intelligent, more willing to play chess than smash the board in a temper. Yet not a coward, by no means, he is truly like me in arms.' He shook his head. 'But Joanna…' He groaned a long note that was almost a howl and the wolves, and the hound pricked their ears.

Nest put her hand on his shoulder. 'And who says she's betrayed you now? And who is the man she is supposed to favour above you, my Prince? Have you asked her? In any case I hesitate to tell you what you should do about this, even as your oldest friend. What would God say? What would Canon Yago say? He's a priest of the Church. Surely he can guide you.'

'Ah, Nest, as you know, the Christian way is to forgive, but I'd find that an even harder battle to be faced for a second time. It is 1228 Anno Domini and I'm over fifty years old, yet I'm torn. I just don't know how to behave in this matter. We've been married twenty-four years and have six healthy grown children between us. And I have my Gruffydd, of course. He remains obstinately all mine, all for

Wales and the Welsh, never allowing that other lands feel the same burning loyalties and loves.'

'And, as you say, we have to live side by side.'

'It is the sensible way. Keep avenues of communication and trade open, yet keep your own land of itself, with its own identity, and defend the right, ay, by God; defend the right.'

Nest let remembrances flood her mind.

Bea, as she watched in her dream-state, heard her thoughts: his and Joanna's son, Dafydd, was Llewelyn's heir. Their five girls had been married to Marcher lords to cement peace with England as much as the alliance of huge wealthy estates. One was even married to de Braose's son, Reginald. Llewelyn was an astute diplomat and sought to find ways to resolve problems other than by massed and bloody battle, not that he avoided such if it became necessary.

But she heard how his efforts at diplomacy were ever thwarted by Gryffudd, his eldest son, Gruffydd the true champion, the warrior, the vigilante, the pure Welshman. He was born to a beautiful Welsh woman, Tangwystl, out of wedlock, but according to Welsh custom and law, was acknowledged as the Prince's legitimate first-born son. They lived and loved at the palace in Aberffraw until she had died in childbed. Yet Llewelyn chose Dafydd as his heir because John of England was his maternal grandfather and he was more of the metal that diplomats were made of, and less of the border raider, as was Gruffydd. Above all else, his own eldest son's happiness included, Llewelyn wanted peace for his people, not war. That was how things were.

'And Dafydd and Gruffydd have never stopped warring jealously since you made the younger one heir. It's that which destabilises the land, isn't it?' she pointed out.

He sat up from his couch abruptly and brought his huge fist slamming down on the chest where his cups rested, causing them to fly off onto the floor and the top of the chest to crack.

'By Our Lady, you need not point that out to me, woman. No one else would criticise their lord!' He was up on his feet in a second and began pacing the room, constantly rubbing his head with both hands in his anger.

'Calm, cariad, calm,' Nest said, from her stool by the fire. 'You'll bring back the headache…What was that you were saying about not smashing a chess board?'

'Don't tell me that, Nest, damn you. I'm your Lord…' he shouted, swinging round so that his red face was thrust into hers.

She was up on her own feet then too and her own face as flushed as his as she demanded, 'Where is it you damn me to? To Hell? I'm a free woman, not of your fiefdom, though we both know how much you value my opinions and my simples. Or if you carry on shouting, I can leave, and then we'll see who'll soothe your head – *my Lord!*'

He roared at her, 'You will sit while I talk.'

'I will sit when and if I choose to,' she replied, her own voice steady and low, and remained standing.

'My head's worse now.'

'It's your own doing.'

'You're an unforgiving woman, Nest. A hard woman. You should go to war. Where're your kindnesses? Ach, you've changed since we loved. I'll wager you don't even remember the dunes…' He roared again and swung round, then throwing his hands on the wall began to bang his head on it, repeatedly.

'That, Llewelyn, is foolish and un-princely,' she informed him tartly and with scorn and sat down on her stool, her back to him. The wolves both raised their heads to gaze at him, and his hound ignored him and turned around on the rushes to make a more comfortable bed.

'See, the animals think nothing of your ravings, and I, I've grown up. Of course I have changed. And yes, you fool, I do remember our youth but now I am a grown woman without a husband and worse in the eyes of many people, I am a woman who wants none. My reputation as a wise woman is what saves me from being thrown off the headland in a storm. I help people in their sicknesses, them and their animals. They respect me for it and that is its own coin. You know it. That and your protection.'

In reply he swung around and brought his first down again on the chest lid and it shattered completely, the painted planks separated, some falling down inside the chest.

'Now look!' was all she said.

Chapter five

Hidden

Good wombs have borne bad sons…

Miranda – The Tempest

LLEWELYN HUNG HIS HEAD, trying to gather his thoughts and still his racing heart. The only sound in the room was the crackle of the fire, the hiss of the braziers and the snores of the animals. When he spoke again it was as though by rote, presenting the bare facts with hard held patience that could evaporate in a single beat of his heart.

'Yes, my sons war against each other; Gruffydd wanted to rule after me to make Wales independent of England once more. But he wants to take this independence by force and his sons will want the same; Dafydd won't want to be left out of such a reckoning nor, in turn, will his sons. They'll want their own piece of Wales to rule.' He began to pace the length of the room.

Nest sorted through her potions.

He continued through gritted teeth. 'And so it will continue until all of Wales, not just Gwynedd here in the north, but all of Wales will be shattered into tiny, petty lordships whose leaders spend their days like rabid dogs, battling for forest rights and bemoaning England's success. By the Blood of Christ, that is to bemoan our own success!'

'It is, my Lord.'

'The Blessed Virgin knows we trade mightily with England, and with the lands over the narrow sea, all the way to the far eastern kingdoms, places where the Lord Jesus himself trod, aye and following the Silk Road, far beyond.'

'I know, I know,' she said and got up to add more charcoal and herbs to the two braziers in the room.

'I named Dafydd heir in an abortive attempt to cement unity with England. But what have I got for my pains? Hmmm? Answer me that. What have I got? I've got a war within my own family. My act of unity is its own undoing. We're a split nation. We're a split family, Nest.'

She sat down and she wondered; she searched his face to find an answer, an idea.

'You didn't say who told you about the Princess Joanna. Who is it that gossips so?' she asked. 'Someone with something to gain by discrediting her or by upsetting you? Why would this person tell you? Is it someone trustworthy? If it be that, then 'tis no gossip and idle chatter, but a friend's warning.'

'Slowly woman, slowly. I know the informant is ever loyal to me, worry not. And I think it is reliable information. That's what I know, but all the same I would that you could look in the future for me, Nest. I need you to tell me what will happen!' He raked a hand over his face and taking up a silver cup from the floor where he had knocked it, he filled it from the ewer and threw the wine back in a single swallow.

She tutted. 'My Lord, strong French wine, especially the black grape, will bring back your headache, either that or shouting,' she chided and snatched the drinking cup from his hand, an exasperated gesture. 'And I can't see into the future; that would be black magic and I have none of that. How dare you!' she spoke softly but with a cheekiness that brought a slight smile to his lips.

She made a wry face. 'If I gaze into the water or the flames, I can see things, but it is only in my mind's eye. I see what people do now in the present, and things that have happened in the past and from that I can suggest what is the best outcome. But that is only if circumstances remain as they are. But you know, my love, that people can change things for themselves if they want to. Are you going to sit back like a milksop and wait for this accusation to come true, doing nothing, being passive? You are the prince,' she said.

'I am but a man with a faithless wife, albeit a wife in name only just now.'

'Lord, no. This may be true in one sense, in that you're a man, but you're a man with more than normal power. And you have no proof of adultery yet. Ask her first; don't you owe her that much? Ask others too. Hold up your head and look them in the eye to see how their gossip fares then.' Her voice became hard, scathing. 'You're behaving like a lovesick boy and not a man.'

He snorted but was thoughtful. 'If I am lovesick it is for my people and their fate. How do you say these things to a man of more than normal power and not fear being killed for your words? And any true lovesickness on my part would be for you. You know it.'

'So many years ago. Time now to be the warrior, the diplomat, the prince. Why would you kill me anyway?' she was incredulous and laughed herself. 'Would it not be silly? Who would soothe your headache? I'm like the fool King Henry keeps at his English court, who says the unthinkable and the unspeakable, so men keep him at a distance fearing his mind is gone, for how could anyone speak so to a prince or a king and live?'

'It is so. Men do fear your truth because it hurts, shames them and, worse, ridicules them in the eyes of their fellows. That's also dangerous, my Nest.' He was serious and concerned and stretched out a hand to take hers. 'Here, the thanks of a prince to his very wise fool, his physician too,' he said and kissed her hand as if she were a princess, then he sat down on his stool and drew her onto his knee.

As he did, the light and the fall of her clothes was such that it showed her body, usually so lithe and tiny, was swollen. He saw it immediately and saw the significance. His face darkened.

'Nest?'

Her only answer was, 'Ah...' She put a hand to her stomach and smiled, sitting there on Llewelyn's knee by the fire.

'Well?' he asked gently, but his expression was strange, at odds with his voice.

'My Irish love, Cormac,' was all she said, and wrapped an arm about his neck.

'*Him?* Cormac the bard? He who came with the Spring?' He didn't look at her, his voice was cold, a muscle in his cheek began to twitch.

'The same one, indeed.' Nest turned his face towards hers, a hand on each side, and looked deeply into his eyes. 'You're jealous, my love?' she asked. She dropped her hands to his shoulders which had the solidity of a tree trunk and her hands were tiny where they rested.

Llewelyn's body had stiffened. He could not answer for a minute, but turned to catch her eyes and held them, at war with his own mixed feelings, recognising the hypocrisy of them.

'We played together as children, we loved each other as young people. Of course, as I am your elder by ten years…'

'More!'

'I had to go away to train as a warrior of my father's court – you know that and that was when I met Tangwystl.'

'Yes, but why tell me what I know? Yes, Tangwystl, the daughter of one of your father's nobles. I remember her beauty, aye and her gentleness and it was me who was the jealous one then, especially when she gave birth to your first son. I wanted that to be me.'

'I did not know.'

'You could not guess? Ahh.' Nest was quiet for a space. He stroked her back, as she continued to reminisce. 'But when your own father, Iorwerth Drwyndwn, died you became the Prince. You could have married me then.'

He hung his head. 'Don't think I don't regret it for my own heart, but I married Joanna to broker a peace with England. And now I love her as my wife. You know that, cariad.'

'*Cariad* now is it? I am not the one burning with jealousy. You are Prince and can decide your own wife.'

Llewelyn growled; she felt his body tense. 'I had to form my court and play the English game. Wales has prospered from my alliances. By the Virgin, do not make my head ache again.'

'It sounds like you threaten me!' She snapped and sprang to her feet, but he snatched her wrist and pulled her back.

'I *beg* you; 'tis no threat, just a headache that spikes at the tiniest upset.'

'Hmmph! Well, worry not, my Lord, I know we are true friends now; we have the best of our relationship, the friendship, and it has had time to mature like a wine in the cask.'

'You have inherited your father's silver tongue.'

'I hope so and I am a woman who is not like others less fortunate. I am no slave or chattel, no man's property. I am a free woman in this land. You said so yourself – and you are the Prince.'

This time he lifted her bodily off his knee and pushed her gently but firmly away. 'Yes, I am a hypocrite, Nest, and yes, I am jealous, I am wildly, deeply jealous.'

'You are a babe, a fool.' She glowered at him, shook her head.

'Careful Nest!' he growled. 'What a child ours would have been, if it had happened. If, if, if! If your father had been a lord instead of a fisherman, then I might have been able to marry you, you know that. But, to the point now; you are old to bear a child, a first child, you near forty.'

'Not so near!' She snorted and raised her eyebrows and shook her head. He was worried for her. He turned her to face him, 'Where is he, Cormac?' he asked, and his tone was bitter.

She said, 'He is gone, back to his country and he doesn't know about the child. I will be fine. Women bear children daily.'

'And they die in agony doing just that.' He put his hand on her stomach.

'I won't die, don't worry. My child will be a girl and I will be fine, my Lord.'

'So, you can see into the future. What do you see for me, Nest?' He was triumphant.

'No, I cannot. Every woman has a feeling about the child they carry. There is nothing magical about it – but no, of course there is, it is the natural magic of birth.'

She did not tell him that of all the powers passed to her by her mother, that her power of seeing did indeed show her the future. She was carrying a girl, one to follow her, and she saw heartbreak for Llewelyn because of his English wife, and she saw death. Late Summer in the life of the Prince and in the year itself.

'I will take care of you, never fear,' he said and folded her in his arms. 'And, even after her infidelity I have love for Joanna, a care of her too; after all the years we have been together and the children. But we know, you and I, that it was at first and foremost the love of convenience and politics. But I do love her now.'

'And me?'

'You I love in a different way; the Welsh way, deeply, truly and forever.'

He kissed her lightly on the mouth, in the curve of her neck, her forehead then taking hold of her forearms with his own massive hands, he moved her away, saying, in a tone that spoke of hard-won determination.

'Come, we go to hall. It is time.'

It was late afternoon and the great hall was ready for the meal everyone shared at this time. The trestles were set out on each side of the hall with the longest one on the dais at the head. At Joanna's insistence it was always covered in a fine tapestry cloth, the English way. A fire of logs and sea coal burnt in the hearth, the fine new stone structure on the back wall with its chimney leading to the roof, to take the smoke of the fire outside. The pot boys moved around the hall filling cups with ale, others brought the thick trenchers of coarse bread that would serve to hold the fish stew and leeks. Fish was always eaten on Friday.

The Prince sat on the dais, usually with his wife and any of their children who visited. But Princess Joanna was not there for the meal that day, she had kept to her solar pleading a headache. Any visiting nobles and relatives sat according to their station on the benches to either side of the royal places, or in the body of the hall if they were commoners.

Everyone had assembled and as Llewelyn strode through the hall to his place, Nest and her wolves followed him some paces behind. There were few who did not know Nest and her companions, but they had never before come to meat in the hall. Nest sat at the end of the long board on the dais for the meal and the wolves lay at her side. Halfway through the Prince beckoned Nest to him to whisper in her ear.

It was simply, 'Look how they're all wondering what I'm saying. Silence can be truly more powerful than any words. Mark me, they'll treat you with even more care than before, Nest.'

He turned and put his hands out to Mellt and to Seren. Their heads were above the height of the board so that everyone could see him fondle their ears. The message was clear and crystal bright as the streams that leapt for ever down Snowdon's crags. He knew his people would keep these two safe, but the wolves of the wild that howled in the night and took their sheep and goats were of the elements, and the people feared them and would kill them when they could.

Nest saw only one person's expression that gave her cause for thought, wary thought. It was the prince's own bard, Ithel ap Deykin. He was a man who found it hard to hide his feelings, even when it was politic to do so, and she had long thought the prince only tolerated him because of his matchless voice. Whether singing the long and lilting poems and songs or speaking a tale, Ithel held people in his thrall. But he also nursed a thriving jealousy of Nest because of her value to the prince. No one else saw the fleeting expression of loathing as Llewelyn whispered. Only Nest's eyes were directed his way and she saw the depth of his hatred clearly, as she had seen it at other times.

As she talked quietly to Llewelyn, she kept a casual yet attentive watch on Ithel and let her thoughts consider him and the others like him.

These bards with their power. How they are revered in lordly households; my own Cormac among them. And how some of them despise their lords and benefactors. If only they knew. Even my Lord, the Prince turns to Ithel to ask him to look in the waters. I wonder, is Ithel one of those that can summon a trance? I don't think so. He has no real power; he is just full of hatred for the English and those of the Welsh who befriend them. He has never liked the Princess Joanna, though his tongue is slippery as eels in syrup.

She sat back and took up her spoon to eat the fragrant stew, rested her hand on Seren's head thoughtfully. Her eyes shone as she remembered something.

My own father was as knowledgeable as a bard, but not such as

Ithel who no doubt grows his worldly influence to evil ends. My father revered the music, the poetry, the beauty of the wild things, not the power of men. He was never happier than when he left the monastery and took up his nets and lines again. I can hear his melodies on the waves and in the wind, lilting notes to rival all the birds. Oh, and the aching beauty of his voice and the thrill of harp as we sung together at the fireside on starry nights. He would always have us join our voices to his, mother and I; each note lighting another star in the heavens.

'Nest?' The Prince's voice made her start a little. He looked at her enquiringly.

'I was thinking of my father and of his music,' she said.

'I remember your voice too, when you sang to me by the river.'

'Hush, my Lord. You are a prince married and I, I am …'

'The friend of my heart.' He smiled. 'Don't worry. I'll remember my place.'

'Humble now, is it? A humble prince?' she teased, and he laughed.

Bea heard Nest's thoughts and accepted this as part of the dream-state where she seemed to exist, sometimes as herself watching Nest and sometimes she felt as though she became Nest for a short space of time. She found herself wishing she could be as confident as Nest seemed to be, complete and refined as a woman, a separate woman with a special status in that society, a woman valued by her neighbours, nothing to shake her poise.

While Nest's attention was diverted by the Prince, she did not notice Yestyn and the rest of the Uchelwr at the back of the hall. They whispered together; their expressions furtive. And she did not see the women behind the curtain, the one which led to Princess Joanna's rooms. Bea saw these things and felt a spike of anxiety for Nest based on nothing more than the way these people looked at her.

Hiding there were the Princess herself and her English maid, Edith, who served her. Joanna's face was dark with anger, and that of her maid no less stirred on her behalf. Joanna had been a beautiful young woman, small with dark hair and delicate English features. Since her return to court after her disgrace, she habitually wore a white coif and wimple and a plain brown dress, much like the simple clothes worn by the nuns. She'd stayed with them for a time after her banishment. Her hair was plaited and confined closely under the wimple; she no longer wore it coiled decoratively and with a jewelled circlet, as in the Norman fashion, in fact she no longer wore jewellery. Instead, she wore a heavy metal cross, a symbol of her supplication and her piety as she strove to put her infidelity behind her.

But as she and Edith watched from their hiding place, Joanna's face betrayed the anger she felt simmering inside her. She'd prayed to put her own jealousy aside, but her face was ashen, her eyes desperate and Edith stroked her mistress's arm gently. She had been nurse to the Princess in England and loved her as the child of her body and her heart.

She whispered, 'Wheesht, my Lady. That woman, Nest, she's common, common born Welsh, one of the fishermen's stock from by the shore, not royalty as you are, Norman royalty at that, my dove. Why my Lord favours her so I cannot guess, her and those wild creatures, those beasts of the mountains.'

Joanna put her pale face near Edith's, 'Watch my Lord with this sea-woman. I don't like her, and I don't trust his feelings for her. He knows I tire of this life at court, but I would keep him close to my heart. You know how I feel about him, Edith. And I need him to be faithful to me, for my own sake and of course for the safety of my boy. I fear for him with Gruffydd. He's wild, uncontrolled, dangerous. Oh, and I love my Lord Prince with a breaking heart. I wish we could go back to our youth when our love was new and unsullied.'

Edith tugged her gently into an alcove further away from the hall where the light was dim, and they were shielded from stray eyes and ears.

Joanna wiped her eyes. 'If only the Prince would curb Gruffydd for everyone's sake. He's forever whipping up hatred for the king and the English generally. Ah, these differences of nationhood. We should all be English, not Norman or Saxon or even Welsh, but God knows the Welsh would never agree to that; my Lord wouldn't, for all he's tolerant of different peoples he still wants a united Wales, a single nation. I've tried to be wholly Welsh. Our Blessed Lady knows that is true from my heart, and I wish nothing else but to serve her and to serve God...and to keep Llewelyn faithful and loving.'

Edith bent her head to whisper in her mistress's ear, 'There, there, my dove, all will be well. I will watch Nest.' She paused to look down the passage and saw no one. 'But I can see that she bothers you no more. I have long thought that your life would be the sweeter without her. And those beasts can be poisoned with ease. Would that be your wish, lambkin?'

Joanna gasped aloud. 'By Our Blessed Lady, no, no. Edith, no! Oh, such a sin! But no, do not tempt me.' Joanna held her head in her hands. 'You must confess the sin of that evil thought. Tell me you will. Tell me you will seek penance and ask for forgiveness and absolution. Tell me. I cannot think of you damned for eternity. What would I do without you?' Joanna rung her hands and tears began to stream unchecked down her faded cheek.

'Oh, yes, my dove, yes. I will do it. Forgive me the thought. I want only your comfort. I was foolish,' Edith cried and held Joanna's hands in hers.

'I can't think for the pain in my head or my heart; I don't know which, but something aches so, Edith. Take me to my bed chamber. This wearies me now. And we can't be rid of the wretched beasts lest my Lord weeps for them as he did his old hound, Gelert, all those years ago. I swear he hasn't wept since. He has sworn to protect all innocent beasts who guard their charges. No, we can't be rid of them,' she said.

Edith reached up an arm to encircle her shoulder. 'Now, now my little dove, Edith will take care of everything. You've done penance enough yourself for one lifetime, by the Holy Mother you have. But I struggle to know why some things are cause for regret. I know you love the Prince but my Lord de Braose was so good for you.'

Joanna looked up sharply. 'Edith, you go too far!'

But Edith knew how far she could go. 'And the light in your eyes when you two were to meet…' she said wistfully. 'But come, I'll mull some wine for you. Come,' she said.

Before she led Joanna away, she stretched up her hand to straighten the white linen coif around her mistress's head and to tuck a little of her long dark hair under it. Edith looked down at the plain brown linen dress the Princess wore and tutted. 'Ahh, you wear the colours of a penitent still, when you should be dressed in rich brocades from the Levant, gauzy silks from the far lands of the East. Oh, and your jewels, garnets, amethyst, topaz, your pendants, brooches and rings.' Edith sighed. 'And your hair, your hair should have pearls threaded through it, not be hidden beneath a rough wimple, my lambkin. You are a princess of the blood and the wife of a prince.'

'He would not look at me as he was used to, even if I did. My Lord has his country and both his sons. I have nothing, but our daughters and our beloved eldest son, my Dafydd, and he will inherit all. That is my reward. I'll try to be content.'

Joanna paused in her step then suddenly making up her mind she pulled away from Edith's arm and said, 'I'll go to the chapel. I'll take no wine until I have asked forgiveness for my jealousy.'

And it was all Edith could do to run after her as she walked swiftly away down the stone passage to the chapel.

Chapter six

Encounter

Be not afeard; the isle is full of noises...

Caliban - The Tempest

IT WAS FIVE O'CLOCK and almost dawn when Bea woke stiff and cold. She heard the trill of a blackbird outside, the answering challenge of a robin; seagulls shrieking as they whirled high above the waves. There was no sound of the wind or rain and when she looked up at the tiny slatted window near the fire nook, she saw the steady drip of water from the old gutter outside, and a touch of blue beginning to brighten the grey dawn in the sky beyond.

The visions lay quietly hidden in her mind with nothing but the occasional nudge of remembrance that quickly slipped away.

She had been lying back in the fire nook against the warm stone with her legs stretched out from the stool. Archie was lying curled up on the sheepskin, high up on the settle and he was yapping in his sleep, his little tail giving the occasional wag. When Bea tried to get up her knees wouldn't unlock, and her feet tingled. She ached all over, but her wrist and her nose throbbed in time, nevertheless there was a kernel of comfort deep inside her to be waking up, even from a heavy dozing sleep, in the cottage. She was here at last. Jeremy was not remotely near her, not even in the same city or country, and that made her want to face the day. But she needed to think. She'd made several life changing choices the day before. At least she hoped they were life changing. Maybe it was a panicked impulse.

Will he come and haul me back and wrap me in a white coat with the arms tied around like a straight jacket?

A tiny panic wormed its way up to her throat and gnawed at her comfort.

He'll guess where I am, won't he?

She realised that she hadn't even considered what she would do next, now she'd managed to get to Nest's Point. She had no idea.

I'll just focus on the present, just being here and then when I feel better, I'll know what to do. The house will tell me.

This had been a favourite notion of Auntie Nest's. She'd say, 'Stay here long enough and you will simply do what is needed; scent the sea, refresh your soul, feel the air around you, feel the stone beneath your feet. You'll know you're home.'

Archie woke up and yawned hugely, jumped off the settle, still agile enough for that, and came to her wagging his tail, licking his lips. A greeting. The electricity was on again, so she made strong black coffee and drank the first mug on the doorstep, doing what Nest said. The tide was coming in and lapped energetically at the highest tussocks of grass next to the stones of the garden wall. There were one or two late sea pinks bobbing jauntily on an island of turf, shells clustered round, bright splashes of sea treasure. A cloud of tern danced and squealed overhead and then were swept off, out to sea on a high air current, spiralling quickly out of sight towards the distant peaks of Snowdonia around the headland. Bea drank in the sharp salt of the breeze, listened to the soft breathing of the sea and felt better than she had for a couple of years.

I've abandoned my job, my career, my calling, she thought and curiously for her, without a pang of guilt.

I haven't told the hospital where I am, given no reason for an unauthorised absence. Right! They'll miss me, well, someone will - probably the patients and the nurses. Why don't I feel bothered? Auntie Nest would know that too.

Bea finished her coffee and heaved herself up off the step to go in for more. Archie had been out on the beach and trotted up the slope, looking expectantly at her.

'Okay, your breakfast. Nothing fancy yet, I'm afraid,' she told him. It was six o'clock in the morning. She looked out of the kitchen window, now able to see the meadow beyond in all its wildflower exuberance.

Someone should paint that with vibrant water colours, with loads of splashes and loose brush strokes. They could call it 'Late Summer

Gloria'.

Bea made herself a second coffee and remembered she had no food for herself, let alone Archie.

Ah well.

As she wandered back outdoors, she glanced at an old driftwood bench to the side of the door and mentally kicked herself for not even remembering it existed five minutes ago.

How do you forget something as familiar as your face? I guess I'm stressed.

She sat.

I know why I'm not bothered about work. Thank you, Auntie Nest. Relax and the answers will come to you. Work? I don't like it anymore. In fact, I loathe it. Why do you loathe it, Bea? she asked herself and decided it wasn't the patients or the other staff, it was because of Jeremy.

I love helping people; the nurses and all the others are great. I love medicine. Jeremy has spoilt that hospital for me. I ought to be able to get a grip, as they say in all the best psychiatric consultations. I'm so self-pitying. Why did I listen to him?

He had beaten all pleasure out of her, emotionally and now physically too. As far as medicine was concerned, he had the old-fashioned consultant's concept of the patient as a project, not a professional relationship. Consultants weren't all like that. He didn't interact on a human level and just because he dealt with the brain didn't mean he understood its emotional function. He didn't even greet patients beyond a slight nod when he arrived at their bedside.

It was awful following him on his rounds after surgery when I was FY1. Well I guess that's what happens to most people in their first year. Being married to him meant nothing. Everyone scoffing at me, saying I had leverage – whatever that is! He was ruder to me than to any of the others. He said all the patients were mentally defective. I think he meant like his junior doctors. At least I wasn't with him when I started my GP training. Hated that though. Not for me. And what a scene he made when I opted for Gynaecology instead - but I love it. Then he accused me of sleeping my way into my Registrar post. God – if only!

Bea still wore the baggy old clothes she'd found in her cupboard upstairs. They were creased and smelly after the night by the fire. She didn't care. Her trainers had spent the night by the fire and were dry but misshapen after their soaking, but she rammed her feet in.

I might get changed – possibly. Maybe not. Hang on. What would I get changed into? That's it; the old jeans that don't fit and my wet stuff from yesterday. Perhaps I'll go to the Post Office for some food. She looked at her watch. *Only seven thirty. Thomas will have all the local gossip. Can I stand it? The Post Office will be open at eight. Should I go? God, I'm not even peckish. I'm just exhausted after that night. Must check on things – what happened to the chimney?*

She looked around, casting her eyes down the beach, along the headland, back across the river to the sand dunes.

Everything looks fine, not too much debris considering the storm. And nothing bad happened at the Prince's llys, did it? Why should it? she thought and then it struck her. *I was out in a storm and not at some llys, some medieval court. Anno Domini 1228? What am I talking about? That was a dream - wasn't it? Wolves! They were with me, not chasing me. Of course it was a dream.*

She shook her head and decided she had low blood sugar.

And there's the chimney! she told herself as she looked up at the roof of the cottage. *I thought the chimney had... where's the turf gone? The roof's slate, you idiot. And there's an upstairs to the cottage. You're still dreaming. Honestly!*

It had been such a vivid dream, a dream about this cottage as it probably looked centuries ago.

That's so weird, it's fascinating! And how come they spoke English, modern English, come to that, if they were medieval Welsh? Well they looked medieval; I mean. Anno Domini 1228? What was the world like; what was Wales like then?

An oystercatcher trilled loudly as it raced down the estuary and Bea forgot the dream in an instant. She spent the next hour sorting out her few things and putting them in more logical places, then on an impulse of panic, stuffing them all in the damp backpack again only to tip it out and tell herself to face it later. She just stepped over the soggy clothes on the floor. She decided to get some food and feed her panic with that instead of with misgivings. She rummaged around, touching base, checking what provisions were still there, and found, as expected, sugar, tea, coffee, salt, flour, all dry and still good, even after months. It had been stored well. She walked round the outside of the cottage and saw how neat the little garden was, as though Auntie Nest herself were still pottering each day.

Perhaps she does, she's my magical auntie after all, she thought. *No rubbish blown over from the sea, after the storm. Funny.*

The tubs were full of nasturtiums, the dog daisies still grew in a huge patch behind the back wall and didn't look at all damaged by last night's weather, but the back yard was sheltered. The flower heads of the giant sedum, Autumn Glory, were beginning to grow pink and glow in the late Summer sun, bees clustering greedily round them, even so early in the morning.

Her new phone had charged in the last hours, so she took it, grabbed her purse and a basket and set out with Archie to walk along the beach to the village. As the tide was almost fully in, she took the higher part of the path, no more than a sheep track really, and in places she had to watch every step. She'd put the dog on the lead when they got to the top fields, in case there were any sheep. Archie was not reliable at all, as far as sheep chasing went. She was halfway down the path and just about to leap over a gap, washed away by the storm she supposed, when a voice startled her.

'So! You must be the woman.' It was a man's voice, deep and the tone withering. It annoyed her instantly.

The dog barked in surprise and Bea stared uncomprehendingly at the man, then lost her footing and slid down the muddy gap with a yelp. Her basket and purse flew from her hands, she let go of the lead and she tried to grasp a thin hawthorn branch nearby, but all she snatched was the air. She landed badly on her back, thumping her injured wrist on a sandy clump of grass and she winced in pain. Archie ran around her, barking at the man.

'Whoa there!' the man called, this time the tone of his voice soothing, exactly as if she were a flighty horse. 'Whoa! Watch out.' He bent to offer her a hand and after throwing him a baleful glance she stretched out her uninjured muddy one.

'Fair enough!' he said and grasped it firmly. He swung her up and onto her feet with little effort. 'You okay? Sorry, must have caught you off guard.'

Who is he?

He bent and retrieved her things and Bea used her muddy hand to tug at her sling and then swipe her hair from her face. She winced as the hand brushed her nose but adopted as dignified pose as she could and held out her hand for the basket. She had to keep snatching her coat as it slid from her shoulders and it was then that she regretted breaking the zip and not drying it thoroughly. She managed to trap the dog lead with her foot and took hold of it, thankful that Archie had reduced his noise to an occasional growl.

'Hey, who punched you in the nose?' he asked, laughing, still holding the basket.

Instead of grabbing it from him she gasped, and her hand flew to her face. She hadn't looked in the mirror this morning.

'Perhaps you fell? Bit unsteady on your feet, yeah? Ground give way?'

She didn't answer.

'Mud on your face too,' the man pointed out unhelpfully, bending towards her and offering a smile. 'Bit of a mess now, aren't we?'

She recovered. 'There's no *we* here, thanks,' she said and snatched the basket from him. She took a step forward to get past him, but the path was slippery, and he held out his arms in a guarding gesture. She glanced at him briefly, unimpressed.

'I'm fine,' she snapped. 'You're just bloody bad-mannered.'

He grinned, and it dawned on Bea that he probably used this manoeuvre often, all those perfect white teeth set in a swarthy face. The perfect permission for rudeness. And what's more, she suddenly recognised him as the man from last night's horror in the storm, the face at the window. He hadn't looked quite so handsome then. He had strong brows, very dark brown eyes and lines on his face that some might call laughter-lines, but she saw them as lines caused by steely determination and intense focus.

Even if he hadn't been well over six foot, he was on a slope and dipped his head as he looked down at her. His shirt neck was open showing a powerful neck. His hands were on his hips and the stance had changed from interfering to quarrelsome.

'So, you're the woman?' he accused her again. He looked to be in his mid-thirties. She thought he looked fairly pleased with himself, arrogant too and this impression was enhanced by a perfect Roman nose and flaring nostrils.

'What woman?'

She suddenly felt fear rise through her body like an electric current. She felt her breathing quicken, a fluttering of panic. *Why am I scared?*

'You're the woman in the cottage. Last night, Gwyn Roberts… We met, and this must be the guard dog?' He grinned, amused, and raised his eyebrows in query.

Archie stood stiffly, kept his eyes on the man, kept up his low growl. Bea felt numb, but the next instant, she felt threatened, then guilty, angry, a range of emotions that was normal for her these days when talking to any man. After her initial bluster, she hesitated with her response. Jeremy had squeezed normal social reactions out of her, rung her dry. But here, at Nest's Point, she was feeling a little more like her old self and it was daylight so meeting the man from the storm was disturbing, but she recognised that she was angry at his intrusion.

She tried to stand up a little straighter and winced. 'We did not meet, actually, you crept up in the middle of the night like something from *Zombie Apocalypse*, crashed and thumped on my door and scared me. What were you playing at?'

Her voice shook a little, and her injuries were throbbing again. She was hungry, covered in mud and had no wish to prolong hostilities with this vigilante bloke, his designer teeth and a reckless fringe that arched over his eyes. She tried to walk past him, face averted, tugging the dog lead.

'Well, excuse me!' His voice dripped venom. 'As I said previously, I was behaving like a good neighbour and I saw lights on at old Nest's place and I thought I should check it out. I mean, it's right down at the end of the beach, quite isolated on that rock.'

She halted.

'*Old* Nest? That's just disrespectful,' Bea gasped. She could hardly get her breath, she was so shocked to hear Nest described like that, even though she was very old. 'And who do you think you are to take on responsibility for the cottage? I mean, saying you were the caretaker. Who said that was your job? Is it your sort of job?' she snapped, surprising herself by the strength of her reaction and the outrage in her voice. She flicked her eyes up and down his body, as if assessing his status.

A headache was forming behind her eyes, the sun was beaming down, and the man's face changed subtly to one with rough cut hair and a long moustache, and surely that was a red linen tunic, a thick leather belt with a long knife in it? Bea rubbed her eyes with her good hand. She realised he was clean shaven and had chin length thick brown hair.

'No, it is not my job. I'm actually a university lecturer and I was merely being friendly,' he said, but managed to look the opposite as well as peppering his words with superiority.

'Right, well, no need.' She didn't feel like rising to the bait and asking what his field of study was. 'As I said, I'm the owner now. Anyway, excuse me. I need to get to the shop,' she said and moved to push past him again, but she stumbled, and Archie skittered away from her legs and she dropped the lead. The path was treacherous after the rain the day before. He grabbed her injured arm.

'Whoa!'

'Let go! I'm fine.' She almost whimpered with pain. 'And as you see, that's sore. Don't touch it, don't touch *me* again!'

She was shivering, and she needed to get away from his gaze and bent to pick up the lead that the dog had trailed in the wet. 'Oh, Archie, come on...' She managed to get the lead and put her hand through the loop.

'Archie? Hmmm. I think you may need to see a doctor,' he said, and she heard an edge of condescension to the remark. 'Old Rhys

Jones is in the village.'

'Another oldie? Well, I won't be needing him.'

She wondered why she hadn't told him she was a doctor herself. Later she decided it was partly because she'd come to hate what she'd become in the job and realised that she wanted to be seen as a person and not a professional type.

'And please stay away from the garden at Nest's Point. Thank you. I don't need you for that either,' she called as he stepped back for her to pass and she made her way down the rest of the path to the road.

'I don't do gardens!' he called after her, but Bea ignored him and stamped up the steep little road, past the chapel and the pub to the village shop and Post Office.

She tied the dog lead to the hook outside and stumbled into the shop; it was crowded with every kind of goods and foods and many eager ears also. The postmaster, Thomas, was inside the tiny security booth counting out some money for a customer, but he saw her immediately and gave her a broad smile. She allowed herself to be grilled pleasantly by several people she knew, asking why she was here, how her clever husband was keeping, when she had arrived, how she was feeling now after lovely Nest had gone, how was the little dog liking it here, what had happened to her arm, in a sling like that, and whether the cottage was to be sold as a holiday home? Her general line was she wasn't selling the cottage and she was here because the clever husband had gone to a conference and was to be the keynote speaker and her arm was a bit of a sprain, thanks for asking. Everyone pointedly refrained from mentioning the wreckage of her face.

The other customers, four women of different ages ,left in dribs and drabs and the postmaster, Thomas, prattled busily as he rang up items on the till.

'D'you know I thought I saw that fancy car of his passing on the road earlier. Must be mistaken. Suppose there's more than one vintage E- type Jag in Regency Red!' Thomas paused and gave her a careful look. 'You all right, love? Don't look your normal self. And covered in mud? What happened? Lose your footing? Archie didn't pull you over did he? And look at that beautiful face. What's happened to you, girl?'

When she gave a brief shake of the head and bent to examine the potatoes in a sack very carefully, she stepped back into a bucket full of plastic seaside spades and bright fishing nets, knocking them over. As she bent to pick them up, she let her hair fall over her face, pretended to adjust the bucket. Thomas saw that she didn't want to be pressed and continued on another tack.

'I've only seen the car here a couple of times, but you know I love the fancy cars. Remember when you were little, and I took you out in that old Sunbeam Alpine I had, the pale blue one? Nest loved that car; so did my lovely Beti, rest her soul.'

She nodded and fumbled with packets of biscuits.

'Don't forget a car like that Sunbeam, d'you?' He served her with dog food, bread, butter, milk, eggs and other essentials. 'And Aberffraw's never seen the like of that E-type either, I'm tellin' you now.'

Bea was shaken and muttered, 'Can't be his, he's in Prague.'

She rummaged in her pockets for her purse to hide her face, she knew her expression would give her away; Thomas was an old friend, a good friend. And she wanted to hide the injuries to her face. Bea hoped beyond hope that her hand wouldn't shake. She caught sight of her ring finger and turned her hand from Thomas's view. It looked worse for the rough treatment she'd inflicted last night when she tried to remove her rings.

'Must need my eyes testing, me. Actually, I do need distance glasses! No, can't have been him! Mind, it was going fast enough for 4 litre engine. It'll be someone else burning rubber on the Rhosneigr road - they always do, these fast car buffs. Maybe someone was going to the racetrack. Seven pounds ninety. Ta.' he said. 'Ooops! Don't worry. There we go, caught it! And here's a dog chew for Archie. Nice to have you back, Bea, love. Catch you later.'

Chapter seven

Alone

O brave new world, That has such people in't!...

Miranda - The Tempest

SOMEHOW, SHE GOT OUT of the shop; the thin crust of calm she had built over the last ten hours was shattered in the heat of Jeremy's psychic search beam and clouded her mind as she walked slowly through the village.

His car. His car's here. It probably was his. Thomas was trying to backtrack.

She decided to give the muddy beach path a miss in case she slipped again and go by the top path, past the church, which meant keeping Archie on the lead. He seemed quite happy to trot along next to her.

Several things dawned on her.

Why didn't I realise? Why would he leave me alone and go to Prague? That's number one. He spent all that time following my every step, listening to every conversation, always watching me with other people. That's two. Then why did I think he'd actually leave me free, even for a weekend? That's three. Why would he let me escape? He's always so possessive. That's four. I'm deluded. I'm dead. How did I not understand this?

The weather brightened from promising to beautiful and a breeze came inland with the tide as she tramped back home.

Home.

Bea was forced to walk carefully because both arms were out of action for balancing purposes. She skirted round the ancient stone church, surrounded by its village of deeply weathered tombstones. They all leaned dangerously at different angles, most of their inscriptions now unreadable and decorated with jewel-like lichens.

Bea remembered; the people had wanted stone and the Prince,

Llewelyn, had given it to them to build a good church on the Christian site, somewhere to worship for the future. Christianity had long ago replaced worship of the ancient gods for all but a few of the people.

Bea shook her head. *What old gods?* she wondered vaguely as she met the narrow path between the modern bungalows; it led straight down to the sandy part of the beach and away from the slippery path near the water. She skirted round a vast tangled carpet of dried seaweed spread across it, high water mark from last week by the looks of it. Last night's storm had left its own high tide just below; tree branches, a plank of wood, plastics of all kinds and many things she couldn't identify that had been thrown there by the waves.

Only last night. Seems like last week.

The tide was filling the estuary and waves danced along towards her. She thought how good it would be for the fishing that day. The men would go out when the tide turned and would be gone twelve hours 'til it turned again. Then there would be mackerel and sand eels for the meal tomorrow and plenty left to salt for the Autumn. Dafydd, her neighbour would get the lobster pots too. The very air was rich and salty, and she breathed deeply. It was a timely reminder for her to tend to the salt-pans, they'd need it for the meat this Winter, even though only a few of the older beasts would be slaughtered, there would be more fish to salt.

What? Bea thought, fleetingly, *Salt?*

She looked up and saw that all the boats in their moorings this side of her cottage were full of activity. There were at least thirty. Men swarmed over them, sorting the sails and nets, getting ready to go out on the high tide. There were other cottages on the ridge where she walked, and their patches of land were marked out from there to the water's edge. Each had a holding trap for fish and at present their boats were all moored, the larger ones with furled sails, smaller ones with empty lobster pots and ropes.

The women were putting washing out on the bushes and tough spiky grass to dry in the heat. A good day. She would do her own washing. She had made plenty of soap last week when the old ewe was killed by her neighbour. The fat and the lanolin were both of use to Nest and she had been given plenty as payment for helping his goodwife at her last child's birth.

The men called to each other, someone shouted in alarm.

It was Bea herself as she slipped on some mud and when she looked up, they had gone. Disappeared. She was stunned. She rubbed her eyes.

'I must be well stressed. Hallucinating big time,' she muttered aloud and hurried on.

As soon as she got back, she brewed more strong coffee, this time with her new milk and added a piece of toast with honey. She gave Archie a crust, which he always took to a corner to eat in privacy. She gobbled the food, more as an antidote to hallucination and shock than because she was hungry, but it did make her feel lighter, more together. Inside the thick stone walls of the cottage it was cool, so she mended the fires. It took an effort with one hand weakened, but it gave her pause to let her mind wander.

I won't think about strange images in my head for now. The brain's a complex thing, as Jeremy is fond of mentioning. But what can I do about him?

She found herself grow cold with apprehension.

Would he follow me here? She tested the possibility. *No? Why go to the trouble of letting me come at all? He's gone to Prague. He wouldn't lie about a high-status conference. Thomas must be mistaken. It couldn't have been his car.*

Her worries grew legs and crawled to the surface of her mind to meet the fears she had hidden since the day before. Such a short time to make a barrier between then and now - the 'now' she wanted to keep.

Maybe I should have gone to one of those shelters for battered wives instead of here. Only I'm not battered, am I? Well, aside from when he left yesterday...and my hair that time. No, I'd feel a fraud going to a shelter. I'm just trapped. She paused. *I was trapped. Now*

I'm here. I'll have to remind myself often.

She moved about the kitchen, putting things away.

I should stand up to him. I should. God, I felt like Superwoman in Med. School. Everyone heaping all that power and glory on your shoulders, bit misplaced with some of our group, and me too, now I think about it. It just went to our heads. It's a good job the nurses brought us all down to Earth.

She managed a smile remembering one or two incidents when she'd been put firmly in her place by a ward sister and then a theatre sister for getting in the way during an operation she was observing.

The thing is, what did Jeremy really think about me? Did he love me? Did he? Was I cherished? I didn't feel the centre of his universe, ever – even when we were first married. I was so besotted I suppose I wouldn't have noticed. But the past year, it's been hell. He's been in my head all the time; pushing himself into my mind. I hate him. Really hate him. Why haven't I got any self-respect? I suppose he stole it.

She didn't know the answer and got herself a refill of coffee then found she couldn't swallow and stood in the middle of the floor holding the mug in her good hand, good, that is, apart from the swollen finger. The other throbbed and her nose was running.

A shelter wouldn't want to be bothered with a case like mine, not when there are women who are beaten black and blue, or beaten to death before they can escape.

She remembered vividly when she'd been doing her rotation in A&E and a woman in her fifties had been brought in, allegedly the victim of someone's rage, a savage attack. Everyone thought she'd been mugged at first. She was well-dressed, wore jewellery and traces of beautiful make-up. It was hard to understand her speech, but eventually she'd managed to scrawl *'husband did it'* on a piece of paper. Bea found that this memory kept resurfacing in the past months. The woman's face was unrecognisable to the relatives who arrived later, and they told the hospital that it couldn't have been the husband's doing, he was a nice man; they had a lovely relationship; there must have been an intruder in their home; and that would be unusual, awful in fact, because it was in a good area.

The woman had been unable to speak much with her broken jaw and a mouthful of shattered teeth, but she'd made an awful choking noise and had tried to move when they said that. She lost consciousness and died quite soon after that from internal injuries, a damaged liver and kidneys. The team in A&E had worked on her frantically; they were waiting for a theatre to become free.

The woman's husband was brought in later that night, covered in dried blood, claiming he'd been assaulted, left in his garage at home. He said he must have been unconscious for some time; he had no memory of anything. He didn't even know where his wife was. What had happened to her? He said he was distraught. He had severe lacerations to his knuckles and the backs of his hands, but most of the blood on his body and particularly his knuckles, turned out to be his wife's. The Registrar in ER had alerted the police when the man had asked if his wife had been brought in here earlier in the evening and eventually the truth had come out. Bea remembered his face. It had been pleasant, ordinary, his eyes inviting sympathy.

People would notice if I was injured physically, but they wouldn't connect it to Jeremy, would they? Anyway, what would I look like then, having so little self-respect that I'd let him do it? But I did let him hit me and lock me up. He locked me up in my room. Could I have stopped him? I can't talk; I've been a prisoner. Maybe women who get beaten up have already lost their courage and sense of self-preservation, lost their identity? Am I like that? Perhaps it gets beaten out of them, or they just take what's given because of the children or something; feel they've got to manage as best they can, nowhere else to go. That's beyond sad. What would I have done if he'd beaten me more than this, if it had shown? I'd have had to take a sick day. No one would believe it of him, ever. But the patients don't take to him and most of the nurses hate him, I know it. But he's Mr. Popular with the senior medical staff, smooth, urbane, talented.

Still standing, she managed to get the mug to her lips and scald them with the coffee and her nose dripped blood into the mug. Archie nudged her leg, whined, but she didn't take any notice.

But what do I know really? I'm just the mousey wife that his friends speculate about, wonder incredulously to each other why he married me, why I'm a mess and he's so polished, why a successful surgeon would want an unsuccessful young doctor and twelve years his junior. I'm not in his social stratosphere, am I? I'm so low status I'm off the scale.

Bea was in the middle of the floor staring at the newly kindled fire in the living room. The sun streamed in through the tiny window and she suddenly roused herself, put the coffee on the flags at her feet and rushed to the front door to lock then double bolt it. Archie watched. He'd gone to his favourite spot by the hearth and sat watching.

Nest had never used the bolts. It had been Bea and her Mum who insisted; there'd been a rash of news items about older people being burgled in their isolated cottages and farms, here in Anglesey. Bea locked the back door and then drew every curtain in the entire house, despite it being daytime. She picked up her coffee to drink it in the fire nook, but by then she was trembling so much she spilled most of it on the stone flags as she got herself one-handedly down onto the stool. She wiped her nose on the back of her hand.

Maybe keeping me as his pet mouse makes Jeremy feel good, makes it look like he's caring for someone needy, because he's such a nice guy he'd take on someone like me even though I'm so unworthy. Maybe they're right. I'm his missionary service, his charity case. But I do look a mess these days; he's right about that. I hardly eat so I don't know why I've piled on so much weight. Should I join a gym? I'm knackered after my shift though. I've just done overtime for three weekends too. Thank goodness he gave me the sleeping pills really. I must have been really exhausted to have such a reaction to them; it's only a mild prescription, after all. But that cocoa! I hate it. I could retch at the thought. He made me drink every last drop...then not letting me go to the loo...

Bea shivered with disgust She had begun to feel worse. She was suddenly assaulted by an unwelcome wave of guilt and tried to look at things from his point of view.

Maybe I'm a bit pushy when we go to parties or have people for a meal. Maybe I should just listen more and not try and join in. All right, the food was a bit overcooked last time – which was six months ago, now I think, and I did get the pud from M & S. Jeremy was okay about it. He didn't actually tell me about it 'til they'd gone. I could get caterers in. Would that be okay, or would he say I should cook, like Alicia or Jocelyn?

She stopped mid-stream as a blinding thought hit her.

Wait a minute. You're talking as though you're going back. Get a grip of yourself Bea. You're never going back. You're here now and you're safe. It's all that talk of an E-type Jag speeding through the village.

She squirmed on her stool and drank the mouthful left in her coffee mug. Then she went to the front window, the one that bloke, Roberts, had peered through last night and pulled back the curtain a little to peek outside. She forgot why she'd drawn them, except it felt safer to be enclosed with Auntie Nest. When she was little, Nest had cuddled her on her knee and said that she was a tiny bird or a little *bee* in a *nest*! They'd giggled. Anyway, now there was Archie, who she loved as much as her mum had. Okay, he was eighteen, which is old by general dog standards, and maybe he wouldn't last much longer, but he was so fit, as many terriers were. He deserved to have a lovely life and not one where Jeremy hated him. Dogs felt these things, and apart from the kicks Jeremy had given him from time to time, he'd locked him up too, in the garage.

I allowed that she remembered miserably.

Outside the sun shone and the sea in the estuary was still, slack water before the tide turned. The cottage was on an outcrop of rock and the front garden sloped down to the high- water mark and it was just an arm's length above the mark that the garden wall stood. There was nothing between Nest's Point and the village, just the long, clean, empty sweep of the beach and the river before it emptied into the sea. At the mouth of the wide estuary, the sea and the sky vied with each other to see which changed the faster, which was more mercurial, more magical, more deeply soul stirring.

Bea was mesmerised by the glinting ripples on the surface of the water when suddenly her eye was caught by a brighter flash of light opposite, on the top of the dunes. A series of flashes followed and then as she jumped back, startled, Bea thought she saw a figure moving on top of the slopes, weaving through the Marram grass.

She yanked the curtain closed again.

'What the hell was that?' she whispered to herself. *It couldn't be camera flash, could it?* she wondered and suddenly felt her chest tighten, her breathing grow shallow. She forced herself to exhale forcefully several times to rid herself of the idea and control her breathing then she inhaled slowly three times, each one slower than the last. Felt better.

No, it wasn't a camera flash.... Yes, it may have been. Don't get paranoid, Bea. No one wants to photograph you here. You're not tabloid-worthy. What would the headline be? 'Consultant's crazy wife legs it to land of her fathers?' Someone was photographing birds is all. The dunes are a nature reserve after all – special scientific interest or something.

She began to wander round the cottage, opening cupboards, drawers, rummaging along shelves with shaking hands, picking up a lump of sea glass, a fossil she'd found in Lyme Regis, a Roman pot that Nest had found here in Aberffraw. Bea was not looking for anything, just feeling the place, trying to become part of it again.

No, I'm not going back, ever. I don't care about money, my salary or what my half of the house might be. I don't. Anyway, it's his house isn't it? I've got the money Mum left me and I've got this place now. Thank you, Auntie Nest. He doesn't know; I hope. I'll get some sort of job when I'm settled. I'll go into Beaumaris tomorrow and see a solicitor, about a divorce. God, a divorce! What will Jeremy say to that? Maybe there's a Citizens Advice place or something. I need to talk to someone, perhaps? But she wasn't sure.

It was early days. All she really wanted was to sit in front of the fire with Archie in Auntie Nest's cottage. She would do the garden, walk on the cliffs, be by the sea where Nest had lived. It was a place of healing.

I could grow even more herbs than Auntie Nest did, get into alternative medicine. What would everyone at work say about that? I could become a medical herbalist or something. I am a doctor, so I do know about treating people. And I like people. I've always wanted to help them. Right, she told herself.

She went to the front door, drew the bolts and peered out of the crack she'd opened, listening carefully. Nothing but the soft swush of the water as the wind freshened, the sound of the grasses trembling in the delicate breeze. Bea laughed at herself and opened the door wide and stepped out into the sandy garden, completely forgetting her fears of being watched, except by Archie who came to sit by the door.

I'm going to be a 'wise-woman', a herbalist, a white witch or whatever people call them. Didn't Auntie Nest make a book of all her remedies? It must be here somewhere.

Bea gazed around her.

This place is heaven and I'm staying.

She flung off her sling and lifted both arms in the air and began to turn around slowly on the spot. She laughed out loud, speeded up and flung back her head as she hadn't done for so long. Her hair whirled about her like a Catherine wheel.

She didn't see the next series of flashes from the dunes further down.

Chapter eight

Unquiet

The hour's now come;
the very minute bids thee ope thine ear…

Prospero - The Tempest

LATER THAT AFTERNOON a dark red E-type Jaguar drew into a sheltered lay-by on the outskirts of Menai Bridge, miles from Aberffraw. Five minutes later it was joined by a Ford Focus in a nondescript blue, driven by an equally unremarkable woman wearing a collection of outdoor clothes in several shades of beige.

Jem Fitzmartin got out of the Jag and joined her in the passenger seat of the Ford. He tried to avoid having people in his own vehicle and the private investigator he had hired was certainly as grubby looking as her job was dirty. Still, as he told himself, he required her services at the moment and needs must...

He turned to look at her and once again decided she was a very unattractive woman. She had medium-length mousey hair scraped back under a black beanie hat and close up it was clear she was in her early forties and not the student she appeared at a distance. But, he decided, close up she also looked a lot more experienced and competent. In fact, she was an ex-police officer, once a Detective Inspector and had taken early retirement from the force to run her own private investigation agency. She came very highly recommended by one of Jeremy's friends.

He didn't waste time with social niceties.

'What have you got for me, Miss Smythe?'

'Dana, please, and quite a bit to start with,' she answered, her voice crisp, professional.

She took her camera out of a bag on the back seat and proceeded to show him a series of photographs of Bea in various locations.

'Looks completely wild!' he muttered; his brow furrowed in

distress.

He didn't seem able to drag his eyes off the image of Bea's blurred face at the window of the cottage the night before. It had been taken with a long lens and given the distance across the cottage garden and the heavy rainy conditions, it was a remarkable shot. An outstanding shot. Bea was holding the oil lamp to the window and a man was on the outside looking in. They both looked crazed.

'Her face looks strange. Oh my…'he murmured. 'An accident of some sort?'

But her face was the second shot because the first was of a man who was battering the cottage door. The light from the little front window and his huge torch illuminated the front of his head but the back blended into the night, the chiaroscuro effect adding a macabre note to the expression of manic fury on his face.

Jeremy turned to look directly into Dana's face.

'Who is the man?' he asked and then without waiting for an answer he continued, 'By the way, I'm impressed by the technical achievement. How did you manage that photograph in the storm? It's really quite astounding.'

Dana ignored the overtly patronising tone of his voice and the quizzical the set of his head and replied politely, 'It settled to a heavy squall and I was lucky, the rain eased off completely for a few minutes and gave me a clear shot just when I needed it. The other bit of luck was there'd been so many flashes of lightning; one or two from me was nothing. The bloke was too intent on banging on the door to notice anyway. Obviously, I tailed her from Manchester as soon as I got your call. Then I followed her from the village car park. Actually, I managed to hide behind the wall - full waterproofs!' She laughed. 'And I had intended to take a look through the windows, see what she was doing but then I saw the bloke coming up the beach path, torchlight bobbing along, y'know. I just got my camera out in time when he arrived. These other shots, here…'

She pointed out ten more pictures of Bea and the man arguing, wondering why a man would be so interested in the technicalities of the photography if he feared for his wife.

'The same man next day. She doesn't seem to like him, see her expression? Look at his too. Possibly a man with a short fuse, but who knows? I found out he's a neighbour. The chap at the post office is very knowledgeable about everyone,' she said, scrolling through a few shots of Gwyn chatting to Thomas-the-Post outside the shop. 'The man's a Dr Gwyn Roberts – university lecturer, not medical. Been here on the island some time, only just moved to Aberffraw,' she told him.

There were several shots of Bea and a tall man standing on the path, mouths wide, faces contorted, Bea looking harassed, her falling, more argument and then her struggling back from the shop with her basket and slipping about. The final shots showed her peering out of the curtained window when she got back that morning. She looked beside herself with fear, but these were followed by several showing her with her arms held wide as she twirled wildly outside on the path. The scarf sling was still round her neck as she'd freed the arm and, swinging as it did, it lent Bea a Bohemian look.

Jeremy said, 'A sling, that cut on her cheek and the swollen nose; she must have had an accident. And the dog…really. It was her mother's. It should be put down – decrepit.'

'I did see her fall on her way up the beach, but I was trying to keep to my own feet at the time, let me tell you, but it was pretty treacherous out there. What possessed her to do that walk in a storm…'

Jeremy smiled, and he appeared grimly satisfied to Dana, who caught the look before he turned his head away.

He said, 'Well, Beatrix certainly looks like a candidate for Psychiatric Patient of the Year. There, if she carries on like this, she'll get herself sectioned before I'm forced to do it for her.'

Dana turned to face him.

'Can I ask you, Sir, is that your intention here? Maybe you feel she's mentally ill, you being a doctor yourself, I mean. I got the impression, when you hired me that this would be a straightforward case of a suspected affair?'

'It may well be that too,' he said and glared at her coldly. 'But about your other comment, are you suggesting I would get my wife sectioned when she didn't warrant it? That would be highly irregular, not to say unethical and against the law. And we are talking about *my wife* here and *I am a doctor*. I have taken an oath, an oath for each status in fact.'

Dana Smythe was a very experienced woman and had been a well-regarded police officer, so she wasn't at all intimidated by this neurosurgeon with money and a massive ego. Her expression was uncommunicative; she had always been able to retain the same poker face throughout the most gruelling interviews when she'd been in the police.

'Sure,' she answered with a smile, prepared to listen longer before deciding what she thought of him and whether to keep the case. After all, being self-employed and having a good police pension meant she didn't have to work for people whose motives she thought suspect.

'Good. Let's keep to the remit then, shall we? I feel my wife is under a great deal of strain, as will be witnessed by our many friends. She will not confide in me and is behaving uncharacteristically, abandoning her job yesterday, her job as a doctor. As you know, I suspect she is having some sort of an affair, and this man may be the one, whether they were rowing or not. But the erratic behavioural development worries me even more, so very much more.' He broke off to look out of the window, as if to steady a tide of emotion.

'May I be frank?' he said quietly, just a slight catch in his voice.

Dana nodded silently, knowing that people who said that were usually intending the opposite.

'I fear someone may be trying to influence her with a view to taking her money from her, if not her sanity. There is a substantial Trust Fund and she has also inherited that ramshackle place on the beach. I feel it is too isolated and unhealthy and has bad memories for her.'

'Ah,'

'She thinks I don't know about her financial windfall, a legacy from her mother. She's been so secretive lately, uncharacteristically so. Really, I... I don't...' He stopped again and clasped his knuckle to his lips, as though pressing back the emotion. 'I don't know what's triggered this whole episode. It's rather upsetting.'

He turned to face the window, several seconds went by, he coughed, cleared his throat. Dana watched him closely, wondering about the depth of the emotion he was showing. In her experience of husbands who suspected infidelity there was jealousy and frustration, anger in bucket loads and often the need to find the man and take revenge, but this man didn't fit he usual type. He was being overprotective of his own emotions if he was supposed to be concerned for his wife's mental health. For a man who took control of others as part of his daily life and took control of their minds in a very fundamental way as a neurosurgeon, Dana thought he was a weird erratic mixture of the restrained and dramatic. When he had retained her services, he had been altogether organised and clinical and far removed from emotional; it was the change that was puzzling her. She decided to keep her own counsel for the time being. He was the customer. For now.

Jeremy continued, 'I really ought to have persuaded her to give me Enduring Power of Attorney so that I can look after her, if the worst happens and she breaks down completely. I'd need to get her sectioned then. You see, there is a history of mental health problems in the family. She was a virtual prisoner there as a child, in that cottage. She was kept away from others and I do suspect there was some abuse. Her family were somewhat peculiar.'

He turned his head away again. Dana took the cue and asked, 'You okay to go on?'

He nodded shakily and continued. 'How she escaped and managed to get into Medical School is a mystery. Indeed, she was on a crash course to failure when she met me, and I paid her fees - helped her finish the course, shall we say.' He held Dana's eyes with his own.

'Beatrix is everything to me, Ms Smythe. And I have already given you the reasons for my having her watched. I do suspect someone has lured her into an affair and she's vulnerable, so very vulnerable. Apart from anything else, I need her watched for her own safety.'

'It's Mrs Smythe, actually, Dr Fitzmartin,' she said, evenly, smiling.

'And that would be *Mr* Fitzmartin, as I'm a consultant.'

'Touché. And of course, you're the boss.' Dana closed her camera up. 'You want me to watch for the rest of the week?'

'As arranged, Mrs Smythe. And it happens that I am staying with friends just over the bridge – the Britannia that is, in Caernarvon, so I am in the area, if needed. You have my mobile number, of course.'

He returned to his own car.

Dana Smythe stocked up on snack food in Menai Bridge and made her way back to Aberffraw to continue her surveillance. She'd booked a room in the pub there. The night of the storm she'd gone back to the mainland and found a cheap chain hotel, one where the staff didn't ask questions about someone arriving drenched in the early hours.

She wondered about the real motives of the attractive doctor. She wondered about the blond hair and celebrity moustache, his obvious pleasure in his appearance, his strange dramatic performance. His blue eyes repelled her; they were simply icy and not comforting as Dana imagined most people would want from someone medical.

She decided that the wife was definitely odd too and, on balance, she felt he might be correct about the mental breakdown. She also thought the wife, Beatrix, was too rough-looking, too obviously disorganised for a doctor and quite the opposite of him; not that the latter made for a bad marriage but what did worry her was that they didn't seem to gel as a couple. She wouldn't have paired them up in a million years. She'd not even spoken to Beatrix, didn't have any idea what her personality was like. She just had a gut feeling. More importantly, Dana didn't get the impression that Mr Fitzmartin adored his wife or even liked her for that matter, despite his dramatics in the car. Then there was the little dog. His antipathy was raw. Dana was a dog lover herself and this worried her.

When she got back to the village Dana checked that Beatrix's old Fiat was still in the pub car park, which it was. People would know it by sight if she was a frequent visitor to the cottage, so it was unlikely the authorities would be alerted for an old car seemingly dumped and, in any case, no one would steal a car like that. Even joyriders had standards. That meant that if it wasn't there, then Beatrix wasn't either. Dana had parked her own in the same car park and walked into the pub, *The Llewelyn*, where she was staying.

Her cover story was bird watching and that she was a mature student doing a Master's, an MSc, in Marine Biology at Aberystwyth University, with special attention to coastal bird life. Her main focus was the oystercatcher and its changing feeding habits. She was in her fourth year as a student and and working on her Master's dissertation. She told people she was particularly concerned to research the amount of flotsam the birds ingested or were injured by: fishing nets, wire, polystyrene, metal cans, and more disgustingly, condoms and tampons. People always looked shocked when she mentioned the last items, as though other rubbish was not that harmful and certainly less revolting.

As part of her cover story she'd done a range of photos of the birds and, as she actually loved photography, they were really good. People in the bar were impressed. She was a very sociable woman and people liked talking to her, but such was her skill that she was never truly memorable, simply a nice woman student, 'bit older than the usual lot'. She blended in.

Dana made her way through the village over the River Ffraw, via the stone footbridge, and up the long, hard sand of the beach on the dune side of the estuary. This sort of open environment would normally be difficult for surveillance because of its very bleakness; there were no people to mix with, no obstacles to hide behind, the whole landscape had a uniformity that would highlight anything out of the ordinary. So, she settled on a bivouac in the dunes opposite Nest's Point and a bird watching hide was as good a cover as she'd ever had in circumstances such as this. Ideal, in fact.

The weather was pleasant for the time of year; windy with the tang of salt on the sea air and quite sunny. She planned to do a fair amount of photography to maintain her cover and she had two cameras with her, one for each focus of her attention.

Chapter nine

Expectations

We are such stuff as dreams are made on...

Prospero - The Tempest

THAT AFTERNOON Bea began to feel a tiny sliver of hope, the tiniest germ of hope and it came in the form of a sense of freedom remembered. It was different from the feelings she'd had on leaving home for university because that was the freedom of happy expectation based on a childhood of love. She remembered that heady, confident independence of her eighteen-year-old self; she savoured the thought as though it were a deep secret.

But she knew this feeling she was experiencing had overtones of panic and thankfulness after her escape from torment, so she decided she would distance herself from the source of the panic and find herself a solicitor before Jeremy found her. The more she thought about it, the more she realised that very thing could happen, so she pushed the idea of him away, firmly, roughly, and tried to focus on the things around her. She wanted to feel herself physically and emotionally in the present, to surrender herself to the magic of the house and the sea, to make herself better, whole again. That need to feel better was what she concentrated on.

After the toast and honey, the sugar rush was moreish, and she had had a minty iced finger she'd bought from Thomas-the-Post. It was flavoured with the nectar of fond memories that surfaced as she ate, memories of mint, lavender, fennel, chamomile, all the herbs she loved. They'd always grown well for Nest, so pushing the last of the bun into her mouth, she went out to the back of the cottage to see what had survived in the pots in the yard.

Mint was thriving in a huge drift, growing in a long, narrow pocket of soil in a cleft of the rock. Although past its very best at this time of the year, it smelled wonderful and she decided to make some mint tea when she went indoors. She cut a whole armful, a sheaf of the stuff and cradled it; she'd hang up what she didn't need, to dry for Winter use. Nest said that the early morning was best for picking any herbs, when the rising sun had dried the leaves and the essential oils were at their zenith of perfection. But the oils would have waned by now. Bea didn't mind.

Archie followed her, wherever she went. When she looked at him, she was doubly glad that she'd taken that chance to run. He looked ten years younger, his tail was up, his eyes bright with expectation. Dogs lived for the moment in many ways.

The cottage stood on an outcrop of rock which rose behind the building and gave way to open land beyond, on top of the low cliff, the headland. She climbed up onto the outcrop and gazed over the meadow, found herself thinking how good it was to have harvested the hay before the storm. It was a second crop in late Summer, all neatly cut and stacked in so many stooks she could hardly count them as they stretched away in front of her.

Stooks of hay? What am I talking about? Bea was puzzled, lifted a hand to shade her eyes and see more clearly without the glare of the sun.

Something slid down her shoulder and, for a second, she looked down at the buttercup yellow brychan and wondered how she came to be wearing it. It had been round Nest's shoulders in her dream, surely? Perhaps she was dreaming now, but when she raised her eyes to the meadow again, she knew she was seeing it through Nest's eyes.

It was a good crop and the overwintering animals would have plenty of Winter feed after Lughnasadh. She always looked forward to this feast, the celebration of harvest's beginning.

What is it the Saxons call this feast? – ah yes, Lammas. 'Tis strange to the ear instead of our own, Lughnasadh. There will be meat and honey cakes, mead and ale. And the dancing! We will be dancing around the fire on the cliff late into the night, she thought. *The sparks will swirl up into the night like new stars rushing to join their fellows. I love this night sky, so full of stars it's like a milky white veil trailed across the heavens by a gentle hand.*

She imagined the night, feeling the joy to come, she bent her head into the sheaf of mint in her arms and immersed herself in its sharp sweetness, its gentle greenery.

A gull cried overhead, almost behind her, and she ducked as it swooped low over the cliff. When she straightened up, she saw that a mist had risen out at sea; a breeze ran before it over the lush wildflower meadow where she stood; the grasses and flowers dipped and swayed - an ocean of colour. The tide was changing already, and Bea realised she must have been on the headland some time. Archie was sitting patiently next to her, but she didn't register that.

What's happened? Where've they gone...? Bea started to ask herself because the stooks of hay had disappeared. She felt round her shoulders to pull up the brychan, but it wasn't there, nor had it fallen to the ground. Instead, a huge gull swept down and brushed her head with its wing. She screamed, flung an arm over her head. Archie set up an angry barking at the gull and jumped up on the spot, trying to get hold of it as it swooped again.

'Arch, come on!' Bea called and ran down to the back door. The dog followed, looking up more than once. The gull itself soared high overhead screeching at others that had gathered. Bea had never liked the herring gulls, the biggest gulls. Her head felt tight. She was certainly tired and certainly tense.

You don't run from someone like Jeremy without exhausting all your reserves of nervous energy; you try to keep your mind intact while he shreds your nerves like so much rubbish,' she thought. The harvest and the longed-for Autumn feast went out of her mind.

Once inside she re-bolted the door and made the mint tea, leaving the rest of the sheaf in the sink, to be dealt with later. She gathered Archie up and they lay huddled on the broad old settle near the fire, her head propped on cushions, grasping the mug and sipping frantically as though the tea were a life-giving elixir. The curtains were left closed and she thought that was for the best. She hated the idea of someone being able to peek through the window at her as she slept, and she intended to sleep until she felt better. What was that odd vision on the top field? She'd felt as though she were Nest herself. Images of waving grasses, stooks of hay, bonfires under the stars and white-winged gulls interwove with the lustre of the sun on the sea; her eyelids drooped, and she drifted off to sleep.

She saw Nest as soon as her eyes closed.

The Prince sent for Nest. The message was given to a page, as it had been last time, but then the boy had been intercepted by Yestyn. Earlier that afternoon Yestyn had ridden out along with his band of brothers, the rest of Llewellyn's Uchelwr, to hunt the rich forest along the coast from Aberffraw.

Nest was at the door when she noticed a boy jogging up the beach path. He halted sharply when he spotted her and the wolves and shifted nervously from foot to foot like a young colt.

'Mistress Nest, will they eat me?' he called up to her from where he'd halted. He was the son of one of the Marcher lords, sent to learn the ways of the llys, the court, with another noble family. This was one of the English customs that Llewelyn thought properly useful to broaden any boy's experience. The boy who stood waiting at the end of the path was Ralph de Warren, and he was ten and tall for his age.

Nest smiled and called, 'No bach, they have already eaten today!'

Then as the boy hesitated, she laughed and beckoned him, saying, 'I am teasing, they'd like to meet you; they're my wolf children!'

'Meet me?' he repeated to himself as he walked slowly towards her, partly reassured by the waving tails of the two wolves which stood as he approached.

'Mellt, Seren, meet Ralph,' she said as both the wolves walked towards the boy, heads dipped, ears folded loosely near their heads. Their bodies swayed gently as they moved, and they licked their lips with the very tips of their huge tongues. Both touched the boy with their noses and rubbed their bodies against him and when Ralph put a hand on each of their backs and laughed, they began yipping and cavorting in front of him. His trews and tunic were soon covered in wolf fur, layering them with grey fur over the brown cloth.

'See, you *are* welcomed, Ralph!' Nest cried. 'And you look like a wolf cub now!'

'How *do* you know my name, Mistress Nest?' Ralph asked as he tentatively stroked Seren who had come to lean against him.

'The same way you know mine, I just heard it spoken, heard that the prince had a page, soon to be a squire, one who was tall as a young sapling birch and as blond as sunlight on a Summer morn. And I know why you are here too.'

'You do? How? Why am I here then?' He looked dumbfounded and Nest ruffled his hair.

'Do not fear. I guessed you come with a message from your Lord and mine. I think he's got a headache because it's a warm and close day; the clouds are massing over the edge of the world and I think there will be a great storm. The heaviness in the air brings pain in the head to some people. And I'm needed to bring him a soothing remedy. Am I right, Ralph?'

He wriggled uncomfortably as she held his eye.

'No, I am not a weather witch,' she said, laughing.

He gulped. 'You saw into my mind, you know what I was thinking,' he whispered and swallowed uncomfortably.

She smiled again and shook her head.

'I *guessed* again because the *expression* on your face told me what you thought, Ralph, bach. I merely looked at the weather, saw you look at the clouds then back at me, a little suspiciously I thought. And I remembered that the Prince has headaches when there is a storm coming. That is all. How do you like Mellt and Seren?'

'They are beautiful,' he crooned and gazed at their sleek bodies, kind eyes. 'I saw the Prince caress them when I was serving his ale. I thought my Lord had magic powers to calm them so.'

The boy walked quietly to Mellt who had gone to sit near the cottage door as he saw his sister being fondled. Ralph stroked his shoulder and the wolf touched the boy with his nose.

'He has, in a way. Do you know what those powers are? They are trust and respect for all creatures. Mellt and Seren feel this and they willingly give it back. They know the Prince feels the same way about me and they love him for it. Now they have met you, they will be your friends too; because I want it to be so.'

The boy beamed with pleasure.

'You'll come to the llys then, Mistress Nest? My Lord said you were to come quickly.'

Nest collected her scrip and her remedies, and they walked together back to the llys and straight into the Prince's privy chamber.

'Snowden's Prince looks ill and pasty today,' Nest said by way of greeting as she laid her scrip on a large painted book coffer and began to unpack it casually.

Her tone was familiar and not a little judgemental. She stood in front of him, hands on hips, her expression severe.

Llewelyn lifted himself up from the long, cushioned settle by the hearth. There was no fire as the day was warm and it was cool inside the stone walls.

'God's Wounds! Is that the way you address your Lord and Prince, woman?' he growled.

'It is,' she answered and pushed him back down again with a single hand.

Hovering in the doorway, Ralph gasped.

Llewelyn heard.

'Don't worry, boy,' he called. 'This Nest and I are childhood friends. We played together on the beach as babes.'

'Ah! I was a babe and you were a youth set to watch me!' Nest corrected him.

He made a face.

'Her mother tended mine until she died. Mind, she's the only one allowed to speak thus to her Lord.'

He put out a hand to Nest to reassure the boy.

'Fetch ale for us, Ralph. Ah, I see Mellt and Seren like you!' he said as he saw the boy ran his hands along their backs when he passed between them. 'That is a recommendation indeed for any person. You will be a true knight and an honest one, Ralph.'

Smiling, Ralph trotted off on his errand.

'Now, my gentle Lord, what ails?' Nest asked briskly as she

rubbed lavender oil into her palms and at a gesture from Llewelyn moved behind him. He had taken a stool and as he sat forward, she reached her hands to his head and began massaging the oil into his temples.

'Ah, that's as soothing as the song of a mountain nymph…'

'And I am a nymph of the shore and the dancing waves, one that rejoices in the sunlight and the west wind!' she replied, her voice deliberately sing song in the style of the bards. She grinned. He couldn't see her face.

'If you would but play the harp too, I'd banish my bard, Ithel, and install you in my hall. He's got a biting tongue at times.'

'I can coax the harp to sing when it suits me. And you know I can, but I don't wish to at the moment. Anyway, if I were your bard you would imprison me, shackle me to the fireside when I belong to the sea and the storm. And yes, Ithel is a man nearer Hell than Heaven, or are we not now told that there is this place they call Purgatory where souls wait to be saved? He will wait there a long time, forsooth, but he is a man of the Druids and the old forbidden ways, and not a Christian at all. Is it he that worries you?'

The Prince was aware that Ithel hated Nest; the man had made his feelings obvious for all to see, including Nest herself.

'Aye, he worries me, but as a fly on a hot day,' Llewelyn said.

'I don't blame you for it, though Ithel might and his friends of the old beliefs,' she murmured. 'Many people still keep the way of the Druids. In fact, many people feel it prudent to have a foot in both camps and hold with both beliefs, even after these many centuries of our good Lord's Church.'

She kept her voice soft to aid his relaxation. She was beginning to realise that he was more worried than she had thought about his kingdom, his warring sons, and his wife.

He turned. 'I'm fine now, I thank you Nest. It was a pretext to speak to you,' he said.

'You, the Prince of North Wales and all Snowdonia need one?' She stood back and stared at him.

'I do not, but I wish to allay suspicion. I don't want people to speak of me using you as my advisor and fuelling the flames of discontent. Many of them come to you for help, and I know, as they do, that your healing is of the natural elements and not those of the dark necromancer.'

'I only use my common sense and my knowledge of the world we live in, cariad.' She wiped her hands on a cloth from her scrip then sat on the settle near him.

Llewelyn shook his head, sighed heavily.

He said, 'I need to be a diplomat, forsooth and keep the favour of the English King. Now John is dead, son Henry, a wily lout himself, is ever ready to accuse me of plotting: plotting with the foul and blackened Druids, as he terms them, and Goodness knows they're well hidden, have been for centuries. I'm accused of plotting with the Church to make our worship here in Wales for the Welsh alone, of plotting with my sons to overthrow English domination of trade and land, of plotting with seers to divine the future, of plotting with witches to make rain spoil the English harvest. God's Blood, it's never at an end.'

'But you still suspect the Princess of infidelity? I wonder why.'

'The Holy Virgin alone knows that! She seems devout. She's contrite. She's seemed so since de Braose's death. She seems deeply shamed and wanting my forgiveness. By Our Lady and Sweet Jesus, I've given it freely enough. She can't believe me. I know in my heart it was lust and boredom that led her astray and I take some blame for being always abroad, away from her side on some campaign or other.'

Nest laid a hand on his arm. 'You'd the kingdom to keep safe.' She watched his face as she asked, 'Does she truly love you though?'

'How like a woman to ask. As much as she ever did, I think. We were passionate when young, aye, but less so now. Her heart has gone from her. She's not a passionate woman with me any longer.' He spoke heavily and gazed longingly into Nest's eyes.

She ignored his unspoken comment.

'More importantly, do you love her? And don't bend the truth, nor play the hypocrite with me.' She held his eyes remorselessly.

'I am fifty years old, but my heart beats with the hot passions of a raw and lusty youth – yet, and I cannot deceive you, my Nest, it does not beat for my wife alone.' His eyes filled with desire.

'Stop that! We're not children.' She turned his face away with a hand and pressed on. 'But you suspect your Lady wife of doing again just what you want to do now?'

He stood suddenly, explosively.

'I'm weak with you. God's wounds, woman, you're truly a witch.' His voice rose and she patted the air to tell him to lower it. To say such things aloud could be dangerous for her, even if she was close to the Prince.

He took a pace or two away; every movement spoke of contained power ready to detonate into violent action. His back was turned to her as he spoke.

'But you know I am faithful for the sake of my marriage; 'tis God's commandment, and for the sake of my people. I can't afford common gossip to undermine my sons or the power of my kingdom. We must keep the peace and trade with England if the land is to prosper at all. I can long for another in my heart only. You know it, Nest. And I listen to gossip despite knowing I shouldn't. By Our Lady, any false gossip or unwelcome truth about my wife can be just as damaging if aired abroad to all and sundry. You know there has ever been a hard core of people who don't trust her because she is Norman born and more because she's John's daughter.' He swung round to face her, his expression determined.

'I've decided I need you to watch her, Nest. I trust you above all others. In any case it is my command, you can't refuse, woman.'

She stood also. 'I wouldn't refuse you anything. I'll watch her to see how she is faring, to see if she needs anything, is in health. I can help that way.'

'And you, you're well?' He glanced at her stomach, it seemed reluctantly. 'When's the child to be born? You didn't tell me when.' He looked away, the muscles on the side of his jaw twitched, his voice was tight.

'In the Spring, with the gales, the melt water and the golden lilies. And yes, I'm well.' She looked uncomfortable and Llewelyn suddenly understood as she unconsciously passed her hand over her stomach; it was a protective gesture.

'You wish to keep this secret for now?'

She nodded. 'Yes.'

'I'll look after you, and the child, Nest.'

'I know that.'

'So you do, I'Truth! You're also the most exasperating woman I know. Take your wolves and leave.'

He grinned suddenly and bent to stroke Mellt and Seren as they ambled past.

'Ralph! Page, ho! Where is my ale?' he bellowed.

The boy came running with a jug held in two hands and two cups pushed down the front of his jerkin.

'Steady, Ralph!' Nest laughed as he tried to negotiate a way round the wolves. 'My Lord will give you one of the cups as I'm not in need!'

Llewelyn laughed too.

'I'll share ale with Master Ralph when he gains his first win with that wooden sword he plays with!'

As Nest walked slowly away from the Llys, Ithel ap Deykin, the Prince's bard glanced out of one of the lancet windows by the gatehouse and watched her. He had been passing the Prince's chamber and saw Nest enter, then had found himself a place in an alcove to listen in privacy to what they said. It had been enlightening and he smiled to himself; it had been surprisingly good to hear his Lord expressing a need for comfort and voicing his worries.

He was in the habit of murmuring lines of poetry or song to himself and thinking aloud was now an engrained habit, especially when he was deeply disturbed. He walked quickly along the shaded passages of the llys.

'He becomes more English by the day. Should a prince of Wales try so hard to keep the peace with the usurper beyond the mountains? Or should he fight to free his people? Gruffydd should be his heir, the son of a Welsh prince and a Welsh woman, a beautiful Welsh woman.'

He closed his eyes remembering Gruffydd's mother, Tangwystl, one of Llewelyn's conquests before he married Joanna. She was the very same Tangwystl, who was Ithel's own first love, dead these twenty years and more. His expression hardened, and he had to steady himself by leaning against the wall until the fit of black despair and pure hatred passed.

'Tangwystl chose Llewelyn, not me and he chose Dafydd to be his heir, half English from his own cursed mother. Choices, choices. We all make them. Well, let's see what choices my lord makes about his Norman English wife.'

He made his way swiftly back to his cell, already composing in his mind the poem he would sing that evening in the hall. It would be of lost love, heartache, fidelity and the feats of the old gods, a poem to make Llewelyn's heart break. He would sing also of the wolves who came from the mountains to wreak havoc and destruction on the llys of men and the feats performed by those men who slayed the vile, ferocious beasts.

The second revelation thrilled him.

'And Nest, what have you done? So, you expect a child. Would it be of royal blood also? This would be interesting and useful, if only it were so....'

He was well satisfied with the information he'd gleaned.

Chapter ten

Unwelcome

There be some sports are painful,

and their labour delight in them sets off.

Some kinds of baseness are nobly undergone ...

Ferdinand - The Tempest

MUCH LATER AND FAR AWAY, the young men of Llewelyn's court turned their horses for home; their pack ponies were carrying much game, mostly deer and boar and a huge cache of rabbits killed by the dogs. They rode abreast along the beach, their horses' hooves splashing in the small waves, and the scent of the sea whirling around them on the spray they kicked up. The mountains of Yr Wyddfa were behind them across the Straits and Caer yn Arfon, on the coast of the mainland, was made a golden town by the last rays of the sun that turned the waves into a flickering field of flames.

They were quiet, quiet in their companionship, replete. It was as they rounded the headland and came in sight of the estuary that Yestyn began to think of Nest. She was much older than him and even as that stood, he wanted her, but knew with a certainty that the wolves would not allow it. He feared her. And resented the feeling.

'But, how to get the beasts away? Surely, now, with all this fresh game? I wonder'... he muttered to himself as he rode ahead of the others.

They walked slowly down the beach, their horses tired yet moving with purpose, heading for their feed and their stables. As Nest's cottage appeared on the headland, the ghost of the moon rose high in the now pale blue sky. Yestyn had an idea.

'I will take a few rabbits to the woman. Peace offering,' he said, and with a grin to his companions; he nodded towards the cottage.

They laughed their understanding and rode on slowly. As the tide was out, they waded across the shallow river, everyone ready for supper and the fire. It had been a good hunt and the game store would be replenished for a month with what they had killed. Yestyn waited until they had disappeared out of sight and hid himself up on the headland for an hour until dark and he was sure Nest had gone indoors for the night. He also watched the fishermen's cottages that lined the beach further down, her neighbours. One by one they all quietened, their lights doused, doors and screens closed as the men were out at sea and would return with the tide in the early hours of the morning.

The beach was empty, the early evening sky vast, limitless, and the sound of the sea soft and hypnotic. As Yestyn waited, his mind was focused on Nest and he gave an involuntary start when a flight of oystercatcher skimmed the shallow race of the river, calling their wild piping notes as they headed out to sea. He shook himself and made his move. He took the string of six rabbits and dropped them to the ground and began to trail them along the beach behind his horse for about a mile, then lifting them up off the ground he retraced his route.

About fifty paces from the cottage, he tied his horse behind some stout bushes around a bend in the path, then taking the string of rabbits he completed the trail on foot right to the edge of the cottage's patch of land and back again to the top of the headland where he tossed them over the edge into the sea. He moved with the grace of a predator. Pausing to check no one stirred here or further along the beach, he returned to hide behind the cottage and wait.

He could hear the wolves snuffling inside the cottage door. They had heard him, of course, but he climbed carefully up onto the turf roof, leaning over the top so that he could watch the front and see if his decoy trail was taken. The wind was in his favour and blew his scent away inland from the cottage but blew the trail he had laid towards the door, and he hoped the smell of blood would be stronger than the traces of himself that would be on the ground too.

It wasn't long before Nest opened the door and let Mellt and Seren out into the night to hunt. Yestyn grinned as the two grey shapes streaked away down the beach. He'd known it was her custom to let them out and they took the trail straight away, following effortlessly and silently towards the cliff and away.

'Now, Nest, you will not make me feel like a child again...' he whispered into the wind, and it snatched the sound away with a conspirator's fingers.

He heard her steps on the rough path as she watched the wolves lope off, and he moved quickly and lithely, dropping down off the front of the roof to stand facing her in the doorway, barring the way.

'So,' she said, 'Yestyn.' She seemed calm, not at all shocked as he expected and wanted.

For answer he lunged forward and grabbed her arm and threw himself against her, pinning her back to the door jamb and with one hand snatching back her loose hair so that her throat was bared to his mouth which he fastened in the curve of her neck, and then slowly drew his tongue from her collar bone to her ear as she struggled. He was a big man, heavy in the shoulder from much training with sword, spear and bow. She struggled to draw breath with his weight pinning her there and he leaned the heavier on her, glaring down into her eyes, laughing.

She shrieked then, a short, angry sound. She grabbed his hair with her fists, trying to pull his head away from hers but he caught her wrists with both his hands then pinned them behind her with one and began to push her back into the cottage. The fire was bright and the place colourful with rugs on the walls and pots on the hob. He pushed his mouth on hers to stop her screaming but she bit his lip so hard that he had to let go. He spat the blood from his wound into her face and she screamed in rage then spat back at him.

'Scream, Nest, scream! You will not be heard. These walls are thick,' he growled.

She kicked out but lost her footing on the earthen floor and Yestyn grinned as she fell. She tried scrabbling away on her back, but he was quick and was on top of her even as he began snatching her skirts up, holding her down with a forearm across her throat and the other still pulling her skirt. In the violent struggle that followed she managed to get an arm free and the next second he felt her hand rake his cheek; he laughed to think she had scratched him, mistaking it for excitement as high as his.

'Hellcat!' he snarled as he pressed down on her, and feeling a wetness on his face, he slapped his free hand to his cheek to wipe it roughly. Laughing again and holding her eyes with his own, he put the palm of his hand to his mouth to lick at the blood insolently, but the light from the hearth caught the mass of colour and when he glanced down he saw that it was full of blood, his blood. No mere scratch by a woman's nails. Instantly he felt as if his cheek were open to the bone and he roared, his face contorted with disbelief. He hadn't expected that. He arched his body upwards and hit her hard across the face with the back of his hand then rose to his feet in a single move to stand over her, ready to hit her again and again.

It was Nest's turn to laugh then and she kicked him away and jumped to her feet, holding the small knife up in front of his eyes.

'Try that again and I will kill you, whoreson bitch, but first, be certain I will have you,' he told her, his voice tight with fury.

Nest stood her ground. She spoke through closed teeth herself. 'And shall I cut your other cheek, Yestyn? You'll need two excuses for your Prince to explain who marked you thus and why.'

He backed to the doorway and stepped outside, roaring in frustration and anger and did not hear the rush of air before the wolves came at him from behind, bowling him to the ground, right there in front of the door. Their growls were deep and furious. One latched onto his forearm and the other had its teeth in his calf. The tough fabric and leather of his clothes was little protection, although the thicker leather of his wrist guards shielded one arm at least, his leather jerkin protected his torso. But the more he pulled against them, the greater pressure the wolves applied, and they shook him and snarled all the while. He gave a single yell of terror. His horse screamed too as it heard the sounds of animal violence.

Nest laughed bitterly. 'Will you attack me now, Yestyn? Shame on you for this! Shame!' she cried above his yelling.

'Scream, Yestyn, scream. There's no one to hear you!' she mocked him with his own words.

He bit his lips to stop himself making more noise as his eyes held hers and he tried to drag one of the wolves off his arm with the free hand, tried to lift the arm and pound its head with his fist. The animal, Mellt, pulled him off balance and he couldn't make good enough contact, only managing to thump the animal's shoulder.

'Get them off!' burst from him but Nest waited a few heartbeats before she called them. They had to be summoned thrice before they heeded and walked stiff legged and slowly to stand crouching next to her, teeth still bared, snarling horribly and their ears flat against their heads, their eyes on the fallen man. Yestyn clamped his hands first on one wound then another as he scrambled to his feet and stood at bay in front of her. He was bleeding freely. Both Mellt and Seren growled and began to stalk towards him again. Behind the bushes his horse let out another scream of terror.

Nest's face was spattered with his blood and her expression was dark as she stepped in front of the wolves, saying, 'Hold there Seren, hold Mellt, leave him now.'

She held his eyes fearlessly and told him, 'Go! Explain yourself to the Prince. But keep away from me now. Do not dare come near again. Go, go!'

He didn't reply, but turned and fled down the path, limping heavily.

Nest held both her hands to her stomach as she watched him leave. He hadn't noticed her swollen belly – she didn't think.

Bea woke three hours later, heavy eyed and drowsy. She felt angry and it was some time before she realised why that might be - it was the dream, the dream of Nest who was attacked by Yestyn.

'He would have raped me...' she whispered. 'I will kill him if he comes near me again or I will let Mellt and Seren finish him...' Bea found herself panting with mingled fear and fury and when she passed a hand over her forehead, she wasn't surprised to find it wet with sweat.

He's bleeding badly, she remembered. She thought how much

blood there'd been, the look of the wound, assessed the likelihood of healing, made a prognosis. *Needs some careful stitches otherwise there'll be a nasty scar on his face.*

She rubbed her face roughly with both hands. *No! I don't care about his scars! But, no, it wasn't real. Why am I thinking it was? It was a dream. A dream about nothing; things I've watched on TV, images from the cottage, the storm and all the upset meshed into a nightmare. All it needed was Jeremy as the villain. It was Nest but I suppose that's to be expected if I'm here; she's always in my mind here. She stood up to him. Maybe I'm crackers like Jeremy said. Psych unit here I come!*

Next to her, Archie whined, and she stroked his head absently, and her gaze flowed around the room, touching all the comforting sights. She was still tired and her body still very stiff, tense. *I just have to sleep in my bed tonight. I ought to get my head down now though.* She let her eyes wander round the familiar room. *No, I'll do that in a little while.*

She spent the next hour drifting about the cottage, agitated, fearful. Archie went to the bed he had in the hearth, right inside the nook. It was a heap of sheepskin and an old cardigan Bea had found.

Bea had felt almost numb after the initial escape from Jeremy, and she was beginning to think that that feeling was a thick pad of gauze on her wounds, designed to stem the initial reaction before all the emotion bled out and killed her. When she'd finally left the house in Manchester she'd had been in a state of chilled turmoil, a panicked efficiency - snatch this, grab that, shove it in the backpack, get Archie's lead, food, bed, get the spare car key quickly, grip it tightly.

But as she moved around Nest's old home, snatches of the dream intruded into her mind. *But it wasn't my Nest, was it? It was one of her ancestors, long ago, one of the first to have that name. When was Prince Llewelyn here? Was it the 13th century? I'm sure it was...God! I'm dreaming about the 13th century! The church in the village is 13th century – that's it. I went past it on the way back from the shop, didn't I?*

She was slightly comforted by this. But the present day and her flight, only the day before, became as distant to her as if she were listening to a stranger's experience overheard on a train; it was as though another person entirely had run out into the Manchester rain. She was exhausted. The long hours she had worked, the busy motorway drive down the coast with long delays under huge stress, the battle along the beach path against the gale and the storm were not the least of her physical strains; but the bone weariness of living with fear compounded all into a gruelling, draining whole. She decided that the dream and the brief hallucinations she'd had were just part of that physical and mental tension.

I could have a complete mental and physical collapse, that, or an aneurism, if I'm not careful. But I'm here. That's a positive. I'm here to stay. I'll never be forced to leave again.

She looked in the small hand mirror on the dresser. Her nose was red and swollen, a livid bruise was developing on her cheek and under both eyes.

I look like I've been in a car crash, a car crash of a marriage... what a cliché.'

But her body needed help and the most pressing need was food, proper food, and then sleep, blissful uninterrupted, safe sleep. She was imagining the feel of the woollen brychen when there was a knock at the door. She'd taken off her scarf sling. Her injured wrist was stiff but not as injured as she'd feared, and she'd decided on a bandage for support, but as she heard the knock her wrist seemed to give a throb of warning.

She started and then froze. Archie began to growl steadily. The knock sounded again and to Bea it was louder, more insistent - one of those, 'I know you're there' knocks. She had to force herself to breathe when the knock came a third time. She managed to move shakily to the front of the room and peer carefully round the edge of the window.

'*Him* - again!' she whispered to herself. Her mouth was suddenly dry. *What can he want now?* She thought.

Outside, Gwyn Roberts tapped his foot. He looked down the estuary, squinting to focus on the shining lemon horizon out to sea. Just as he put out his hand to knock again, a voice called from behind the door.

'Yes?'

'Ah! I just called to see if you'd got back safely, and…and if you were alright,' he said.

'Fine,' Bea answered.

'Oh, for God's sake!'

He took a step back then with a scowl he changed his mind and knocked again, loudly which now made Archie bark.

'Hello! Can I have a word? Hello!'

Bea opened the door a crack and Archie tried to push his nose through, still barking. The safety chain was on. She had been rooted to the spot, her body rigid, ears strained to catch his retreating footsteps, feeling that her slight hold on peace had been shattered.

'Well?' she called, but it was difficult to hear over the noise of the dog.

All she could see through the tiny gap was his waxed jacket, the hood up. She tried to look past him. He was blocking her view of the outside; she thought she'd caught one of those flashes of light again, camera flashes perhaps.

'What do you want, *really*?' she managed to ask as Archie drew breath.

'As I said, to see if you're alright. It's all right, okay!' he said, directing this at the dog. 'Ignoring me, I see. Loud, isn't he?' Gwyn commented, but Bea remained silent. 'Face no better then? Oooo, sore. I only called last night because I was being neighbourly, and I thought we met awkwardly this morning as well. I wanted to put things right, that's all. I get this all the time…' he finished with a rueful smile, pulling down his hood. His fringe bounced agreement as he shook his head.

She was gripping the door with one hand and had her foot behind it so it was difficult to bend and scoop up the dog, but she managed it and Archie exchanged the loud barking for a persistent growl. The door chain gave her a vestige of confidence, so she answered with more asperity than she had used for a long time.

'Right, well I can't say I'm surprised you get this reaction when you're so rude,' she said and stared at him through the narrow opening. She could only do that with one eye.

'Rude?' He was shocked. 'That's rich, seems to me it's the other way around. But I suppose some people can't see a celebrity as a normal human with feelings. They just take the opportunity of a face-to-face meet to vent their jealousy.'

Celebrity? I thought he said lecturer.

He was cross, almost petulant and he sounded as though he were voicing a pet rant. She opened the door a little wider, against the chain.

'Jealousy? Why would I be…what? Are you saying you're a pop idol or a footballer or something? If so, I'm not interested in either.'

She tried to close the door, but he put his foot against it.

'No more am I! I'll clearly have to tell you,' he began but she pushed against the door.

'No, you don't, really!' she said.

'Look, I'm an historian, the TV one.'

She carried on pushing the door, but he stood firm.

'I'm on *Pictures of the Past*. You must have heard of it? Gwyn Roberts? Yes?'

Bea stopped pushing and put her head round the door.

'I may have done; probably not as I know nothing about history. Anyway, that doesn't give you the right to keep bothering me. I don't have time for much TV. Will you just go away? Just go!'

She was close to tears by then. Archie began barking once more, sensing her distress.

'Sorry. Look I just brought you this as a peace offering. I'll leave it here shall I?' he shouted above the noise.

He fished a bottle of red wine from a deep pocket inside his jacket and put it next to the front door. Bea glared at him, terrified, as though he'd offered to pour it forcibly down her throat and he was about to say something to that effect when there was a shout, loud enough for them both to hear. It came from behind the cottage, a man's voice. There was another shout and another.

Chapter eleven

Rescue

Full fathoms five...

Ariel – The Tempest

GWYN SAID, 'AHH. VISITOR? I'll make myself scarce then.'

He'd given vent to pure sarcasm and he sketched a wave as he stalked to the end of the building, but when he glanced around the corner to see who was coming, he pulled up short.

'Hey, what's up?' he called, instantly serious. It was a man struggling to carry something large and loose in his arms. Water streamed from the man and his burden. At that distance it was difficult for Gwyn to see what it was; it could have been a goat or deer, a carpet or a person. The man was trying to negotiate the steps that led down from the flat area above the cottage, down to the front door. He was panting with the effort.

Gwyn went forward, calling, 'Need some help?'

The stranger gave a nod and accepted the help wordlessly. Gwyn managed to get his arms under the bundle so that both men were taking the weight, and as he did, a sound came from the burden. It whimpered and turned its head. It was an animal.

'Ah, a dog,' Gwyn murmured. 'A big chap!'

'It's a bitch,' the other man told him.

'Yours? An accident?' Gwyn asked, and the other man shook his head.

'Found on the beach just now. Washed up, I reckon. Anyone at home here?' he asked and nodded towards the cottage. He had a soft Southern Irish accent.

'Yep, could be, but not too welcoming,' Gwyn answered.

The other man gave a low laugh, incredulous.

'What?' The man was puzzled. 'Nest is always at home to sick creatures.'

'Erm, it's her niece I believe, and a bloody noisy dog, one of those annoying small ones.'

They were moving slowly around the corner to the front door.

Gwyn cleared his throat and said, 'Look, Nest died, I'm afraid. I'm sorry if she was a friend. I knew her too.'

The man was shocked. He checked his stride.

'No! I'm that sorry, I am. Ah, Nest.' He shook his head. He was completely shaken.

'Sorry to tell you like this then. I'm Gwyn, Gwyn Roberts – live down the beach.'

'Lorcan Macarthy. I've no idea who *she* is though,' he said and nodded towards the unconscious dog.

They shuffled round the little building and stopped at the front door in unspoken agreement. Bea was behind it, still trying to breathe calmly, hiding from whatever was next to come. Anything but the briefest most superficial social contact left her short of breath these days. She jumped when a knock sounded.

'Go away, I said!'

Gwyn raised an eyebrow at the other man and whispered, 'The niece is strange – bit of a bitch herself I'd say.'

He knocked again loudly. 'We need urgent help. Sick dog.'

His voice sounded an imperative note. The whole tune was now familiar to Bea. She opened the door a little and the first thing she saw was the lolling head of the dog between the two men. She saw at once that it was in a bad way. It was a big animal with brown curling fur, eyes closed, silky wet ears that were heavy with the water. Her heart lurched.

'Oh,' she murmured, 'Okay, okay, bring it in, bring it in.'

She stepped back and unlatched the door allowing the men to squeeze past her into the living room. Archie was unusually quiet; trotted round all the legs, jumped aside once or twice. Both men seemed familiar with the layout and that caused her a stab of fear as though her sanctuary had been discovered. What if it were a ruse to get in? Perhaps they'd drugged the dog? What did she know of the angry stranger, the so-called Dr Roberts? Who was this man with him? Some low-life?

Her heart was fluttering wildly and her breathing coming in tiny snatches, sucked desperately in through pursed lips, but when the dog made a small whimpering noise it broke through her panic. It made her focus on the dog's eyes which were screwed shut for a second or two as if reacting to a spasm of pain.

'Let's get her near the fire,' the Irishman said, then over his shoulder to Bea he called, 'Have you got blankets, towels, hot water or something?' A soft voice, educated.

'Yes,' she said, automatically but stood there watching, mesmerised by the sight of the poor animal and at the same time recognising this man, the stranger, had an Irish accent.

She hadn't reacted, so he prompted gently, 'We'll need them then.'

Bea shook her head in apology and went in search of the things, returning quickly.

They had laid the dog on the mat by the fire and from the swell of her belly it was obvious to all of them that she was pregnant. Archie had crept up to the dog and sniffed her body, then he sprang onto the settle and watched.

Bea knelt and drew a coarse blanket over the dog's rear half then she rubbed its head gently with the towel; she felt her own breathing becoming a little more settled.

'What happened? Is she yours?' she murmured as she pulled her hair over her opposite shoulder. She bent to put her head to its chest.

Lorcan stroked the dog's ear. 'I found her on the beach below the headland, lying on her side. Looked as though she'd been washed up. I tried to rouse her, but I don't know how to do CPR or anything on a dog, or even if you can do it, I mean. But I thought of Nest straight away,' he said.

He took the towel from her hand and began wiping the dog's flanks. 'She's always good with animals.'

'Nest died.'

A bald statement. Bea was shocked to hear herself speaking so bluntly.

'I just heard,' he said.

'I'm her niece, Bea, Bea Johnson.' *Yes, Johnson. Never Fitzmartin again. I should never have agreed to the married name...* 'Well, great niece as it happens. We live here now. Me and Archie.' She nodded at the little dog. She kept her head down, coughed to hide the moment.

'I'm Lorcan,' he said. He reached out and ruffled Archie's head briefly; the dog allowed it.

Bea lifted her chin a little, in acknowledgment.

She said, 'She doesn't need CPR because she's breathing and if she's breathing, her heart's beating. CPR is only needed for re-starting the heart and lungs together. But her breathing *is* quite shallow and slow. She's fairly stiff, in a stupor.'

She lifted the dog's jowls at one side.

'Very pale gums.' She pressed a finger onto the gum.

'Sluggish circulation. Probably low blood pressure. Moderate hypothermia, at a guess but hang on, I need to get something. Cover her, keep rubbing gently, just very gently all over, just to absorb the water.'

'Sure, I will. Don't know what I'm saying about CPR, do I? I can do it on a human – somehow didn't know you could do it on a dog, y'know?'

'I suppose it can be done on any living creature with a heart and lungs – in theory, I mean...'

Gwyn Roberts stood with his arms folded and raised his eyebrows and dipped his head as though in appreciation of her speech. 'Most I've heard you utter...*Bea,*' he said. 'We haven't met formally, as it were. You know, where I say something such as, "I'm Gwyn Roberts" then you say...'

'Oh, yes, I suppose I shouid...' she muttered. 'Erm, Bea Johnson. 'Excuse me. I need to...' She pointed to the stairs.

He stepped back in exaggerated haste and held out an arm to direct her theatrically past him. As it was, she was forced to edge between his body and the wall, keeping her back to him as she did, then moving quickly around the corner to go upstairs.

She wrenched her stethoscope from the backpack where she'd pushed it earlier, then to the bathroom downstairs, where she found the new digital thermometer in the first aid box. Despite Nest's protests, Bea had insisted she have one for those people, visitors, who weren't into herbs, moonlight and chanted spells. Nest had laughed heartily.

When she got back into the main room, Lorcan was still methodically dabbing the dog's body dry, and Gwyn was in the fireplace, putting more logs on the fire. He was facing away from her as she came into the room, but even his back annoyed her and frightened her. Right then she was forced to use his help, so she gathered some courage and touched the very edge of his shoulder to get his attention.

'Could you put the kettle on? We need a hot water bottle. Nest had an old one for visitors' use – the pantry cupboard I think.'

She took the stethoscope from round her neck where she had unconsciously draped it, ignoring the returning pain in her wrist.

'Dog's heart's here,' she muttered, glancing quickly at the other man, Lorcan, and gently pulled the dog's front leg forward to put the end of the stethoscope on the ribs, just behind the point of the elbow. There was no doubt in her mind now that the dog had had some major trauma. She listened carefully. 'I've no idea what is normal for so big a dog. Her heart rate at the moment is …' she looked at her watch, 'Fifty-five beats per minute. It sounds too low and her breathing is … eight breaths per minute.'

'Kettle's on, bottle found,' Gwyn said as he returned. 'Not a vet then?' he asked, and she found she couldn't even look at him. Instead she said, 'Do you have an iPhone? You could Google it? Dog's heart rate, breathing and temperature.'

'Do I have an iPhone? I couldn't exist without!' Gwyn told her as he fished out a phone and began to work the keyboard. He sounded smug.

'Don't have mine with me,' said the other man. 'I was a good friend of Nest's,' he added, glancing up at Bea. 'I'm so sorry for your loss. I loved that woman, I did.' His voice was gentle, low.

'Thanks, me too,' Bea muttered.

She saw he had nut-brown eyes, with thick lashes any woman would envy, she might have envied if she'd been feeling more like herself. His blond hair was as unkempt and wet as the dog's. He wasn't a good-looking man by anyone's standards, stockily built and obviously strong as he'd carried the big dog from the beach and over the headland. He was scruffily dressed, but so was she. What she did feel was good; she thought he had a heart. That would disqualify him from being in league with Gwyn Roberts. There was something gentle yet wholly passionate about him and his voice was soothing, unlike the other man's academic Welsh uplift that grated on the edge of her teeth.

Maybe, she thought, *it grates because he's so insistent, so pushy, unlikeable. I love the Welsh accents on Anglesey; after all, I'm half Welsh myself.*

Gwyn gave a triumphal gasp. 'Heart 60 to 140 beats per minute, breathing 10 to 35 breaths – all depending on size...' He glanced down at Archie, who was now lying on the settle watching everything intently. The dog stared back.

'Of course,' Bea mumbled. 'And the temperature?'

'Ah, 37.8 degrees - below 36.7 degrees is very dangerous...'

'And the animal is hypothermic. Right,' she said, absently as she fished the thermometer from her pocket and passed it to Gwyn. 'Can you just sterilize this? Do you know how to do that?'

'Of course,' he replied in the same tone she had used, but with a smirk. 'Consider me your lackey,' he muttered and went off to do the job.

Two long strides and he was out of sight.

'Who's your posh friend?' Lorcan asked. He stroked the dog. 'I've not rubbed her too hard, only enough to dry her off a little. I guess I know about human exposure more than dogs'; but it must be similar? Y'know, if you encourage the blood to the extremities then it's moving away from the body's core where it's needed. Yes? This poor girl was well exposed, just found her there lying on the beach as if she had been washed up by the tide; just flotsam.'

'I guess you're right about the exposure, but I don't know him; just a neighbour, not a friend at all. I only met him yesterday, came down myself then. Auntie Nest died in the Spring, with the golden lilies, as she called the daffodils. She always said she would.'

'How?'

'Heart failure. Old age really, she was ninety something. She said it was time and I was with her. She smiled, took a little breath and was gone. Gently so. I'm a doctor, by the way.'

'Wouldn't have guessed,' he said, and smiled himself.

Bea decided it was something he did often because he looked suddenly attractive as all the lines and shadows were smoothed away.

'Have you been away? I mean do you live here or in Ireland?' she muttered, suddenly feeling a moment of panic that she took even a slight interest in another man, still obeying Jeremy's ban on simply talking to other men. Even though he wasn't there with her, the habit of the last years was hard to break; his shade stood behind her and held her shoulders in a clawed grip.

'Live here. Been away for a year. British Antarctic Expedition; research opportunity. I'm an apprentice plumber.'

'What?' she said this as a simple conventional query, not really listening, her focus moving to the dog.

'Actually, just joshing; I'm an engineer and I was looking at water supply and sewage, litter too, global warming; interesting stuff.'

Bea didn't answer. Gwyn returned with the hot water bottle and the thermometer.

She wrapped the bottle up in a towel and put it near the dog's stomach, not touching it, then she lifted the dog's tail and took her temperature. The dog whimpered a little.

'Just on 37 degrees. Not really hypothermic, but she would have been if she'd been left much longer,' Bea said.

She cleaned off the thermometer with cotton wool.

'Could you take that and sterilize it again?' she said as she held out the instrument to Gwyn without looking at him. She tossed the cotton wool on the fire as she focused on the dog.

'Well, okay then, *doctor,*' he muttered childishly, clearly having heard that part of the conversation when he was out in the kitchen. He snatched the thermometer but when Bea didn't look up or react to his tone of voice, he prompted, 'You don't work round here do you?'

'No.' These days even a hint of mockery could feel like criticism to Bea and she didn't turn around or encourage the enquiry.

Gwyn shook his head, a gesture of exasperation and took the thermometer out to the kitchen again.

Lorcan stroked the dog's head. 'What do you think? Should we take her over to the vet?'

'I've forgotten where the vet is on the island. I've never needed one here,' she said.

'Nearest one ? Let me see… over near Menai Bridge. Take half an hour to get her to our village, carrying her, as the tide's only just turned, not fully out yet. Another half hour or more on the road…'

She sat back on her heels. 'Too much added trauma. We're doing what we can here, I think.'

He said, 'The thing is I do have a good friend who's a vet, round here too, but she's away on a course in Scotland and I know there's little reception where she is, so no point even trying to contact her for advice at the moment.'

Bea put her stethoscope onto the dog's distended belly, listened for a little while then smiled. 'There're pups in there; well, I mean, I think there are. And I think I can hear at least three different heartbeats, but then I'm not actually used to listening for multiple births like this – for a dog, that is. They do all sound very regular and what I'd guess to be strong. You found her on the beach?'

Bea found herself full of pity for the poor dog.

Lorcan smiled too. 'Yep, just taking a beachcomber stroll before supper really. She was just on the edge of the tide. Good job it's going out. I thought she was a seal for a minute, I did sure. Nest would know what to do for her, wouldn't she?' he said, looking into her eyes. 'You know you have eyes exactly like hers, don't you? Sorry if that's too familiar, it's just that I knew her well, stayed here for a few weeks after me dad died. She told me about you too.'

Bea dropped her eyes quickly and stammered, 'Yes, she would know about animals.'

She ignored the rest and then she smiled down at the dog.

'Hello to you,' she murmured as there was a tiny whimper and the dog licked her lips and tried to open her eyes, half lifted her head.

Lorcan stroked the dog's shoulder.

'There my beauty, there, you're okay now, okay there.'

'Ah, waking up, are we?' Gwyn muttered peering round the door to the kitchen. 'I'll make some tea.'

Bea bit her tongue. 'I'll come and do it, thanks anyway.'

'I have been entertained to tea here before, don't worry. I know where things are,' he called and disappeared.

Lorcan grinned. 'As I said – posh and pushy!'

So, she let Gwyn do the job because just at that minute, the dog raised her head and threw an anxious look at her flanks. Bea laid a gentle hand on the dog's belly.

'You know, I think that was a contraction. Pity if it's starting now; she's exhausted, isn't she? Exhaustion isn't a good place to begin labour.'

Archie jumped down from his perch, walked slowly over to the other dog's head, as it lay on the blanket, and sniffed her muzzle delicately. Her response was to open her eyes and move her nostrils to scent him. She didn't seem to have the energy to lift her own muzzle and closed her eyes again. Archie lifted his front paw, a gesture that terriers use to show either uncertainty or stalemate, then he hopped back on the settle.

Lorcan grinned. 'Tactful little guy, he is too.'

Bea found she could smile. She listened to the dog's heart and checked her breathing again.

'Better heart rate,' she muttered, 'and, better breathing rate too. Only just though, and that may well be from building distress, not returning strength. It's a little fluttery. We'll just have to hope there're not too many pups or we may lose her. It's a tiring business, giving birth.'

The dog drew back her lips and tried to fling her head back to her flank, but after a half-hearted attempt she subsided back with a groan and it was then that Gwyn returned with a tray of mugs.

'Whoa! What's going on? Tea's up, though.' His voice was loud and Lorcan motioned with his hand for him to lower it.

'Yeah, right, right.' Gwyn used an exaggerated whisper as he put the tray down on the hearth.

Lorcan got up and took a mug, raising his eyebrows in thanks.

'I think the doc will manage fine, I do. I know a natural touch when I see one.'

'You a doc too then?' Gwyn asked, sipping his own tea, his voice sounding heavy with expectation of the negative.

'Plumber, mate.' Lorcan grinned.

'Very handy,' Gwyn commented promptly and heartily.

Bea thought she'd never heard anything so blatantly insincere, but she couldn't be bothered to correct Lorcan's own description.

Lorcan turned to Bea. 'You wouldn't have an old towel I could dry meself with? It'll be me that's hypothermic in a minute, else!' He smiled.

Bea blushed. 'Oh, of course, you're soaked too. There's one in the bathroom, out back,' she said. She made a move to get up, but he was up before her.

'I'll go. You're wanted here, look,' Lorcan said, moving his head in the dog's direction.

The dog groaned and shifted her weight.

'All right, my lovely, all right,' Bea crooned as she knelt by her.

Out in the dunes, Dana had taken a string of shots showing the dramatic arrival of the dog and the two men. She opened a packet of crisps and decided that she would wait it out then check in with her client, *Mr* Fitzmartin, later.

Jeremy himself had arrived in Caernarvon by then and it didn't take long to settle in with his friends. He'd been to Medical School with the husband, Don Macintyre, and loved visiting Don and his wife, partly because of the long friendship, partly the sailing on Don's boat on the Straits and partly because of his lovely wife, Mairi. In fact, he had always been very attracted to the lovely wife and avoided bringing his own on sailing trips, so that he could devote his time to the friend's.

They'd had an early supper and had settled in the den to watch the sun go down across the sea. The den window filled the whole of one wall and showed a spectacular view of the estuary beyond the castle to Anglesey across the Straits.

'So, pal, what's up?' asked Don, topping up Jem's glass with more of the old single Malt.

Mairi's eyes radiated her sympathy for whatever the erring child-wife had done to upset or humiliate him now.

'Ah, that obvious is it?' Jeremy asked, his voice theatrically subdued for the observation and he took a long breath before he answered.

'Beatrix has run away and I'm dreadfully afraid she may harm herself,' he admitted. 'She's on the island now, in that benighted place, the witch's hovel, as I call it.' He managed a self-deprecating laugh. 'I've no idea how to help her any longer. I simply don't know what to do.'

'Cheer up, pal, she's stressed is all. I always think Bea throws herself into her work. Perhaps she needs a holiday. Run away though? Sure about that? She doesn't seem the type. What do you think, darling?' he asked Mairi.

'I think Jem's right. She needs professional help,' she said and rose gracefully to top up the men's whisky glasses. 'Probably mine.' She caught Jeremy's eye as he held up the glass and there was a smile hovering round her lips.

The contrast between the two men couldn't have been greater; Jeremy was slim, held himself proudly and behaved with well-tuned arrogance. Don was built like a wrestler, wore his hair in a crew cut and was bluff and honest in all his interactions with other people, whoever they were. People wondered why they were friends.

Chapter twelve

Suspicion

Misery acquaints a man with strange bedfellows...

Trinculo – The Tempest

'THERE, THERE, BEAUTY,' Lorcan whispered as he stroked the dog's head.

She'd settled down again after a brief spell of discomfort when she'd first arrived and was sleeping, sleeping and dreaming. Her paws twitched, she growled and whimpered and once she thrashed her tail as though wagging it in the dream. Archie lay with head on paws, alternately watching the other dog and dozing.

Bea came back into the room. She had shut the front door after Gwyn Roberts, who had, he announced, a pressing matter to attend to.

She gazed at the dog, trying to assess her state. She was used to humans, and although animal biology differed between the species, she decided that the general principles of care would apply; warmth, shelter and rest. For now.

'At least the sleep will do her good. Must have been a false alarm earlier. I've no idea how far along she is, when the pups could be due – I don't even know how long it takes for dogs. Gestation, I mean.' Bea felt at a loss.. 'I'd make more tea but I... I mean, I...' she began and pulled her sleeves down over her hands to hide their shaking, focusing on the top of the dog's head to calm her mind.

She was avoiding Lorcan's eyes. It was difficult to be alone with a man, any man without worrying whether Jeremy would find out. Her confrontations with Gwyn Roberts had been bad enough. She could feel the sympathy coming off Lorcan in waves and she realised that she felt guilty for inspiring the sympathy and uncomfortable being alone with him, by the fire. It was too intimate for her. She'd been desperate for Gwyn Roberts to go because even on so short an acquaintance she found him irritating, too assertive and with a shock, she saw that he reminded her of Jeremy. Perhaps it was his confidence, because they were nothing alike in appearance.

But Lorcan sat back, relaxed against the corner of the fire niche.

'Thanks, I've my fill of tea for the moment. Glad your friend decided he had more pressing matters though.'

'He's not a friend,' Bea said hastily. 'As I mentioned, I only met him last night. Well, not so much met him as he came banging on the door in the middle of the night…no I didn't let him in,' she added to Lorcan's look of shocked enquiry. 'I know nothing about him, or you…'

She stood on the other side of the fireplace, next to the dog's head, away from Lorcan.

'They know me in the village,' he said.

She thought he seemed anxious to prove his credentials as he added, 'I've a small cottage up the lane, with the pigs – the field where they are, I mean. And Nest knew me very well. I told you, she spoke about you all the time, she did. I usually come here every Spring; fish, walk, paint. But as I said, the Antarctic winds beckoned last year.'

'How come I didn't hear about you from Auntie Nest?' Bea said.

She had spent the past two hours in this man's company and so far, it was surprisingly soothing, but now she'd had enough. She'd felt no warning prickles of fear about him, only the guilt that Jeremy had generously given her. And Lorcan himself had been good company, pleasant and tactful; he clearly liked animals. And he hadn't quizzed her about her injuries or why she was here or what she did; he just spoke softly about the island, the wildlife, the weather. She found him quiet, restful to be with as they watched the injured dog, waiting for something to happen.

His voice was gentle as he answered her question.

'Oh, Nest could be very close when she wanted. Maybe she felt there was nothing to say about me, even though she knew me as a boy, for all of my childhood, as it goes. I came here every year with me Da, holidays, stayed in the B & B in the village, apart from the two years we were in Ireland at me Granny's place, before she died. Da finally bought himself a place here. He died too.'

'Oh?' Bea felt tired suddenly. 'Right. Yes, Auntie Nest could keep her own counsel.'

She got up and went over to sit next to Archie. He yawned hugely and settled back against her, catching her mood. She'd begun to realise that this swimming tiredness, along with a feeling of being in the moment, not thinking back or forward in time, not focusing on anything other than the fire, the sky, the moving grass, the waves – these things seemed to herald a slip into the dreams. Maybe they were hallucinations. She didn't care, just felt herself moving with the flow. She forced herself to stand up straighter, took a step forward; it turned into an awkward gesture, a panicked one.

'Look, Lorcan, I wonder if I can ask you to go now? I feel so tired. I think the dog looks settled for a while and she can certainly stay here, until we find her owners. And Arch doesn't seem too bothered, for an old chap. I'll be with her and, to be honest I'd rather be alone.'

He took a long look at her then gave the dog a final stroke and got up. He smiled.

'Sure y'can. I'll call on you later after supper. A two-minute chat at the door; yeah? See if everything's all right for the night, before someone decides what to do about her. That be okay with you?'

He sounded genuine, concerned. He said he was known thereabouts.

'Yes, of course,' she said and made a mental note to check with Thomas-the-Post. *If it's not too late by morning... Who have I let into the cottage? I don't know him.*

'Anyway, it's time I got some dryer clothes before I get meself pneumonia!' He laughed.

'Oh, no. I didn't think. You were soaked too, weren't you? I only gave you a towel. So sorry.'

'Hey, no matter really, the front of me's dried by the fire.'

'Right. Sorry.'

'Be seeing you.'

She had barely shut the front door after him, and bolted it top and bottom, caught up the chain, before she felt her feet dragging. The dog was snoring and wasn't too near the fire. Archie lifted his head to watch Bea.

'What can we do about you, girl? Puppies too. Is someone missing you?'

Bea sat down on the settle and felt her wounds.

I'll be bruised on my back and arms, she thought. She ran her hands over her belly. Everything felt calm, the babe stirred slightly, so she sighed, relieved. *Thank Goodness there is no lasting wound on me that the Prince might notice.*

Her eyes flew open. *What baby? Wounds? I can't be pregnant! I'm not pregnant. It'd be an immaculate conception! And it couldn't be Jeremy. Impossible, unless he drugged me.* Then she thought, *Would he?* Her heart slammed painfully. *Did he? I don't want it... And he said he didn't want children.* But as this thought ended, she felt the flutter of the babe in her womb again, light as a crystal wave skipping over the pearled pebbles of the shore.

She smiled to herself.

Yestyn will have to account for his wounds though.

The strange dog, lying asleep by the fire, woofed gently in her sleep. Bea bent to caress her head and quietly lowered herself onto the settle next to Archie, but before she'd stretched her arm over him, she slipped into her dreamscape and the other dog whimpered softly in her own.

'Ah, Mellt, cariad, Seren, my love. You saved me again,' Nest stretched out a hand to each of them and they pushed their heads under her fingers. 'But we don't need thanks, you and I, do we, my loves?'

After sniffing the ground where Yestyn had thrown Nest, Mellt scratched at the patch of earth where his blood was and scented the air by the door, then he sent a jet of urine onto the place to re-mark it.

It was a while before they could be persuaded to lie near the fire again and when they did, they stayed alert, listening for strange sounds intruding on the night. There was not much blood spilt, but Yestyn would bear three scars for his actions. Nest knew the wolf bites would have broken the skin, and possibly one of the smaller bones of his arm. His clothes must have soaked up a fair bit of the blood and he would be bruised purple and blue, but the blood on the ground came from her knife wound to his cheek.

Who will he ask to tend his face? He will need it cleaning at least, maybe stitched. But that's his reward. The wounds may go bad. Should I tell my Lord? I'll think on it for a while. As it is, Yestyn will leave me alone now, at least for a day or two.

Nest closed the door against the night chill. It was not locked because she normally had no fear of intruders, no one did in the village or the llys. Her door had no lock or bolt in any case. She examined her feelings. Anger? She felt anger. Fear? Only for the safety of the babe. The babe that nestled in safety, for now. Yes, fear then. She straightened her clothes and sat by the fire. The wolves settled nearby, but with pricked ears.

She rested her arms on her knees and looked into the flames that danced brightly over the turves and sea coal.

But what happens now, this hour in the Prince's llys? What of my attacker? She asked the flames and as she gazed, she saw figures moving in the hall.

'Nest, Nest. What will happen now?' Bea whispered to herself as she watched and waited to see what unfolded through her eyes.

Chapter thirteen

Treachery

At this hour, Lie at my mercy all mine enemies…

Prospero –The Tempest

IN THE PRINCE'S HALL, everyone was gathered for the meal. Ralph served Llewellyn his wine, wiping the lip of the jug with a cloth. It was something Llewellyn classed as one of the more amusing niceties his wife had brought from the English Court. The boy finished the ritual with a flourish not lost on his Lord, and he stepped back to his place.

Ithel ap Deykin sat in a corner of the dais allowing his fingers to caress the strings of his harp. The instrument sang softly and quivered with pleasure at his touch. His role as the Prince's Bard was not to provide background entertainment while people ate, he would have broken his beloved harp had he been forced to that desecration; no, he was merely pleasing himself before he gave Llewellyn and his court his latest poem, a song from his heart.

He glanced around the hall. His eyes lit on the Uchelwr, those of the noble houses of Wales, but did not find who it was he sought – Yestyn.

'Where are you, my weasel? I would have those nuggets of information you promised me. What of Nest? What of the child she carries? Do you know of it, Yestyn?' he crooned, his voice sounding only as the notes of a song, undecipherable to all but himself. He caressed the strings of his harp and it sang wild, wailing notes, telling the true feelings of his heart; it sang of injury, torment, endings.

Behind the curtain at the rear of the dais, Edith, Joanna's handmaid, stood shadow-like to listen. She wasn't concentrating on the bard, but she glanced at him and curled her lip in disdain; instead she was listening to the people while they ate, relaxed, unwary and careless in their talk. This was her regular habit whenever possible, in case she could glean some information that would be of interest to her mistress. The Prince dined today with visitors, lesser lords of the Marches, both Welsh and English, each with small lands on the borders and as ever, he fostered peace in his kingdom and welcomed people.

Edith pulled the thick woollen cloth aside slowly, and just a little. She scanned the hall until, reaching the very back, her eye lighted on Yestyn's face on the edge of the torchlight, near the door. He was gone in a lark's breath but not before she saw the bright splash of red on his cheek. She allowed the curtain to fall, as though by the efforts of a draught, and made her way quietly down the passage. She paused on her way to find a maid to take the Princess a jug of wine that she herself had promised to fetch.

Ithel ap Deykin had also glimpsed his informant and like Edith, he made his way stealthily out of the hall, going first to put his harp in the safety of his own chamber. He needed to hurry; the Prince would miss him soon. From there he made his way to the kitchen buildings outside the hall, where each of them, unknown to the other, guessed Yestyn would go. And it was Ithel who found him first in the biggest of the buildings.

'A wild cat, Yestyn?' he asked, his voice faintly amused to recognise a knife cut on the man's cheek.

'One whose claws I will cut off and leave her bleeding stumps to fester,' he answered through his teeth.

The kitchen was empty save for Yestyn who sat in a corner near the fire and beside him, one other, a strange wild woman that Ithel recognised. She had told him she was called Sister of Air, Chwaer Awyr. He often saw her coming back from the beach with a sack of noisome sea-gleanings. She was thought by some to be a black witch, one who used live creatures, crawling, poisonous creatures in her spells to summon dark spirits. Others thought her harmless and Ithel himself knew she had some skill in hiding wounds, lessening scars.

'You kill me, woman!' Yestyn swore and knocked the crone's brown hand away from his face, raking off the large leaf she had plastered there with a foul mud-like substance.

Edith arrived just then and gasped, a mixture of shock and outrage to see the young man's face. All was lit by a spurt of flame from the fire, writhing shades of orange overlaying the red of his blood, his black stubble and the woman's grey ointment. Edith threw an angry glance at Ithel as she strode towards the group then rounded on the other woman.

'Away, you filthy hag, you spawn of the brothel, away to your cesspit, away to your heathen devils. My Lady will hear of this!'

She snatched the woman's arm and dragged her across the floor, kicking her.

'I'd have you banned you from the llys, you foul creature.'

The woman snarled but nothing stopped Edith.

'You poisoned the girl, Angharad. She was my Lady's favourite maid. Get up! Away, I said. Away.'

And she kicked the fallen woman again and again until Ithel took hold of her arm. The woman lay still, but watchful, tense; keening a low note at the back of her throat, a feline noise.

'Steady, woman.' He spoke to Edith; his eyes bored into hers. 'Angharad died in child-bed, the child breached. Have you no dignity? She serves a purpose. Your Christian God will be angry with you,' he hissed in her ear.

'There is only one God, you heathen. Let go of me, fool. She poisons him with her unwholesome messes.'

'Why do you care what becomes of his face, Dame Edith?' Ithel asked, always alert to nuances of behaviour.

'My Lady values him as her guard. What other evil have you in your foetid mind? Are you jealous? Is that it?' she goaded, and he took a step towards her as though to strike her but Yestyn stood between them.

'*I* care how I am marked and by what,' Yestyn growled.

His hand was clamped over his cheek, the sinews of his forearm standing out, the veins throbbing under the skin. He stood unsteadily.

'Take heed, bard. What is it to you?' He glared at Ithel.

Edith drew her lips back in a grimace and darted around the men to get at the crone.

'Get out, unnatural fiend!'

She pushed her to the floor again with her foot, but the woman turned on her a face of such loathing that even Edith flinched for a second. Then she gathered herself and reached out her hand like lightning to yank the woman's head by the hair, screaming at her.

'Go, begone, I said!'

The woman rose in a single lithe motion, albeit she was forced to bend in Edith's direction and when she was thrown towards the doorway, she did not stagger but resumed the seeming-bent form of an old woman, yet in the manner of a spring. The rags she wore were black and grey and her face was plastered with red ochre streaks. Her hair, which was decorated with twisted grasses, feathers and twigs, hung in heavy ropes down her back and her scalp had been lathered with grey mud; it was now a cracked cap that resembled old hide. But her bowed back could not hide the fact that her body, as she stalked out, was strong and supple.

'Why did you go to that creature, Yestyn?' Edith demanded.

'She knows cures; she makes scars more pliable, sometimes invisible. That is the reason I sought her out. My brothers have been tended by her in the past,' he muttered, turning away, but Edith snatched his shoulder and moved him gently.

'I thought you warriors valued scars as battle honours. I can tend wounds, as you know. Sit and let me do my work,' she told him as Ithel drew a stool near the fire.

Yestyn looked at both of them with suspicion but allowed the attention.

'Why do I need you both, or either one of you?'

It was the bard who answered.

'I value your services, as you know. I see Dame Edith is of similar mind,' he said, turning his gaze on her as he spoke. 'And I would know why she had a burning desire for information that you can supply, Yestyn. Perhaps she will divulge her secret.'

He smiled at her, but she returned it with a vitriolic glare and answered him harshly.

'As I said, my Lady values him as her guard. Nothing more.'

'Come now, Dame Edith, do you not burn to know who did this to him, and with a knife? Do you not guess that sea-witch, Nest, is responsible?'

Edith hissed her contempt for Nest, shaking her head and Yestyn growled with fury.

She said, 'Perhaps you do not want scars that are not gained in battle then. Is this true, and as I see, with a knife? Why?' she demanded as she twisted Yestyn's head to the firelight to get a better look at his wound. 'Why would she need to wound you thus? What have you done? Have you harmed the filthy beasts she harbours?'

'She hates me. I know not why, but I will kill her or mark her in like fashion…' he began and winced as he lifted his bitten arm to touch his face but swaying suddenly he began to slip sideways off the stool.

Ithel reached out to stop him and inadvertently nudged his calf where he had his second bite wound, causing Yestyn to yelp with pain this time.

Edith was quick to see what had happened. 'So, knife and teeth, was it not? Did you try to molest her and get these injuries from the beasts for your trouble? Hmmm? I am right, am I not?' she said, but her voice was concerned rather than gloating, Ithel noted.

'Just leave me,' he said and turned to the fire to nurse his wounds, hunched over.

Edith persisted. 'I will tend the wounds; my Lady would wish it. She has no love for Nest.' She glanced quickly around, to confirm the place was still empty, save for them, adding, 'I will not take refusal over this.'

'Allow my help, Dame,' said Ithel, and he managed a disarming smile when Edith looked affronted. 'For all that you are Norman…'

'I am Saxon, Welshman,' she interjected but he carried on smoothly as if she hadn't spoken.

'I know of your own healing skills and I would learn from you,' he said.

'I think not! But I see you have a motive; one you keep to yourself.'

He did not answer her, merely said, 'You've a private chamber near my Lady's solar.'

Yestyn was groaning now.

'As you well know, and I have stuff to tend wounds; calendula salve for the broken flesh and comfrey for the bruising, plantain for any fever that brews and to draw out poisons.' She touched Yestyn's knee to catch his attention. 'I have poppy for the pain too,' she told him. 'You can trust me to treat you fair, unlike the hag. Why would you seek her unwholesome touch? What filthy mess is this she has smeared on your face?'

Yestyn hung his head, grabbed the injured arm and winced.

Edith turned to Ithel, saying, 'No one will disturb us. He will need two people to support him. Come, I will take your offer, though I do not like you, Ithel ap Deykin, and I am sure the feeling is mutual. I surmise we share a nuisance - a person, who, like a niggling thorn stuck in the flesh, persists with being an irritant until it is pulled, and the skin purged of poison. Do I judge you rightly, Welshman?'

She held his eye as he pushed back a smile.

'I have no wish to be friends, it is true, but we may be of service to each other. I will help then I must return to the hall; the Prince, who will be waiting, may call for another song. Come. Come boy, we will assist you. Come.'

Edith spoke quietly in the young man's ear.

'We will help you, Yestyn, and keep your secret if you help us in return; if you listen to the soldiers' gossip and discover what services she does for our Lord, the Prince. You agree?' Edith asked as they lifted him to his feet.

'Yes, yes, help me. And I will listen, and I will watch her also, but she will not know of it,' He gasped with pain as they manoeuvred themselves to support him. 'And I will watch the wolves to see how best I may kill them.'

'And that without detection, you mean? It must be done with caution. The Prince values them for their mistress's sake,' Ithel added.

Yestyn yelped as they hoisted him between them. 'I would kill her…' he began, then he lost consciousness.

In her cottage, Nest looked deep into the flames of her fire and far into the future, seeking her unborn child, but saw other futures instead. She saw Llewelyn much older; she saw his English wife in a convent, a convent at Llanfaes, not yet built. Then she saw a stone coffin carved on the sides with Christian images and words, and on the great lid, the effigy of a woman, a royal woman, Joanna herself.

The vision changed, and she saw that same sarcophagus empty of a body, broken and alone, in a field by a stand of bushes and full of water. Cattle were nearby. Nest looked deeper; the flames flared. She saw the coffin once more, this time in a strange room with oaken doors, an antechamber that led into a huge Christian church she did not know of. It stood in a crowded village with many stone buildings and a half-finished castle on the shore of the Straits. Dead leaves blew around the sides of the vacant coffin. The air was redolent with tears.

Nest sat back and sighed deeply.

'So, I see no tomb for my Prince.' She spoke aloud, and the wolves twitched their ears at her voice; Seren licked her lips, sensing sadness in the sound.

Chapter fourteen

Stillness

Thought is free…

Stephano – The Tempest

IT WAS EVENING and the fire had died down when Bea woke, and for a moment, she stared at the dog on the rug next to her wondering why it was brown and not grey and white, and why there was only one lying there when there should have been two. Archie whined, and she saw there were indeed two and she stroked his familiar rough fur, drew him close to kiss the top of his head. Her eyes were prickly with sleep; she rubbed them carefully as her nose hurt and she had been breathing through her mouth, which was paper dry. She also had a headache and a raging thirst. The strange dog woke and gave a whimper, looking as bleary as Bea had done to wake somewhere unknown.

'Hello girl,' Bea said, sitting up and resting her hand on the dog's head. 'How are you doing? Hmmm? How're the babies?'

The dog whined softly and licked her lips, so Bea reached for the bowl of water that was on the side of the hearth; Archie had a little one in the kitchen. She guessed the Irish guy had put this one within reach. *Thoughtful.*

'Thirsty? I sure am.'

She offered the dog the bowl and smiled when she took a long drink.

'No collar. What do we call you, I wonder? Are you a Beauty? Maybe a Dasher, Lily, Maisie – hmmm?' Bea said and tried a few more random doggie names that came to mind.

'Well, I think you're a Girlie – a beautiful one at that, even though you're a bit bedraggled at the minute. Where have you come from though?' Her voice was soft and soothing, and the dog seemed to recognise the kindness it held. 'Is someone missing you at this moment? Where are your family?'

She caressed the dog as she talked, soothing her, trying to make her relax and eventually she did; she sank back with her head on the hearth rug and closed her eyes.

I'll have to get something for her to eat, but what? Maybe some scrambled eggs? Something light in a couple of hours. Maybe Archie's dog food is too rich and anyway, I've only a little left. Maybe the Irish guy, Lorcan, I mean, will get me some dog food from the village? He said he'd come later. Hang on. Relying on a new bloke. What am I thinking? And Jeremy doesn't even know I've gone yet, I hope.

Bea felt the familiar wash of fear whenever he came into her mind, but she forced herself to concentrate on the dog as she got herself up and began by fixing the fire and then made some tea.

While she was out of the room, Archie jumped down and went to sit near the other dog, settled himself and gazed into the fire. The dog pushed herself upright and rested on her elbows and they were sitting companionably together when when Bea came back. Both dogs turned huge brown eyes to hers.

'Hello, girl,' she said. 'I see you met Archie. You two okay? Y'know what – I'll see if you want a biscuit. Arch loves them. Not good for teeth, but what the heck.'

She dashed off and came back with a digestive which she broke into pieces and offered to both dogs.

'Aren't you gentle?' She stroked the big dog very gently on the head but snatched her hand away from her own dog. 'Careful with my fingers, Arch,' she chided, playfully.

Archie's biscuit was gone in seconds, but the other chewed the biscuit slowly, and at last sank back on her side. Bea gazed at her.

'Wonder when your puppies are due? Do you know?' The dog sighed. 'You're just exhausted, aren't you? Poor Girlie. I'm calling you that. Hey, do you even understand English? Perhaps you fell overboard from some ship from Norway or something. Nope; don't know any Norwegian.'

The dog's tail wagged tentatively, only a couple of tries, flopping against the floor with each slow beat. Now that she was dry, her fur was a light chestnut and it was rough and slightly waved and her tail was feathered like her long ears. Suddenly, Archie sat up, cocked his head to one side, listening. The other dog's ears pricked and seconds later Bea heard what they had caught first; footsteps on the sandy path outside. All three of them were frozen in attitude and started as a knock sounded on the door, but Archie didn't bark this time.

It was a polite knock and with it came a strong Welsh voice.

'Hello there, Bea! Thomas here. Only me. Got a minute, have you, love?'

Bea breathed again, thankful to hear a friend and one of the familiar voices of her childhood. She rushed to the door, opening it without the fear of earlier that day.

'Got a bit of news you might want to hear,' he began and stepped inside the cottage as she welcomed him. 'Oh, hello young Archie!' he cried as the dog trotted to him and raised himself up for a pat by resting a paw on Thomas's knee.

'Eighteen now!' Bea said and Thomas replied automatically, as if they had used this formula before, 'Spring chicken…' He undid his jacket, took off his woolly hat and scarf. 'It's about our Dr Roberts,' he said, and she caught the downward lilt of his tone as he said the name and wondered, with a contrasting lift of her spirits, whether it could rightly be interpreted as derision.

'I gather he's been to call? Very sociable, you could say, our Dr Roberts.' Then as he spotted the dog on the hearth, he smiled and added, 'Oh, of course, this must be the shipwrecked dog then. Duw! On the shore. Dear me! Heard about her, I did.' Moving slowly, he bent to stroke the animal's head.

'Have to call Dr Roberts *ours* because apparently he's here to stay. Bugger's a celebrity – on the telly, no less.'

'He has mentioned that already, soon as we met. What on Earth else has he to say, Thomas?' Bea found her voice and found also that she was annoyed with Gwyn Roberts, annoyed and not a little worried. *What's he done? Said? Is he some sort of animal rescue vigilante? Has he found her owners?* She found it surprisingly painful to think of that possibility.

'Seems he knows everything, our Dr Roberts. I gather you met on the night of the storm? Listen to me! Was that only last night? And young Lorcan; he found the dog earlier, I hear.'

'Yes, yes he did. Why? Is this Gwyn Roberts taking the credit? The other guy, Lorcan, brought the dog for Nest to see to. Didn't know she'd died. Goodness, I'm glad you've come, Thomas. You need to get me up to date. Why are you standing there? Sit down, sit down.'

She felt a rush of love for her old friend. Thomas had always been a bit of a comfort blanket for Bea. She filled him in with her version of the dog story so far, how Lorcan and Gwyn Roberts had been involved in their different ways and before that, how she'd arrived at the cottage with Archie.

'So, you've told me all I want to know about the annoying Gwyn Roberts but what about this Lorcan? Who is he? What's he like then, as a person? Do you actually know him well? Is he okay?'

'Full of questions, our Bea, always has been.'

Thomas smiled affectionately. Bea wanted to hear Lorcan was trustworthy beyond doubt, didn't want to hear he wasn't known locally and was some sort of spy of Jeremy's.

That's being a bit paranoid... she told herself.

'Don't fret. Known him since he was a little'un. Used to help my Beti collect the eggs many a time. God rest her; she loved to be with the little 'uns. Lorcan's mother died some time ago and he and his da, Damon Macarthy, came regular like, once a month at least, from Dublin. Bought the old cottage from Griff-the-Grave when he went to live with his daughter. At eighty-four, well, it was time he gave up digging graves, or it might have been the death of him!'

They laughed easily together.

'Damon and his boy knew Nest well, they did. Why, you got a problem with Lorcan too?'

He smiled down at her, a teasing smile hovering around his mouth.

'Sort of. Nest never ever mentioned him, and I never met him when I was here. Strange.'

'Maybe, but...things just work out that way sometimes. Some

people keep passing each other until one day…they meet and hate each other instantly. Or they might meet and cause stars to burst in each other's hearts. It's just the way it's meant to be, girl. You should know that with Nest as your auntie *and* your Godmother – not saying which gods, mind!'

'Hmm, I suppose so. I don't know why I'm so suspicious these days. I seem to have lost my magic, as Nest would say.'

'Ahhh.'

'Anyway, this dog was washed up on the beach past the headland. Fancy being washed up in a storm. She was spotted just as the tide was going out. And I don't have a problem with your Dr Roberts; he seems to have one with me. I just want *never* to see him again; that's what I want.'

Bea found herself growing hot and feeling she might actually burst into frustrated tears. It had been a bad forty-eight hours and still she was being manoeuvred by a man, another man, two men she didn't want. Thomas wasn't in her tally. Her words came out with a sob and she had to hide her face as she turned and bent down to the dog. Archie pressed close to Thomas's leg, scratched himself.

'Hey, steady on there, love. It's only me. Known me since you were shorter than the Marram grass out there, haven't you? I might run the gossip shop, but I can keep my mouth shut when it's one of my own.'

'Okay, okay,' she reassured him and sat down on the floor, next to the dog, and he followed, perching on a low stool. He scooped Archie up onto his knee.

'Funny how dogs know when a person or another animal is sick; they don't hassle them, do they? And how're you feeling? Hmmm? That bruise is all over your face, girl. A nasty fall that! Well, that's what you get for tramping up the beach in a storm.'

Bea tried a smile. She was thankful that he believed her lie but it disturbed her to have to tell it to such an old and trusted friend. It didn't sit right with her at all.

Needs must. If he knew Jeremy had done it, he'd go mad.

Bending to fondle the injured dog's ears Thomas said, 'She's a lovely one. Actually, before Mr Nosy came in, young Lorcan called to get some milk, told me about finding her and he asked me to bring you some dog food. I would have brought some more for young Archie in any case. Lorcan said he wouldn't bother you again tonight. Asked me to see if it would be alright tomorrow though, just to peep through the door for a minute? What d'you think?'

He reached over to where his jacket lay on a chair and fished a couple of cans and a small box of dog biscuits from the pocket.

Bea's face lit up.

'Oh. Right. Kind. I'll think about the offer of a visit. Suppose I'll have to, as he found her. Dog food for her? I was thinking that maybe I should keep it simple for a while and just give her a spoonful of scrambled egg? She's exhausted; don't want to overtax her body, especially in her condition.'

The dog had looked up at Thomas's voice and finding nothing fearful in it, sank back, her head now on Bea's knee.

'Well, you're the doc round here, animal or no. Looks like a mix of Setter and Wolfhound, if you ask me,' Thomas offered. 'And that's what our Dr Roberts decided and Lorcan agreed. That's what the description said too...'

Bea's head flew up, her eyes startled, her voice near panic in an instant.

'What? Her owners have been found? Oh...that's why you came.'

'Now, now, wait a minute – just about to fill you in, love. Roberts heard from Mick-the-Lifeboat that they'd been out to a bad wreck on the night of the storm. Big sea-going yacht, out of Dublin no less, heading for Beaumaris and blown too close to our estuary. Apparently, it foundered mid-channel, coming in on damaged engines, no sail. Capsized. Found belly up. Family all on board with their friend. Seems it was two parents, two teenage kids, one middle-aged friend – *and a dog*, a big dog. Only the friend survived and he's in a middling bad way, in the hospital now at Bangor, with two broken legs and a broken arm, plus a bit of exposure for good measure. The helicopter that picked him up did have a look for the dog, which the rescued chap was worried about, but it was a big sea and Mick and the lads searched too.

Nothing – until now.'

'Poor Girlie,' Bea said, stroking the dog. 'Fancy taking a heavily pregnant dog on a boat like that.'

'Apparently she's called Stella,' said Thomas and the dog pricked up her ears, looked round sharply.

'Stella?' Bea asked her, and the dog wagged her tail decisively, just once. 'Stella, the star! Fancy that. I wonder if she's Seren y Bore or Seren Mellt?'

'Remembering your Welsh afresh? About time, girl,' he said, smiling.

'Wish I could get my grown-up tongue and brain round it, Thomas. It's easy when you're a kid. No, a story I've heard somewhere about two wolves; those are their names, I think. I'm a bit mixed up these days.'

'That why you weren't overjoyed that I spotted the fancy Jaguar, hey? Bit of trouble is it? You thought I didn't notice, didn't you? Thought you were a bit distant with old Thomas, love.'

Bea bent her head and let her hair hide her face.

'Sorry. I suppose so. I can't speak just yet. Help me if you will and let me know if you see it again. Don't tell anyone, anyone strange that I'm here, will you?'

He rubbed a rough hand over his thatch of white hair, then reached over to squeeze her shoulder with the other. 'Don't even mention it again, love.'

He was a big, vigorous man, in his late sixties, a soothing man. Bea trusted him.

'So the friend will want her when he's out of hospital?'

She tested the idea, glanced at him.

'Our Dr Roberts says not, and he knows everything, he does. The friend isn't into dogs and anyway can't cope with puppies. Said she'll have to go to the rescue place on the mainland. There's no other relatives to take her.'

Bea was alert and desperate.

'I'll have her. I want her. Thomas, can you get in touch with the hospital for me to tell him or the police or someone. I can't go there myself; a hospital is the last place I want to visit just now.'

'Like that, is it?' he interjected.

Bea's eyes were shining.

'Can you tell the friend she's got a new home here. Fix it for me, please.'

She suddenly felt more alive than she had done for months and her heart gave a lurch of pure joy.

'Okay. I can do that for you. And it's what Nest would want too, isn't it?'

'Oh yes, I think she would.' She cradled the dog's head. 'And what will we do with these puppies is the next thing, assuming I can have her. You wouldn't mind, would you, Arch? He likes puppies. You will find out about her soon won't you, Thomas? What do you think, Stella?' she asked, and the dog yawned and shuffled a little, lying on her forearms. Her head nodded. Her eyes closed as she sat there with the glow of the fire gently bathing her worn and strained body.

'I'll find out tonight about that, girl. I'll phone the ward. You can rely on me, just in case our Dr Roberts wants to get a finger in the pie. Can't see him as a dog man, mind.'

The sky was dull outside as the night approached and blanketed the estuary. The tide was out, the sand looked wet and cold.

'You look tired, love. What if I give Lorcan a ring and tell him I've seen you both and it might be okay for him to knock on the door tomorrow then? And I'll knock on Dr Nosy's door on my way back to the gossip shop; tell him firmly to keep away. You'll be able to settle down for the night. Get some proper sleep. Look like you could do with a bit, lovely. Okay then?'

Thomas stood and hands in pockets, waited until she'd nodded slowly in agreement before giving both the dogs a soft pat on the head and making for the door.

'Bolt it after me. Got enough wood in the store there?' he asked.

'Thanks, yes. And I will.'

She gently disengaged herself from Stella to follow him to the door. Archie trotted after her.

Once Thomas had gone, she busied herself with preparations for the night. She checked the doors and curtains, brought in more wood, put a fireguard in place, made herself and the dogs some scrambled eggs, which Stella managed slowly, and Archie wolfed down. Stella hadn't offered to get up or show any signs of wanting to relieve herself, so Bea let her be and decided she might feel like it later, when she was more rested. She brought pillows and the knitted cover from her bed and lay down with a dog on each side and fell to thinking about her own future, perhaps with two dogs now.

Bea knew it was a flight of fancy in a way. It was tempting, soothing to think that a new life was unfolding here in Aberffraw. Her Manchester home and career seemed as far distant as the Aberffraw of so long ago that had haunted her dreams, and Jeremy seemed a remote figure, someone from her past that she would never need to see again; an idea almost too good to be true.

How strange is the mind? It arranges things for you without being asked sometimes. I feel as though I've got a force field round me, she thought.

She turned all the lights off except a little table lamp and was soon asleep with her arm over the dogs again. An hour of the deepest, blackest sleep and Bea woke suddenly to find the dogs had gone. She put a hand on the blanket and found it warm and heard behind her, at the front door, a little whine. It was Stella with Archie at her side.

She leapt to her feet, scrabbling her hair out of the way and flew to the dog.

'Okay, Stella? What's the matter? Ah, need a wee? Right, you too Arch? Just a minute.'

She snatched a length of hemp rope that hung with other odd things by the door and tied it loosely round the bigger dog's neck.

'In case you get scared and run off, well, waddle off.'

It was dark by then; the sky was an indigo velvet cloak, strewn with diamonds thrown carelessly from an emperor's cache. It took her breath away. The sea was invisible, its presence heard as the quiet breathing of a huge creature. Both she and the dogs stood by the door and breathed the sharp night air, looked around them, felt the moment. A pearly moon had risen and coated the sands with the same precious gleam.

Nest, that long-ago Nest, must have looked at this same sky in the 13th century, never changing in all our little lives. What's happened to her now? What will she do with the baby?

Bea shook her head slowly.

Don't be daft. It was a dream. There's no baby really. But what if this really happened in the past and I'm just getting a sort of replay somehow? People do say that stones can hold a memory of events and people. And computers hold memory in microchips, don't they? If only I could switch it to 'play' like a DVD and watch what happened next.

Stella whined. Archie was already sniffing and scratching round the front path.

'Okay, come on,' Bea whispered to Stella as she led the dog onto the rough ground in front of the cottage wall. Whispering didn't disturb the peace of the night.

'There you go, girl.'

The dog got herself down with a grunt that made Bea laugh softly.

'Poor thing, you must be near your time, I reckon!'

She tried to lead Stella a little further down the beach, but the dog pulled in the direction of the cottage door.

'Know a good place when you find it, hey?' She looked seaward. 'The tide's turned, feel that little wind?' she asked the dog who replied by pulling for the door and the fire. Archie beat them to it.

Chapter fifteen

Temptation

The clouds methought would open and show riches...

Caliban – The Tempest

THAT SAME HOUR, in Caernarvon, Don Macintyre lay sprawled, snoring open-mouthed on one of the Chesterfields in the den. For hours, he and Jeremy had talked and finally laughed over their malt and Mairi Macintyre had kept refilling her husband's glass. Eventually he had fallen asleep and the glass rolled from his hand to land soundlessly on the deep pile of the rug. She'd made espresso half an hour earlier and poured Jeremy another cup.

'Well?' he said.

'Well.'

He threw back the last of his coffee. She rose and took the empty cup from his hand, dropped it on the rug next to the glass, then took the hand and led him to the open balcony, overlooking the sea. She closed the doors behind them. They leaned together, face to face on the rail at the far end, out of sight of the window and in the deep shadows. The breeze played with her long hair as he looked down into her face.

'How beautiful you are, for a malevolent and completely immoral bitch.'

She smiled. 'Two compliments in one sentence. No, three compliments!'

'I want you to do something for me, something well within your excellent skill range. Say you will before I tell you what I want.'

He put his hands on her shoulders, pulled her closer into his body. She smiled.

'I will, but you know how practised a liar I am. Why, I'm almost at your standard.'

'Mmmm. I swear, if you were cut, you'd bleed only sugar syrup, or arsenic.'

He glared steadily at her for several seconds.

'I'll just have to trust you to remember how...how...' He made a pantomime of trying to think of adequate phrasing, '...how *open to censure* we both are, shall we say?'

'Got me there, Doc – oops, *Mister!* What's the favour? I'm all agog; panting for it, actually.'

She licked her lips, threw back her head. Her hair rippled over her shoulders and, as she leaned backwards, the soft light that spilled from the den made a bronzed halo of it. Jeremy dug his fingers viciously into her shoulders. He laughed quietly at the lack of visible physical reaction.

'I am actually very worried about Beatrix. No, don't laugh.'

She put a hand over her mouth.

'Whatever is happening between you and me, I *do* care about her. I've done everything in my power to keep her in work, functioning on a very basic level, I'll admit, but functioning on this very basic level so that other people notice - and comment...And now she's run away.'

'No wonder you're so good at Poker; your expression gives away nothing,' Mairi said, her own expression was a pantomime of admiration. 'Marvellous!'

A little moue of regret touched his lips. 'Sadly, I've been absent from the tables for weeks now. Looking after the welfare of a sick wife has meant I've been confined to barracks – so to speak. Had to resort to online actually. But it's not the same; there's little glamour, no need for the DJ, the martinis, the glitz.'

'Yes, you do enjoy the whole Casino Royale experience, don't you?'

'I could do with the millions that go with it.'

'Running up a little tab? Hmmm? Oooo naughty.' She squirmed with delight as his expression hardened.

'Couldn't have gone better last night, actually. Private game at my favourite hotel across the water. I did well, very well.'

'So...' she drawled. 'What's next in the main game – the sick child-wife?'

'So,' he said with exaggerated patience, 'I want you to find an excuse to go walking on the beach at Aberffraw and *accidentally* bump into Beatrix. Feign shock, concern, an embolism, whatever your sinful mind can conjure. I want to find out how she is, how she's coping, what she's planning now she's fled the marital nest.' He shook his head slowly. 'It's a huge shock to my ego to find she really did want to escape my care, my caresses.'

'Ooo, there, there, baby…' Mairi pouted.

He took hold of the end of her chin with finger and thumb.

'That's why I took myself off to a spurious conference, to see what her reaction would be. I told you before that I'm worried about her, very worried.' His face became serious. 'You and I both know she's close to breakdown and, well, I don't want anyone to take advantage of her.' He smiled.

Mairi grinned. She took his hand from her chin using her own thumb and forefinger. 'You mean, except you, you delicious bastard? I'd lay odds she has more money than you think. Is that it?' She reached up her hands and grasped the hair on either side of his head, snatched his face down to hers and kissed him fiercely.

He kissed her back angrily, violently and she laughed, then reached up to smooth his hair but he caught her wrist.

'Don't touch my hair,' he told her coldly.

She reacted by laughing at him again and then, with her hands on his chest, she pushed him back roughly and as he wasn't expecting the strength of the push, he staggered against the waist-high glass wall of the balcony.

'Consider me warned. Now apologise or I'll tell Don you tried it on,' she drawled, but Jeremy could see her body was quivering with indignation, fury almost, and he wanted her more than ever. She was so much more alive than the child-wife.

'Tell him. Tell him whatever you care to invent. It'll be all the same to me, Mairi. I need to know about Beatrix soon and I know you'll not let me down. I'm off to bed.'

He didn't look back, just strode back into the house.

Don was deeply asleep and destined to spend the night on the Chesterfield as he was too drunk and too heavy to be helped to bed. On her way across the room, Mairi dragged her husband's legs up on the seat and tossed a throw over them. She didn't put the light out as she went off to their bedroom, smiling.

Chapter sixteen

Confusion

Sometimes a thousand twangling instruments will hum about mine ears; and sometimes voices…

Caliban - The Tempest

BEA WOKE AT FIVE the next morning. She lay still and watched as the dust motes danced along a beam of sunlight that edged between the front curtains. A seagull called in the distance and behind that high note the sea snored steadily. Bea took a breath as she listened to it and realised that the room smelled of lavender, mint and salt; the blended perfume of scent and sound she would always identify as Nest's Point. But there was another earthy note to the perfume now - dog. She stretched, feeling a little more rested than she expected, and smiled to see both dogs sit up and yawn just as she had; they'd both finished the night by the fire, warm and companionable.

Stella shook heavily, and walked over to the door, asking to be let out, but when Bea opened it and stepped outside with her, the dog merely squatted on the sand near the door to relieve herself. Archie walked underneath her, which made Bea laugh, and went down the beach himself, but Stella trotted back indoors and glanced fearfully over her shoulder at the incoming rush of the tide as it coursed down the estuary.

'A bit worried about the water, is that it?' she asked the dog. 'It's okay, you're on dry land with me now.'

Stella gave a short, low wag of her tail and licking her lips, she whined expectantly at Bea.

'Ah, thought transference now? Hungry? Food, Stella?' she asked and as the dog pricked up her ears and seemed to understand this, she went off to the kitchen and gave her small portion of the tinned dog food on an old saucer. Archie rushed in expectantly, as though he'd heard the sound of a can opening from down on the beach.

'Okay, you too. A little and often, hey, Stella? Don't want to tax your insides too much after the strain of yesterday, do we? And you, Arch, you're allowed tiny snacks because you're a mature gent.'

He bounced up and down on his forefeet as she put his food down.

When they'd finished eating, Bea took the dogs back to their beds by the fireside.

'A stroll later, you two. And you, Stella, you need rest after yesterday. Doctor's orders.' *Listen to me! Very twee. You idiot.*

She made up the fire and as she broke twigs and fed them into the embers she gently blew them into life and on a sudden whim she searched the strengthening glow for images, any images.

'*Maybe,*' she thought, *Maybe I should try to look in the flames, like Nest did and see what's there? What's happening to Nest now? I should say – what happened then, I suppose? Maybe Nest's power has been passed down so that I could 'see' whenever I need to, like she did?*

She sat with her back against the settle, her arms round Archie and Stella. Gazing into the flames, she felt their fascination but not any of the downward spiralling sensation that she'd experienced before. She didn't feel as though she was slipping away into the past. Try as she might to free her mind of thoughts, as she supposed one should, at least in meditation, nothing happened. She was tired but not receptive in the way she thought one should be when deliberately trying to 'see' into another time.

But I do feel quite buoyant and sort of, sort of... centred. It's as though Nest's in the next room and is about to say something. And with that thought soothing her mind she dozed and didn't dream.

Sometime later her phone rang. It was Thomas and he'd just left the hospital. He'd phoned ahead, and the survivor of the shipwreck had agreed to see him and was delighted that Stella had found a new home, and as Thomas had told him, an excellent 'forever home'. He loved the dog himself. He was called Martin Shawcross and he felt he owed it to his lost friends to do what he could for Stella. Once he knew she'd survived, the best he could do was give permission to rehome her with someone who would love her. Apparently, there was no other family or any friends who could take a dog, a large one, that is, and in whelp. A small dog would be different.

And Thomas had more news; the father of Stella's pups was a black Labrador. Martin thought the birth was to be fairly soon but couldn't be sure. It was a neighbour's dog and the mating had been an 'accident', he said. Apparently the family had been besotted with Stella, couldn't bear to be parted from her, so she'd accompanied them on the trip, all their many trips. Pete, the father owned an IT company, the mother, Jenny, was a vet. The two teenage boys, Sam and Tom, both wanted to be vets too.

Thomas said Martin talked a long time about his friends, cried too, and Thomas reckoned it did him some good to know Stella was safe. She was beloved, Martin had said, and asked that Bea keep in touch; let him know how Stella was doing, tell him about the pups. Martin had experienced a huge trauma, physically and emotionally. Yes, she would keep in touch. Martin should visit. Must visit.

Bea breathed deeply, relief tinged with both joy and deep sorrow for Stella's lost family; she would miss them; Bea was sure of that. But just then a wave of emotion engulfed her.

'Stella, you can stay. You can stay here with us. Oh God, I'm so happy,' she told her, tears streaming down her cheeks, and, as she threw her arms round the dog's neck, she realised that she'd not felt anything like that for months, years in fact. Even the fear of being found by Jeremy receded into the background; for a time. The events of the distant past receded too.

'You two get on with each other, don't you? How great. I'm going to get you checked out by the vet, Stella, then we'll get a better idea when to expect your family, and just how many of them.'

Bea spent a wonderful half hour tidying things, making plans in her head, hugging herself with sheer delight. Then when Stella got up again and showed she'd like to go out, Bea took her piece of twine and another baggy jumper, which she tied round her waist in case it was needed later, and she set off for a walk.

With my dogs...she announced to herself.

'Come on, my lovelies. We'll just toddle up behind the cottage to see the view and you can have a rest before we come back. It's just us three now, so it's about time you saw something of where you're going to live. Arch knows already, but he loves a walk, don't you? Not too near the water though, just yet. I guess you've had enough of the water, Stella.'

So, with Bea chattering away, Stella with tongue lolling and slow steps, and Archie bounding ahead, they made their way up the back of the cottage. From there they made slow, steady progress to the top of the cliff, where they sat to enjoy the lure of the tangerine horizon as the sea sparkled against it. There was little wind and it was slack water, so the sea basked beneath a blue, a cerulean blue sky. Both dogs flopped down next to Bea and, when she looked down at them, they both noticed and responded with a companionable wag.

Think Stella likes me, and Archie is remarkably cool about her too! Bea decided and with no thought other than that, certainly none of Jeremy, she hugged her knees and gazed out to sea, her mind relaxing and gently floating on the waves.

Hello, she said to herself, as her eyes adjusted to the distances, *Someone's out sailing early. No, wait. Easily six, seven – ten boats!* She sat up. *Maybe there's regatta along the coast or something. Quite early for classes to start. Wonder where? Isn't it a bit late in the season though?* She raised her hand to shade her eyes, scanning the open sea. *Strange colours on the sails, strange shapes too, single and double masts.*

'Where are they going, hey dogs?' She bent to stroke them, but Stella was already asleep and snoring, her jowls rippling with exhaled breaths and then dream-barks. Archie lay with his head on his paws, looking at her.

Bea carried on talking. 'Look at those square sails and is that an animal head – a dragon on the prow?'

'Mind, they don't look like any of our boats, more like those of the

Irishmen who came in the Spring. One of those boats that brought Cormac.' She passed a hand over her belly and smiled. 'Wait! Is their mission peaceful?'

Nest spoke aloud; she often did so to the wolves.

'Last time they brought war bands to protect their raiding parties and big ships to carry the stolen cattle. I expect someone will have spotted them by now and will have told the Prince, after all, they come openly in daylight. Maybe they learned their lesson after they were beaten and forced to pay for what they stole. Am I doing them a disservice? It could be they come for peaceful trading.'

She gazed past the horizon to distant lands, thinking, *How wonderful to travel so far to the lands of the East and bring those fabrics full of golden thread the Princess used to favour, that pottery of fine clay ware, those beads and beautiful ornaments. And for us to sell our goods to them; our pelts, our wool and our hunting dogs.*'

Nest put out a hand to touch the wolves' warm backs.

'Come, my dears, our neighbours may know. And I need some more of that fine green glasswort for my pottage; there's a good patch at the opening of the river, close by the edge of the salt marsh. Come Mellt, come Seren,' she called as she rose to walk back inshore across the newly shorn grass of the sea meadow.

The day before, the whole of the village had worked to gather in the stooks of hay and take them back inland, piling them into a fine high stack. It was the fifth stack they had made this year; and although the grass had been cut late in this meadow, it was not unknown for a second cut in a season. A good year with much hot sun, plenty of fodder for the Winter and plenty to be thankful for Nest decided as she and the wolves strode down the beach. It was a fine dry day and the gulls wheeled high overhead.

On her way she saw one of her neighbours, Madoc ap Dafydd, who, now he was too unsteady on his feet to go out with the fishing boats, spent his days mending nets in his yard by the estuary mouth.

'Madoc, how now?' she called. 'Your fingers fly faster than the spiders who weave in my roof space.'

'Ah, Nest, girl. I do this in my sleep. In fact, I'm asleep now, and dreaming a vision so lovely that it warms my old belly, aye and more besides!' He grinned at her, his face alight with admiration. 'You grow more beautiful by the day, Nest. You know our Christian neighbours say you have a pact with the devil and our neighbours who still favour the old gods say you have a pact with the Mother Goddess, and *that's* how you stay so lovely, as lovely and youthful as the start of the Spring, promising a beautiful Summer.'

Nest put her basket on the low yard wall. She laughed.

'Madoc, you talk like a young warrior in the first flush of strength and paying court to a maiden.'

'And me all of eighty-five years this Winter solstice, but aye, with the same wild passions in my heart as I had when twenty! Ah, I was a fine strong young man. You would not have been able to resist!' He laughed.

Nest laughed too, and the wolves lay down on the gritty shore when she sat on the wall.

'What of those boats approaching us? They come from the direction of Ireland. What have you heard?' she asked. 'Come, I know you see and hear everything,' she teased.

'A crow may have whispered on the wind...' he conceded, 'Trade, it seems; so I'm told.' His voice dripped disbelief. 'They came with the Spring to raid the mainland and went away with tails between their legs, yet now they creep back on their bellies like whipped curs to lick their master's hand and to try and out-bargain a Welshman. Ha!'

'Do you tell me truth?' Nest was incredulous.

'Indeed I do and I hear that our Prince is well pleased. Now, do *you* know different, my girl?'

'Oho, Madoc, I know nothing, which is why I ask. You are still a fisherman, are you not? A fisher of information,' she said and added, smiling, 'As am I. So, what do you know of that would be interesting to me?'

'A silver tongue, my lovely, a silver tongue you have.' He laughed. Although Madoc's hair was white it was thick, and his eyes were as blue as the Summer sea. 'I did hear that many a message has gone to England from our Prince's Lady wife. I did hear that her waiting woman (I don't call her a *maid*, for it sullies the title I give to our own pure young girls), I did hear that she has been seen very thick with that boil, that canker of the soul, Ithel ap Deykin.' He paused and looked deeply into Nest's eyes. 'I also heard that Yestyn has been wounded by a wildcat and keeps out of his Lord's sight for the time being.'

Nest held his gaze and spent a little time to consider before saying:

'Yestyn is a strutting young cock and too fond of himself and of getting his own way by force. He thinks to have me. I taught him a lesson, which may indeed make him angry, but I would that my Lord Prince knows nothing, for he would surely kill him. The boy has his way to find and I, in turn, find that I am not afraid of Yestyn's anger at all. It's through him that I can see what others are doing; others like Ithel and that woman, Edith, as you say. I fear them both for the Prince's sake.'

Madoc nodded and, grabbing her hand, said, 'If I were but five years younger, I would kill Yestyn for even thinking about you, Nest. By the gods I would! I would gut him as easily as I do a fish. As would my Lord Prince, if he hears of it. He values honour in his Uchelwr.'

He flushed with anger and truly she believed him.

'On my oath, if Yestyn comes near enough for my old legs to carry me I swear I'll do him harm. Trust me.'

'Oh, I do, and I thank you. The Lord God is forgiving, but the old gods will deal with him. I've seen his punishment travelling on swift wings. It won't be long.'

'Ah, you looked in the flames or the water, as your mother before you?'

'I saw. That is all I will say, Madoc, bach.'

'Everything is safe with me as far as you and your wishes are concerned, lovely. Knowing you since you were born makes me feel like a second father to you. Yours lost at sea! Ah, lost at sea and like my own brother. We never part with one of his ilk without regret. He often asked me to look out for you if anything happened to him; a sacred trust, he said. So have no fears of me. I will fish for you as long as I have breath in my body,' he told her and a muscle in his jaw tensed. 'And I wish that body was not so old.'

Chapter seventeen

Disdain

A pox o' your throat, you bawling, blasphemous,

incharitable dog!...

Sebastian - The Tempest

THEY PARTED affectionately, and Nest carried on to her cottage. She went purposefully indoors, so the wolves took themselves to lie in the open doorway where the wind could lift their fur and bring them interesting scents. She took a wide earthenware bowl from the shelf and setting it on the board, filled it with water from her jug. Next, she lit a small bronze oil lamp, a gift from Llewelyn, and positioned it so that the light gilded the surface of the water. Her movements were practised, efficient, quiet, and she was soon ready. She took her stool and sat on it straight backed, which meant that she could look directly down into the water. After this she took five slow, long breaths to focus her mind.

'So, Ithel, how goes it with you?' she murmured as she took hold of the bowl very gently and tilted it this way and that until the water began to swirl slowly around in a miniature whirlpool. She concentrated on the movement of the water and the bright flickering wavelets created by the light; then she drew a single long, slow breath and, as she exhaled, she closed her eyes briefly.

'Ahhh, now...' she said and opened her eyes to see figures in the stilling waters, figures moving in a darkened place.

'Where are you, Ithel?'

Her voice was no more than a breath, yet it had a pure musicality that made the wolves prick their ears.

The gleaming water-window showed Ithel ap Deykin clearly; he was in Caer yn Arfon and it was midnight.

It was the darkest night in the month with heavy cloud dousing all the stars and the sickle moon. As if affected by this sombre mood, the sea slapped the shore peevishly. It tossed its usual flotsam of branches and leaves, scraps of rotting vegetation, sometimes dead creatures, all in an ungainly high-water mark at the foot of the castle palisade.

There were already long strands of kelp stuck to this wooden outer defence, flung there by previous high tides and glued there by sun and wind. The wood was also festooned with dead barnacles, broken crabs, feathers, wings and even a glistening jelly fish new washed up from the deeps. Lower down the shore, the most recent branches and roots lay tumbled in huge heaps, not yet foraged for fuel by the local poor. The night was still and the sea calm.

Along the top of the ramparts two torches could be seen moving slowly towards each other. They moved in measured paces then took a minute's halt as the guards holding them on the walkway patrol exchanged words in passing. But their torches were dimmed by the shrouding darkness.

Below the palisade and crowding on the very edge of the high-water line was a spillage of shanties that stretched beyond the castle to higher ground. Their numbers were kept down by the castellan. He had them cleared by his soldiers whenever they became too numerous or noisome, or whenever the garrison had to defend the castle and town from invasion. The shanties and their inhabitants were dispensable. Yet to Ithel, one of these dwellings held three creatures that were very valuable indeed to him, that is, until they had served their purpose. He called them creatures because to him they were less than human.

Under the blanket of the night and cleaving his way through lingering mists of strange odours, he made his way to an isolated shack on the shore. He'd been there before. It was tucked right against the palisade, almost invisible under the many arms of a stout bramble. The approach was surrounded by a layer of offal too rotten even for the roaming dogs and pigs. No other shelters were within listening distance.

Ithel wore a long dark cloak and pulled up his hood to hide his face, as if his long dark hair did not usually do that service adequately. He was not as robust or as broad as many of his countrymen, but he carried a stout staff and could defend himself. It was best to be prepared on these shores. He used the staff to part the bramble and slap the leather curtain which served for a door cover. It was strange that this valuable leather item survived in a poor neighbourhood so close to death and sickness, but the other shore dwellers knew who lived in the dark shack under the castle wall and let it alone.

'Ho, you hags within. Come forth,' he whispered, bending to the doorway. He repeated his slapping but had not beaten more than thrice before a hand reached out and grabbed hold of the staff itself. Ithel was not in a mood to be controlled or prevented from having his way, and he yanked the staff from the hands so quickly that a small figure, still clinging to the other end, was pulled out from under the hanging. It was black from head to toe, shrouded in rags and long greasy hair and it was a woman. But she didn't lie there stunned, as an onlooker may have expected; instead she rolled lightly to her feet and stood braced and hissing to face him. Her bared arms were decorated with complex swirling patterns painted with a blue dye, similar to those the Druids once wore. She was Chwaer Dŵr, Sister of Water.

Ithel kept his ground; his expression showed nothing but disdain and hardly changed as the leather cover was drawn aside by another hand. This one was white as a lily, smooth as that of a high-born lady, yet the figure that emerged from the shack was dressed in rags as numerous and as black as that of the first. There was a difference though; this woman had careful red lines drawn horizontally across her cheeks and forehead as though by fingers dipped in blood, and her hair was long and red. She stood tall and proud and met him eye to eye, this Chwaer Tân, Sister of Fire.

No sooner had he met this challenge than a third and final figure emerged from behind the curtain. She was forced to stoop sideways to get through the gap and, although Ithel kept his expression under tight control, each time he saw the woman he was mesmerised by her size. She was huge, the size of a warrior, twice Ithel's size, with hands that could cover the top of his head like a cap, the weight of which he remembered as she had once forced him down onto a low stool in the hovel. Her hair was short, spiked with grease and black as the night around them. She wore rags that had once been blue, and her dress hung open to the waist exposing huge and pendulous breasts that had forced many men off their guard before she killed them, crushed their necks with her warrior's hands.

Ithel kept his eyes on her face. He spoke quietly although there was a razor edge to his voice as he asked, 'You have what I need?'

The big woman eyed him with a stare that probed beyond words, nevertheless she said, 'What is your intention, bard?'

'My intentions are my own, hag.'

'I am called Chwaer y Ddaear. Speak me fair or go your ways without your desire.' Her voice was calm and deep; strangely melodious.

Ithel dropped his head so that his hair and hood would hide the smouldering fire of his eyes. He composed his voice carefully to speak with the very dangerous Sister of Earth.

'I beg pardon, Chwaer y Ddaear. I have an enemy. The Lord Prince Llewelyn has the same enemy. I wish to be of service to my lord, but without him knowing,' he said.

As Nest watched him in the water window, she saw his thoughts clearly written on his face; he would like to rid the world of Y Chwiorydd - The Sisters, and he intended to see this giant, unnatural Sister of Earth in the very earth she was named for before he was finished.

'How so?' Sister of Earth murmured. She stood relaxed in front of him and dominating the confrontation with her confidence.

'I would see a son of Gwynedd as its Prince.'

'We *have* a son of Gwynedd as our Prince,' she replied.

'Indeed, but he has not named the rightful heir. Gruffydd ap Llewelyn is the one and not the English usurper.'

'Ahhh!' She laughed. 'You wish to cleanse the throne. I see. I see also that you lie.'

Ithel tensed and held his rage in check with difficulty.

'There is also a woman who bars the way, one who is a pretender to the arts that have been gifted to you and me.'

He inclined his head, a gesture to humility.

She merely smiled her derision this time.

'We share no arts, man.'

Although they did not join the discussion, the other two women were not inactive; they moved like drifting smoke on a still day, slowly weaving and twisting, touching and floating around the pair, extending their long fingers to graze his arm here, his leg, his cheek, his throat there, and as they moved they each hummed a single note, one higher than the other. But Ithel had visited The Sisters before, he knew their ploys to unsettle a man. He radiated anger; he wanted their spells, more importantly he needed their mind-altering potions, their undetectable poisons.

Sister of Earth spoke calmly.

'Nest it is you speak of. We know your passions, Ithel ap Deykin. We know you allowed our sister, Chwaer Awyr to be kicked and beaten by the English bitch, though she was helping the soldier. Sister Air is precious to us. We *see*, as you pretend to, Ithel the Bard. We see you in the smoke from our fires. We see that you fear, and you desire Nest of the Shore, how very much you desire her. We see that you would unsettle the kingdoms and bring more strife and war to Gwynedd. Llewelyn got his first born, Gruffydd, with Tangwystl, and we know she was also your own first love. You have loathed him from that day, loathed him for taking her and not marrying; she was willing for both events. Yet you serve him, serve him with rumours and he trusts you. Trusts you. But, did you know that she loathed you, Ithel ap Deykin. Did you know that? Tangwystl despised you. Could you not *see* it?'

Chwaer y Ddaear chanted her words on a single note, but let the volume rise up and down until they matched the rhythm of the waves that beat slowly on the shore. She stepped back and joined her sisters as they wove a dance about him; their arms and bodies were graceful and lively as water flowing round stones, and as they moved they were joined by tendrils of grey, lilac, sage coloured mist that wrapped him in ropes of power until his eyes finally showed fear. They laid hands on him then and ripped his robes, tore his hair, bloody from the roots, rent his face and arms and legs with their long nails and when he fell to the ground, they kicked him until he was senseless.

Finally, when he lay still, they moved back to their den as quietly as babes breathing.

Nest, watching in the water window, murmured to herself:

'Ahhh, The Sisters: Chwaer y Ddaear, Sister of Earth, and Chwaer Tân, who is Sister of Fire and Chwaer Dŵr, Sister of Water. And here at Llewelyn's llys, Chwaer Awyr, Sister of Air. I love you all, my friends, and I know you are powerful and fearsome. Strange and wonderful in the way of Earth's deep magic.'

Nest bent to take a final look. She saw the dawn breaking and the tide beginning to rise up the castle shore. There lay Ithel on the water's edge. When the waves slapped his face he began to stir and in a daze he finally rose and as he realised how exposed he was to the sight of men, he stumbled quickly up the shore and into the woods. Of the shack under the bramble arms, nothing could now be seen.

Nest used her hand to ruffle the waters of the bowl and sat back, thoughtful.

Bea rubbed her eyes, the glare from the sun on the sea was giving her a headache. She shaded her eyes and looked around thoughtfully.

I saw Nest watching Ithel. She was a seer. It was as clear as day to me; I was there with her, with Nest. And why am I seeing these things? It can't just be hallucinations; it's too much like a story unfolding, everything is in an order and they progress from one event to the consequence. What's going on? Who'd believe me? Will Nest tell the Prince of her fears or about the danger she's in, or about Ithel's treachery?

She looked down as Archie nudged her with her nose. Stella sat up with difficulty.

'Archie, Stella. I almost forgot you. I was so caught up in things.

God, my head aches. It's these dreams or visions, whatever they are. They're so real to me. Who'd believe me if I told them?'

'I would,' said a woman's voice.

Bea whipped round and Stella barked, a warning note.

'What? Mairi? Mairi – *is it you?* Oh, erm, what are you doing here?'

Chapter eighteen

Conspiracy

Your tale, sir, would cure deafness…

Miranda - The Tempest

MAIRI SMILED. 'Hello you! And in answer to your question, I'm just going for a walk,' she said. 'What are you doing here on my favourite cliff? Well, not really a cliff is it? More of a high bit with a drop! You going for a walk too?'

Her auburn hair was loose, and it flew in the wind like an untethered sail. She laughed disarmingly. She tried to tame it and push it inside her jacket collar but gave up on it with a pretty wave of her hands and instead turned so that the wind cleared her face of her hair. She was wearing a pale blue outdoor jacket, matching all-weather pants and obviously new walking boots.

'I have that problem with hair,' Bea muttered and pulled it out from inside her jumper, as if to prove her point and let it fly in the wind too, then, despising herself for the childishness of her action, she grimaced nervously and stuffed it all back inside the neck of her jacket.

'Gosh, what a lot! I didn't know it was that long, actually longer than mine. I thought you liked it all restrained and pinned in place?'

'No, no I don't, not really. That's what Jeremy likes,' Bea said and despised herself again for mentioning him, thinking about him at all.

Archie had started to growl softly when Mairi arrived and he sat and watched her. She seemed not to hear and turned her attention to the bigger dog that lay with her head on her paws.

'And who's this lovely person? My, oh my, is she pregnant? What a whopper!'

Mairi bent down to fondle the dog's ears, but Stella was aloof and silent.

'Whose is she? Someone you know? A friend?'

'Actually, she's mine. I just got her this morning really. She needed a home in a hurry.'

Bea's voice was quiet, almost lost on the wind. 'Why are you here, Mairi?'

Mairi ignored the question, laughed lightly. 'Oh? Needed a home…? I wouldn't have thought Jem wanted another dog, Bea, especially as he didn't want your mother's old one. Mind you, I suppose he can't last long; he's a bit ancient, I believe. What's changed Jeremy's mind?'

Her tone was light and teasing, friendly, woman to woman on the vagaries of husbands.

'She's not Jeremy's dog. I told you, she's mine, as is Archie, and they live here in Anglesey with me.' The assertion was ruined by the fragility of her voice.

Bea had begun to shake as she tried to struggle her way through the sticky mire of explanation. Mairi still appeared not to notice, instead, she sat down next to Bea and, making herself comfortable, she held forth on the view as familiarly as if they'd just had a brief interruption in an intimate conversation, two close friends. Stella lay still and Archie moved, stiff legged to explore the grasses near by.

'Gosh, it's just divine on the island. I keep saying to Don that we should move over. Where we are in Caernarvon is so full of tourists in the season. I positively hate it.'

She reached to her left to catch the mass of hair and this time, treating it like a wayward curtain, she twisted it round into a rope and pushed it inside her collar, zipping it firmly in place, competently, decisively.

'D'you know, you can get some lovely unspoilt properties here, well off the beaten track, places that would cost another hundred thousand or so on the mainland. I mean, I realise Don works at Bangor but that's an easy commute, no distance from the island and he just loves his work, as do I, and, well, Jem too, I guess. How about you?' She nudged Bea playfully with her elbow and rolled her eyes. 'Tough when you're just starting, I know.' There was the attempt at an intimacy that Bea did not remember having with her.

Bea managed a muttered repost to Mairi's assertion. 'But I haven't just started; I'm a registrar…'

Once again, Mairi acted as though she hadn't heard, and Bea stiffened with tension as she rattled onward in her conversational hopscotch.

'Did you know Don's just applied for the new Clinical Director post at Bangor Hospital? I'm absolutely positive he'll get it! I know he loves his traumas but ortho is so energetic, isn't it and he's past his first flush of youth. Actually, we could afford something really splendid on the island, and as far as travel goes - I mean, from here, rush hour to the mainland is two cars, a builder's van and a bike, for Goodness' sake!'

Bea found herself growing pale with the strain wondering why Mairi had suddenly materialised from the ether; Mairi, who was the wife of Jeremy's best friend.

Jeremy.

She felt her throat drying and she thought that her panicked breathing must surely be obvious.

'Why are you here?' she repeated. 'Do you always come over here for a walk? How did you know I was here?'

'I didn't. It's pure chance, lucky chance.' She smiled. 'And I do come over here if the mood dictates. Day off today. The air is so much more alive here than is our own spot in on the edge of town. I think it's because, here, the wind blows straight at one from the sea, rather than being deflected by the island, as in our case. So…' Mairi paused and gazed intently at Bea, 'are you here for the day, or what? Have you got a day off too or some holiday going on? Jem didn't mention it to Don, or perhaps he's here?' She looked around brightly and although it was an obvious theatrical pose, Bea couldn't help but look round too.

'You all right, chérie?' Mairi murmured and she laid a hand on Bea's arm.

Stella growled, lifting her head a fraction from where it rested on her paws and Archie threw up his head, alerted, and began barking at Mairi.

'Shh, Arch. Shhh. Yes, yes. Of course. Why?' she asked. Suddenly awash with fear, she caught Archie's collar and lifted him up under her arm.

Bea began to chew her bottom lip, a habit when she was worried or annoyed. She hated Mairi's pretentious use of endearments from other cultures; French were her current favourites, last year it had been American, everyone had been called 'honey'.

'Why? Well, you've gone a bit pale. Is it those headaches and visions? Hmmm?'

Bea ignored that.

'Is he here? No, he can't be, he's in Prague, at the conference. Have you seen Jeremy?'

'He's at a conference you say. So, you're on your own, are you, Bea? Are you sure? Where are you staying?' Mairi's voice was soft and she spoke slowly, dipped her head, smiling.

'I'm at my Aunt's cottage – down the way.' She waved her hand vaguely, hoping to put Mairi off enquiring further or worse, asking to be shown round.

'Look, Bea,' Mairi began, shifting her position and moistening her lips with a pink kitten tongue, as though she rather feared that the unfolding conversation would be uncomfortable for Bea, and that, she, Mairi, was sensitive enough to make allowances for that. 'Are you taking your tablets okay? They are important in your treatment. Jem's in a desperate state about you actually.'

The pink tongue hid the needle-sharp teeth. Mairi looked pleased with herself.

'Tablets? What tablets? No, I mean I'm not on any medication for anything at all…Well, he did give me some sleeping stuff, but I don't need it here.'

'Oh, dearie me.'

'What do you mean?'

'I mean that you really need them to keep you on an even keel, especially with your condition. It's always the way; people take the meds, feel better and decide they don't need them anymore. Then there's a relapse.'

She shook her head, a gesture more like a disapproving nanny than a concerned friend, and Bea was puzzled.

Mairi continued. 'With the right medication, people can lead a virtually normal life and hold down a good career. I mean, think of your patients, if not Jem.'

'What condition? What do you mean? I haven't…'

'Chérie, don't take this wrong, it's kindly meant; Jem did say he thought you were in denial actually.' Mairi's voice and manner were the epitome of patience, kind concern and sympathy. She closed her eyes briefly and took a steadying breath, as if deciding whether or not to put some home truths on the table.

'Bea, you're bipolar. Remember, darling? And you also have schizophrenia and manic depression – poor you, poor, poor you.'

She put out her hand and gently rubbed Bea's upper arm, patted it.

Bea flinched.

'I don't, Mairi, really I don't.'

Her stomach gave a sickening lurch at the emotional jolt Mairi's words gave her and the physical contact too. She couldn't speak for a minute then she licked dry lips and said:

'Jeremy apparently told someone I was depressed a while ago, and the person asked me about it. I was shocked because I'm not ill, I haven't seen a psychiatrist – *ever*. I don't need to.'

She found it hard to keep her voice steady. She'd never really felt comfortable with Mairi, although she'd made a conscious effort every time she was taken to the Macintyre's for the weekend.

'Right, right. Everything's going to be fine, you'll see,' Mairi soothed. 'So, you say Jem's at a conference? Actually, he did phone us, to say you'd disappeared.' She let the words hang on the air. 'He was quite distressed. But he's not at a conference, is he? Hmmm? Did you just run away from everything, Bea? Just felt you had to, had to get away? Is that it?'

Bea was visibly shaken, and Stella sat up, nudged her with her nose so she slid her free arm round Stella's neck, squeezed her.

'It's okay. It's okay, girl.'

Next minute she found herself twisting her rings round and round with her thumb until her finger became so sore that she had to make a fist of her hand to prevent herself crying with the discomfort of it, but also with sheer frustration and fear at having been ensnared by Mairi.

Mairi's expression radiated concern, her voice was soft as she reached over and rested her hand on Bea's to still her agitation.

'Don't chérie, don't, you'll hurt yourself. To be honest, Bea, I don't blame you one bit for taking off. Has old Jem been a bit hard on you? I mean, I suppose if you're not well, you don't want someone as intense as him bearing down on you all the time, do you?'

She shuddered ostentatiously, and Bea didn't notice the spark of amusement in her eye, the flash of her dimple.

'And we all know how intense he can be, don't we?' she said.

'I told you; I'm not ill.'

Mairi passed over this and said, 'Okay, that's fine. But in case you feel you want to really get away from it all, from Jem, I mean, I have got contacts. I would have, wouldn't I, being in this field of medicine. Actually, I do do know of a really good private place, sort of a sanctuary, one of these guru-led meditation places. I know several people who've been for a 'rest'. Maybe you...'

Bea stood up and Stella dragged herself to her feet, wagging her tail a little uncertainly.

'I'm not ill. Did Jeremy actually say I am?'

'He did say you may have to go into hospital again, chérie.'

'I'm not going back to Manchester. I'm resigning.'

Bea was blurting out words, decisions she'd only just made, unable to look the other woman in the eyes.

'No, I meant he said you may have to go in again for a little help, you know, *as a patient*. You know *I know* that's true, don't you? Don and I visited last time, remember? I think it was after your mother passed away. You looked so sad.'

Bea gasped, and she shook her head, trying to get herself calm enough to answer without shrieking but as it was her voice sounded weak and uncertain.

'As a patient? It isn't true. I can't listen to this, Mairi. I'm not ill. I haven't been in hospital as a patient - ever. And no, I don't remember because it didn't happen.' Her voice was still shaky but it had risen with her panic.

This sounded like a plea. She got up and called the dogs, turned abruptly to walk away. Archie cast baleful glances at Mairi as he followed.

'I've got to go.'

Mairi glanced round at the retreating figure. She dropped her head back so that her hair was snatched out of her collar by the wind and flew about her head making her look like a new-age, perfectly and fashionably dressed Medusa.

Chapter nineteen

Influence

The baseless fabric of this vision...

Prospero - The Tempest

'HELLO THERE!' a man's voice hailed. Mairi leaped to her feet and seeing that the voice belonged to a young man, she smiled and waved, calling hello herself.

It was Lorcan. He had been striding across the higher ground towards her then stopped abruptly when he saw her.

'Oh, hello to you too.' He said, 'Didn't see you down there. You rose up like a sea nymph out of the waves, sure y'did. I'm awful sorry; it was the other girl I was trying to call.'

Mairi smiled. 'Well, thanks for the 'girl' at least, oh, and the nymph too! So, are you a friend of Bea's? She's one of mine too,' she added as he smiled. 'We've just been chatting.' Mairi turned on all her considerable charm.

Lorcan brushed his hair from his eyes. 'Only just met, but I'm hoping we can be friends, you know?'

'Indeed, I do...' she said, falling into step as he nodded downhill, smiled an invitation and began to stroll onward. 'I'm Mairi by the way,' she told him and once he'd reciprocated, she asked casually, 'How did you come to meet poor Bea, Lorcan?'

She kept her voice friendly and curious, with a note of concern for her friend. It was slightly at odds with the frank appraisal she gave him and the look of appreciation she wore as she spoke.

He explained what had happened the previous day and then in turn he wanted to know what she meant by 'poor Bea'.

'I shouldn't really have said that. I mean she is a friend, along with her husband, that is...'

'Husband? Ahh...'

'Old med school pals with mine –well, my almost ex, I should say.'

The look she threw him then was one of undisguised invitation, yet her voice became serious once more as she said, 'But about Bea, she's run away from hospital, the psychiatric unit, actually. She's been terribly depressed; voices, visions and that sort of stuff, if you know what I mean?'

Lorcan said he didn't really and Mairi wasn't surprised; she'd given him some tantalizing information, that begged to be explained.

She looked at the ground as she walked.

'I did hear her screaming something at that poor dog, the big one. The other one just ran away. She was certainly looking angry when I landed on the scene and I'll admit it's not like her, but I do worry. She usually likes animals.'

As they neared Nest's Point, he said he'd run on down and see how the dog was doing and let her go on alone, if she didn't mind.

'But I do mind, Lorcan. I rather do mind. I'll be walking on the top of the headland there at this time tomorrow, if you should be going that way yourself,' she said. 'Be kind to my little friend, won't you? Her husband's a brute,' she called as she sped up and strode across the trickle of the river and on to the other side. 'A really vicious brute…!' she murmured and smiled broadly. 'Brutish, savage, unpredictable and delicious.'

A sudden thought of Don, her husband, interrupted her daydream. Don, who was so lovely and rich, even richer than she herself, but her attitude was, why not more? But then Don was so reliable, so solid and boring. His bank balance was his salvation as far as she was concerned, and he did turn a blind eye to her occasional liaisons, although she wasn't sure he noticed in the first place. However, one never knew, and she intended to get a little nest egg of her own from Jem and to have him maintain it well into the future. She was positive Jem would oblige her. Reputation was everything to him and he wouldn't want his tarnished, would he? Mairi had plans.

Lorcan watched her heading for the dunes and the trek down to the village road. But she was gone from his mind in seconds as he walked up the cottage path. He knocked gently on the door and called, 'Hello indoors, only me, Lorcan!'

There was a short bark from inside but no other answer, so he knocked again and after a few seconds Bea called through the closed door.

'We're fine thanks, Lorcan. The dog's fine, really.'

'I brought something for them. I'll just leave it here will I?' he said and he stooped to put a bag of dog treats by the door, but before he straightened up Bea had opened the door slightly.

'Hi, sorry. I'm feeling a bit stalked at the moment.'

'I'm not surprised,' he said and when Bea looked puzzled, he added, 'Your friend, Mairi, was it? She said you'd not been well, been in hospital.'

Bea' hands flew to cover her mouth, her face flushed.

'No. It's not true, any of it. I haven't – well, only to work. What did she say?'

'Only that really. You mean she was mistaken? She said she was a friend. Is she?'

Stella came to the door with Archie and they both pushed themselves out to nudge Lorcan's leg, interrupting Bea before she could answer.

'Hello there, girl. Hello to you too, laddie!' He stroked them both and looked up enquiringly at Bea, but she was struggling to keep herself together.

'No, she's not a friend. I don't know, I, I…'

'Look, tell me to go or I'm coming in to make a brew. I think you and the mum-to-be, and the soon to be dog-uncle need a sit down and a chat. Yes?'

By way of reply and permission Bea said, 'The mum-to-be is Stella, she's called Stella and she's mine now, officially. So, I'm owner of a pack, it seems.'

'Now Nest would say that's magical, I think!' His voice was warm.

She managed a slight smile and stood back to allow Lorcan inside. Mairi had always inspired disquiet in Bea, and in contrast and as much as she wanted to be totally alone again, she felt Lorcan wore an aura of comfort, and she was desperately in need of that.

He made her sit by the fire. It seemed that was all she'd done since returning to Nest's Point. He made tea and produced chocolate biscuits from his jacket pocket. He told her that Thomas had phoned and filled him in on the change of ownership and the condition of the surviving friend, and some of the other events he hadn't heard about that had led to Stella being washed up on the beach.

He quietly coaxed her to agree to have a vet check Stella over; he'd a friend on the mainland who was a vet and would come over if he asked. Bea realised that he also thought he'd be saving her a job that might prove too much for her, as well as for Stella herself, so she said,

'I'm really not ill, you know. I don't know why she'd say that.'

'What about your husband? How does he feel?'

She blanched and the hand that held her mug shook suddenly. 'I don't want to talk about him. I can't. I'm living here now, at Nest's Point.'

'You're going to get a job over here then?'

It was only a normal, gentle nudge that anyone would voice, but she felt a frisson of fear, fear of the future. She shook her head.

'No, I'm giving up medicine and staying here. I'll think of something else when I'm ready. I've just had enough of medicine.'

'I guess it's stressful?' he ventured, but she wasn't to be drawn.

'Yes, but, that's not it. I just want to get away and stay here for a while. I just don't want to talk about him, I mean, my husband. I just don't. Can you just trust me for the moment?'

He smiled and told her to take as long as she needed. His voice was reassuring.

'No reason you should tell me at all,' he said.

He chatted about the beach and the weather for a few minutes, but then, standing up he said, 'Just let me know if you need anything or if they do, of course.' He nodded in the direction of the dogs. 'Here's my number,' he said as he took up the pen from the table and jotted it down on a piece of paper there.

'I'd better be getting along. Bye for now, all of you.'

Across the water, lying in a new spot in the dunes, Dana Smythe caught the visitors to the cottage on camera. She'd watched Bea through her long lens as she fled back to the cottage and with a big dog as well as the little terrier. The big dog had moved very slowly so Bea's flight was really at her speed, Dana reminded herself. It was just that Bea had the appearance of someone desperate to get away from another person; glances over her shoulder, worried expression, much urging of the big dog and the final slamming of the door.

That was after the obvious unwanted meeting with the woman on the cliff. The body language couldn't have been clearer to Dana; Bea had wanted to get away as soon as the woman joined her. And she was curious about the identity of the woman and mulled over the possibility of her being a wronged wife; Mr Fitzmartin had said he feared Bea was seeing another man, she decided it might be possible for this to be the man's wife, although, at the end of the lens, the woman had seemed very relaxed, not confrontational at all. Appearances could deceive.

So, her curiosity thoroughly aroused, she followed Mairi to the village to see if she had a car and, when she discovered that was the case, she noted the licence number of the brand-new Range Rover, just so that she could identify it when she saw it in future.

'Well, plenty of cash there. A spanking new Range Rover Velar, 3 litre, HSC,' she murmured. 'What I could do with a car like that. Over eighty grand, easy. Must have a good job.'

If Dana wanted to know where the woman lived, she would simply follow her. She made it a rule never to use her old police contacts, never called in favours with serving police friends; she always veered away from gathering any black marks at all. You never knew what would come back to bite you.

While she was in the village, she went along to the Post Office and was buying some snacks when in walked the young man she'd seen on the beach, heading to the cottage. She recognised him as the man who'd staggered down there with the wet dog yesterday. She'd heard from Thomas that the dog had been shipwrecked and was staying with a friend who lived at the cottage on the beach, which must be Bea. The dog had done well to stagger along as it had, she thought.

Thomas looked up from the till and when he saw who it was, smiled.

'Oh, hello there, Dana, isn't it?' Then he saw the younger man. 'Everything all right then, Lorcan, bach?'

Lorcan replied with a non-committal nod as he and Dana ranged round the shop picking up various goods.

Thomas quickly tilled them up and handing Dana the full bag said, 'Ten pounds fifty, ta. Stacking up for a midnight feast, is it?'

'What? No! Bird watching essentials.' Dana laughed. 'I spend a lot of time in the face of the wind. Need to keep up the calorie intake.'

'What're you after then?' Lorcan was beside her at the till. 'I've a keen interest in bird-watching myself, as it happens.'

'Oystercatchers, me. I'm doing some research into the effects of litter on the oystercatcher population of the North Welsh coast. Yes, I know, sounds a bit heavy doesn't it?'

She laughed again, and it was infectious; both men smiled.

'I'm into photography too so I'm after that competition-winning shot, y'know, the BBC Countryfile calendar cover?'

'Don't get me started on litter,' Lorcan groaned. 'The bane of my life here on the coast. You on holiday? Live here?'

'Staying at The Llewelyn round the corner for a few weeks, maybe less. I'll play it by ear.'

'Right. I'm in there tonight, watching the darts. I could stand you a drink and bend your ear about your research; might have contacts you could use. I'm a researcher myself but it's rather bigger litter occupies me time, let me tell you.'

Thomas chipped in.

'A big-wig he is, our Lorcan. *Professor* Macarthy no less. Just back from Antarctica, a year's work there.'

'Wow,' Dana said, adding, 'I'm Dana Smythe; not even doctoral status, yet.'

'By God! Don't be calling me Prof though, I'll never hear the end of it from the lads in the darts. Pleased to meet you, Dana. I'll be there around eight then?'

'You're on.'

She left with her shopping and looked forward to finding out about his relationship, if any, with her subject, Bea. Bea out there in her lonely sea-swept cottage. She had no idea whether he'd known Bea before he staggered down with the dog in his arms yesterday.

When the shop door closed behind her, Thomas asked Lorcan how Bea and the dogs were fairing.

'Seem fine. Only thing is, I saw her on the top of the headland with a woman just now. I thought your Bea looked upset by the chat they were having, then she rushed off. When I caught up the woman made a big deal of telling me Bea had run away from a mental hospital.'

'Never!' Thomas interjected.

'Said Bea's husband was worried. Seems she knows them both.'

'Husband. Yes, there is. And a nasty little bugger, if you ask me. Better off without him. Never reckoned much to him myself, nor did Nest. I think there's something going on with Bea, something odd, but *mental*? Bea? *Never*. She's from a long line of strong women and she's a lot like our Nest, rest her soul. I think she can handle most things. Bea said nothing to me about being ill. She's got a nasty injury to the lovely face, but that's what happens when you traipse about in storms at midnight. Otherwise, she looks fine to me, same girl as I've always known, but a bit strained, if you know what I mean?'

Thomas had a feeling Lorcan might be interested in Bea herself, not just because of the dog.

Outside in the village square, Dana had stopped to put her things in her rucksack when she saw that Mairi was still around; by then she was in the driver's seat of the white Range Rover parked at the side of the Chapel. Her window was open and her hair lifting in the breeze. She had her phone in hand, as though ready to make a call. As luck would have it, the chapel was open and even better, the street level windows were all open too.

Dana recognised a chance when she saw one; she strolled over and walked casually in through the front door. There were one or two women cleaning at the far end of the hall. It took Dana only seconds to locate the window in the vestibule that was next to the parked Range Rover.

'Maybe...' Dana murmured to herself, 'Y'never know...'

She strolled to the table under the open window and smiled when she heard a woman's voice. Her accent was English, educated, very confident and what's more, Dana decided it was also angry - livid in fact. She picked up a pamphlet from the display stand on the table as 'cover', while she listened to one side of, what was clearly, the telephone conversation. She also pressed record on her own phone. You never knew what evidence would be handy, for whatever reason.

'Look Jem.' The woman spat the words.

Dana almost gasped. How many Jem's were there in Anglesey that knew Mr Fitzmartin's wife? And how many times had she heard Jeremy being shortened familiarly to Jem? She'd also known Jezzer to be used, but was fairly confident Mr Fitzmartin wouldn't tolerate that.

The woman continued. 'I do have better things to do, more rewarding things actually, my own work for instance.' There was a pause to which she replied, 'I'd say you have no alternative but to trust me.' Another pause and she added coldly to some comment he'd made, 'Yes – me, Mairi. I told you I can easily fathom a mind like Bea's. It is my job, after all. Why, are you, 'dreadfully afraid she may harm herself'? Wasn't that what you told Don and me? It was so sweet, I almost believed you, had I not known you so much better than that.' Listening again and then she laughed. 'Things will work out, but you need to know I'm not one to be crossed, especially not by you, my sweet.' Another listening pause. 'If only you had the nerve it might be quite arousing, Jem darling. Au revoir,' she drawled and disconnected.

Dana pocketed her phone and, returning the pamphlet to the stand, she strolled out of the building. She smiled at Mairi, who was preparing to drive off, and she headed back to the beach and the dunes. She would make her 'report' to Mr Fitzmartin about the woman she had seen in conversation with his wife, although he would clearly know who she was, and what was more, by the sound of their talk they were intimate. She would need to discover exactly what it was that Jem, Mr. Fitzmartin, was planning with regard to his wife because the last thing she wanted was to be involved in some gigantic fraud, financial or emotional.

Chapter twenty

Design

To work mine end upon their senses

that this airy charm is for…

Prospero - The Tempest

AS SOON AS LORCAN LEFT, Bea closed the door, shot the bolts and leaned gratefully against it.

Thank God he's gone. I've got to be alone or I'll burst. Well, alone apart from the dogs. A friendly face is okay for a short while, as long as he doesn't come over every day. I don't want that. I hardly know him, apart from what Thomas said and even if Auntie Nest did like him.

The tiny entrance hall smelled of salt and there was always a shimmer of sand on the floor that whispered underfoot, counterpoint notes to the wind that whistled its way under the door. Bea's heart was racing and the skin across her forehead felt as though it was stretched tight with tension.

But what was Mairi really doing here? Bea had been dumbfounded to see her. *She doesn't do walks. She said Jeremy had phoned them; said I'd gone, escaped from a psychiatric unit? Why is Mairi lying? Is she lying? Did he say that about me and she, they, her and Don, believed it? She didn't seem to know about the conference in Prague. What if he's not actually gone anywhere? But where would he be then? Why would he let me think he'd gone and let me leave?*

She felt a waterfall of fear drench her from the crown of her head and down through the very core of her being. There were too many unanswered questions. She found it deeply worrying, as if Mairi's appearance itself hadn't already unsettled her and diverted her from the timid pleasure she'd felt with the dog. She couldn't think why

Mairi would be involved with anything to do with her. They weren't even friends. It hadn't occurred to her that Jeremy might have phoned his friends down here to check up on her, and by all Mairi said, to worry because she'd run away, absconded from some psychiatric unit, no less. In any case, she was convinced that Jeremy didn't know she'd inherited Nest's Point so there was no reason to think she would even be on the island.

But if he really thought I was ill, why would he leave me alone in Manchester and go to a conference? Have I imagined it? I wasn't ill after Mum died. I was devastated. I was sad, grieving. There's a bit of a difference between a very natural grief and clinical depression. Anyway, I had Auntie Nest to help me and we were sad together. I'm sure I wasn't in any mental hospital. What am I saying? I do know I wasn't. I'd hardly forget something like that. I think I'd know – wouldn't I? But what about those people at that party, saying they'd heard from him that I was in therapy? She pushed herself away from the door and shook her mane of hair, a gesture she always called 'lightening the brain'. *I will need therapy if I go on like this.*

Archie and Stella were sitting in the middle of the floor, looking intently up at her and Archie gave a slight wag of the tail, the sort that meant, 'let's do something' or 'I want something'.

'You are so right. This is getting to be a habit. I keep shutting myself – us, indoors. I've spent all that time being locked in by Jeremy and now I've escaped, I'm locking the door on myself. But, y'know what? It's staying locked for the time being, just for safety's sake and because I'm the one doing the locking. We're going to do some organising – but first, you two need a little dinner, don't you?'

Archie shot away to the kitchen and Stella, who obviously knew the word too, heaved herself to her feet and padded happily after Bea to the kitchen where both dogs were given another small meal. Both finished their food quickly, but Stella just stood and gazed up steadily at Bea.

Bea bent to stroke her head. 'I bet you're missing your family, Stella. It's been awful for you, hasn't it?' She took the dog's head in her hands and looked deep into her brown eyes. 'Poor girl. You're grieving. Poor girl. I'm going to look after you, and your babies, don't worry.'

The dog gave her a brief wag of the tail and then padded back to the fire where she settled down again, head on paws.

Bea found a notepad and pen and sitting on the settle by the fire, she began to make a list of things to do, positive things and only a short list that could be easily achieved. It was a habit her mother had taught her. Archie leapt up and sat next to her. So, she wrote three things fairly quickly: *get solicitor, get vet for Stella – microchip check (change ownership)* and *resign job.* Then she moved to more mundane things such as: *stock up on food - me and dogs, get wood delivered, put Calendula ointment on finger. Ooch, sore.* She added, *clothes?* to the list because she had brought very few clothes with her and as the season was changing; she'd soon need colder weather things.

It was early Autumn but there could be ferocious gales in September and October on the Welsh coast, yet a mild Winter to follow on their heels. There again, there might be an Indian Summer, which, she had to admit, was more likely on the island with its balmy maritime climate. She recognised her need for gathering supplies in the cottage to be something like preparing for a siege in Prince Llewelyn's day.

The pen rested on her lap as thoughts crowded in, stirring up her fears and terrors of Jeremy. Was he right? Could she possibly be mentally ill? She knew that making a list and organising herself was a rational activity, but there again, patients she'd met on her Psych rotation as a student doctor had often behaved just like that for short periods, but their own strange behaviours would keep surfacing, bursting to the surface like drowning swimmers to put themselves or someone else in harm's way.

One patient, a middle-aged man, was highly intelligent and knowledgeable and she'd had many interesting conversations with him, but each week of his stay in the unit, his elfin-like and very elderly mother brought in a brand-new cotton shirt for him.

She remembered. *When his mother had gone, he'd cut the collar off the shirt and wear it like that for the following week until she came again. He said he did it to stop his mother's shirt strangling him.*

Another patient came to mind, one that held quite some significance for Bea because of her own experiences since she'd come home to Nest's Point. It was a young woman who sometimes felt driven to take off all her clothes in a crowded public place, fold them, and then replace them. When she was committed to the Mental Health Unit, she said her hospital room was in a Nazi Concentration Camp.

She believed it was 1943 and her room was crowded with people of all ages, all of whom had no clothes and were dreadfully starved. She said she was one of them sometimes. She said they prayed together and, although she was not Jewish herself in the present day, she could recite, in Yiddish, the prayers the mothers used to say to their children.

During the final week of Bea's rotation, the woman walked out of the ward unnoticed, and made her way to a local bridge over the Manchester Ship Canal from where she jumped to her death into the water far below. Bea had been devastated.

But didn't she behave exactly as I'm doing – apart from the clothes thing? My brain keeps taking me off to the thirteenth century. It's so real I can smell the fires and the sweat, taste the food, hear the shouts, feel the pain, see the blood. I felt the baby move inside me, I felt it. What if they're right and I'm absolutely deluded? I don't want to be sectioned. What did that other patient say to me in the ward that day? His name? What was it now? I asked him what it was like to be there in the mental health unit and he said, 'You've got to be bloody mad to stay in here!' He used to buy himself clothes from the local charity shops every day and change his trousers seven or eight times a day. Plenty of so-called sane people do that, so what is madness, what is it to be clinically insane? Not the medical definitions we had at med school. Definitely not.

Stella barked in her sleep and Bea wondered if she was dreaming of her lost family, chasing her ball down the beach, smelling the scents as she stood on the prow of the boat. Maybe she was playing with the children; dreaming, dreaming, maybe longing for them too. Wasn't dreaming a kind of fantastic time-slip into another dimension, a kind of time travel?

'What do you think, Archie, am I mad as Jeremy says I am? I don't know what to think, except that you're a lovely dog and so is Stella.' She stretched out a hand to rub the big dog's back and Stella lifted her back leg to join in and scratch her flank as energetically as her bulge would allow.

Bea rose from the settle; she was weary and, as she began to turn, something moved just out of her vision, something green, and deep red, she thought. She whirled around to try and catch sight of it and there in the corner of the room, near the kitchen door was a shadowy figure. It seemed to be wearing a long green robe or dress, with a russet border to the skirt. The figure, a woman, was bent over a hearth of some kind, then straightened and for an instant, looked at her, looked straight at her.

'Nest? Auntie Nest?' she breathed but as she strained to focus her mind on what she thought she saw, it faded away and she was looking at the door.

Was it Auntie Nest? No. She rubbed her eyes; they were as clear as ever, but her head swam, she felt nauseous and she fled to the toilet, only just in time to throw herself on her knees, grab the side of the bowl be thoroughly sick. She turned around on the floor, slid her legs out in front and leaned back against the toilet.

I'm seeing things; well I've done it before but this time, it wasn't a dream, was it. It was like seeing a ghost. She felt suddenly in command of herself. *It was, wasn't it? The ghost of that other Nest, or rather, her spirit. What if other dimensions do exist and events actually get recorded in the rocks, or the earth, the stones of a building? What if all the emotion of their lives is packed in every crack and crevice, has soaked into the plaster and wood so that you can breathe it in, hear it, feel it? But why did she appear to me just then? Does she want me to do something, know something? Out there this morning, I saw thirteenth century Nest. She was in here and she was looking in the water, scrying, I think it's called. She was watching the bard, Ithel. But is she back there in the thirteenth century, watching me in my time too? Can she see into the future? Is my time happening at the same pace as hers but in another dimension? This is getting a bit Sci-fi for me. I'll be calling in some Ghost Busters at this rate, or maybe one of those American ghost hunting reality shows we used to watch on night shift. Bit boring mostly, but made you think. Well, those of us who had half a brain!*

She smiled at the memory of herself and some of the other ward staff taking a break in Sister's room or in the Junior Common Room; it gave her such an instant shot of longing for that companionship and energy that it was like a physical pain. Then it was gone, replaced by the sound of Jeremy's voice whispering in her mind, a comment he often used, 'You stupid little slut.' When they first met it was, 'You're so charmingly unspoilt, so fresh, my darling.'

Bea's head felt as though it would burst, and a pain was building behind her eyes. She went back into the living room, over to the corner where she'd seen the figure, where she'd seen Nest. She wanted to touch the stone wall, stand on the spot where Nest had appeared to stand moments before, to see if she could truly feel any presence, any sort of vibrations from the past. She didn't.

'Where are you, Auntie Nest – *my Nest?* Why can't I see you instead of the one from Llewelyn's time? It's not fair,' she told the walls of the cottage then she sat down on the floor and sobbed until her eyes were raw and her throat and head really thoroughly aching. Archie was snoring, fast asleep on the settle, but Stella waddled over to lie down at Bea's side, pressing close.

Chapter twenty-one

Chance

You fools, I and my fellows are ministers of fate…

Ariel - The Tempest

DOWN IN THE VILLAGE, Mairi had finished her call and was satisfied with the response she'd had from Jeremy and delighted with her earlier encounters on the cliff. She started the engine and swept out of the little village square with the speed and panache of a rally driver. As she rounded the bend that led to the main road, she saw a man leaning over the gate of his cottage. The sun caressed the buttery yellow wall of the building and, set against that, his dark hair and khaki jumper combined with his natural swarthy complexion put Mairi in mind of a TV presenter she admired who fronted programmes on wildlife and adventure.

The man at the gate smiled as she looked towards him. She could see that he was very comfortable with admiring glances from strangers and his smile broadened when she stopped the car. She backed up until she was level with the cottage.

Opening the window, she called, 'Hello, I wonder if you can help me?'

He said, 'I do hope so.'

Mairi turned off the engine so he opened the gate and stepped forward into the track at the side of her car.

'I'm Gwyn,' he said and made himself comfortable with his hands in the pockets of his jeans. He looked relaxed and confident. He nodded at the car.

'Brand new? Latest? It's a Velar I see. Lovely.'

'Gosh, yes. My husband's obsession.'

They smiled at each other.

'How can I help you?'

'You're not local?' she asked, and he answered with pursed lips, a rueful grin and a shake of the head.

'Noooo. Just moved in actually.'

Mairi said, 'Oh, well, you may not know the answer to my query then, but I'll try you out. The little cottage at the end of the beach; I heard it was for sale.'

He looked surprised. 'More than I've heard. Why, are you interested? We could do with some attractive neighbours.'

She smiled her thanks at the compliment and said, 'I think you've got one already. There seems to be a young woman living in that cottage, or at least, she's staying there, I presume.'

'Ah…' was all he said but raised his eyes heavenward.

'Is there a problem?'

'No, no. To be fair I don't know her really. Only met her the other night, in a thunderstorm, as a matter of fact. I went down there in the middle of the night when I saw a light on to see if there were intruders. Let's say, she wasn't exactly welcoming. I was only doing her a favour,' he said, without taking his eyes from Mairi's.

Both her front windows were open, and the wind streamed through the car and whipped her hair out of its confines again, pulled it away from her face to flow out behind her. She scooped it round her neck with a graceful movement and saw that the gesture wasn't lost on Gwyn.

'You know, you look like some figure head on the prow of a three master! Lovely hair, gorgeous colour.'

She simply smiled. Apart from anything else, she enjoyed flirting with handsome men. She assumed her most innocent, yet puzzled expression and said, 'I just met the women on the cliff, at least I guess it was her as she went into the very cottage. But I have to say I didn't like the way she treated that poor dog, the big one who seems to be pregnant. Oh, and there was a little scruffy white terrier thing too. It ran off.' Mairi shook her head, as if at the distasteful memory.

'Why? What do you mean? What happened?' Gwyn asked, suddenly more alert and sounding very concerned too. 'The big one's a very needy dog. I was involved a little with her rescue – well, sort of. I was there when one of the locals carried her down to the cottage. Apparently, he'd found her on the beach. Seems she was washed up there after a shipwreck during that storm the other night. She was in a bad way and in-whelp too. What did the woman say then? Her name's Bea, incidentally.'

Mairi was all righteous indignation as she told a tale of Bea shouting, pushing and dragging the poor creature by the neck with the lead and all the while complaining that she'd been landed with the dog. She said she was contemplating phoning the animal rescue people or the police to come and take it off her hands.

Mairi was delighted by his response. He looked aghast.

'Really?' he said. 'She didn't strike me quite like that, seemed fairly quiet to me.' And he added, 'She's a doctor, apparently.'

Mairi leaned out of the window and swept her gaze quickly around as though checking for eavesdroppers as she said:

'No! You do surprise me. You'd have thought she would have some compassion at least. Actually, I did hear something she was saying – to herself as it happens. She was, well, how to put this politely? She was raving, talking to the wind I suppose, or maybe the voices in her head at least. She was telling someone she wasn't going back to the unit. She didn't want the shock therapy again. As she was dragging the poor dog, she kept screeching, *No, no, I can't, I can't. It hurts so much. Don't. Don't.* The little one kept up a constant yapping. Awful. It was strange when I heard her voice as I came over the tops. The wind blew the sound towards me, but she was turned away and didn't see me for a minute. When she did, her face was just thunderous. She wasn't a bit shocked, simply angry, I thought.'

'Wow, interesting, I must say. Must make some enquiries about the dog then. I hate animal abuse myself. Thomas at the Post Office knows everything. He knows Bea too. I'll see what I can find out. The guy who rescued the dog from the beach is a local, as I said. He seemed okay though, plumber apparently. Maybe he'd take the dog on.'

He glanced behind in the direction of the Post Office and gestured over his shoulder with his thumb.

'Well, fancy that. There they are, Thomas and Lorcan; that's the plumber, the younger of the two.'

She glanced over his shoulder and saw two men who were looking their way as they stood chatting themselves, near the bridge.

'Ah yes, I met the younger one on the cliff, earlier. Seems nice,' she said and then gave a sigh of relief. 'So, you'll do something? How wonderful. That would put my mind at rest. And I am looking for a pied-à-terre on the island. Myself and my husband are separated actually, but I'm taking custody of the cars, let me tell you, new or not. His little *friend...*' She said the word and gave a tiny shake of the head with a look she hoped was one of distressed significance. 'His little *friend* will not be getting her hands on them, nor will she have any access to the marital house.'

Mairi slipped her hand slowly into the front of her jacket and moved it gently around as Gwyn watched her. She found what she was searching for in the inner pocket; it was a card, which she handed to him.

'My number, should you hear about any the sale of the cottage, or the dog's welfare of course. Do let me know. It's been enlightening to talk to you....I'm Mairi. And you, what do they call you? Did you say Gwyn?'

'Oh, yes, Gwyn, Gwyn Roberts.'

They shook hands slowly as she stared at him intently, a quizzical smile hovering on her lips.

'Not the guy with the maps and medieval sites, *surely* not the TV historian - are you? Gosh, say you are! You certainly look like him.' She was suddenly so enthusiastic that she almost leaned out of the window, but had to catch her hair again, as it blew over his face.

There was a moment of laughing confusion as they both fought their way through it.

'Yes, for my sins – *Pictures of the Past* – that's me. I'm always surprised when anyone notices.'

Gwyn looked anything but surprised, she thought. He looked as though he enjoyed the admiration and was used to publicity and the wiles that fans employed to start up conversations.

'How lovely. I always watch,' she lied and resolved to watch at least one on catch-up TV before she saw him again, because she decided he was definitely worth another encounter. Very attractive.

She had seen a trailer for the programme and having a good memory for faces, she'd recognised him quite legitimately. Her lucky day. It occurred to her that someone like him could be so helpful to her in so many ways. She reached for the ignition and wore her most bashful expression and downcast eyes but at the same time her smile was simply encouraging.

Gwyn said, 'Oh, thanks. Always glad to please the punters. Well, you know where I live. Do call any time, Mairi.'

He stood away from the car and waved.

She returned the wave and roared away on to the main road.

Thomas and Lorcan had walked up the road from the bridge and watched the exchange between Mairi and Gwyn as they chatted themselves.

Lorcan nodded at the Range Rover as it drove off and they continued on their way to the Post Office.

'Y'know, it was her I met on the cliff. Your Bea had just fled down the track with the dog. The lady in blue, with the copper-coloured hair. Sure, she's a taking sort of woman. All batting eyelashes and flirty looks. Not quite one to trust, as me Da used to say. It was she that told me about Bea having mental problems, so she did.'

Thomas was firm.

'Never. I told you and I'll stake a lot on that. But I'm wondering what she and our Dr Roberts have to chat about, I am.'

'Mmmm. They could make a likely pair, so. Keep your eyes open, Thomas, man. I've work to do.'

'Never doubt me.' Thomas said as Lorcan strode off home.

Dana had been halfway down the long beach on her way to her bird-watching hide when she glanced casually behind; it was her habit when on surveillance. She saw Mairi's car and she'd seen Gwyn Roberts in his garden when she walked past to the beach track.

'A coincidental meeting or what?' she wondered aloud.

She took out her camera, which had a powerful telescope and fired off a few shots of them chatting. It was even more obvious that things might not be exactly as Mr. Fitzmartin had told her. Dana was curious to know more of Mairi's involvement, considering the telephone conversation she'd overheard. She wanted to know where she'd come from and now, what she was talking about to Gwyn Roberts.

From her own observations, Gwyn Roberts was not that well received by Bea. Furthermore, it was crystal clear to her that Mr. Fitzmartin knew Mairi, and probably very well indeed. He'd said he was staying with friends in Caernarvon. Maybe she was the friend.

When Mairi and Gwyn Roberts had parted, Dana continued walking to the hide.

Chapter twenty-two

Recollection

What seest thou else in the dark backward

and abysm of time?...

Prospero - The Tempest

BEA PACED THE FLOOR of the cottage, her list in hand, worrying about how and when she could get to a solicitor, how to write her resignation letter to the hospital and how to avoid getting over friendly with Lorcan, but get him to bring his vet friend to see Stella.

She needs to see a vet, that's for certain. She's got to be the priority. I'll just have to play it by ear with Lorcan. Maybe I can get Thomas to come and then they can all leave together.

Bea made up her mind to phone Lorcan soon, be decisive. She took a deep breath, congratulating herself on making at least one decision, the most important. The paper in her hand was a symbol of that decision. She read and re-read the list and her eyes began to blur and she felt that almost dizzy sensation and she suddenly felt the urge to sit down on the spot, before she fainted.

The fire crackled in the hearth and there was a smell of herbs on the air as Nest looked down at the letter in her hand. It felt warm. She loved the feel of parchment. The letter was written in an elegant, educated hand with the best of inks and she admired it even as she read.

Her mind was suddenly filled with warm memories. Her father had insisted that she learn to read and write, as any great lady would do, never mind that she was a humble fisherman's daughter. He'd said, 'The Lord Jesus Christ held fishermen in high esteem and to him, all men were equal and women too. And you are Dafydd ab Ivor's daughter and as good as anyone's.'

So, every time she felt a high-quality parchment, Nest felt a surge of love for her long dead father and memories of her childhood flooded her mind. He was at the very centre of all the good times.

How he loved to write, whether on the wet sand with a stick or on scraps of parchment that the scribes at the llys gave him.

She immersed herself in the joy of the memory. Her father was a fisherman by the time she'd been born and had stayed so throughout her childhood. But as a child himself he had been given, by his own parents, to the monastery at Penmon as a child oblate, a gift to God.

The Augustinian brothers cared for him well, he always said so. And he loved them well. They taught him to read and write and he learned the stories of the New Testament. How eagerly Mother and me listened as he told them by the fireside.

And she treasured the tale of how, when he was a young man, the time had come for him to take his vows, but he'd asked to be excused. The Abbot was learned and kind and had seen that the boy, Dafydd, was not suited to the monastic calling so he had released back into his family's care. He'd become a fisherman, like his father before him.

When he walked away from Penmon that day, he met his love, Generys, on the shore of the Straits. They met on the edge of the dancing waters and so, I have always been a child of the sea, Nest remembered as she listened to the sound of the waves trickle in through her open door.

Her father had said, 'Our meeting was meant to be. The Good God wanted it so. There she was, Generys, her hair a bright cloud about her shoulders, stooping to gather the riches of the sea in her skirt.'

Nest's mother would add to the narrative of their meeting.

'They were to decorate St. Francis's shrine on the wayside, you remember, Dafydd? I always used the old homes of the little sea creatures there because he was the patron saint of animals. I cared for all God's creatures, as St Francis did, and it was Easter, so I wanted the decoration to be an extra celebration.'

Then Nest's father would say the final line, 'And so, from that day the feast of Easter, that of St Francis and the Abbot himself have always been doubly special for us.'

Nest remembered; *Father took a barrel of salted fish to the Abbot every year of his life after that. Ah, when I was born, he took me to be blessed by him and named, Christened. Oh, and such a wonderful Christening gift the Abbot gave me – my beautiful little psalter, my book of psalms, handwritten and illustrated by the Abbot himself in his youth. I'll always treasure it.*

Her father had vowed that Nest would have all his learning.

'I'll teach you myself, all I know, cariad. We'll read together by the crackling fireside or on the misty shore and you'll learn to write your name for the first time on the glistening sands, by the light of the silvered moon or the glorious sun – whichever shines upon us.'

She had been the only child of Dafydd and Generys.

And my mother's special gift is the knowledge of animals, herb lore and healing. How much I owe them both. How I loved them – still do...

Somehow, Bea knew all this as she felt the parchment in her fingers, Nest's fingers, and looked down to read the words that had been written, not by Nest, as she had assumed, but by the Princess Joanna. As she stood and read, Bea floated between the worlds and between identities. Sometimes she felt that she was inside Nest herself, had become her for a moment, and sometimes she watched Nest, a spectator only.

This time she watched. She stared into the hearth and saw that it had changed. A fire of peat and dung was burning well, and an iron pot hung over it on a trivet; the tendrils of fragrant steam made her hungry. She recognised the aroma of rabbit cooked with thyme and sage. The curtains at the window had disappeared, along with the glass panes and she saw only the wooden shutters. The door into the Victorian extension was not there, only a stone wall and against it was a board on trestles. On it were laid out bunches of herbs, small pots and jars, and a pestle and mortar.

Bea became aware that Llewelyn was there only when he spoke, and she watched as Nest smiled and put down the parchment to pour a cup of small beer for him. He took it absently, sighed heavily.

'You see?' He nodded towards the letter. 'What if my wife is plotting against me now?' he whispered, as if afraid the fire or the sleeping animals lying there in front of it could hear his words.

'My Lord, she does *not* say that in this letter. No more was she plotting all those years ago, merely writing to her father, the king. You are giving way to black thoughts. The letter asks for Sir Roger's help on a journey, nothing more.'

'Nest, Nest, you cannot quiet my heart by twisting the truth yourself. She has asked another man to provide an escort, which is bad enough. Am I just the wind in the trees? No. I am the Prince, Lord of Snowden. As it is, she wants an escort to take her to the convent once more; she wants to go into seclusion, *away from me*. Why did she not ask me? Why? Is she escaping tyranny? I am her husband, her Prince. I'Faith, she shames me by this action.'

His voice had risen as had he and he began to pace the floor.

'Cariad, she is merely trying to plan for a future. Maybe she thinks you no longer want her, not really. Maybe she knows the people still have not accepted her even after all these years. Everyone knows that Gruffydd has not, for he does not hide his hatred.'

'Aye, true, true. But what of me? She knows I have forgiven her. Have I beaten her? Have I berated her, shamed her before the people? She has her freedom here, as you know. She is the Princess.'

'Her freedom, you say, but not free will, not her privacy. You have her unsent letter.'

'God's Truth! Privacy…?'

Nest opened her mouth to speak but he held up a hand, his face was thunderous.

'That needs no answer, as you know. Why would she need privacy from her husband? Why would she run away thus? You are the wise-woman, so answer me that!'

'You are not like other husbands, cariad. Maybe you shamed her by your forgiveness,' she said. 'And I am sorry.'

Bea heard Nest speak the last words next to her ear, as if she were in the room with her. She turned, expecting to see the apparition she had glimpsed earlier, wanting to see it, speak to it – to *her*. People often spoke of ghosts as being fearful, but Bea instinctively knew that this was no such thing. She, the ghost, if that's what she was, had a benevolent aura.

In her hand Bea still held her list; its smooth modern paper felt flimsy in comparison with the warmth of the parchment and the significance of the letter. She looked at the sleeping dogs by the fire. They were snoring gently.

She got up and put the paper back on the table, leaned her arms on the window sill and pulled the curtain aside gingerly. Massed clouds were scudding across the sky, the Marram grass on the dunes opposite bent horizontally, flicking whip-like fingers inland. The sun, escaping the clouds by the second, was a beloved child playing chase, bursting out to surprise onlookers with its aching, golden loveliness, then ducking back out of sight. Bea watched with a moment's stolen pleasure before her mind opened up to the familiar dread.

I escaped from Jeremy; no letters involved there. I wonder if he's shamed like the Prince? I don't think so, or maybe he is. What will everyone at work say when they find out I've gone for good? One thing's for sure, no one will mention it to him. He's going to be livid. So I guess he might be a bit shamed. What will he tell people? What about Mairi? I definitely don't want to see her again. What if she comes here, what will I do?

The sharp sweet scent of mint drifted across the room and halted her panic. She'd put some in a stone jar and a great bunch was hanging from the beam in the kitchen. Bea wondered what the cottage had really been like in the thirteenth century.

I'm only imagining it really, at least I think that's what this is.

She felt a moment of longing for that time, for herself to live with the Nest who visited in her dreams, her visions. The medieval Nest was a woman who felt her own worth, knew her mind, and Bea felt she might be losing her grip on her own, so maybe Jeremy was right. She simply couldn't handle life.

She felt a sob rising from deep inside her, felt it trying to escape and when Archie came to sit in front of her and whined, she thought for a second it was the dog that had made the noise, but when she felt the tears running down her face, she knew it was she that was crying.

    He moved to her side and looked up at her, wagging his tail so she sat down with her back against the wall. Archie lay down next to her and a moment later, Stella joined them.

Chapter twenty-three
Advance

Graves at my command have waked their sleepers, oped, and let 'em forth by my so potent art…

Prospero - The Tempest

BEA FELT SO TIRED. She was aching all over. She'd spent the past hour or so sitting on the floor mostly crying, sometimes just stroking the dogs. She struggled lethargically to her feet and went to the kitchen. It was just six o'clock, but still the sun and clouds played their celestial game. She caught sight of herself in the little mirror on the kitchen wall.

Is that really me? Nose splattered; look at that bruise coming out now. Thank God it wasn't broken. Puffy eyes, three chins at least. My hair used to be shiny; must be the salt air that's made it so dull, that and I haven't washed it since the morning I left Manchester, and that's three days ago - I just got doused in sea water instead.

She tried finger combing her hair but only succeeded in causing more twists and tangles. *Tangwystl,* she thought, linking the sound.

Tangwystl – Llewelyn's love before Joanna, but after myself. It was not to be, not to be…

Bea shook her head. She'd heard Nest's voice in her head. It was real; she wasn't imagining it. She knew she could be drawn again into the events of the past and she realised that she welcomed it; it was an escape from the woven threads of the present but one that she wanted to resist for the time being.

I need to feel clean, take charge of myself she thought.

Aloud she said, 'I think I'll wash my hair and then give you two a brush. I'll do Archie first. He's smaller and less tangled. Maybe we'll all feel better. What d'you think?'

They wagged their tails. It was lovely the way Archie had accepted Stella straight away. How uncomplicated dogs were. She brushed them with an old hairbrush belonging to her Nest. Then she was relieved that she recognised her Nest and the medieval one as different people.

Proving I'm not mad.

Stella was delighted to be brushed and grunted contentedly. Archie stood it for a short while then walked away.

'You're even bigger today, my girl. When are the pups going to make an appearance? We'll find out soon as we can,' she promised. 'I'll sort out a vet.'

She fed the dogs again and pushed herself to deal with her own hair. It was so long and so ragged with neglect that it took her almost an hour to boil enough water, find shampoo and organise herself in the bathroom. When she finally rinsed it with an infusion of rosemary and lemon balm, both still growing well in the little back yard, she sniffed the cloud of scent that swathed itself around her and felt a calmness hovering like a shawl about to be laid gently over her shoulders.

It took another hour by the fire to comb the hair and dry it. She finally plaited it loosely in a single heavy rope over one shoulder, telling herself that she would wear it loose when it wasn't windy, but this was the new look - casual, free. At the very least it wasn't dirty any longer; it would take some time to look good again, so she stood in front of the mirror and decided to be positive, told herself she looked a lot better.

'How did Llewelyn's Nest wear it?' She took hold of the end of her plait and wound it around her head like a coronet.

As she turned her head this way and that the mirror image became slightly out of focus and she froze when a man's face appeared behind her in the reflection.

Llewelyn said, 'I didn't give you that mirror so that you could preen yourself endlessly, woman!'

'Well, that's what it's for, *my Lord*! I've seen you looking in it often enough,' Nest retorted, then as she turned and put down the silver hand mirror, she suddenly gasped and grabbed at her side.

'Oooo. That was …' she began.

Llewelyn took hold of her, swept her into his arms and off her feet, quickly striding to the settle by the fire and sitting her on it.

'What happened? Was it the babe? Speak to me, Nest, speak to me!' he said, desperately as she continued to gasp and rub her side.

'I'm well don't fuss. It was nothing. Yes, the babe! It kicked is all that happened. Do you not remember with your own children?'

She slapped his hand away from her arm.

'I suppose I should, but no, I don't. I was always away on some journey or unconscious in sleep. But you, my witch; is all well really? When is it to be, the birth?' he asked, kneeling on the floor at her feet.

'Two more months yet, cariad. Don't worry. I'll be fine and no, I don't want any women from the llys to help me, so please do not send anyone.'

'Morgan tells me there is a wise woman who comes to the kitchens to sell potions and the like…perhaps?' he said, with a note of enquiry.

'Ahh, Sister of Air, Chwaer Awyr. I know her well, she is indeed a wise one and not one for dark arts, rest easy. But I do not need help. I thank you. My babe will be born in the early Spring, after the Christmas feasting is well over; so I may dance and sing in the revels, my Lord. You may rest easy and feast on each and every one of the twelve days and give some time to your wife.'

'Be serious. I will do anything for you, my Nest.'

'I know. But now you speak of Chwaer Awyr, I heard that she was recently sent away, and harshly, by Princess Joanna's maid, Edith. I also heard that she and your precious bard, Ithel, plot together, suspecting you and me of being more than the old childhood friends that we truly are, cariad. They would like as not want to discover that we are lovers.'

He groaned, rubbed his hands roughly over his face and head.

'Would that we were…'

She tutted.

'Well…' he raised his eyes to hers.

'Listen to yourself, my Lord, for I shall not. I have more urgent things to attend to.' She rubbed her side vigorously. 'Ooo, like this little elbow in my ribs. Think, will you? Why would Joanna's maid be plotting against you and me, when Joanna herself wants to get away because she feels you have not forgiven her? What can be brewing I wonder?'

He was quiet for a time.

'It is a mystery, and one I will discover. But Ithel, Ithel.' His face was thunder, storm, gale. 'I thought Ithel was my man. I support him, I pay him. He's let me down, but then he's always an enigmatic one, seems to wear mystery like a cloak of office.'

His voice was dangerously even and quiet.

'Beware, my love, beware. I've a feeling about him.'

Llewelyn sat next to her and turned her towards him.

'You're all right now?'

He put his hand lightly over her belly and she covered it with her own and smiled to reassure. The babe chose to kick just then he smiled with delight.

He said, 'Lovely, like its mother!'

He became serious again as he remembered something.

'I also hear things, this time from Morgan, and he is one I trust, as I trust you. I hear that my man, Yestyn, was wounded by a so-called wildcat. And he seems strangely absent from my presence these past two days. What do you know of it? There's another rumour that he was cut with a small knife. A strange cat.'

She heard the danger in his voice.

'I also heard that and count him well punished for whatever he did,' she said, but did not look at him.

Llewelyn tried his best to bully her into telling him more, especially what Yestyn's offence had been, and against whom, and he said he knew it was a woman he had offended because such a wound could only be a woman's doing.

But Nest knew how harsh Yestyn's punishment would be at the hands of the Prince. She'd decided that the pain of the wounds, the vigilance of her wolves and the threat of shameful disclosure would be his best punishment and also her best defence against him.

Llewelyn stood abruptly.

'I'll send for him. I've a feeling I should kill him myself and quickly, but I'll hold my sword, for a while. He is one of my Uchelwr, and his family will be broken if he shames them in my court. So, he will live at my pleasure alone. But I will kill two birds with one stone instead, my Nest. I'll use him to escort my Lady wife to her nunnery. It's what she wants. I have to give her this. May she find peace and return to me soon enough. An unquiet mind is a poor crown for her, and she deserves better. I'll write to Sir Roger myself and tell him my wife has no need of his help. I am her husband. Yestyn can escort her and stay there with her as her personal guard, for as long as she wills. He can take six of the foot soldiers with him, no others of my Uchelwr for company either; he is not worthy of the company of other nobles.'

His voice was quiet and cold. He stood abruptly.

'In the meantime, I'll think what to do with him on a more permanent basis. I'll also speak with Ithel ap Deykin before I am much older!' His expression was grim. 'Gelert, to me!' He roared for the dog suddenly and Gelert leapt to his feet and trotted out quickly with his master.

The prince called over his shoulder. 'All will be well, Nest. I'll make it so, on my life.'

'My Lord...my Lord...' Nest began, but he was gone.

'My Lord...' Bea repeated as she gazed in the mirror but as her image grew into sharp focus, she dropped the end of her plait. Her arm was aching both from holding the plait up in that position.

God, my hair is heavy. I look like Nest, or perhaps it's the other way round, she thought with a shock. *My Nest was my godmother and my great aunt, Mum's aunt. And she had no daughter of her own; no children, poor Nest. No Nest to follow her, only me. And the old family photos; Mum and Nest are so alike, and I'm like both of them. How strange and lovely.*

She didn't know why, but it was suddenly important that she looked like her own version of herself, made her own style, so she scrabbled the band off the end of her plait and quickly undid it, then using her fingers as a comb she divided it in to two and made up two thick loose plaits instead, one on either side of her face.

'Archie, Stella, I'm going to pull myself together. First of all, you need to go outside for a wee, and then we all need some food before an early night. That's my prescription. I'll phone Lorcan and set up the vet thing. In fact, I'll do it now,' she said as she found her phone.

It was a short conversation because he was actually in Bangor with the vet at the time and they arranged for them both to call in the morning. The vet, a woman, had a day off and they were out shopping together, but would be back on the island later that day. Bea phoned Thomas to tell him they were calling in the morning and he said he could take half an hour off to come too, anything for her. His response had been just what she needed.

So, feeling as though she'd advanced her plans a little, she breathed a sigh of relief and took the dogs up onto the headland for a short and very slow walk. They'd not got far when it became obvious that going uphill was too uncomfortable for Stella; she was panting heavily and kept stopping. Just as they turned around to go back, she thought she saw a figure in a bright blue coat at the end of the beach, on the opposite side of the river. She hurried on in and bolted the doors, closed the curtains. Mairi wore a coat that colour.

Chapter twenty-four

Trust

Remember I have done thee worthy service,

Told thee no lies, made no mistakes…

Ariel - The Tempest

DANA STROLLED DOWN the beach on her way back to the pub. She needed a break. She'd seen Bea walking back to the cottage and gently encouraging the big dog to hurry up, coaxing her along. The dog wagged its tail when it glanced up at her, clearly not frightened, not abused. Even without her long lens, Dana could see the dog looked weary, and huge. The small one looked happy enough, scampering around the other. She passed a man in a blue coat taking his own dog up the beach but no one else was around as she walked through the village.

She stopped at the Post Office, just as Thomas was closing up and, with a little charm and a wearing a weary expression, she got herself invited to have a cuppa in the back room. She'd spent a lot of money there in the past couple of days and each time she'd met Thomas he'd come across as genuinely friendly and kind, and perhaps a bit lonely she thought. She was glad of the opportunity to talk to someone who knew Bea well.

It didn't take her long to get the talk round to Bea. She told him she'd seen the young woman with the terrier and the pregnant dog when she was in her hide on the dunes; she'd already showed him all her bird shots taken there that day. He began looking through them again, going through the string of shots on her camera as she'd shown him.

'I'm getting the hang of this digital stuff now, aren't I? They're fabulous these photos. You a professional photographer then?' he wanted to know. 'This camera certainly looks the business.'

'It is, and in a way, I suppose you could call me a professional; certainly at the moment. The photos are for some research on oystercatchers. They do have a hold on my heart,' she told him and, using her cover story, she explained about her project.

'I would like to take some shots from the other side of the river as the birds seem to rise up in their flight just as they hit the wide bit of the river front of the cottage; you get a good spread of the flight pattern. Would that woman mind if I stood on her terrace?' she asked him.

'No, I don't expect so, Bea's lovely, she is. She's here for a rest, mind; give her a break if she says no, though I'll put in a word for you, if you like.'

'Thanks, will you? She's having a bit of a rest? Work problems or something? That's most people these days isn't it? Stress and stuff. I guess you know her well.' She threw out the questions with disarming rapid fire, hoping for a hit. She took a long drink from her mug. 'Mmmm, lovely brew. I'd die for another of those, Thomas' she said, pointing to the shortbreads he'd put out.

'Go on then, help yourself. But Bea, trouble? No! Just an old-fashioned rest. Heard the story about the shipwrecked dog then?'

She said she hadn't but had seen a couple of men carrying a big dog into the cottage the other day. So, he filled her in, adding that the dog now had a permanent home with Bea.

She asked, 'Known Bea long?'

'All her life. Lovely girl; spent a lot of her childhood here. Would have wanted a daughter of mine to be just like her, but it wasn't to be, lost my wife recently you know. In fact, I think of Bea like a daughter.'

She nodded with sympathy.

'Looks a bit isolated for a child, that cottage on the beach, I mean. Not in the middle of things for village life, is it?' Dana prompted.

'Never a happier, sunnier child than Bea, I can tell you. Hasn't had it all smooth though. Her father was killed in a plane crash. He was the pilot too. Her mother was injured in the accident and was in hospital for a long time after that. Bea was ten at the time and she spent a year here with Nest, that's her auntie and godmother who used to live in the cottage. She learned Welsh too; forgotten most of it now, mind! She went to the village school too, made loads of friends. Mother was a millionaire you know, a famous author, no less. She did biographies of the rich and famous. But she never spoiled Bea, not one bit. She always worked hard with her studies, she did. She's a doctor you know. I always imagine she's lovely with the patients.'

Dana saw that he was clearly very fond of Bea and enjoying the reminiscences.

'Pilot, you say. I hear that's a tense sort of job. My friend is one of the cabin crew on a French airline. You should hear the tales she tells about the pilots losing it. Stress. And the party hangovers...my!'

'Yes? Well, not Ivor – that's Bea's dad. Tea-total, as we say here, and ex RAF, then a test pilot for one of the big multinational companies. None better, girl, none better. No, the accident was just a freak thing. Bird strike; a flock of geese actually.'

'Whoa! Awful thing.'

They were quiet for a minute.

Dana said, 'I was an only child too. I always felt as though I had to live up to expectations. Both my parents were ambitious and so successful; not planes, banking. I couldn't wait to grow up and leave and just veg-out, you know? Whoa, the homework I did! Never got to play out. I don't know why I'm telling you this. You must be a good listener, Thomas. I guess that when I hear about another girl...like me...'

Thomas sat up straighter, pushed away from the table a little.

'Now, don't get the wrong end of the stick. Bea had wonderful parents, both highfliers, literally, but nobody pushed Bea. She was the happiest, most carefree little bird I know, especially when they were all down here with Nest. It's a shame about yours though.'

Dana realised she wasn't going to get any suspicion of family abuse or strange behaviour, as Jeremy had told her, simply tales of a happy childhood, until the accident, and Bea seemed to have weathered that. She turned the talk to Gwyn Roberts.

'By the way, clear something up for me if you can. The guy who lives in that yellow cottage near the bridge – d'you know him? I've seen him somewhere before.'

Thomas laughed. 'He's a celebrity himself, presenter on an historical programme, BBC2, no less!' He made a wry face.

'Oh, wonderful. I may have watched him then. I love history, next to birds that is. Didn't he do something about Llewelyn the Great, here in Aberffraw? And y'know, he looks like one of the blokes I saw helping get the dog in at the cottage. Funny old world.'

'He was. That was him.'

After a little more chatting about the weather, the tides and the storm the other night, she thanked him and left.

She wasn't due to meet Lorcan in the bar until eight o'clock, so she spent the time having a bath, relaxing. She needed to see what information he could give her about Bea too. By 7.30 she was finishing a meal in the small bar and had half a glass of dry white in her hand when Lorcan strolled in. He'd come from the tap room where the darts match was ongoing, and the roar of voices followed him out as someone scored.

He approached with a smile and a grinning glance over his shoulder.

'Sure, they take things to heart, the lads…Hi there, Dana isn't it?' he said.

'Hi, Lorcan? What can I get you?' Dana said and they shook hands casually.

'Lovely, a half of, yes, y'guessed, draft Guinness.'

Once the greetings were over, they found they could talk easily. But Dana did have a special talent for making people open up which was always useful when she was on the Force. She genuinely liked getting to know people, and in the case of suspects, what and who they knew or what they had done. But Lorcan wasn't in her sights as any rival to Jeremy, and Jeremy's suspicions bothered her more and more. If Bea was having an affair as well as being mentally unstable, well, it had happened before, but Dana just wasn't feeling it at the moment.

'So, *Professor* Lorcan is it?' she asked.

'It is! Just got the job. I'm what they call a visiting professor. Lucky me. I've a great life, Dana; love me work, passionate about the research. I'll give you a bit of a run down if you're interested – you being in the same area, so to speak. Waste and the oystercatchers isn't it? I may have some students and doctoral researchers who could help, y'know, networking, global chatter and that, spin-off work done in your field.'

'Sure. Great. I can tell you're as worried as me about the effects of waste dumping...' she began, leaning forward, arms on the table, keen to share.

She gave him a brief outline of her fictitious work; having been careful to say she was only beginning her dissertation and she'd come to Anglesey because of all its beaches. Dana was absurdly thankful that she hadn't said she was at Bangor University, though she realised he would have contacts aplenty in his research field, and probably at Aberystwyth, where she said she was based. She needed a plausible explanation, quickly, but reverting to her real purpose she asked:

'But I wanted to ask someone, someone local, and it's off the research theme completely, you'll think me a gossip. Y'know the cottage on the beach, right out there on the estuary opposite my hide; well, there's a woman there with two dogs. I was asking the nice guy in the Post Office, Thomas, if he thought she'd mind me taking some shots on her terrace; different direction for the flight pattern at different times of the day, y'know? He said she's fine but someone else I spoke to said she's a bit strange and they'd heard one of the dogs was stolen or something. I've seen nothing odd over there while I've been out on the dunes and believe me I'm out in all weathers. I love dogs, so I do take a special interest in any I see.'

'Ho, I see, local gossips at work. I was the one who rescued the dog on the beach, so no kidnapping involved or whatever the term used for a dog would be. But the lady, only just met her meself, when I found the dog. Have to tell you she comes with the highest credentials. Her aunt was Nest, who owned the cottage until she died, this Spring. Lovely Nest may have been ninety, but we were good friends. I know about Bea from Nest, but our paths never crossed, trust me I'd remember that one. And Thomas-the-Post, he's known her all his life and if they both say she's honest and upright, believe me, she is.'

He smiled broadly and pointing to her glass, stood up to go to the bar.

'Please. Dry white,' she said in answer to his unspoken query.

'Right y'are, then…Oh, hello there,' he said as a man approached. It was Gwyn Roberts. 'Get you one?' Lorcan asked and Gwyn raised his eyebrows, nodded and pointed to Lorcan's Guinness glass.

He sat down at their table when Dana moved a chair out.

She held out a hand saying, 'Hello, I'm Dana. You joining us?'

Gwyn Roberts shook her hand.

'Seems I'm invited. I'm Gwyn. You two together?'

'No, only met today, in the Post Office. It's a bit of a melting pot, isn't it?' she said. 'Seems Lorcan and I are in the same line of work.'

'What? A lady plumber?' he sniggered. 'Sorry, that's not very PC is it? But I'd have a lady plumber any day!'

He raised his eyebrows suggestively.

Some of the worst criminals and several senior police officers in the North West had tried insulting Dana, tried every suggestion in the book, but she remained untouched by their efforts and their hands. She had a healthy sense of her own worth.

She laughed disarmingly. 'Well, it's true that we're both concerned about the waste people generate, but more on the environmental research side than the flushing away side, if you know what I mean. I'm beginning a thesis for my Masters, and he's visiting professor with Bangor University, British Antarctic Survey being his latest stop-off, apparently.'

Gwyn was speechless and glanced at Lorcan who was standing at the bar collecting the drinks.

Knowing exactly who Gwyn was, she assumed a politely puzzled expression and said, 'But haven't I seen you on TV or something? Were you in some ad for yoghurt? Am I wrong? Sorry,' she added as his face registered shock and then contempt.

'Well, some of these yoghurts do generate a lot of effluent for us plumbers!' she said, then she laughed at him as she lifted the last of her wine in mock salute.

Gwyn was stunned for a few seconds, but he suddenly threw back his head and roared with laughter.

'I can be a pompous prat at times!' he told her when he'd recovered, his shoulders still shaking.

She laughed with him then said, 'Actually, wasn't it, *Pictures of the Past* where I've seen you strutting your stuff once or twice?'

'Ahhh!' He smiled and shook a finger at her.

'Hey, don't get excited, it was a slow drama night, is all.'

She smiled up at Lorcan as he returned with the drinks.

As he put the Guinness down in front of Gwyn, Gwyn said, 'Thanks Prof. I hear it's Professor of Plumbing at Bangor? I'm there myself, although we'll only need plumbers in the History department when we move over to water closets from earth pits!'

'Ah! *Bangored* to rights, I think. It's a fair cop. I'm a brand-new prof, though, and more on the practical side than the pipe and slippers type. Sure, it's more pipe and wrench for me. Y'know, you *were* judging a book by its cover the other day at Nest's Point, when we took the dog in.'

Gwyn took a sip of his Guinness, smacked his lips and answered, 'Maybe, maybe.' But he smiled and added, 'Not many attractive young women round here.'

Dana coughed and prompted, 'Er, present company excepted, I'm guessing?'

'There I go again. Two left male-chauvinist feet. Definitely present company excepted. My apologies again.'

Lorcan looked from one to the other.

'You two getting on fine?'

Gwyn said, 'Oh yes, now I'm put in my place. Talking of which, I seem to have rubbed our new neighbour up the wrong way; Bea, over at Nest's Point. Seems a bit prickly.'

'Oh, I like her fine, I do,' said Lorcan.

Gwyn snorted.

'Well, I can't say or do a thing right for her apparently.'

'Oh?' Dana asked, smiled her most interested and encouraging smile. 'Something wrong?'

Gwyn told them then about his meeting a woman, name of Mairi, when she was driving past his cottage. He told them what Mairi had said about Bea abusing the poor dog, but both Lorcan and Dana contradicted him strongly.

'I've seen nothing like that at all and I've been on the dunes for days. Did hear the gossip though.'

Lorcan added, 'I think she's fallen for that dog well and good. I've a friend who's a vet coming over to see her tomorrow too.'

'Seems I got the wrong end of the stick yet again,' Gwyn said. 'Why would that Mairi woman say otherwise though? If she's a stranger to Bea, what's in it for her?'

Lorcan took up the point. 'Not what she said to me. I know the woman you mean, Gwyn. Sure, I met her too. Apparently, she's not a stranger though, some sort of friend. Mind, not the sort I'd like, spilling all sorts of private stuff to someone you met on a beach. She said she's run away from a psychiatric ward. I know she's wrong about Bea mistreating the dogs, so probably about the mental health thing too. Thomas said there's no such problem.'

Dana was beginning to have some sympathy for Bea, especially in the light of her own discoveries about Mairi.

They all resolved to keep an eye open for the fickle 'friend', Mairi, and passed onto other topics of conversation; TV work, the Antarctic, the Welsh coast and holiday visitors leaving litter.

Later on, and back in her room, Dana put through a call to Jeremy, her client. She passed on the scant information she had for him, namely that Bea had had several callers, all men, and had also spoken to a woman on the headland.

She sent him photos of Mairi chatting to Bea and then Lorcan later, and Gwyn and Thomas calling at the cottage at different times. When she asked him what he wanted her to do next, he told her to let things rest for two days. He was going to phone a friendly psychiatrist, a colleague, and get her to call on Bea, hopefully persuade her to come home to continue her treatment.

When she'd disconnected the call, Dana said to the empty room, 'I think I'll have a chat with Bea, get to know her, see for myself. Tomorrow, if I can.'

Jeremy had taken the call in a hotel room in his favourite and very exclusive hotel on the banks of the island, just outside Menai Bridge and overlooking the Straits and the Welsh mountains. As he put down his phone, he decided to take a walk on the beach, but not just any beach. After all it was only ten o'clock, so he'd drive over to the other side of the island. After speaking to Mairi that afternoon, he thought it best to move out of the Macyntyre house to infuriate her and keep her on her toes; she was a little too intense at the moment and needed a lesson in control, his control that is.

The night had closed in as he headed off to Aberffraw, but he knew that the scant light of the sickle moon would be perfect for what he had in mind.

Chapter twenty-five

Fear

What strength I have's mine own…

Prospero - The Tempest

JEREMY LEFT HIS Jaguar at the hotel and borrowed a small car belonging to one of the young male staff. It was a handy arrangement that he'd used before and involved the payment of fifty-pound note, on the understanding that no one was to know he'd gone out that night. The young man was happy to help.

He drove the car to the parking space by the dunes at Aberffraw, then continued on foot over the old bridge to the village side of the river. He wore black. Taking the beach path, away from the houses and out to the estuary, he was forced to use the light on his phone to find his way. But even though he'd been walking beside the swelling waters, his mind didn't register that; it was on pleasures to come and he'd gone about a hundred metres before he realised that the tide was in and the final approach to the cottage would be blocked by the waters. So, he was forced to make a detour and go by the higher path through the village and across the top of the fields. That annoyed him intensely.

The village was quiet as ever; the only public nightlife was in the pubs and after the storm, people were indoors, hugging their fires as they felt autumn creeping quickly forward. Outdoors there was little light and a brisk wind, both of which suited Jeremy because they would shield him from sight and mask the sound of his feet from the few bungalows he had to pass.

Even so, he was relieved once he had passed those obstacles and the way was open before him; but still, he closed the field footpath gate carefully to prevent the tocsin of its usual loud clang. He set off across the field, but before he had realised why the turf was so short, he had walked into the back of a sheep lying straight across the path. It leapt up with a startled cry; the wind had hidden the sound and scent of the approaching man, and it ran with the rest of its flock, scattering in all directions, all bleating loudly. One of them even careened into the back of Jeremy's legs causing him to fall heavily. He swore viciously.

He'd dropped his phone and, unusually, the light had gone out. It took him several minutes to locate it by feeling the ground on hands and knees. This was not quite the way he had hoped the trip would play out, but he was a patient man, one who relished the long game, so he brushed himself off and strode on resolutely across the three fields, heading for the back of the cottage.

He could hear the sea clearly and feel its vast presence as he approached the lane leading to the cottage. It sloped down between dense hedge banks. The ground was pitted and rough and he had to concentrate to avoid stumbling, so he was startled by a sudden flapping noise and the explosive eruption of an unseen bird from the depths of the hedge. It was straightway followed by an owl swooping over the lane, so near his head that he felt the downdraft from its wings. It shrieked, searing the silence. He ducked instinctively, then almost laughed aloud at the pure thrill of his clandestine adventure. A fox barked in the distance; the sound, for some people, eerie, lonely. Not to him. He was immersed in the night, a part of the wildness and untameable time. On a high point in the field he glimpsed a rabbit in silhouette on the grey horizon, its body frozen in the moment, sitting back on its haunches, but its jaws still furiously chewing as it stared at him. He moved his head a little and the creature scudded away, faster than thought, a tuft of grass flung up in the air as it fled.

When he rounded the final bend in the lane Jeremy saw the old cottage; it was touched by the ghost of moonlight, pale and weak in the dungeon dimness of the night. He had worn thick-soled hiking boots but still moved as carefully and as silently as he could across the loose stony track to the back of the building. The curtains were drawn but the light from within gave the small windows a warm peachy glow. He could smell the wood smoke on the air and smiled to think how cosy and safe Bea must feel – for a little while more at least.

He walked unhurriedly and carefully around to the front of the cottage, listening intently; dogs could hear the slightest noises that humans couldn't pick up and he was pleased that Dana had mentioned the new animal's presence. At the front of the building there were two windows, one only dimly lit, one of the kitchen windows, and the other in the main room. He smiled; this one was bright with light and he noticed a tiny gap where the curtains didn't meet.

Moving his head very slowly he put his eye against the gap and felt a frisson of pleasure to see Bea lying on the settle by the fire. The two dogs lay on the rug below and as if sensing his presence, they both pricked up their ears and lifted muzzles, scenting. Archie stood up, listening. Jeremy didn't dare breathe. Bea hadn't noticed anything; she appeared to be asleep, lying on her side, face towards the fire.

The wind was freshening, and he hoped it would hide any noise of his footsteps from the listening dogs. He watched Bea sleeping and then, his face alight with pleasure, he raised his hand and beat a sharp rhythm on the window pane with his finger tips, keeping his eye on the scene within. The dogs were alert instantly. They both threw up their muzzles and barked, deep and furious intruder barks. Archie bounced forwards on stiff legs, but the bigger dog he didn't know began to struggle to her feet and Bea jerked upright, shocked. Her loose plaits fell over her face and she scrabbled at them as she tried to get to her own feet, but Stella was in her way.

'Who is it? Who's there?' she called, her voice reedy with panic, and almost drowned by the cacophony of barking.

Jeremy listened, smiling. He repeated the tattoo a lot louder, to be heard above the barking, but in any case, he knew the dogs would hear if Bea didn't. He moved quickly to the corner of the building, out of sight of the window, and jumped down behind the sea wall to watch what happened next through a clump of sea lavender. He guessed she wouldn't open the door to confront any intruder and was rewarded by seeing the light within dimmed and her frightened face appear at the opening between the curtains. She gripped each curtain tightly and her hands shook as she tried to overlap the fabric to cut off the line of vision. All the while, the dogs kept up an outraged baying.

Jeremy sat with his back against the wall and enjoyed the night: not the pulsing iron grey beauty of the sea with its rippled silver stripes lent by the sickle moon; not the green, salt-laden scent of the wind nor the dry shushing of the dancing grasses, but the very idea of causing another person to feel ice cold fear. It was intoxicating.

He relished the feeling for a good ten minutes then rose as silently as a thought to creep to the back of the cottage. The dogs had quietened down, and he waited, basking in anticipation of the fear that would surely course through their bodies - soon. It was a power-filled moment. He remembered that there was a small high window near the fire nook, un-curtained, but as the moon did not light that side of the building, he wasn't worried about being seen when he beat gently on that window pane. It was impossible to look into the living room without standing on the bank, so he used his imagination to watch Bea start up as she had done before, this time primed for fear, her face would be ashen, the dogs on their feet again and now facing the window at the back. The big dog was baying in deep booming bursts and Archie kept up a furious staccato yelping. He was probably leaping onto the settle and scrabbling at the cushions to try and jump at the window.

Jeremy was pleased. He slid round to the bathroom window to scrape his nails down the glass and then on the back kitchen window soon after, paused for thirty seconds then walked round to the front to tap loudly on the second kitchen window there. The wind was picking up and whistling under the eaves of the cottage; the waves splashed loudly nearby, and the dogs kept up the deafening noise. Jeremy decided to take up a higher viewing point and quickly strode to the back of the building to jump up on the rocks and tuck himself behind one of the bigger boulders. He had decided to leave a longer period before he induced the next round of terror and had considered the possibility of her phoning someone for help, in which case he'd be in a good position to see an approach and make his escape, if need be.

Fifteen minutes went by, not quite long enough, he judged, for a rescuer to stride up from the village, if indeed one were coming. He decided it was time to continue and went straight to the back door, which was hidden from the path by a small outbuilding. He thumped loudly on it with his fist and then sped round to the front and repeated his assault on the front door.

The dogs howled. Bea screamed loudly, a piercing scream that rose above the wind and the noise of the animals.

'Who is it?' she shrieked from behind the front door. 'What do you want?'

Jeremy couldn't resist and putting his mouth close to the keyhole he called out, 'Beatrix!' just once.

His voice was loud and distinctive. She couldn't fail to recognise it. Neither did Archie. He recognised it and his bark changed immediately to a fearful yelping shriek and he fled to the back of the living room and scrabbled himself under the dresser there.

Jeremy had his ear pressed to the edge of the front door and heard the electronic beeps of a phone being dialled, followed by a pause filled with rasping, sobbing breaths he recognised as Bea's and her whimpering cry when she got through to someone.

'Help, help me. Can you come? Please come.'

She screamed then, a long, terrified note and then he heard a thumping and clattering noise followed by another volley of barks.

Deeply satisfied, he began his walk back to the car. He had just crested the top of the lane by the cottage when he saw a light bobbing towards him across the field and recognised Thomas by his shape and gait. Jeremy pulled up his collar to hide his face.

They met near the corner of the churchyard and with his face averted Jeremy smashed his own shoulder into the older man's chest then grabbing his shoulders he spun him away from himself and sent him sprawling on the ground. Thomas lay there writhing and cursing loudly.

Jeremy didn't bother looking back and within the hour was back in his hotel room with a malt whisky and a steaming bath.

Chapter twenty-six

Kindness

The direful spectacle of the wreck,

which touched the very virtue of compassion in thee...

Prospero - The Tempest

BEA LAY SLUMPED and unconscious behind the front door amid a tumble of sticks and boots and Stella approached her anxiously, whining, licking at her face, nosing her hair and neck. After a few seconds, Bea opened her eyes and stared at the dog, confused. The light spilled into the tiny hall from the main room, but it was dim, and Bea tried to focus through her tear gummed lashes and strands of hair.

'What's happening? Who... why is there a dog here? Who...?'

Stella nudged her hands with her nose and whimpered, her tail wagging low down as she watched Bea struggling to sit up. Bea felt herself drifting in and out of consciousness; she remembered falling; she thought she'd heard Jeremy.

'Was it him? He doesn't know where...When's Thomas coming...?' she began and then slid back as darkness enveloped her again.

Further down the beach, Thomas banged on Gwyn Roberts's door, and with an effort, let himself lean heavily against the door jamb. He heard the approach of swift footsteps and recoiled when the door was snatched open hastily and Gwyn thrust out his upper body.

'Yep?' he said by way of greeting then, recognising Thomas, he added pleasantly, 'Oh, it's you.' A second later, 'Steady...' he said quickly, and grabbed the older man who had staggered backwards.

'You okay? Come on, come on in. Watch where you put your feet, the light's not too good.'

'Ta – I'm fine, fine. It's just my ankle. I got bowled over, you could say.'

Thomas accepted the arm under his shoulder as he was helped into the cottage and onto a chair by the door.

He took hold of the younger man's arms and said:

'I need your help as it happens – quite urgently.'

He grimaced as he tried moving his foot.

'I was on my way up to Nest's Point, just heading for the top path through the fields and not far from your wall - black out there, it is - when out of nowhere, some bloke just rammed into me, spun me round and away from him, grabbed my arms and spun me, he did; knocked me right on my arse then just left me! That's how my ankle twisted. The bugger.'

'Who? You've lost me.'

'Couldn't see, pitch dark up there; but I've an idea. More importantly I need you to go up to Nest's Point and see if Bea's all right.'

'Bea? All right?'

'She phoned me just now, well, ten minutes and more. No idea.... Quite frantic she was, and the dog barking fit to burst; some intruder's outside; must be my bloke. I'd know him anywhere by the stink; lathered in some aftershave muck, he was. She's scared witless, poor girl. Oooo! That's sharp.'

Thomas winced and bent to rub his ankle and then nodded thanks as Gwyn produced a stool with a cushion and gently lifted his injured leg to rest on it.

He said, 'I'm on to it, except that she'll think the intruder was me. We're not the best of friends, she and I...' Gwyn shook his head, his expression one of wry acceptance even as he reached for his jacket. 'I'm going, don't worry. I can handle myself too. We academics love a punch-up,' he added and snatched a torch from the window ledge by the door.

'She'll be all right if I phone her. Damn.'

He looked at his empty hand, realization dawning.

'But no, dropped my phone out there on the path somewhere. I don't know her new number. You'll just have to tell her I sent you.'

'But she'll still…'

'Look, take this, as a token,' Thomas said, dragging his scarf off he handed it to Gwyn. 'Wave it at the window or something and she'll recognise it. She made it for me last Christmas.'

He gasped again and bent to grab his ankle.

'Damn ankle's giving me grief all right. You going, or what?'

He gave Gwyn such a look of desperation that the younger man responded without any further comment, fastened his jacket and patted his pocket for his own phone.

'I'll call the landline here when I get to the cottage to tell you she's okay, so don't worry, I'll wave the token above my head. Not exactly on the same 'trusted messenger' level as a lord's signet ring, but as a modern knight errant, one can't be too choosy!'

'Go on, lad, go on!' Thomas growled, more in pain than anger as he waved Gwyn out.

Bea lay behind the door in the cottage, still gripping the phone and slid effortlessly into her dream, clutching her stomach. Stella nosed her repeatedly, but she felt the dog's presence recede as Nest filled her mind. Archie crept out from under the dresser and joined Bea, pushing himself close. He hid his nose right behind her back.

Nest drew breath sharply. The babe had been very active since the Prince left and the last sharp kick had been low down in her abdomen; a dull, gnawing ache was building there, coming in little waves too. She'd never felt anything like it before and it was as fearful as it was exciting.

'Not quite time, babi annwyl, baby dear. But you do jump around so, like a little fish in the sea; a sea baby, you are,' she whispered, both hands rubbing round and round her swollen belly, soothing herself and the baby at the same time.

Nest felt her muscles begin to tighten and a second later came a pain so fierce that she doubled up and slid to the floor from the settle, grasping the seat with one hand and her stomach with the other as if to prevent it splitting open. The wolves were both alert, both sat near her and watched her, licking lips, noses testing the air.

'Don't worry, my loves. I am well,' she told them and leaned against the settle, breathing deeply. *It is too early for the babe to come, but sometimes the womb tests itself for the birth, I know,* she remembered.

She'd helped other women through pregnancy and birth before, many times, but this time it was different of course. She wanted this baby so badly and she knew full well she was a little old for a first birth.

Many things could go wrong, but, I hope not, I hope not.

The wolves lay down next to her and she made herself comfortable, willing herself to relax and after ten minutes and no more cramps, she knew her womb would be calm for the time being. So, she put a cushion behind her back, and prepared to rest a while and gaze into the fire and if sleep came, well, she and the babe would be better for it. The cushion was one filled with goose down and with huge sprigs of dried mint sewn inside it so that each time she moved the soothing scent was wafted around her. She did she gazed into the flames of the fire, speaking softly to herself.

'Will I have a live babe, I wonder? Oh, I will. I have seen it. I must not worry. Will she live long? Oh, what will she do if I die at the birth?' She felt her heart tighten. 'But many mothers do die at the birth, even the very youngest. I have seen so many and some who follow their babes, broken in heart and body. Can I look into the flames and see what will happen?' she whispered. 'Dare I do it?' The wolves twitched their ears and rested noses on paws. Outside the day was darkening and the sea rising; the wind whistled sharply under the door.

'I will look,' Nest said and focused on the flickering fire, emptying her mind, feeling the familiar sweeping sensation in her chest rise up and up until it took over her consciousness.

'There,' she breathed and smiled as she watched shapes and figures appear in the dancing gold of the flames.

She saw her little house, or at least she thought it was hers; it was very similar and assuredly on the same site, she would know those rocks and the curve of that headland anywhere. Nevertheless, the house she saw was bigger, taller, and with a roof made of hard slate tiles by the look of it, and, what were those structures? - strangely shaped windows that were thrusting out of the roof itself. There was a stone structure on top of the roof and smoke coiled gently upwards from the top to drift away on the breeze; some kind of smoke-hole, she guessed.

It seemed to be harvest time; she could smell the newly-cut hay and there was a basket of apples, big green apples by the door of the house. Nearby, a small white dog, a little terrier, sat on the garden wall and scratched itself and, on the path in front, a few russet brown hens pecked at the grit. One of them began stabbing its beak at the apples but fluttered away with a squawk as a woman threw open the door, indeed it was the very same oak door of Nest's own house, and she shoed away the hens by flapping a light cloth that was tied around her waist.

She looks like me, Nest thought, surprised. *But what clothes does she wear? The robe is tight round the top of her body and the skirt so wide and free and so short like a man's robe. Leather boots too – well laced. Her hair is the same as mine, and what's that? A netted filigree decoration around her neck. She looks like the wife of a rich prince.*

Bea saw this also, but she recognised it for a woman in the everyday, working country dress of the 1920s and the cottage looking very much as it did in her own present day. The woman took a pride in her appearance; everything was bright and clean. She wore a white apron over her russet cotton dress with a cream lace collar fluttering at her throat.

But to Nest, these were only strange differences that next minute were made trivial when she saw a small child push its way out from behind the woman's skirts. It was a girl, a dark haired, laughing little girl who ran towards the hens waving her arms, making them scatter and retreat a pace or two with insulted clucks, as if used to such treatment but nevertheless affronted. The dog stood up and wagged its stubby tail frantically and dipped and danced on the spot to see the child.

'Oh, Nestie,' cried the woman, bending forward with a laugh as she caught the little girl and swung her, squealing, into her arms. 'Leave the hens alone, my tiny chick; they'll not lay big eggs for you if you make them fly away.'

Both Nest who watched the flames, and Bea as she dreamed, smiled and felt their hearts sing. For Nest knew that they were her own descendants, and Bea felt equally sure that she was seeing her own Auntie Nest as a child.

Nest turned from the fire and laid a hand on each of the wolves.

'My child will be well.'

She felt a moment of blissful calm but then Mellt suddenly tensed. He rose, his hackles bristling and Seren leapt to her feet too and they crept to the door, snarling deep in their throats. Their grumbling was interrupted by a smaller sound, a distinct rattling of something small being thrown at the door, pebbles perhaps. Nest watched as the wolves, now quiet, listening, trotted forward and put their noses to the ground, taking the scent on the air that seeped under the door. Then they both whined and looked back at Nest.

Can it be the prince, back so soon? Nest wondered as she opened the door and prepared to step out into the light; clearly there was no danger because the wolves were calm, indeed, so sure that nothing was amiss that they slipped past her and lay down on the ground outside the cottage. They were relaxed, but watchful.

'Ah, I see,' she said to herself. 'Welcome Sisters,' she called. She'd seen a small movement by the water and knew who was there.

One by one and slowly, four figures emerged from the landscape. From the edge of the river a seeming boulder unfolded itself into the small frame of Sister of Water, the sunlight touching the bright blue of her decorated arms which she moved like the rippling wavelets.

'Chwaer Dŵr, welcome,' said Nest, smiling.

Across the river, the dunes rose majestically, undulating in waves as huge as those that were thrown up by a Winter storm at sea. The grasses atop the dunes bent obediently with the wind blowing out to sea, and from among them rose **Sister of Air**, her wild plaited hair and sinuous body echoing the dance of the grasses.

'**Chwaer Awyr**, I welcome you also,' Nest called to her, even as her eye was drawn to the direction of the bright sun; a third figure appeared to walk from within it and towards her along the beach. It was another woman, **Sister of Fire**, and her long red hair and painted face were as bright as the rays of light themselves.

'**Chwaer Tân**, welcome,' she said, even as she felt a presence behind her. She turned expectantly at the sound of a voice. The wolves merely flicked their ears and sat still, watching.

The voice was deep and kindly and Nest watched with a smile as Sister of Earth dropped down from the rocks next to the cottage and came to her side. 'We are here for you, Nest of the Shore. Did you think we would forget you when you are in need?'

'I welcome you my sister, **Chwaer y Ddaear**,' she said. 'Now you are all here.'

They surrounded her and holding hands, there in front of the cottage, they walked slowly around her, chanting a melody that was as lilting as the wind and waves, sparkling as the fiery sun and as deep as the earth itself.

When the song was done, each of the Sisters kissed Nest and then together they sat on the ground in front of the cottage. Nest went indoors and fetched out bread and cheese and some small ale and they ate in companionable silence. It was quiet all around, save for the breathing sea and the cries of high gulls, wheeling lazily in the blue above.

'The men are all out with the tide, their wives are home,' Nest said, indicating the other cottages along the beach, beyond the sheltering rock. 'But, for all they are good women, I would only have you at this time, Sisters.'

All four women smiled and nodded their heads.

'Your babe is precious and will be the second of your long line. We will stay by the shore until she is born,' Sister of Earth said, and gesturing for permission with a smile and a nod at where Nest's hand lay on her stomach, when Nest smiled back, she knelt and reached under her skirt and laid both hands on her swollen belly. She felt all around it very carefully; her touch was confident, experienced and reassuring.

'She is well grown; not yet down the birth passage but she will turn when the time is right, in the next few weeks. You are well, Sister?' she asked and as she helped her straighten her skirts, Nest answered.

'I am indeed. I go about my usual business, as I will after she is born. The Lord Prince knows of my child but no one else,' Nest said.

Bea tried to speak, to tell her that Ithel knew, Ithel who hated Nest and wanted her at the same time, but all that came from her lips was an incoherent mumble. Stella licked her face then growled when she heard the footsteps outside the door.

Sister of Air spoke.

'Sister Nest, we know of the Prince's man, Yestyn. I treated his wounds before I knew who had given them and why. He is tended by the woman, Edith, and I, Chwaer Awyr, owe her a debt of revenge for spurning me and I will fulfil it when she least expects it.' She hissed, folding her arms across her chest, her eyes fierce with hate. 'But the man, Yestyn, will be well served by the wounds your companions gave him, for they will be some long time healing, if ever they do.'

She smiled at the wolves.

The women rose and Sister of Earth took Nest into a warm embrace, saying, 'Nest, we will be close by and will not show ourselves unless we are needed.'

Nest returned the embrace willingly; she had known them all for many years, but as she drew away, Sister of Earth kept hold of a hand and added, 'Nest, one more thing before we leave; the bard, Ithel ap Deykin, you need to be wary of him and his influence, nay, his appetites. He tried to use us in his own plot to harm the Prince and he has suffered because of it.'

Nest drew breath sharply. 'I saw, Chwaer y Ddaear. I watched in the water. He is an insidious worm; one not to be underestimated, one that can be dangerous for the Prince and for our land, for all he spouts his Welsh fervour and hatred of the English, aye, be they Norman or Saxon. I will try to help the Prince understand this. And I know Ithel lusts after me, even though he loathes me; a dangerous mixture, you are right, but don't worry, I'll be guarded at all times.'

Bea felt a wash of relief as she heard the confidence in Nest's voice.

It took Gwyn Roberts about ten minutes to reach the Nest's Point and he scouted around the whole area of the cottage before making his way to the front door. He'd seen nothing to worry him, nothing obviously suspicious, and all was quiet when he went up the path; but when he stopped outside the door to listen, he heard the low growl of a dog behind it.

Sister of Air smiled pleasantly and said, 'Would that I had been there with my sisters, but I will just have to bide my time until I have paid the hag, Edith what I owe her.'

'Wait a moment, Sisters, wait...' Nest began to say something else as they turned to melt away, but then there came a bellowing and thumping noise so loud that Bea felt a stab of fear. What was happening? Would Nest and the Sisters be harmed?

'No, wait,' Bea called aloud. 'Wait. Don't leave her alone in case he does come.'

The thumping continued, and Bea began to feel awkward and stiff, finally becoming aware that she was lying on the floor behind the front door of the cottage, but no longer in the 13th century.

The present day and the horror of the past hour slammed into her mind instead. It had been Jeremy's voice on the other side of the door; he'd found her, and he hadn't left.

Now someone was banging loudly and continuously on the door; it was him, he was just on the other side of the wood. She felt as though he only had to reach his hand right through it to snatch at her. She screamed, throwing her arms over her head, then feeling a surge of anger instead, she shouted, 'No, no! Just go away. Leave me alone. I'm not coming back.'

The banging on the door carried on and an unexpected male voice roared, 'Are you okay? Hello Bea. Are you okay? Open the door. Come on, it's me, Gwyn Roberts; you know me now. Thomas sent me. Said there was an intruder prowling outside. Is everything okay?'

Stella had started to bark again when she heard his voice and it was difficult for Bea to make herself heard, or to get Stella to stop. The dog was incensed, throwing her head back in fury, her front feet almost leaving the ground with the force of her barking. Archie joined in. He knew this wasn't Jeremy.

'No! Go away. You can't scare me like this. You're mad. I'm calling the police,' she yelled. 'Leave me alone. I'm not coming back, Jeremy.'

'It's not Jeremy. It's me, Gwyn Roberts. Thomas really did send me. I've got his scarf as proof,' he shouted, knowing it wasn't proof of anything as he might have taken it from the man himself. 'He said a bloke knocked him over. Said he might know who it was. Was it this Jeremy? Come on. I'm here to help you, really. Put the chain on and open the door. No need to worry. I'll give you my phone, Thomas dropped his when he was knocked over. You can talk to him at my house, on my landline. He can't walk just now; twisted the ankle. Come on!'

'Are you sure you're on your own?'

'Yes. It's just me and the night time – again!'

'Who's out there with you? Is he there? Are you helping him?'

'No, no, it's just me and I'm alone, really I am.'

Gwyn's voice was beginning to have a coaxing note to it, and Bea wanted to believe him, but fear gnawed at the ragged edges of her bruised mind.

She struggled to her feet, then yelled, 'Wait a minute! I'll have a look.'

She went around all the windows of the house and peered out into the night but saw nothing of significance out there.

He might be hiding.

Bea went back to the front door and putting the chain on, and with the dogs still barking, she managed to take the phone held through the gap by Gwyn. He'd got Thomas on his home landline and Bea heard his voice.

'It's all right, all right. Let him in,' he said.

Bea listened to the confidence and reassurance in his voice and finally opened the door, but it was some minutes before the dogs quietened down and threw themselves on the hearth rug, completely exhausted after all the excitement.

'I'm only here to help you, really,' Gwyn said, holding his palms up and facing her, and she nodded slightly and stood back to close the door. She kept hold of his phone which was still connected to his home landline, where Thomas listened.

Chapter twenty-seven

Balm

O, wonder! How many goodly creatures are there here...

Miranda - The Tempest

'THOMAS IS THAT YOU?' Bea said, her voice wavering. Her knuckles were white as she gripped the handset, and if it were a fraying rope holding her from a fall to her death, she couldn't have been more desperate.

'Course it is! Are you okay, love?' he said.

'I might be, I think, in a minute.' There was a long pause. 'He came, Thomas. Jeremy came here. He hates me. I wanted to tell you, you know. He's trying to scare me into going back and I'm not. I'm never going to. He says I'm mad, Thomas. I'm not really, I'm not. It's him, it's him.'

''Course not!' His voice was soothing. 'Nasty little bugger.'

'Why won't he leave me alone?'

'That I don't know, girl. But we'll sort him out somehow and I'm here for you and Gwyn Roberts is too. Now don't say anything else; I know he's bound to be listening. I think Roberts is okay; perhaps not as bad as I painted him – at being a pain in the arse that is. But he's big and strong and can probably handle himself against a reedy thing like the almighty brain surgeon. Now I know you're one of these independent, modern young women, but you could delegate for once, accept a bit of muscle when it's offered. It can't harm when you've been attacked, like tonight. Yes?'

'What d'you mean?'

'I mean, *be nice*. Ask him to stay 'til morning, if he will; then we can get someone else to come and have a look around to see if anything's damaged or moved. I'm stuck here at the minute. I was on my way up to you when some bloke pushed me over, twisted me ankle. I'll lay odds it was the great Mr. Fitzmartin, the bastard, as you say. That's why I had to send Gwyn Roberts; I was right near his place. And I'm going to ask Dafydd from next door to come and help me home from here. Tell Roberts I'll lock up for him. Dafydd's Muriel can help me in the Post Office 'til I get this ankle looked at. It could be fine by morning anyway. Now do me a favour, set my mind easy and let Roberts stay; I mean *ask him* to stay, because I haven't; he just ran straight off to the rescue, girl.'

'Oh, Thomas, what am I going to do?'

'Just as I said. Now off you go, cariad, off you go. We'll have a chat about the brain surgeon when I next see you, in private. Didn't tell me things were quite that bad, did you?' His voice was gentle, and he added, 'But the most important thing to remember is that I've got your back. Okay?'

'Okay.'

'Night, night then.'

He hung up.

Gwyn Roberts was standing just inside the room, bending to stroke the dogs when Bea handed him his phone, saying, 'Thanks. Thanks for coming.'

'Glad to help. Thomas said you'd had a visitor.'

'Not exactly a visitor. Not a great choice of word.'

'Look, sorry. I couldn't help but hear some of that. I mean you've had someone prowling about and it was someone you're scared of, I guess. Can't be nice for a woman on her own,' he began but she flared up immediately.

'A woman…? Scared? A woman on her own? You mean a woman needs a man to watch her back? Is that it? Bit patronising really.'

Why am I angry with him? I am losing it...

They stood face to face.

'No, didn't actually mean it like that. I meant for *someone*, a person on his or her own in an isolated spot and with a pair of dogs that are, well, vulnerable just at present, and well, the little guy is old, isn't he? That's all I meant. Right?'

'Right.'

Bea struggled to keep her voice from sounding waspish but knew she'd failed when Gwyn stood straighter and faced her squarely.

'I believe you wanted Thomas to come out here in a hurry. You did ask for his help, didn't you? Now I'm just doing a neighbour a favour and that's extended to you too, even if it is the middle of the night, again. Thomas was injured as he was on his way here. However, as I am clearly surplus to requirement, I can go and help the old guy get home. That's really no problem. You obviously feel I'm here to sabotage your independence and shred your psyche,' he said and began to zip up his jacket which he'd opened when she let him in. 'All in all, I'll leave you to plaster metaphysical balm on your wounds.'

He began to step past her when she took a huge, shuddering breath.

'Hey, are you cr…'

'I - no, no I'm not,' Bea said quickly, dragging her hands over her hair and then down her face.

She looked shocked to find both palms were wet.

'You are crying, really. Come and sit down. I'd give you a neighbourly hug, but you might punch me. And I'm sensitive about being punched.'

Bea said nothing but walked slowly over to the settle by the fire. Gwyn followed; hands thrust deeply into his jacket pockets. He stood in an awkward, uncomfortable pose by the hearth and looked down at her.

'Look, I'm really sorry if I upset you. I know you've not been well,' he began but when he saw her expression, he slapped his own forehead in frustration.

Bea answered abruptly, 'I'm not ill. There is nothing wrong with me. I am not ill. Is that clear?'

He held up both hands palm facing and nodded agreement quickly. She knew she was being unreasonably surly; after all he had come out here. An image of him on the night of the storm flashed across her mind.

Okay, it's different now, he's here to help, I suppose. I was in shock then, still am, if I'm having all these dreams and visions, whatever they are. And I'm not ill. Anyway, he might be able to frighten Jeremy off if he comes back.

He said, 'Yes. No you're not. Okay – not ill…'

'I'm just scared, that's all,' she said. 'Frightened to death, if I'm honest.'

'Frightened? Frightened of what, Bea?' he asked, trying to look more closely at her but she turned her head away.

He took his hands out of his pockets and relaxed his pose.

'Everything. Him.'

'Right. You mean the guy that bowled Thomas over, I take it. The intruder? The one you were talking about. What's his connection to you, if I might ask?' He sounded worried, genuine, sympathetic.

Bea decided on a leap in the dark, to trust him.

'He's…he's my husband,' she said. 'He's followed me here. He said he was going to a conference, but he hasn't gone. He's here somehow, somewhere, out there. He's stalking me.'

Gwyn edged over to the stool and sat down hesitantly.

'And you didn't want to be followed here, I take it?'

'Well, no, clearly I didn't! Who wants to be followed in the dark? No! I'm not going back. I'm staying here, for good,' she said and nodded as if to reassure herself.

'You actually saw him outside, your husband?' Gwyn spoke gently.

Bea didn't answer for a moment, the sound of his voice, the banging, the darkness, Stella's insistent baying, Archie's fear. It was all a horror.

'No, no I didn't actually see him, but I heard him. He said my name, outside the door. I know it was him. He tapped on every window. Archie fled. He knows him well. I thought I'd die of fright.'

'Right,' Gwyn said. 'Sounds weird.'

Bea was hunched up on the edge of the settle, staring into the fire, rubbing her hands together.

'Cold?' he asked and when she nodded, he got up and began to tend the fire, poking it expertly to send air under the low remnants and adding a couple of logs from the basket and with a small shovelful of sea coal, it was soon blazing nicely.

'There,' he said, sounding satisfied. 'Mind if I take off my coat for a minute. Bit warmer now. I can make you some tea, if you like.'

He dropped his jacket on the floor by the stool and underneath he was wearing a rough old jumper and jeans and looked at home in them, a man at home with himself too. He raked his hand through his hair. It made him look dangerous she thought, dangerous and in control. Gwyn went out to put the kettle on with the ease of one used to looking after himself. Bea realised she didn't know anything about his personal life, any part of his life. He was a stranger, a mystery. Thomas had been a bit scathing about him but seemed to have changed his mind and she knew he was doing her a favour by coming out in Thomas's stead.

Maybe I'm being a bit prickly. I don't know how to behave, do I?

He soon returned with a tray with two mugs and the milk jug on it. Bea was still rubbing her hands together, trying to make up her mind about what Thomas had advised. She glanced through the shield of her hair at his stooping figure as he manoeuvred the stool with his foot, so that he could rest the tray on it.

'Thomas suggested I should ask you to stay here tonight, just in case. I wondered if you would. I do have a spare bed, but I'm going to stay down here with the dogs.'

Bea's voice sounded strange to her. It was not only the request for help, but also the fact that she had not got on with him in their short acquaintance. It was also a tacit admission, not only to herself but to others, that she now needed active protection from Jeremy.

She watched for Gwyn's reaction through the privacy of her untidy hair; most had escaped her plaits and hung over her face. She didn't dare turn her head in case he gave her a scornful rejection, but from the corner of her eye she saw something she didn't expect, and she jumped. She quickly dragged the hair behind her ear to try and catch sight of whatever it was and as she did, Archie stood up from his perch on the settle, staring intently at the man, the fur on his back lifted.

What's that he's wearing? It's long, and of fine wool too. Is he wearing long leather boots and a dark blue robe? A brooch, gold. That sword...that sword...I've seen it before. His hair's long too, and that long moustache...' she thought, then the next instant the image of a medieval lord was gone, and she saw dark blue jeans and walking boots and an olive-green jumper.

Archie seemed to see this too and relaxed his posture, licked his lips, lay down again, watching.

Bea's mouth was as dry as the dunes in a hot July. Gwyn stopped fiddling with the tea things, saying affably:

'Of course I'll stay. No problem. Glad to help.'

She managed a slight smile, feeling both relieved and exhausted.

Gwyn went back to the kitchen and returned with the teapot. Once the pot was ceremonially stirred and the tea left to brew, he sat down on the floor with his back against the fireplace, a hand resting on Stella's flank. She hadn't woken and was snoring steadily.

'D'you know, I think she's getting her milk. Her pups must be born soon, don't you think?' he said as he ran a hand over the dog's belly. 'Not that I'm a dog expert; just saw a vet programme the other week.'

Stella woke with a grunt and swung her head round to touch her flank. Bea watched, suddenly alerted but before she could make any comment Gwyn continued talking.

'By the way, I met a friend of yours today. At least she said she was a friend; her name's Mairi, I gather, but she was a tad negative, it has to be said.'

He told her the gist of Mairi's comments.

Bea started in shock and knocked the tray on the stool so that he had to dive to catch it.

'Whoa!' he said, as he righted it. 'Is she important? Quite a smooth sort of woman. Confident. Actually, overconfident, in my opinion.'

Bea began to pour the tea, anything to divert the conversation away from Mairi. Her hands were shaking, and the teapot spout tapped on the edge of the mug.

'So, not a real friend, I take it?' Gwyn asked and gently took the teapot from her, finished the pouring and handed her a half-filled mug.

'She's a friend of my husband's, well, she and her husband that is,' she said. Her voice was quiet, subdued almost.

'She said you'd been ill and in hospital,' he told her.

Bea shook her head vigorously. 'How many times? No, I haven't.

Well not unless I was working, that is. I am a doctor at a Manchester hospital – *I was*, I mean. I've resigned. Well, I'm going to. I hate it there now.'

'So, you're not ill?'

'No. I already said…' Bea began and then stopped as Stella gave a groan, a deep, uncomfortable groan. 'Stella, okay, girl. Okay.' Bea got down and knelt at her side as she was speaking.

'Not giving birth I hope?' Gwyn asked as he bent down next to her.

'I don't think so. I don't know, but I've never seen pups born before. Have you?'

'Not in my job description.'

Stella rolled over onto her back with an effort.

'Looks like a beached whale,' Gwyn commented.

Bea laid her hands on the dog's swollen stomach and felt carefully all over.

'Hang on!'

She ran both hands gently over the dog's belly and then looked at Gwyn as she felt another spasm.

'Y'know, yes, that was a contraction, I'd say. It was a strong one.'

She kept her hand in place and as Stella tensed, she said:

'I'm pretty confident she's in labour now. Would you get my stethoscope for me? It's somewhere on the floor upstairs in the back room.'

'On the floor, hey? Coming up,' he said and stood immediately, looking ready for anything. 'Hot water and towels? Isn't that what people usually go for? I mean for babies.'

'I suppose they would come in handy for dog midwifery too.'

She kept her attention on Stella but suddenly leaned back.

'Wait, wait, Stella,' she said as the dog rolled back onto her stomach and began struggling to rise.

'Come on there,' Bea said and put her arms under the dog's belly to give some support and Gwyn rushed back to lend his own arms, and after some heaving and pushing they stood back and Stella managed on her own.

Jeremy was forgotten by both of them in the excitement.

'A graceless business, this pregnancy lark,' Gwyn muttered and went off to get the things Bea needed.

She stood in the middle of the room watching as Stella began to prowl around, sniffing in corners, doubling back on herself and nosing the blankets on the floor, banging into the log basket then the stool, almost knocking the tray off. She spun round, her tongue lolling, panting loudly and as her eye fell on the settle she rushed forward and took hold of the blanket in her mouth and dragged it onto the floor. Archie, who was using it as a bed, scrabbled to jump off before he fell. Stella stood perfectly still for some seconds, her head hanging low and then suddenly she turned right around and began to scratch at the hearth rug, rucking it up into brightly coloured cloth waves before she lowered herself carefully down in the middle of the heap.

'Poor girl,' Bea said and laughed a little at the dog's confusion. *The pups are coming. How wonderful*, she thought and then a worry punched her heart. *She's got to be okay though. She must be okay.'*

'Any sign yet,' Gwyn asked as he reappeared and handed Bea the stethoscope. Any idea how long it lasts? I mean is it like shelling peas for animals? They just pop out, don't they?'

'I bet they don't...' Bea said.

'I'll Google it shall I?' he asked, iPhone in hand.

Bea gave him a tentative smile. 'Yes, why not?' she said as she knelt next to Stella and listened to her heart and lungs. 'Breathing steady, strong pulse, slightly elevated. Normal, in the circumstances, I'd say. No major distress.'

He busied himself with the keyboard and quickly came up with results.

'Seems labour can last any time at all, depending on the dog, its general health, whether this is the first or second stage of labour, whether she's been 'nesting', restless, prowling around, or none of these - but maybe the position of Saturn in relation to Venus or wind currents in the northern hemisphere.'

Bea ignored the wry comment and knelt down next to Stella.

'You *have* been restless today and you've not wanted to eat much, have you?'

'Does she ever actually answer you? Whoa!' Gwyn exclaimed as Stella gave an audible groan and they saw her abdomen tensing as she rolled a little to one side.

Bea stooped forward and listened to Stella's heart with the stethoscope. 'Gwyn, can you time fifteen seconds for me?'

She listened intently as he signalled the start and finish of the timing.

'Seventy beats per minute,' she said, when they'd done, 'a little elevated but not too high. She is working hard, after all.'

'You should have been a vet perhaps?' he suggested, and she smiled at him properly for the first time.

'Maybe you're right. Auntie Nest was good with animal ailments and I think I'm like her.'

'Look,' he said, 'she seems to be doing something this end. Is this it?'

'Could be,' she answered and moved round to Stella's back end, gently lifted her tail out of the way. 'I think so. She seems to be well dilated. That was quick. Maybe I was too wrapped up in myself to notice.'

Stella made no noise but panted a little as Gwyn said, 'There, see.'

A dark, wet bulge appeared, and they could clearly see little nostrils through the glistening birth membrane.

'Bloody hell! That was fast!' he said. 'I've never been at a dog birth before, a dog lying-in, I should say. I am a Medievalist after all.'

Bea gasped with excitement. 'Look at the little nose, Gwyn.' She hadn't felt so excited for a long time.

Stella had another contraction and as the whole head was pushed out, they both cried, 'Yes!'

'Good girl, good girl!' Bea crooned gently and stroked the dog's head.

There was a brief pause, another great heave of Stella's belly and the pup slithered out. It was covered in the glistening birth membrane and a little fluid and blood.

Stella panted quickly and then heaved herself around and gave the wet bundle a cursory lick then set about nibbling the cord straight away. Once done, she pulled at the membrane with her teeth and carried on licking until it was all cleaned off.

'Maybe she's done this before,' Gwyn said and handed Bea a towel.

'Isn't she lovely?' Bea said and picked up the pup to place it near Stella's nose as the dog slumped back to lie on her side. 'It's bitch. Wow,' she whispered.

Stella suddenly swung round and began to lick the pup with such energy that Bea had to laugh. She didn't seem to mind Bea holding it up to her cradled in the towel. The tiny pup wriggled and snuffled. Bea cleared its nose with her fingers, and it gave a hearty squeak, stretching out its tiny front paws.

'Perfect tiny thing, look, Gwyn, look,' she whispered.

'What colour is it supposed to be? Looks like particularly ripe estuary mud to me,' Gwyn said. 'Shouldn't it be having a drink or something?'

'I'll just clean it off a bit more,' she said, gently wiping it with the end of the towel. 'I suppose it should feed now. They can feed straight away I think.'

Gwyn was busy with his iPhone again. 'Says here that there can be anything from twenty minutes to two hours between pups. Lord above! Afterbirth should come with each pup and you've to count the pups and the afterbirth and match the numbers or I guess it's trouble.'

'Right,' she said and placed the puppy with its nose against one of Stella's teats. 'Look, Gwyn, it's interested alright. It's sniffing. Isn't that great? Look, look, it's pushing its little paw into her, kneading her. Maybe it needs a minute.' Bea's throat was tight, her heart was full, and she didn't bother to wipe away the tears that spilled.

Stella turned to lick the pup several times before she was satisfied, then lay back again.

'Charming,' he said, looking at the puppy and made a grimace of distaste as, after a few minutes of nuzzling her belly, it finally found a teat and latched onto it, sucking greedily, pushing at the swollen skin with miniature paws.

'Oh, look. Its little claws are like pearls,' Bea murmured.

'D'you think she's got ten in there? Certainly big enough for ten!'

Then as Stella turned her head to clean the puppy noisily with her tongue and spent the longest time on its bottom, he added, 'Oh, too basic for me. Are they always this bloody disgusting?'

'Dogs are pretty straightforward, yes. Well, that rug's messy enough to throw away now, let alone if she has another nine pups on it! Not that I mind really. I'm just so pleased for Stella. She's a good girl. Seems to be quite calm with the giving birth business, from what I can tell, well, better than a lot of humans.' Bea shook her head, a wry smile on her lips. 'Actually, I've not attended many human births either.'

'D'you know, you're very lovely when you smile,' Gwyn told her, adding in a serious tone, 'if I might say…'

Bea flushed awkwardly and stroked the dog. She couldn't think how to answer that.

'Perhaps this has helped put the intruder out of your mind for a little while?' he suggested, and she nodded.

'Yes, for the moment at least. Dogs have a way of putting things right for you,' she said. 'Where's Archie?'

He sat up on the settle when he heard his name and cocked his head, looking at her intently. He'd been perfectly still and had watched the event. Bea patted her leg. 'C'mon, Arch. Come over here. You're an uncle now. Come and have a look.'

Stella glanced at him as he came to sit on Bea's knee.

'They're very good together, aren't they? Possible rise in status to stepfather perhaps? Hmmm?' Gwyn murmured.

Bea grinned.

Chapter twenty-eight

Respite

Now I will believe That there are unicorns…

Sebastian – The Tempest

STELLA HAD THREE MORE puppies: another bitch and two dogs, each at roughly hourly intervals, and each one born in a different part of the room because Stella wandered around intent on finding a new site for each event. The new arrivals were all lined up and feeding by three o'clock in the morning. Gwyn had made a bed for the family from old rugs next to the hearth. He surrounded it with a wall of dry logs laid lengthways to prevent any wanderers rolling away and into danger for the next couple of days. Stella had allowed Archie to sniff the puppies and he had gone to sleep on the sheepskin in the fire nook.

By four o'clock Gwyn was asleep by the fire and Bea was in the same state on the settle.

At eight o'clock he was woken suddenly by the harsh scream of a passing gull. He sat up quickly and banged his head on the wooden rocker next to him.

'Bloody hell,' he said, and Stella raised her head from the nursery bed to stare at him with a look of complacent motherhood; her puppies, tiny gourmets, were suckling hungrily and murmuring; their closed eyes gave them an air of appreciative intensity. Gwyn watched them for a while before rising quietly and making his way out to the kitchen.

He made coffee for himself and Bea and put her mug on the hearth before retiring soundlessly to the rocker to sip from his own, but when he raised his eyes from the mug, they met Bea's through the steam.

'Ah, awake. Made you coffee.' He indicated with his eyes.

'Thanks.'

Bea felt awkward as she sat up and she moved her loosened plaits over her shoulders, reached for her coffee to cover up her confusion.

The intense hours they'd spent together as Stella whelped had been curiously intimate, yet the day before he'd infuriated her and the night she'd arrived he'd frightened her so much she'd been immobile with shock. But in the morning light she gazed at the new family, so contained and satisfied, then at her old dog, Archie, calm and accepting of the newcomer. She watched Gwyn as he rose and moved around, busy with simple domestic tasks: stirring the fire to life, drawing the curtains, letting the smell and sound of the sea into the room through the open window. Bea was shocked to find the atmosphere felt safe and good.

'Good morning, Stella, Archie,' he said and the sound of his voice talking to the dogs brought Bea fully awakened from the homely scene and aware of the reason he was there in the first place; Jeremy had found her, and the illusion of safety evaporated. But then in the next moment Stella's new family dispelled the feeling and replaced it with pure joy. The dog looked up at Bea and gave a low whine and Bea went over to crouch next to her and the litter.

'Good morning, girl. How are you? Did you sleep at all?' She stroked the dog's head and Stella wagged her tail, flicked her ears back and smiled up at her. She turned to pick Archie up. 'Come on, my sausage. I won't forget you, don't worry.' His tail seemed to vibrate, it wagged so fast and he licked Bea's ear vigorously.

Gwyn joined her. 'I think she did, actually. And he was snoring his head off. It was an exciting night, all things considered. But the main star is thriving, isn't she?'

'Yes, she looks as if she is, and the little ones too. They all look darker than her; quite chocolatey and it looks as if their fur will be rough like their mum's. Apparently, the dad is a black Labrador. What a wonderful thing, all those puppies and she's come through it fine, hasn't she?' She glanced at him and realized how much he'd done to help. 'Thanks for being here. I don't know what I'd have done otherwise, well, you know, with my, erm - with the upset, as well as with Arch and Stella's big event.'

'Don't give it another thought. I'd only have spent my evening savouring a fine claret by a roaring fire with a priceless first edition in my hand, the work of an eminent medievalist scholar. Instead of which I get to race to the rescue of a damsel in distress, again.'

Bea stiffened straight away, her mood swinging away from contentment. 'I'm not doing this on purpose you know,' she told him, more sharply than she intended but felt a stab of the familiar fear. *I'm not safe yet and now I've got Stella and the pups to look after as well as Arch! All vulnerable. What'll I do?*

He began to stand, held up his palms in apology, a rueful smile on his lips. 'I was only teasing; trying heavy sarcasm but to no effect, clearly. Really, honestly it was no problem, my coming up here, especially as Thomas was injured. Tell you what, though, I'll give him a bell, shall I? See how he's doing after all the drama.'

Bea drew in a shocked breath, her turn to feel wrong footed. 'I've forgotten Thomas. How could I?' She was instantly awash with shame, felt the heat of it rising in a deep blush up her neck and cheeks.

Gwyn held up his phone in an, 'I'll sort it' gesture and began to make the call while Bea sat frozen in her attitude of embarrassment.

He'd not made the connection when there was a knock at the door and a man's voice they recognised called a greeting. It was Lorcan.

'Hello the house. Only me.'

Bea was still immobile, but Gwyn strode over to throw open the door and welcome him in.

'Hello, I know it's early, but I've brought the vet. I promised I would,' he said as he walked in then straight away saw the new family. 'Sure, I see we're too late. What beauties!' he cried, adding, 'This is my friend, Heather, our vet of the hour!' He drew a woman in gently by the arm and presented her to the others with an attitude of pride. Archie dashed to the visitors, gave a single welcoming bark.

As the woman stepped into the room, Bea reeled, gasped for breath. She saw a tall, well-built woman with close cropped black hair and an ankle length blue woollen dress, belted with a leather thong. Hanging from the thong was a long silver scabbard, showing the carved hilt of bone-handled knife. She wore a long sheepskin cloak and leather boots. A woman with money and power; both were needed to be able to dress like that.

Chwaer y Ddaear, Bea thought. *Why is she here, now?*

She swallowed; her throat was so dry suddenly. Archie stared up at the woman, every muscle stiff, eyes fixed on her. Bea she passed a hand over her eyes; surely the blue was fading? The light from the window blurred Bea's vision and the woman's appearance changed subtly as she turned to face them. Her hair was the silver of moonlight, no longer black. Bea stood to greet them, her breathing coming fast. Archie relaxed a little. No one else reacted in the way they had and she was relieved to see they were more intent on introductions and puppies.

She saw that the woman, Heather, was tall, much older than Lorcan, in her sixties, slim and beautiful with a vibrant complexion framed by long straight grey hair that wove around her like a gossamer veil on the air.

'Hello there, lovely to meet you all,' she said. Her voice was soft, and her accent was lowland Scots. 'Is this the mum I've heard so much about?' Heather said, looking intently at Stella.

She flashed a smile at both dogs, then focussing on Bea and Gwyn, offered her hand to each of them. 'What a lovely house. What gorgeous dogs and lovely contented pups too, I see.' She moved quietly to crouch next to Stella and began to murmur softly to her. Stella licked her lips and gave a slight wag.

'I'll give you a minute then,' Heather said to the dog and rose to join the others. 'She's a tad uncertain. I think she'd like to get the measure of me first, before she commits herself. How about you?' she asked Archie and bent to hold out her hand. He stayed where he was but wagged a greeting.

'Okay then.' Heather smiled.

'Well, there's a surprise,' Lorcan said, smiling broadly at the pups then turning to Gwyn he said, 'What happened? Thomas phoned me late last night and said he'd been injured, and you'd come over here to see about an intruder. Have I got that right?'

'We were about to phone and update him, check on him too.' Gwyn said.

'Done it already. Sure, he's fine apart from a bit of a sprain and wanting a second round with the bloke who bowled into him. Already back at the Post Office with a mug of tea and a neighbour's wife to boss the whiles. He's not heard the good news from here though.'

Gwyn handed the phone to Bea. 'Like to tell him, Bea?' He looked at her searchingly, kindly. 'You all right?' he asked, his voice low.

She shook her head, let her hair fall protectively over the side of her face. She was still self-conscious about the bruising. 'A little shell-shocked by all that's going on, is all,' she told him and took the phone to the window to lean into the deep recess. The others chatted quietly while she made the call. Thomas was delighted by the news and was all comfort and support, warm and strong as she'd always known him. As she ended the call, she felt overwhelmed with emotion and quickly left the room, saying she'd put the kettle on again, but she shook so much that the kettle rattled against the tap as she filled it.

What's happening to me? Jeremy must be right. I'm losing it. I'm ill. I'm overreacting to everything. Seeing things. Sister of Earth! No, she's not real. I'm definitely hallucinating now – not even dreaming. Did Jeremy actually come here last night? I don't know anything anymore. But I've got all these dogs now. I can't be ill. I've got to get hold of things. Sort everything out, somehow.

She was fumbling with mugs when Gwyn came into the kitchen.

'Right, I'll do that, you look a bit upset. You obviously need a hand here. It's been a tough night for you, hasn't it?'

Bea was stunned that he'd noticed her distress and she was affronted too; she was sure he was being judgemental, not to mention officious.

Who does he think he is? Prat! I'm not married to him. He sounded just like Jeremy then. Why can't he just shut the hell up? She gripped the edge of the stone sink, her knuckles white. *I'm married to Jeremy and I don't want to be. I'm just pathetic. I'm even thinking like an extract from a woman's magazine, a bleating letter to the agony aunt.*

She swung round to face him. 'Look, I'm fine, thanks. Perhaps you need to get home now? Have you got a lecture or TV show or something? I think I can manage on my own. It's high tide at 10.05 am so the beach path is open for a little while yet. Thanks for everything.'

Gwyn stood and stared at her for a full minute without saying anything.

'I was actually imagining we had become friends of sorts during the night, or at least achieved a truce, but pardon me for my presumption. I'll be on my way then.' He slammed the mug he held down on the table with such force that it cracked in two. 'Bollocks,' he said. The words came out between his teeth.

Bea's shoulders slumped as she felt a wash of shame drench her.

'Oh, I'm sorry. I really am. You're right.' She found she couldn't say anything else and she stood staring at the floor and wondering what to do to make things right again.

He swiped a hand over his head. He said, 'Look I'm sorry about the mug. I am a prat. I'll call in later, if I may?'

She forced herself to look at him. *I used to get on with people so well. Now look at me; snapping and breaking down, pushing people away.*

'I really am sorry. I overreacted; I'm just so tired. I wouldn't have been able to manage without you last night, and that's unusual for me,' she said.

'No, no, it's good for me to be put in my place from time to time - everyday, if I'm honest.' He smiled, relaxed. 'But, apart from my being pushy, what puzzles me is why you are being so bloody hostile. I came to help. Look, I'm tired myself and I'd love some tea and to hear what the vet says about our patient. Would it be all right if I stay a little longer?'

'Of course, and will you make it? You're right and I'm sorry. I have been hostile to almost everyone here. It's not like me. Really, it's not. Please stay.' She was suddenly overwhelmed with embarrassment and just needed to get out of the room. 'Look, I'm just going to see Stella,' she said and edged quickly out of the kitchen. Gwyn filled the kettle, shaking his head.

As she walked back into the living room, she saw the woman in the blue dress again, the one with black hair, Sister of Earth. She was bending over another woman who sat on a low stool by the hearth. Bea saw it was Nest and that she was heavily pregnant and sat with her legs apart, skirt stretched over her knees, bracing herself, her eyes closed, mouth set in a line of discomfort. But she was calm and nearby the wolves lay sleeping in the warmth. The air was full of the scent of lavender and rosemary oil from the small earthenware oil lamps burning around the room. She noticed the Prince's bronze lamp, his gift to Nest, on the board. She thought it burned more brightly than the others and wondered if Nest valued it because he'd given it to her.

Bea felt suddenly peaceful. She stopped and breathed in the scent of the herbs and also caught the unmistakeable smell of dog, or rather, wolf, which made her smile as she recognised it. She walked forward slowly, feeling intensely curious to discover what was happening and not at all worried by her apparent slip into the thirteenth century again. It was becoming familiar.

But before she reached the hearth, the scene she witnessed quietly morphed back into her own time and there were Lorcan and Heather sitting together on one side of Stella's bed. Bea found she didn't mind. Archie was on his settle perch and staring intently at the place where she'd seen Nest. Did he see? She felt suddenly in possession of a thrilling knowledge, no more confusion, no more disorientation or fear of hallucination and breakdown, no more loneliness. It might not be her own childhood's Nest she saw, who she visited, but it was still Nest. Bea felt the relationship, felt that Nest was with her whatever happened. And what comforted her more than anything was that Archie seemed to see what she saw, and he wasn't frightened.

But now I'm slipping off into the past with other people all around me in the present. What will I do if they notice anything odd?' she thought. *Maybe I should just go with the flow, take a leaf from Nest's book and be my old self.*

She crouched down with the others and Stella thumped her tail.

'Well she certainly likes you,' Heather said with a smile. 'She's bonded with you very quickly from what I'm told. That's so good. And lucky for her because of the whelping and the shipwreck. How terrible. Poor family. Want me to check her and the pups over, Bea?' she asked.

'I do actually. That would be great. I feel so sad for her family. I'll keep her safe. I'm sure they would have wanted that. They'd be pleased with the pups I bet.'

'Oh, yes. They're great. By the way, is he okay with things?' Heather asked, nodding at Archie.

'He's more than okay.'

Lorcan handed Heather her backpack and she said, 'I find it easier to put things in here if I visit patients off-road, so to speak.'

The pups were asleep and when Heather asked Bea to pick one up, Stella allowed this readily, so all four were transferred to Bea's lap while Heather checked the dog's heart and other vital signs, palpated her stomach and examined her carefully. Stella accepted all her examination and then pointedly looked at Bea, as if to ask for her puppies to be put back in place, which she did, gently.

Lorcan smiled and said, 'Y'know, I've a fancy for one of those when they're ready. They are magical, aren't they?'

Bea found she was able to smile back and nod. 'She's going to be a great mum. I bet the pups will all be calm like her; she wasn't distressed during the births and each one was quick. We checked the afterbirths and got rid of them – well, Gwyn put them outside for the tide to take,' Bea told her.

Heather said, 'She's in good shape, considering the shipwreck ordeal. I'll give her an oxytocin injection while it's not long since she whelped – six hours I hear. That'll help close down the uterus and promote let-down of the milk. She'll feel a bit better too. Mind, she does seem to have plenty of milk, and you say the puppies have been feeding well.'

'I'm so glad you came, Heather. I needed to hear that,' Bea said and Gwyn, coming into the room then, added, 'It all seemed to be easy really.'

'Dog's don't often make too much fuss. If you like, I'll call in tomorrow too. In the meantime, give her more food, small portions, something very nutritious, lots to drink and don't worry if her faeces are dark for a few days – it's normal. Okay?' Heather said.

Lorcan put a hand on Heather's arm. 'I've a couple of errands for Thomas. Why don't you go over to my place and wait for me there?'

She nodded pleasantly at him, but on impulse Bea said, 'You could stay here a while if you like. Keep me company.'

It was agreed, and Gwyn left with Lorcan, both to see Thomas, both promising to return later with supplies. Bea felt good.

Chapter twenty-nine

Arrivals

Blow til thou burst thy wind…

Boatswain – The Tempest

NOT LONG AFTER the men had gone, the tide was lapping energetically at the garden wall, helped by an offshore wind. Low scudding clouds bowled along the horizon, galleons setting sail on a voyage as a flight of gulls screeched their hurrahs.

Indoors the fire was cosy, and the puppies slept. Heather was easy company, warm, undemanding and interesting; she talked about her work, dogs, life on an island far from her native Scotland. For Bea it was balm to her soul. The terror of the night before when Jeremy stalked around the cottage receded into the far distance and there were small pockets of time when she forgot him altogether. She knew she was overwrought, and she imagined her nerves as fine wires stretched almost to the point of infinity. In recent months she had existed in a cloud of despair and loneliness, but since she'd escaped, she lurched from wild alarm to a delighted denial of the fear. But her subconscious whispered that indulging in little episodes of happiness is pure escapism and sooner or later you will finally have to face him.

Heather offered to make lunch for them.

'You see how easily I invite myself,' she said, laughing as she walked into the kitchen. 'Do you have salad?'

'I've got bacon. It's actually healthier and I should know, I'm a doctor.'

'Is that with healthy ketchup as the vegetable part of the meal?'

'It is; please, lather it on. And it's all I've got anyway.'

'No bacon for you, my laddie,' Heather said to Archie, who had come to sit by her. 'I think he likes me now. It's usually the smell; a combination of cows, cats and horses.'

Bea smiled. *She's so nice to be with; calm. I wonder if she and*

Lorcan...? Bea tested the thought and decided she felt comfortable enough to ask the very question. 'Heather, can I ask – are you and Lorcan together?'

'Good heavens!' Heather laughed delightedly. 'Och, I'm flattered you think a lively young professor would be attracted to an ageing vet; but no, Lorcan's father, Damon, was my love. We lived together for about ten years before he died and when he did, I moved off the island to Bangor and let Lorcan have the cottage. There's no one else for me. And I'm more of a mother to Lorcan.'

'Ah.'

'What about you? Lorcan says he's heard something about a husband...?' Heather said.

Bea was leaning on the wall at the side of the kitchen range. She let herself slide slowly down so that she was sitting on the old rug, her arms tightly round her knees.

'Yes,' she said softly. 'Heather, I think I'm becoming ill, mentally ill that is, losing it as they say in all the best psychiatric units. At least everyone I know in Manchester thinks I am, and Jeremy, that's my husband, he says I am. He's told everyone.'

As Heather cooked the bacon, made butties and coffee too, Bea talked. She told her how she and Jeremy had met, how she'd been blinded by his charm, flattered by his status and warned by her friends and her mother, but to no avail. Nest, her own Nest, had been silent but non-judgemental about the subject of Jeremy.

It felt right to talk to the older woman. Bea watched her face; there seemed to be nothing disapproving in her expression or in the way she picked up the tray of food and nodded towards the living room.

'Come on in here, Bea. It's warm. Come on,' Heather said.

Bea cradled her cup but didn't touch her food. She told her how things had deteriorated to the point of her nightly imprisonment for the past few months since Nest had died.

'The thing is, Heather, I know he shouldn't have done that to me, but what bothers me more is that *I let him*. I think I made him worse, indulged him in his vices, as they say. Why didn't I stop him, refuse to be locked up? I must have some compulsion to be hurt. I think, I *know*

I'm depressed, just normal depression, not clinical that is. My head seems heavy, woolly. Maybe I should go and see a doctor down here and get a therapist or something.'

'Maybe, my dear, maybe. Why not wait and see? Sometimes I think animals need only rest and time to get better from the less obvious injuries, usually the anxieties some humans lay on them, causing a build-up of tension. Maybe you're suffering from an emotional overload, Bea.' She poured herself another mug of tea and filled Bea's up. 'You've certainly had enough to cope with. One remedy for that is the sea; it calms the troubled breast, as my mum used to say. And this house, cottage or what you will, I think it suits you. Nest lived here all her life. Och, it's full of her presence. Yes,' she smiled in response to Bea's look of enquiry. 'I did know her. She was fey, sure enough, and wonderful, and I think being here will help you see things right. Now don't think that means I won't help. I'm not abdicating the trust you've just given me. You can talk to me any time, anytime at all. And while I think on, who wouldn't be depressed to be treated like that by a person you thought loved you?'

The moment was interrupted by the puppies as they stirred with tiny squeaks and Stella began cleaning them noisily.

'She'll probably like a feed and a wee once they are settled again. What have you got in the way of feed?' Heather began, but the next interruption came as a knock on the door.

It was Dana. She introduced herself very smoothly and quickly mentioned her work and Lorcan as her contact. She asked if Bea minded her lurking on the beach next to the cottage. She'd like to get some shots of the oystercatchers from a different angle, along with some of the other coastal wildlife on this side of the estuary.

'Hopefully my hide will be as camouflaged to you, as I think it is for the birds and beasts,' she told them.

Bea hadn't asked her in, but she warmed to her instantly, so she said, 'I'd be glad of someone outside, but it might not be safe for you. I have to tell you, I think I had a prowler last night and Thomas-the-Post was coming up here to help me and he was bowled over by some bloke running away in a hurry. Perhaps you'd better stick to the daytime?'

'Wow, I'll be on the look-out. Thanks for that. I'll keep it to the daylight hours anyway,' Dana said, then looking past her into the gloom of the indoors, she asked, 'Can I hear puppies? Is that your dog? I thought she looked in-whelp, when I saw you from across the river. The little Jack Russell yours too?'

Bea smiled, 'Yes, They're both mine and yes, she has had the puppies – four. Want a quick peep?

Dana shook her head at the same time Heather called from indoors, 'Might leave it for today in case she gets stressed. She's seen a few new faces already today. It'll be better for her in a few days.'

'Yes, you're right, both of you. I wasn't thinking,' Bea said.

Dana waved at Heather over Bea's shoulder. 'Thanks, but another time I'd love that. Must get on and move my hide over. Be seeing you!'

She walked off with a wave, wondering just what Mr. Fitzmartin was doing last night and resolving to go over all her notes on this case. She needed to get to know Bea a lot better before she decided what she would do. Things were not what they seemed, as they say in detective novels. One thing she did know was that Mairi was passing on the story of Bea having escaped from a mental health unit and blatantly strangling the truth about Bea and the dog. Dana had seen that for herself.

As she crossed back over the river and made her way up to the dunes, she saw a woman walking towards her from the direction of the sea and heading back to the village. She recognised her distinctive blue jacket. It was Mairi.

'Well, think of the devil and she's right there...Thought she'd gone,' Dana muttered to herself and wondered if Mairi would stop to chat.

As they approached one another, Mairi smiled and called, 'Nice day!'

'Always is here, whatever the weather.'

'You come here often?' Mairi asked. She stopped walking, looked relaxed, ready to pass the time of day.

'Quite a lot. Doing some scientific research; oystercatchers and how they cope with litter; all those plastic bottles and nets, you know.'

'Oooo. Interesting. Sounds out of my league. I'm just here for the beauty and the wonderful air,' she said, giving a clear message that to enlightened people like her, things scientific were, by definition, soulless.

Dana said, 'Do you live hereabouts?'

'No, no. Caernarvon actually. I'm just keeping an eye on a friend's wife.'

'Oh, why's that? Is she ill? Or, is it something dodgy? Has she run off with the milkman?' Dana said, opting for officious gossip to provoke a revealing reply and using the old adage with an irony that pleased her.

'No, nothing so easy. Simply sad. She's run away from a place of safety you might say. It was a mental health unit. We're all worried about her and I'm the one who's free in the day, so I said I'd keep watch, so to speak.'

'Is she running wild and naked along the beach or something?' Dana enquired, smiling. 'I've been here most days recently, and all day as it happens, and I haven't seen anything odd.'

'She's in that cottage over there.'

She indicated Nest's Point. Dana was intrigued by the new slant. She'd heard the version Mairi had given to Lorcan and Gwyn. She recognised that Mairi wore an air of caring competence and was warmly invested in the friend's wellbeing. That was quite different to the conversation she'd overheard through the chapel window, entirely different.

Mairi continued, 'Her husband's devastated. Doesn't know what to do. I'm walking here every day, hoping she'll speak to me and let me help. It's beyond tragic. We can't just go over and get her because she's threatened to harm herself; you know the sort of thing.'

'Oh, God!' Dana nodded in sympathy. 'I'm going to be here for most days. I'll keep my eyes open. Y'know, I've seen a young woman over there, so I'll make a note of anything and if she seems to be doing something dangerous, I'll phone the police shall I? Or an ambulance perhaps?'

'Oh, no. Don't do either. Really. We want to get the poor darling back without any more trauma, you understand. Here's my number...' She took out one of her cards and handed it to Dana. 'Please do ring. I'd be so very grateful.' She glanced at her watch. 'Blow. Look at the time and I do have to go but good luck with your science thing. Maybe I'll see you here tomorrow?'

'Probably will. Don't worry; Mairi, is it?' she asked, looking down at the card. 'I'm Dana Smythe.' She handed out one of her own private cards, not her business one.

They parted as new acquaintances, smiling and seemingly in complete accord to anyone who saw them.

As Dana continued along the beach to her hide, she was struck with how quickly Mairi had got to the point, and with a stranger. However, she knew she had always inspired confidences; people usually did tell her their secrets, except that when she was a police officer, it usually took a little longer and some persuasion.

When Mairi and Dana had stopped for a chat, Bea had been leaning on the window sill in the cottage, watching the clouds race and she recognised Mairi immediately. Her breath tightened, and she jumped back so quickly she collided with Heather coming back from the kitchen.

'Oh, whatever's the matter? Seen a wee ghostie?' she asked. 'Bea, Bea. Look at me. Look. You okay?'

All Bea could do was point at the figures across the river.

'That's Dana who came here, isn't it? Does she upset you?'

Bea shook her head, continuing to point. 'No, no. Not her, the other one in blue. It's Jeremy's friend. I told you about her. She's here again.'

'She's walking on now, look.' Heather stuck her head out of the window and craned it to see the retreating figure in the blue jacket, then went outside to the end of the building to get a better view.

Bea was rooted to the spot until she returned.

'Gone. Really gone. I saw that bright jacket get in a Range Rover, a white one, and drive off and away. So, don't worry. Look, why don't you take a walk on the cliff, stretch your legs the whiles, get the air? I can mind the livestock - the nursery, I mean. Take wee Archie.'

Bea considered. 'You know, I'll do that. You're right, Heather. She's gone. I'll feel safe with you watching Stella and the pups.' She grabbed her coat, pulled her hair from its plaits and went out. 'Just for ten minutes then. Come on, Arch, just you and me, hey?'

He was at her side in a second and with his front feet on her knees, his tail wagged furiously. He gave little grunts of pleasure and as soon as the door was ajar, he was out and yapping, doing pirouettes and leaping up.

Not bad for your age, Arch!

Bea and Archie took the cliff path behind the cottage and she relished the wind in her face, letting her mind wander to the far horizon that stretched out before her. She walked quickly, recognising that she wasn't fit but enjoying the effort and after about ten minutes she began to feel more in control. The wind took her hair and made a banner of it, pressed her old coat against her like a breastplate and filled her with its power.

She felt the babe give a mighty stir.

'Ooooo,' she murmured and passed her hands across her belly, the familiar caress, and wondered just when this baby was going to make her entrance into this wild, wild world. She breathed slowly and steadily, recognising the smell of the herring as they raced before the fishing boats on the horizon, the scent of the pines from the distant forest down the coast and the sharp tang of the great sea itself.

Mellt and Seren streaked along the beach. 'Away my beauties!' Nest called. They were hunting a hare which raced to the dunes beyond and soon disappeared in the sunny haze of blown sand and sea spray. She laughed and held her heavy belly in a joyous embrace.

'Another false alarm, my cariad, babi annwyl. Even Sister of Earth thought you were about to burst into this world last eve,' she said quietly. 'Ah, the air smells of Winter snows gathering too. The old year is ending, and the new will come soon with you, my little one.' She closed her eyes to imagine the land covered in snow and the fierce storms to come.

The vision was interrupted by a small sound, louder than the wind and the sea. It was a scuffing sound behind her, a boot on the rough stone path. Nest swung round and froze.

'You!' She spat the word. 'Stay away from me. I'll have none of you!' her voice rang out above the drumming of the wind.

Bea felt a spear thrust of fear pierce her body.

Chapter thirty

Dread

I'll manacle they neck and feet together

Sea water shalt thou drink

Prospero – The Tempest

THERE WAS NEST on the cliff top and in front of her was Ithel ap Deykin, crouching like a beast about to spring, and in his hand, he brandished a long sharp knife. Several emotions flitted across his countenance like jagged, broken branches and shredded leaves on a Winter gale: fury, fear, longing, disgust, uncertainty.

But he mastered himself. He stood fully upright and his expression settled into one of burning hostility mingled with lust.

'Ah! Great with child, I see. At last you show yourself to the world. Our Lord Prince will acknowledge it, of course,' he drawled. He paced towards her. 'If the brat sees the light of day.'

Nest laughed. 'You! You threaten me, Ithel ap Deykin? You who cannot get a woman, let alone get a child on her.' She adopted a conversational tone and she had her double-edged reward as he lifted his arm and pointed the dagger at her belly.

She laughed again, but Bea felt her fear as she said, 'The Prince did not father my child as certainly as you would never get the chance to.'

He took a pace forward. 'So, perhaps it was the young warrior you marked with your knife in the throes of your lust, woman.'

'How would you have any knowledge of what men and women do together? And as you seem to know what Yestyn did, you must know he is not the father of my child and I tell you now, should Yestyn come near me again I will kill him, Ithel ap Deykin. Mark me! I will kill him or anyone else who touches me when they are not welcome.'

He laughed himself then and with the dagger he began to trace a design in the air around her, an outline of her body.

Nest stood straight and still and fixed her eyes on his face.

'You will die soon, Ithel, very soon,' she told him, her voice took on the prophetic note of a bard, but Bea could still feel her trembling, despite her bravado.

'And, will that be at your hand?' he asked and sprang forward suddenly to hiss in her face, 'Or will you set your beasts on me?'

He pressed the point of the dagger into the side of her neck, under her ear and she flinched and made to step away from the edge.

'Move and you die, by the knife or the fall.'

She felt his spittle on her face and wiped it off with the back of her hand, defiantly. He roared; his voice powerful even above the noise of the wind. Slowly he pressed the point in so that a thin trickle of blood began to run down her neck. She did not cringe or move away then, kept her eyes locked on his.

Bea felt Nest aching to flee, but she was trapped.

Nest felt the blood running down her neck, over her chest and between her breasts. She smiled grimly.

'I wonder at your fate if you harm me or my unborn babe?' she said as he continued to glare at her, his face so close that she could smell his breath. It was foul.

'You will not be here to know, will you?' he hissed and pressing the dagger into another spot he reached up his hand and took hold of her breast and twisted it so that she cried aloud at the piercing pain and dropped to her knees.

His face was ablaze with excitement and hatred in equal measure and he stepped back to watch her writhing on the cliff top turf, threw back his head and laughed. He licked his lips but as he took a breath to speak, his arms were suddenly gripped from behind and he was dragged away from his victim. He had dropped the knife and cried in alarm, twisted round to discover his attacker, but each way he threw his head he saw nothing but black fronds of fabric, felt the hands holding him bite into his arms like the iron jaws of a man-trap. He screamed, a high short note and tried to gain his feet, scrabbling his heels, squirming his body like a viper in its death throes.

Overhead a race of gulls screeched. 'Ah, the devils come for me,' he cried and let out a thin wail like a terrified girl.

A hand shot forward and stuffed a rag in his mouth so that his cries were ended and only his bulging eyes showed his terror, the whites showing bright against his swarthy skin and greasy black hair. He looked frantically from side to side but then one of his captors took hold of his head firmly and kept it facing forward, even as another bound a black cloth efficiently about his face, save for a gap for his nose, and then round and round his body until he resembled a giant chrysalis. All the while he bucked and squirmed but nothing stopped his captors' progress.

Nest got to her feet unsteadily and looked into the eyes of one of her rescuers, saw one lay a finger on lips and kept silent. There were four of them, the Sisters. Three picked up the wrapped man like a bundle of used animal bedding and carried him off. They walked quickly and purposefully down the slope to the beach, across the trickle of the river, up between the giant sand dunes where they disappeared.

Nest stood and watched; the wind teased her hair from its plaited coronet and made it a corona. She held a protective hand over her belly, but her head was held high as Sister of Earth put an arm around her shoulder to guide her away from the edge of the cliff. Of the wolves there was, as yet, no sign.

'Are you hurt, Sister Nest?'

'Yes, but it is passing now,' she answered as she pressed a hand over her sore breast. 'My pride is more hurt because I did not hear him approach and I should have stopped him. I should have been wary, but the day was fine, and my wolves capered as if they were cubs. I was in ecstasy with them as they ran. If they'd seen him attack me, they'd have killed him. What will you do with him?'

'We will take him to our home in the forest, deep in the forest. Don't concern yourself with him, Nest. All will be well for you and the babe.'

'You'll know if I need you? When my time comes?'

'We will, surely,' she said, smiling.

'Chwaer y Ddaear, how did you know what was happening to me

here?'

The other woman smiled broadly, her face transformed. 'Sister of Air hates him and after we left you that day, she undertook to be his shadow. She would have been on his back like a wild cat if she hadn't slipped and fallen on the rocks below. Such a simple accident but the time it took for her to recover it cost you pain, my dear.'

Nest massaged her bruised breast with one hand and held her belly with the other. Her face showed signs of the strain. She was ashen.

'But you all came. How did you all know? Were you watching?' The Sisters were seers and gifted in the supernatural arts, as was Nest, but she was curious to know how it was they had come to her aid so swiftly. 'Did you fly perhaps?'

Sister of Earth laughed merrily; her face softened and was full of good humour. 'Why, nothing but a bird's whistle. We all have our own bird, the one we can mimic faithfully, and we use the sound to call our sisters in times of great need. We others were in the dunes, yonder and we heard our whistle. That's all.' She laughed again. 'No black arts, so fear not! I told you we would all be nearby.'

Nest smiled. 'Walk down with me, Sister,' she said but as she turned ready to step down the stony path, something moved on the edge of her vision. She stopped abruptly and stared to her right.

''Tis the woman again, the one who has a look of me...' she whispered and reached out a hand. 'Her form glistens in the sunlight. She has a small white dog...Look, can you see her?'

Bea felt the wind buffet her, and as she reached out a hand to snatch at her hair, she saw that Nest was still standing there, but with her own hand outstretched and a smile of wonder on her face. Bea looked down as she felt something touch her leg. It was Archie, pressed against her, watching something intently. 'Can you see her, Arch?' she murmured.

Chwaer y Ddaear looked at Nest. 'I've seen her shadowing you before,' she told her. 'Do you know who she is, recognise her?'

'I feel she is part of me, but a part that is somewhere else, somewhere far distant. Where is it? Who is she?' Nest wondered – but not with any fear in her tone.

'Do you feel any harm coming from her?'

'No, no. I feel I know her in a way. It's wonderful and frightening at the same time,' Nest whispered. She hadn't taken her eyes off the shimmering figure with its long hair streaming in the wind, as if to do so would allow the image to blow away on that very wind.

Sister of Earth said, 'I sense that she is one of your family. She lives in the distant future – yes!' She laughed. 'But she also lives at the very same time that we live here. Nest, Nest, how often have you seen your long dead and still beloved animals out of the corner of your eye, then turned to get a better look only to find they have disappeared. And people, your mother and father? You've seen them when they travel from the spirit world.'

Nest looked at the tall woman with her short black hair, cloaked in kindness and wisdom, then turned her head to Bea again.

'Oh, wait, wait,' she cried as the figures on the cliff edge began to dwindle.

Bea called out to her, 'I'm still here. I can see you, Nest.'

'She's gone,' Nest said, and her voice was bereft.

'I know.'

Nest turned around slowly, her eyes closed, trying to free her mind as she often did when she was looking in the fires or the water. 'How can I reach her when I wish it? Show me the way, if you know.'

'I think you are learning the way unaided. Never fret. These worlds lie next to ours, like the layers of a bulb. She is not gone. I will show you how to draw back the curtain. Come, Nest, come home. You need to rest now.'

They had reached the beach when there was a rush of air behind them, the sound of splashing and a series of quick, joyful yips as Mellt and Seren bounded up. But no sooner had they both pressed their noses against Nest's body, their attention changed to inquisitive and from that to suspicion. The wolves caught wisps of Ithel's scent that clung to her clothes and body. Both lifted their noses into the air and seemed to see the path he had been taken on.

'Come my dears. He has been taken care of. Come, come,' Nest called as they approached her cottage.

The wolves cast baleful glances over their shoulders at the dunes as they trotted after Nest and Chwaer y Ddaear.

Bea followed their gaze across the river, wondering where the Sisters had taken Ithel and what they had done to him, and when she turned to see if Nest and the Sister had reached the cottage, she saw that there was no one on the beach at all. And there were no other fishermen's cottages and boats, nothing but Nest's Point with its Victorian roof. She also realised with a slight shock that she was on the beach and not on the cliff head. She had no recollection of moving at all. She took a few steps forward. Archie trotted closely by her side, his little muzzle lifted high as he watched her.

Chapter thirty-one

Meetings

His art is of such power…

Caliban – The Tempest

BEA WALKED towards the cottage and shrugged off the strange, but not unpleasant feeling of disorientation that always clung about her when she had visited the past. That was how she described it to herself, paying a visit and she understood now that she'd see them again, which lent a buoyancy to her step. And a further marvel made her glow with pleasure; it seemed that Nest could see her, was aware of her in the future. She also saw Archie and Bea resolved to watch him whenever she had another experience; she was desperate to find out what he would do.

'They say animals can be more sensitive to these things than humans, Arch.' He bounced along the path as she spoke. And it's wonderful to be going home to something as marvellous as Stella and the babies. There's Heather too,' she told him as they neared the cottage.

She felt quite close to the older woman after they had exchanged a few details of their lives. Even though she'd worked in a busy environment, she had missed the company of other people because Jeremy had isolated her as surely as if he'd left her on a desert island.

The tide had turned, and the swollen river was beginning its seaward rush, rippling eagerly along to join the limitless oceans. It reminded Bea of children at the end of the school day, running homeward. The earlier clouds were swept away, and the sun had the whole sky to itself to play on the water. The little wavelets became golden serpents racing for the horizon. There was a light in the cottage window, and it felt welcoming. She jumped from rock to rock, not yet with her old agility but promising herself walks and fitness to come and simply a life without the overpowering, stifling presence of

Jeremy.

Heather smiled as Bea walked in. She was sitting by the fire with the dog family.

'Ah, lovely. See how happy Stella is now,' she said as the dog thumped her tail and gave a low welcoming rumble.

'Hello girl,' Bea greeted Stella and the pups. 'If I didn't know they were pups, I'd say they were guinea pigs,' she said, adding, 'but adorable. Your puppies are lovely, Stella,' as the dog heaved herself out of the nursery bed and licked Bea's face, tail wagging low, submissive, secure. She glanced over her shoulder as the little terrier sniffed the puppies and turned back to Bea.

Heather got to her feet. 'Look at him; typical terrier, one front foot held up. Anyway, Bea, I'll be needing to go. Will you be okay? I'm wanted elsewhere; a farm-based emergency at the other side of the island. Another vet is there but I'll have to assist, as I'm on the island already and because it's my day off!' She made a wry face.

'Of course, you go. I'll lock the door and I can always phone my other new friend, Gwyn, should I need anyone. He insisted I put him on speed dial; seems to like being a knight errant!'

They parted fondly, and Bea felt quietly confident about being alone. It felt as though a crisis had passed somehow. She rubbed her hands together absently as she watched Heather walk down the beach and was turning her rings round and round when a thought struck her; the swelling in her finger had gone down and the rings felt a lot looser. She went indoors and found some hand cream to lather over her fingers and after some little pain and much skin pulling and re-application, she finally drew them off. Her finger throbbed.

'There,' she said. She felt relief, surprise and a surge of ice-cold resolve. Grasping the rings in her hand she fetched a hammer from under the sink and went outside. Both dogs looked up briefly and Bea was reassured by their calmness; surely they would hear if anyone were approaching, if there were any danger.

She put both rings on a flat stone on the garden wall and brought the hammer down on them with a force she didn't recognise as her own. Both were ruined in that one blow, but she carried on hammering them, pounding them until both were flattened slivers of white gold and the diamond was powdered to dust. Even before she'd finished her frenzied work the fragments began to move in the breeze, so she fetched a dustpan and brush to gather it all, then she went down the beach a little way and threw it into the wind.

Gone.

Just at that time, Jeremy was standing in front of the window of his hotel room, gazing at the view. He was naked. His arms were folded across his chest and his expression was severe. The whole of the Snowdonia range was before him and the waters of the Menai Straits surged past the island, beautiful and deadly.

'Do come back here before you get too chilled. And don't worry, I'm not being wifey and worrying about your health, I just can't stand cold flesh, chéri,' Mairi told him.

She stretched luxuriously and then wriggled herself up to lie across the huge pillows of the four-poster bed. It was hung with deep wine-coloured velvet and gold brocade. Her hair was spread rippling about her, a cloth of bronze and copper.

He turned and threw her a glance, saying, 'You look like Lucrezia Borgia with your hair so wild and abandoned and all that faux-Renaissance drapery.'

She laughed. 'My God! If only I had half the panache Lucrezia was supposed to have had. I can bring several people to mind whose sudden death by poisoning would benefit society hugely; or perhaps I'll be honest and say, benefit me.'

'That's more like it. Be true to your nature.'

'As are you, Jem. We are two of a kind, chéri.'

'Maybe, maybe,' he said, turning to face her. His expression was dark, and enigmatic. 'But, speaking of pairs, isn't it time you re-joined your loving husband? Shouldn't he be heading for hearth and home about now?'

'Maybe, maybe. But do come here first. I'm not quite ready to go.' She patted the pillow invitingly.

'And yet, I am. So...*do* - go now.'

She didn't move. Her expression remained smiling and confident.

'Is this all the thanks I get after my masterly performance with poor Bea? I actually felt sorry for her and convinced myself she deserved to be cared for in my state-of-the-art psychiatric facility.' Her tone was playful, but he didn't respond.

'Indeed, which is where she will be, as I intend. You've played your part well with Beatrix, so far. I'll say that. And you do give value for money, Mairi, in *all* you undertake. Don should cherish you more. Assets are always worth preserving, I say.' His tone was conversational, casual.

'But do you give value for money, Jem? Remember what you promised me. You are expecting a substantial windfall, you led me to believe, from Bea's inheritances. You're the one with debts, and one of those debtors is me. You promised me a share in the spoils of our little game. Remember?'

'I'll repeat myself, Mairi, maybe, maybe...' He hadn't moved, except to rest his hands on the window sill behind him, his arms outstretched.

Slowly she swung her legs off the bed and sat upright to reach for her hair. Still unhurried, she twisted it into a loose knot on top of her head then secured it with a clip from the bedside table.

'While we're talking about assets, chéri,' she said, and flicked her eyes up and down his body, 'Let's not over-inflate your own worth. And furthermore, it would be a grave error to make me feel undervalued.'

She slipped off the bed to her feet and began to dress, unhurried. She had only a thong, red high-heeled shoes and a nut-brown jersey dress which she slid into last of all.

'Am I to suppose that is intended as a threat?' Jeremy asked, his voice incredulous, as he turned his back on her to look at the view.

She picked up her handbag and took out her car keys.

'Of course, what else? Au revoir, chéri. I imagine we'll be in touch. Now don't go upsetting poor Bea. We don't want her carted off just yet. Now that's my professional opinion, Jem, and you'd be wise to heed it.' Her tone was sharp, clipped and cold.

She walked slowly to the door, opened it wide and without a backward glance, she left. She didn't close it behind her.

'Now,' Jeremy muttered to himself, after he had closed the door and locked it, 'time to pay another visit to my good wife.'

He gave Mairi no more thought at all. His mind was entirely on Bea.

He dressed quickly but, this time, not in black. He fastened up his walking boots with a feeling of anticipation and much satisfaction. He was energised and excited as he snatched the keys of his car. No need for disguise and subterfuge for a man trying to make contact with his sick wife, a wife sorely in need of his help.

The early evening sun gilded the peaks of Snowdonia as he drove along the coast road to Beaumaris. He'd decided to go through the town to take the road to Aberffraw from that side of the island. The tide had turned but the Straits were full and there was a peculiar vibrating flatness to the water. The sandbanks were still invisible, along with the treacherous currents that ran deep and unseen. He loved the danger of this water whenever he sailed with Don MacIntyre. He enjoyed the danger of Don's wife too, but he didn't love her any more than she loved him. She was right that they were two of a kind in some respects.

He increased his speed to 60 mph, dangerous on the narrow and twisting coastal road but he thrilled as the car hugged the road and began to eat the miles. The evening sun glinted on the waters of the Straits and the trees lining the road blended with the waters beyond with a strobe-like effect. Jeremy rarely felt fear and enjoyed the expressions of terror on the drivers of a couple of cars going the opposite way. Laughing he pressed a single key on his hands-free and heard the ring tone.

'Ah, Mrs Smythe,' he said when it was answered.

'Hello there, Mr Fitzmartin.'

'Do you have anything to tell me?'

'I have been waiting for you to make contact again, Mr. Fitzmartin, and I think you asked me to step back a little?' There was a question in her voice.

'Nevertheless, I believe you are staying in that god-forsaken place and I wondered if you had overheard something that I'd be interested in. These villagers are inveterate gossips, I find.'

'I'm glad you asked me actually. Do you want to meet? I'm doing some shopping in Beaumaris at the moment. Maybe…'

'Perfect. I am heading through there shortly, on my way somewhere else. Perhaps a meeting in the bar of the Buckley? About ten minutes.'

'See you then.'

Dana was in the hotel bar in five minutes and she sat at one of the tables, facing the entrance. She had a coffee. When he strolled in, she was a little surprised to see him look so relaxed and remarked to herself that this was not the aspect of a man with a sick wife that desperately worried him. This was a man who had possibly spent some time catching up with a friend, an intimate friend. Dana would have bet money that the friend was called Mairi and she smiled to herself. Things had just become a whole lot clearer in her mind. After the greetings and the offer of coffee, which he declined, Dana produced her camera.

'I have been in my birdwatching hide each day, partly because I do like photographing birds, and it's really great cover, my being in a hide, and handy for keeping a low-key eye on things.'

'And…?'

'She's acquired another dog, from a very recent shipwreck, actually off the island the other night, during the storm, well, when she arrived. Anyway, she seems fond of the dog. I can't say I've noticed anything strange about that. A few locals have visited: the Post Master and a couple of younger men, an older woman. Nothing to note about them. No suspicion of her having any intimate involvement with the men, or the woman, for that matter. Your wife seemed to behave quite rationally, insofar as I can tell from watching her only and having no way of hearing anything. The only person to get an adverse reaction from her seems to be a young woman she met on the cliff when out with the dog. The woman was a little older than your wife, at a guess, I've got a photo of them.'

She showed him the string of shots of Mairi talking to Bea. Mairi appeared relaxed throughout and even solicitous in her gestures and expressions, but Bea looked increasingly panicked and downright horrified by the end of the photo series as she made her way back to the cottage, trying to encourage the big dog to move, her little terrier following.

'Do you know the woman at all, Mr Fitzmartin? Is she a family friend perhaps?'

He smiled, sadly. 'Ah, yes. In a manner of speaking she is, because she is my wife's psychiatrist. And I have to say it would be the reaction I'd expect her to have when faced with Dr MacIntyre. She did escape from her care, after all.'

Dana dipped her head as she put her camera away, thankful to avoid his gaze legitimately because, although she knew her face would be under control, she didn't underestimate his searching glare.

He said, 'Beatrix looked all right otherwise, didn't she?' His voice sounded hopeful to Dana and she watched him carefully as he continued. 'Hmmm. It was when she was faced with the hard truth that she crumbled. Dr MacIntyre has told me about the meeting. It's always the way with people who have a tenuous grasp on the real world. They simply invent their own environment and then panic when it disappears.'

Dana waited.

'So,' He took a slightly shuddering breath and Dana found herself wondering if she had things wrong, whether that woman, Mairi, was really a psychiatrist. She'd check, for sure.

'Yes?' She hoped her tone was suitably encouraging.

'So, I'll contact Dr MacIntyre again to hear what she thinks is the best way forward. I want you to carry on with the surveillance, make sure she's safe actually. I'm on my way to the wretched place now. I don't mind telling you that it has always been one of the most sinister places I know. I just want to say hello to her and reassure her that she can stay there as long as she wants to, if that's what's going to keep her in one place until Dr McIntyre can arrange to get her back to hospital.'

Dana nodded.

'I also need to tell you that, sick as she is, I do still think there may be another man. I've known for some time. She's rather demonised me, I'm afraid, and another man will seem as if he were her salvation, so Dr McIntyre tells me. I need you to keep on working out there. She doesn't think I know she's there, so my arrival may be a shock. Dr McIntyre did advise against my visiting, but I'm desperate to see her. I have to go. I'll only stay a minute. Can you be there on the beach and keep an eye for the early part of the evening, in case she simply runs again? In which case, I'll need you to follow her. Just keep her safe, Mrs Smythe. Keep her safe.'

He stood and offered his hand. 'I'll be in touch.'

They shook briefly. He strode away.

Dana was puzzled and took out her phone to look up Registered Psychiatrists. She was wondering if it was some new approach to treatment that required a psychiatrist to engage in damaging gossip about their patients with strangers they met on a beach – which is what this so-called Dr McIntyre had done after all, not only with Dana herself, but also with Lorcan and Gwyn.

She ran her finger down the screen of her phone. 'Well...well. Who'd have thought?' she said aloud when she found exactly that entry she wasn't expecting.

The barman was passing. 'What's that, Madam?'

'Oh, nothing. Just got some very surprising, unbelievable news. Can't believe it.' She saw his look of anticipation. 'No, not the lottery!'

They both laughed.

Chapter thirty-two

Moment

I pitied thee, Took pains to make thee speak,

taught thee each hour One thing or another…

Prospero - The Tempest

JEREMY STRODE along the beach. He moved like an animal, a predator on the hunt with contained violence in every sleek movement, ready for deployment at a second's notice, aware of everything around him while his eyes were fixed on his prey. He smiled as he approached the cottage. Gulls wove a raucous cloud above him. He was intoxicated with his own feeling of power and anticipated the pleasure of the forthcoming confrontation, confident that he would control every sentence that was spoken, every gesture, every emotion Bea felt. As he neared the cottage, he couldn't help but think about Nest and savoured the surge of triumph that filled him to the core.

'Dead,' he said aloud and smiled.

Jeremy had loathed her from the very first meeting. There was a distinct aura of power surrounding the Welshwoman and he felt drawn to her with the fascination of a mongoose for a snake. And now, finally, she was dead. Gone. The loathing remained finely etched, burnished pleasantly on every fibre of his being each time he brought the death to mind.

He was a hundred metres away when the door to the cottage opened and Bea herself stepped out. She closed it softly behind her and strolled towards the end of the cottage wall that faced the estuary and there she stopped. Her posture was relaxed, and her back was to him. He didn't alter his pace at all and in half a minute he reached the cottage path. He allowed his boot to scuff the gravel and alert her.

She swung round. Her expression was calm with a smile of

welcome hovering on her lips. She froze when she saw it was him.

'Bea, darling,' he called pleasantly and continued his approach.

She swallowed but otherwise she didn't move, caught in the arc of the turn.

It was then that a volley of barking came from the cottage and Archie erupted from the door. When he saw who it was, he balked and his voice altered from aggressive guarding to one of terror, high pitched and squealing. He backed away from the opening of the storm porch to the door and remained at bay, leaning back on his hind legs, screaming his fear. It lasted seconds then he turned and pressed himself into a corner, crouched and shaking.

'It's only me, Beatrix' Jeremy said. His voice was soothing and when he reached her, he took hold of her arm gently, bending a little towards her. 'Aren't you going to say hello at least?'

She said nothing. Swallowed. Her breathing quickened.

'Oh dear. Still not well?'

'No! I mean…'

'Now, now, you don't really know what you mean, do you?' His voice was kindly, concerned and Bea's expression was puzzled.

'You rushed off from home. I've been so very worried, my darling.'

'I…what?' she stumbled through the words.

Jeremy's smile didn't falter.

'Not asking me in for tea? I think you should,' he said and put a little gentle pressure on her arm.

'How are you here? Prague…? It *was* you last night. I knew.' She shook her head. Slowly and with a growing look of confusion, she turned fully to face him and lifted her arm vertically out of his hold. She stretched the hand out in front of her, palm up and stepped back.

'Go away. Go away.'

He sighed. 'A little melodramatic, don't you think? And last night? Hmm, bad dream? What am I going to do to a big strong girl like you? And you are a *big* girl now, aren't you, Beatrix? I did suggest you work on getting to a healthier weight, didn't I? But here with all that bara brith and Welsh butter. It's going to be a bit of a temptation to pile on the kilos, more kilos!'

He stepped a little closer and looked down at her, holding her eyes with his own. His expression radiated compassion.

'Don't come near me.' She dropped her arm, took a step back and felt in her pocket for her phone. Her voice was unsteady.

'I'm going to phone someone,' she said, taking it out. She was shaking and gripped the phone with whitening knuckles. She threw a quick look at the cottage.

'Friend? Phoning a friend? A man, of course. There are always men, Beatrix. Always men.' He shook his head slowly. 'Looking in the hovel for him? Have you got a man waiting in there for you now?' Jeremy's voice held a note of outrage. The breeze caught his fringe and ruffled it angrily.

'No, no. My dogs. Only my dogs.'

'Dogs? More than one? How is that mangy terrier still breathing? Disgusting, isn't it?'

She dragged her eyes away from his and tried to locate the keyboard. It was hard to focus. She found the single key she wanted and pressed.

'Oho, speed dial? Close friend? You know you're not well. You're not making healthy choices at present, are you? I'm your friend, Beatrix, your only real friend, husband, soulmate…' He smiled slowly and held out both his arms, letting them hover for a short time on either side of hers as though to contain a flighty animal, then finally, with an air of failure, allowing them to drop heavily.

'No.'

'No? Again? Is that the only word you can manage?'

There was the tinny sound of a man's voice answering her phone call. 'Hello? Bea?'

'Do answer it, darling,' Jeremy said.

He held her eyes with his own as she moved like an automaton and lifted the phone to her ear.

'Can you come?' was all she could manage before her fingers trembled so much that they released their hold on the phone and it dropped to the floor. It landed on a stone and broke open. Jeremy still held her eyes and he smiled again.

'What do you want from me?' she asked. Her hair had come loose from its plaits and was lifting in the strengthening breeze.

He glanced at her hair in distaste. 'I'm going to get that cut off for you, don't worry. It must be such a nuisance.'

He perched himself on the cottage wall, patting the space next to him. When Bea didn't move, he said, 'Come on, you never know who's watching. At least pretend to be normal and sit next to your husband.'

Bea's expression brightened an instant.

'There's a woman birdwatching in the dunes; she'll see you. She'll help me.' She blurted out the words.

'Birdwatching? How conservation minded.' He patted the wall again, but she didn't move.

'You don't need anything from strangers, Beatrix; I'm with you now. I'm going to take you to a hospital. You'll get help there; you know that. And lovely Mairi will be there for you. She has a clinic this afternoon. Did you know? She's just got a partnership at the private place on the mainland, just outside Bangor. Very exclusive, beautifully secure. No one will know you're there, don't worry.'

He chatted easily, smiling compassionately.

'No. I'm not ill. I'm not going anywhere near Mairi.' Bea's voice was a little stronger and she turned to face him.

'You told me you were going to Prague, to a conference.'

'I did, didn't I? But here I am, here to look after you.'

'You hit me, you punched me. Why would you do that?'

'You were drugged up, my darling. You fell.'

'Drugged? Drugged with what? Did you give me something?'

His expression didn't change, and he didn't answer. He blanked her out.

'I want you to go.' Bea's heart was racing, pounding.

'You think it's going to be that easy, do you?' He laughed, and his tone was pleasant. 'You've always been deluded. Always suffered from an over-ripe imagination, enjoyed pretending, haven't you? But then I suppose you get that from your mother. I'm surprised you didn't take after her and write books. She did so well. All that money and acclaim for making things up.'

Bea was silent.

'What happened to it when mummy died? The money I mean. Hmmm? Oh, I know the party line; she donated it all to literary charities with a few animal ones thrown in. How heart-warming. I'm confident that she passed on a secret little nest egg to you, my darling, but preferably a very large nest egg. Well, what's yours is mine. We are married after all. You really shouldn't keep secrets from me. It's simply unfair. I'm always honest with you. I married you for the money, didn't I? Mummy's money and you an only child, now an orphan too.'

Bea gasped.

Jeremy arranged his features into an expression of deep concern and his voice dripped honey.

'You didn't know why I married you? You thought I latched onto a rabid bitch like you for your personal charms, your witty conversation, sophisticated tastes and alluring body. You supposed I wanted my friends to think I had lost my mind, as you have?'

'You locked me in. You took everything from me.'

'For your own safety, darling.'

He tried to take her hand gently and to anyone who saw them from a distance it would look as though his were the pleading and kindly gestures, hers the aggressive.

He continued. 'A depression like yours can lead to some difficult behaviour patterns. For instance, running off to the wilderness like this, to this ramshackle place on the beach.'

'It's not ramshackle…' The words came out as a plaintive cry.

'Running away from me as though you were fearful. I've had a bit of a job explaining your behaviour to people at work.'

Bea made a sudden movement towards the cottage, but Jeremy stood and took a single long step to block her way. He took hold of both arms again before moving to her side to put one round her shoulder. His every movement was controlled, firm and to someone watching at a distance, it was all compassion.

'Do you know, when we came here before we married, when auntie was alive; oh, she's dead too, isn't she? - well, I did sense that auntie disliked me a little, whereas I positively hated her on sight.'

He turned her so that her face was lit by the evening sun and she had to shield her eyes with a hand.

Inside the cottage Stella began to bark. Bea pulled away from him and moved into the storm porch then to the door. She opened it a little to allow Archie to scurry past her and into the safety within, then pulled it shut and stood with her back against it. The sun was behind him and his outline flamed leaving his features and body darkened and indistinct.

She took a ragged breath; she was desperate to get inside to the dogs, but she had the feeling that the dogs would push past and try to defend her and then he might hurt them. Bea felt the familiar surge of panic welling inside, pushing to explode in one long rending scream.

It was then that she saw a movement behind Jeremy, a blur of blue and black. She froze, stared. She recognised the figure instantly, at least she thought she did. Surely it was Sister of Earth, glimpsed briefly through the hazy veil of gathering mist tumbling down the headland rocks. Then came a spark of light to Bea's left, and down at the water's edge another nebulous figure detached itself from the glint on the waves to stand and look at her before pouring itself back into the flow, Sister of Water. Next, she found her eyes drawn up to the top of the dunes; the dancing grasses flurried urgently then parted for only an instant to reveal amongst them a woman with a streaming hair, Sister of Air. Finally, as the evening sun blazed out fiercely and horizontally across the sea, Bea saw that within the rays themselves stood a figure with long red tresses and red painted lines on her face, Sister of Fire. They were all with her. She felt them. Waiting.

She said quietly, 'This cottage is mine now, Nest left it to me, just to me. I'm staying here for good.'

'We are married. We share all our monies in law. If you remember, we didn't have one of those rather tortuous pre-nuptial agreements, did we? Should you imagine in your wildest ravings that divorce is possible then I'll simply have you committed to a psychiatric institution, probably and NHS one as opposed to the comfy place Mairi runs for the very rich, and then I'll obtain an Enduring Power of Attorney. Mind you, I'd only send you there initially to Mairi's place to preserve my good name; can't have my wife wallowing with the dregs. Then I'd have to develop a narrative that ended with you being expelled from all that caring luxury because they couldn't handle your psychotic episodes – other patients' safety and all that. Actually, you may end up in a secure mental health unit run by the State. I do have a considerable reputation to maintain. I'll be quite distraught, naturally.'

Bea stared at him. Stella didn't stop barking. She was behind the door. She didn't hear Archie.

'There, there, Beatrix, darling, this cottage will be mine, *is* mine. D'you know, I think I may keep it as a holiday let for people on Benefits who need to recuperate from, whatever. The NHS will pay.'

He smiled. His expression was one of a man enhancing a pleasure by taking it slowly.

'Now, we'll go inside while you pack your rags, for form's sake, and then off we go. My car's down by the bridge. I can have you safely in Bangor in an hour.'

'No. The cottage is mine alone. Nest had the deeds tied up tightly in a Trust and I am one of the trustees. It can't be broken.'

He shook his head sadly.

'You have always believed everything people tell you. I should know. You really are quite, quite malleable. A lump of clay, *lump* being the best description.'

Bea stood up straight. It was an awkward feeling because for so long she had been trying to make herself smaller, to disappear. She forced herself to face him squarely.

'I'm not going anywhere ever again with you. You should go now. My friend is here.'

She looked over his shoulder as a figure emerged from the glare of the sunset.

Was that a cloak – a raised dagger?

She blinked, the image was gone but what wasn't, and in itself surprised her, was the strength of her conviction as well as the strength of her voice as she spoke to Jeremy. Both had let her down in the past.

He reached out to take her arm again, but she stepped back.

'No, don't touch me – don't ever, ever again!'

'Come quietly or not. It's all the same to me, Beatrix, but you're coming.' His voice was soft, but his tone held menace and certainty.

'I am not coming. I'm not.'

Jeremy started to reach for her again, but another man's voice stopped him mid movement.

'She said she wasn't coming with you and I think you should listen.'

Jeremy turned slowly to confront the intruder. He took in the appearance of the newcomer. He was tall, powerfully built, dark, angry. He had come down the path from the cliff.

'Who's this, Beatrix darling?' he asked Bea, over his shoulder.

The man answered for himself. 'I'm Dr Roberts and I am a friend of Bea. I said I think you should listen. She wants you to go.'

Jeremy smiled; composure unbroken.

'My wife has a doctor already, thanks. She needs to see her now, as a matter of fact. As you seem to know each other, perhaps you could see to these dogs for a while? It sounds quite frantic in there. I need to get my wife to hospital,' he said.

'Jeremy, I am not going to a hospital. I don't need to go. Please just leave me alone. I'm getting a solicitor. He'll contact you.' Her voice was low, but she faced him.

Jeremy gazed at her steadily, his expression laden with regret and pity. He turned to Gwyn Roberts and told him, 'I'm afraid my wife has been ill for some time, despite what she tells people. It's a complex problem. Probably not within the remit of a local GP.'

Gwyn said, 'Probably not, if indeed the diagnosis of a GP were needed, or any diagnosis for that matter. You're under a huge misapprehension, both about Bea, who isn't ill, and about me. I'm not her GP, I'm her friend.'

'Friend? Really?' Jeremy's tone was amused and tolerant. He shook his head, smiled. 'Yes, my wife does have a talent for making new, and rather temporary friends. Beatrix, darling, do come now.'

She stepped back, kept her eyes on him and Gwyn moved to stand by her side.

Jeremy said, 'Fine. Have it your own way then, darling. I can see I'll have to leave her here for the short term, but I'll be back.' He took hold of Bea's arms as before, tenderly, gazed down into her eyes. 'All right don't worry. Look, you stay here if you want to. Another few days may do you good.'

'I'm never leaving the cottage.'

Gwyn Roberts stepped into Jeremy's path. He was slightly taller than Jeremy and much broader in the shoulders, and although he was much slimmer, Jeremy was lithe and muscled. They were face to face, could feel each other's breath.

'You heard her,' Gwyn said. 'I think you need to give her some space. Never mind suggesting she stays *for the short term*. She can stay for as long as she needs to, surely?'

Jeremy's expression showed puzzlement, his voice polite disbelief.

'Excuse me? Beatrix is my wife. *My wife.* So, it's not for you to say where she will be, or for how long. And I'll be looking after her and not some casual local friend, or whatever you think you are to her.'

He inclined his head slightly and made a slight gesture of the hand to indicate he wished to pass, but Gwyn was immobile.

'Get out of my way,' Jeremy said, quietly and using both hands he pushed Gwyn violently in the chest so that the bigger man was forced to stagger backwards. But he kept his balance and in a single lithe movement he came forward again and punched Jeremy in the stomach. The action startled Bea. Jeremy doubled up but made no sound other than a soft 'oomph!'. He straightened slowly until he and Gwyn were face to face again. He didn't appear to be in pain.

'Don't come back,' Gwyn said. 'And that includes any midnight prowling you had in mind.'

'Move.'

Gwyn stepped aside with insolent ease and Jeremy stalked away down the path and on to the beach.

Jeremy called to Bea over his shoulder, 'See you soon, darling.'

Chapter thirty-three

Then and now

By foul play, as thou sayest, we were heaved hence…

Prospero - The Tempest

'OH GOD. OH GOD,' Bea whispered. She remained against the door, stiff, shaking.

'You *married* him? *That's him?*' Gwyn was incredulous. 'What a cool bastard. What were you thinking? Fit too, and I don't mean I fancy him either.' His expression was grim. 'I wasn't punching a cushion; almost broke my fist! I'll have to hit him harder next time he comes throwing his weight about.'

She shook her head, not listening, staring after Jeremy's striding figure. 'I don't know how I came to marry him. I think I remember liking him…it's all a blur.'

'You're crying again, Bea.'

'Am I?' she put her hands to her face and looked surprised to feel the wetness. 'No wonder I'm crying. You would,' she said.

'No. I'd kick him senseless daily. Yeah, just for the smug look on his bloody weirdo bastard face.' His own face was red with anger, his voice savage.

Bea stared at him. 'Yes,' was all she said. Her hands dropped to her sides.

He took a long look at her and let out a long breath that was more to expel his temper than to exhale.

'You look drained,' he said gently. 'Come on, let's get you inside, out of this bloody blinding sun, for one thing. Trust the sunset to do a wow display just when you don't need to celebrate.'

He gathered her towards him and away from the door but before he could reach round her for the door handle, she was in his arms and sobbing uncontrollably. All he could do was stand there, with his arms round her, pat her and occasionally murmur the standard, 'There, there.'

Both dogs began barking again.

'Come on, Bea. Inside. The dogs and pups need you and you need to wipe your eyes on a proper hankie and not on my shirt. Good Lord, I'm all soggy now – ewww, is that snot too?'

She stepped away from his arms.

'Oh sorry – probably. I do need a hankie, sorry.' She wiped her hand down the mess on his shirt front and then transferred it to the side of her jeans.

'Great. Let's go,' he said. He planted a kiss on her forehead as he turned her bodily to face the door. 'Oh God, sorry! You seemed to need it.'

'Did I? Sorry,' she answered automatically as she opened the door and let out the frantic dogs. Behind her in the room, Stella's puppies were stirring and mewing loudly.

'Look, we've said enough sorries for a lifetime, Bea, and I've only just met you. Look, take the dogs down the beach for a wee or something and I'll get the kettle on.'

The dogs took themselves onto the little pebbled garden patch and were back at Bea's side in a minute. They went indoors together, Stella to her pups and Bea to sit on the rug beside her, stroking Archie who had flown onto her lap.

She stared into the glowing embers of the fire and, before she could drag her eyes away, she felt the familiar draw of the distant past. She wiped her eyes with her palms. She caught the scent of herbs and smoke mingling and then another scent, something cooking in the pot that hung over the fire.

Pottage, she thought and glanced down to look at the pups but saw only the familiar curve of two grey backs, her wolves.

'Not mine, not mine. Nest's …it's Nest…'she murmured.

A voice called to her from the other side of the hearth.

'Bea, Bea, can you hear me? You all right? Bea…' said the man.

'Llewelyn? Why are you here again?' she asked but he looked puzzled and didn't answer, just stared.

She rose, spilling the terrier onto the floor and staggered over to the settle. She lowered herself clumsily but urgently onto the rug in front of it, moving as if in great discomfort.

'My Lord Prince, what ails? Help me, do,' she gasped as she rolled onto her knees and grabbed hold of the side of the settle, trying to get up again, wincing, as though in pain now.

He was shocked. 'Llewelyn? Prince? What...? Bea, it's me, Gwyn. Are you okay?'

Bea said, 'My Lord, help me up, would you? I fear I am the size of a cow. And this babe is so desperate to enter the world it wriggles like a shoal of herring in the net.'

Then she laughed and stretched her hands up to him. Gwyn took them, and he pulled her up then holding her round the waist he led her to the wooden rocker by the hearth and lowered her into it.

'What chair is this, Lord?' She glanced at the rocker's arms but then lost interest and carried on her own theme. 'You did not think to become a body servant at this time in your life, did you, cariad?'

Gwyn bent down to look into her eyes, searching for a physical sign of this strange behaviour. He leaned forward and rested each hand on the arms of the chair so that he could look into her eyes. He was worried.

'Llewelyn, Lord, even a body servant should not be so familiar!' She pushed him gently away, smiling up into his face, then as if on an impulse she stretched up and taking his face in both hands she kissed him on the lips. It was a gesture that seemed to Gwyn to be familiar to her. He shivered suddenly.

'Ah, someone brushing my shade,' he murmured.

'Why, Lord?'

'Oh, nothing. Do you know me?'

'Do I know you? Do I know myself? Now why would you ask me that? What's the matter with you? And you didn't tell me why you are here again.'

The bastard husband had spoken of a psychiatrist and for the first time Gwyn wondered if he were speaking the truth. So, he decided to follow where Bea led in this strange game. He said:

'I'm here to help you, you know that. Go on, give me my full title. I like to hear it.' He spoke with a confidence he wasn't feeling.

'And how well I know it. You are shameless, wanting to hear yourself addressed thus, but I'll indulge you if the babe allows me respite for a breath.' She sat back and took a few deep breaths. 'You are my own Llewelyn, Prince of North Wales and Lord of Snowdon, and more importantly my own true friend and first love. Obviously, Cormac loved me too,' she said and looked pointedly at her stomach and patted it.

She smiled, gazing up at him and waiting for his next question.

'Do you know the year, cariad?' he asked, using the familiar endearment she had used to sooth her too.

'What? Why the questions, Lord? You seem strange, out of sorts. I will humour you. 'Tis the year Anno Domini 1228. So, are you content?'

Gwyn smiled at her. 'I am content, cariad,' he said then asked, 'What do I look like to you?' He patted her hands. 'Tell me. I command it.'

'Look like? Look like? Are you becoming vain in your old age, Llewelyn? There is my silver hand mirror, the gift for my birth day. You may gaze on yourself.'

'Humour me.'

She pretended to study him, turning his head this way and that, tilting her head to get a better view.

'You look as ever you did when you were a raw boy throwing water on me out there on the beach.'

'I insist. Describe me, what I wear, my clothes this day, anything. There is a strange look in your eyes, and I think you might be running a fever, or you may have sand blurring your vision. You are flushed as a berry.'

She sighed in pretend exasperation. 'Blurring my vision! I'Faith, I shall tell. You wear your dark green surcoat, black doeskin boots, hose...let me see...' She bent forward to lift his jumper, 'Ah, yes, dark blue. Your belt is decorated with chased silver florets and holy crosses. Now, more...Ah, your cloak, over there on the trestle is wool, a rich deep red; the embroidery on the hood and collar was done by the Princess herself, and it is fine and beautiful indeed. You want more?'

He nodded sternly, which made her grin.

'Well, the design is of leaves and roses worked in thread of gold and silver with a touch of red on the roses. There is black wool as the design base behind the motif and on the shoulder of your cloak is a fine and fierce red dragon. The silk thread will have been costly and most likely came from a land far away, the far East lands across the seas. Will that suffice, Lord?'

He smiled then and knelt in front of her, resting his hands loosely on the chair arms.

'Go on; now describe my person, my body.'

'Why?'

'Why? Because it is my wish. Your eyes have a distant look and I think you may faint. I wish to keep you awake so that you can birth this babe.'

She laughed heartily, and he found himself joining in. In fact he'd had no rouble adapting himself to the medieval phrasing she used as she spoke. It was his own specialism, after all.

'Dirty hair,' she said and pulled out a long strand. 'This could be washed with a rinse of rosemary for dark locks.' She bent forward and sniffed it. 'Pheeww. Yes, a wash.' She pulled at his face, 'A shave, apart from this of course, and that needs a trim, a princely trim.'

He felt a tug on his upper lip and put his own hand there to find his fingers on hair, a moustache, a long one, but the discovery was not shocking. Of course he had his moustache, all nobles and princes in Gwynedd wore face hair thus, but there was one more detail he had somehow misplaced in his mind. It niggled at him.

'Indulge me again, cariad, so that I can be sure you are well after that little fall you had. I fear you banged your head.'

'I did? I cannot recall!'

'There, see. So, indulge me further and say which of the endearments I use for you, my friend and love, do I use the most? Hmmm?'

Gwyn was confused by Bea's sudden change of perceptions and at the same time he had a strong sense of déjà vu. The few facts she gave him were familiar to him as a historian yet the relationship she was beginning to describe was also something he felt wholly familiar with and valued, something that was part of his very existence. And Bea, Bea was someone he valued above riches, any riches: gold, silver, precious gems, land – his very crown. The lead he offered her was one he hoped would say the name she thought she owned just now. He had to be sure, that little niggle had to be quietened.

She rubbed her side and her belly and settled herself more comfortably then pretended to think deeply.

'Let me ponder this. Now, the usual one is *witch*, but I would that you did not call me that in the hearing of any other because we know full well the way people and of course, the Church, view witchcraft. Then there's *cariad*, of course and *my love*, and *little weasel* then *woman*. Mostly you say, *my Nest.*'

She held his eyes with hers with an intensity that made his breath quicken.

'Nest,' he said, wonderingly and took hold of her hands. 'Nest.'

'Nest, yes. Why, my Lord, have you forgotten?'

'No, my Nest,' he said. 'I have remembered I married Joanna of England and perhaps I should have married you.'

'Too late, Llewelyn,' she said cheerfully, 'We are old loves and comfortable, but while the babe is quiet, do you bring this up because something has happened with the Princess? What is it?'

'Nothing has happened. It's just I feel so content here, with you. I am the Prince and you are Nest and I would guess that your child will be a girl and will be Nest also. Am I right?'

She nodded. 'Of course. The babe is quieter now and rests herself. Did you know that? Babes go to sleep when they are in their little nest and they wake up and wriggle, just as when they come into the world. Llewelyn. Llewelyn are you asleep?'

He was sitting on the floor next to the rocking chair by the hearth, his head resting against her shoulder. The dog, Stella, and her litter slept, Archie lay sleeping on her knee again and Gwyn slept too, but what Bea saw was Llewelyn and her wolves, all dozing, and she closed her eyes contentedly and joined them.

It was dark when Stella woke and began a noisy cleaning of her pups as they wriggled and rolled over each other, squealing and grunting. Eventually all four found a teat to latch onto and began suckling. Archie jumped off Bea's knee and went to the water bowl near the hearth, lapped determinedly. Of the humans, it was Gwyn who roused first.

'What on Earth...?' he muttered as he straightened up and then grimaced. 'Eeew, stiff neck.'

He screwed his face up as he rubbed it and his eyes fell on the feeding pups.

'Noisy little piglets.'

'What?' Bea said drowsily. She rubbed her face with both hands, tried to focus her eyes.

'Ah, awake now?'

'Obviously. Why are you here?'

'You called me, remember? Jeremy, the arrogant arse husband. Recall him at all?'

'Jeremy.' Her voice was toneless, resigned as though speaking his name was a statement of fact. 'Yes.'

'You've been asleep, well, we all have, the family included. Must have been the strain. Are you all right, Bea?'

'I don't know, I really don't. Sometimes I think I'm going mad. That's what he says too. Maybe he's right.'

Gwyn got up to mend the fire. 'No, no,' he soothed, 'But I think you need to tell me a bit more about him, what he's done. I hated his guts on sight; so don't think you haven't got a sympathetic ear,' he said.

She didn't answer, covered her face with her hands, hiding it.

'Okay, maybe you're right,' he said, 'You've not known me long and I can be an interfering prat, don't argue...' He watched her for a reaction and when he got none he said, 'Okay, you're not arguing. Fair enough. Tea then? Wonder what they used in medieval Wales when they needed the equivalent displacement activity, ice breaker, palliative? Hmmm? Don't know? Tea it is then.'

He went to make it, wondering how to talk about what had happened earlier, her hallucinations, murmuring to himself.

'She thought she was a medieval woman, Nest, in fact. Wait…' He stopped, holding the kettle under the dry tap, his hand poised to turn on the water. 'Me too - but not the woman bit - I had a moustache. I was…I was Llewelyn, Llewelyn Fawr.' He felt his smooth upper lip with his free hand.

He turned on the tap. 'Maybe there's something in the water here? Powerful hallucinogen?'

He made the tea in a daze and didn't notice the weather had turned and rain was hammering against the kitchen windows. When he took the tray in to her she was drawing the curtains and ran past him to do the same in the kitchen.

'Feel better now?' he asked and handed her a mug when she sat down again on the rocking chair and took Archie on her knee. Gwyn took the old settle on the opposite side of the fire.

'Not really. Gwyn…?'

'Yes?'

'What did I do earlier? Was I myself? Y'know, did I sound as though I was me? I mean, Did I get mixed up about things?'

He took a long drink of tea, trying to compose a tactful answer but finally he decided the simple one would be kindest. If he were to get straight to the point with no messy prevaricating and strangled tactless stumbling it would also be the quickest way to discover what had happened earlier to her and to him too, and perhaps what had happened to her in her marriage.

He said, 'Not mixed up, in fact you were very clear, but as *Nest*, medieval Nest, who once lived in Aberffraw, maybe in this very cottage. It has got medieval walls on most of the downstairs, hasn't it?'

She said, 'Yes. It is medieval and yes, Nest, the first one lived here. Llewelyn Fawr had it built for her. I know all about her, Gwyn. I visit her life, if you know what I mean? Can you imagine it? Was I talking as though I were her?' The explanation tumbled free.

'Yes, you were. Bloody hell. It was a bit confusing at first, then I got interested, as it's actually my own field of study. Then...' He paused and looked into her eyes. 'I was there too. I thought I was Llewelyn for a few minutes. Funny thing was, I felt a moustache on my face, physically felt it, a long one, long and drooping at the sides. You were pregnant, weren't you?'

'Nest was.'

'What am I saying? Yes, of course.' He laughed. 'Go there often?' he enquired. 'The past, I mean.'

Taking him at face value Bea answered, 'Only since I came here. It's always been a magical place, but now I've come here to live, it's wrapped itself round me, the magic of the place and the past, past events, I guess. I've been seeing what happened to Nest, what she's doing as though it's happening right now. I somehow hear her thoughts and sometimes I feel as though I *am* her, so to speak.'

'I've got all night, well, not *all* night. I'm not inviting myself; I meant all evening. Will you tell me everything? I mean, please, please tell me,' he begged. 'I'm really interested, not just saying it. I pride myself, as does the wider academic community, on being somewhat an expert on the period in question.'

He was staring at her intently and it took a little while for Bea to focus and begin to speak. What didn't help was that when she met his eyes, they seemed to be in a swarthy face with a long dark moustache and with piercing dark eyes.

'It's just that...' She shook her head, unsure how to tell him what she wanted to.

'Go on, I'm fascinated. And I mean it; I'm not making fun.'

'It's just that you look so like him, Llewelyn, the Prince. Llewelyn Fawr.'

He laughed delightedly.

'He's one of my greatest heroes; you know that? No of course you couldn't as we've only just met.' He paused, thoughtful. 'Only just met, but I do feel that you are familiar to me, so very familiar, even more so after your little time travel episode earlier. See? Yes, I do believe you. I might be an historian and as such work with facts much like a scientist or a detective; but, as a man I have a great inclination to believe in parallel worlds and ghosts, spirits, presences, whatever you like to call them. I'm in sympathy with the very concept. Maybe that's because I'd give ten years of my present life for an hour's time travel to see and feel for myself what it was like in 13th Century Gwynedd, Llewelyn's Gwynedd.'

His face was lit with the passion of the idea.

'I've done it, Gwyn,' she told him quietly. 'I know that the first Nest lived then, and she and Llewelyn were friends.'

'They were teenage lovers, it seems, from what you said earlier,' he reminded her and as his eyes met hers again, he felt a jolt of energy so powerful that his body tingled with it.

'I know, I know.' Bea stared at him, her own expression puzzled.

'Tell me what's happened to you, Bea,' Gwyn said. 'Tell me why you married that arrogant sod and why you ran away; that's what you did, isn't it?'

She nodded and as she searched for the words, she began to loosen her hair and comb through it with her fingers.

'You look like Nest, don't you?' he said. 'I've seen photos of her when she was young. I mean the present-day Nest of course. Thomas has a snapshot of him and his wife, Beti and Nest, sometime in the 1960s. It's pinned behind the counter,' he added, almost as an afterthought. 'But I've got a feeling you look like the medieval one too. Am I right?'

'I think so, *if* I've been sort of time travelling or dreaming and not having an elaborate psychotic episode. The Nest I've seen, does resemble me, or I her. There is a family likeness. Nest and Mum and me all looked alike. I loved that.'

'All beautiful then?' he said, his voice quiet, serious. Bea didn't register the comment. 'Tell me about what he did to you, Bea – Jeremy, I mean; why you had to leave.' He shook his head. 'No, what'm I thinking? No, tell me what you've been seeing since you came back here. I'll only be raging mad if I hear what your husband has done. I want to hear about what you've been seeing first, so…'

She looked uncertain. 'I've not explained all of this to anyone else. I thought people would think I'm mentally ill, with Jeremy saying just that and telling everyone at work. While I've been here, it's been so strange, petrifying at times, but truly, truly wonderful too.' Her face was lit with excitement.

So, she told him all about Nest and Llewelyn and the period in their lives that she had slipped into. He was absorbed by her story and whenever she mentioned any historical fact, he would nod slowly, occasionally he asked her to explain where something was located, such as a forest down the coast, the fishermen's cottages on this beach, the shape of the estuary and the dunes which changed all the time. He wanted to know about agricultural and domestic details, the weapons and use of horses, their harness and the decorations they used, the saddles. He was fascinated by her detailed descriptions of the Prince's llys, the fabrics, ornaments, floor covers, everything.

He was thrilled with her knowledge of social hierarchies and ownership of goods and animals, such as what estate of man or woman was allowed to own a fine palfrey, a destrier or the different hawks for hunting. At those moments he would consider and murmur comments, 'Of, course, only the Prince would have the Spanish-bred destrier. And, you know what, Bea, they were astounding craftsmen; metals, jewels, fine pottery and silks, yes, trade with the Far East was lively…' or he would say something such as, 'Definitely could be what happened. I could check evidence of coastal erosion.'

She talked for almost two hours and he asked questions, very sensitively, checking her story for continuity and asking for details of the culture, the principal people, their relationships, attitudes and what she had heard of their ambitions.

Gwyn wondered, 'How come you understood the language? I expect the people spoke medieval Welsh and early English, possibly Norman French at times.'

'I don't know. I just understood everything as though I was one of them.'

When she'd done, he said, 'God! How I wish I could travel with you! How fantastic. I can hardly believe it. Y'know, you couldn't make it up, Bea, well, not unless you were researching in my field, at my level. It was so consistent it was like a novel. You should write one.' He was excited.

'Mum was a writer, a famous one, as a matter of fact. Biographer,' she said thoughtfully.

He smiled. 'Must be in the genes then. But if you're crazy, I want some of that. Right now, what I want is food. I'm starving. Got any eggs?'

He was up on his feet before she could answer and off to the kitchen where he made them omelettes which they ate with chunks of bread and washed it down with coffee. They ate it by the fire, but before they did, he'd given Archie and Stella some tea and let them both out of the door. It was still raining hard and both dogs were only out for a minute then came dashing back to the shelter of the cottage.

The meal over, Bea sat back and wondered what she'd done. He seemed to believe her, she felt sympathy coming off him in waves and he was enthralled by her knowledge of the 13th Century. She was positive she hadn't heard all the historical detail anywhere else. She knew she couldn't have absorbed all that information from a couple of documentaries, and she didn't read non-fiction even when she had time to read.

'Gwyn, I was wondering… I mean…can you stay over tonight?' she asked him, and he grinned, the sort of grin she would have found intensely annoying if she hadn't begun to like him. 'I mean, with me and Archie, Stella and the kids.'

'Kids – yeah, I like that. You don't think Jeremy would ever be dissuaded from his plans by bad weather?'

'Never,' she answered. Fear wormed its way into her heart.

'Well, it's only nine o'clock. On a more serious note tell me about what Jeremy has been doing to you, if you feel up to it, that is. I've a feeling this is the creepy psychological thriller, showing in the next cinema studio in a multiplex. I've heard the block buster historical romance. Time for a touch of the nasties.'

She sat down next to Stella on the hearth and stroked her. Almost absentmindedly she picked up two of the pups and lay them in her lap as she tried to get her thoughts in order. Archie sat next to Gwyn on the settle and he made a pantomime of shock before giving the older dog a scratch behind the ears, which Archie didn't seem to mind.

'It's funny, it's feels okay to unburden yourself to a stranger. Yes, okay...' she said as he raised his eyebrows and looked offended. 'You're less of the stranger now, I'll admit. It's just that you're not someone who has known me for a long time and already has an opinion of me that can be altered, perhaps for the worse. I told Heather, the vet, a little about what he's done because she was so sympathetic and wise, and it was quite a relief in a way. She wasn't a bit judgemental. But when I told Thomas who I've known all my life, I was just ashamed of myself for letting Jeremy treat me like that. I only told him a little as it was, and I felt awful. I couldn't bear to have him think badly of me. I should have known better. If I'm honest I do wonder if I'm beginning to experience a mental health problem. Maybe I was – I am – losing grip on reality and that's why I allowed him to treat me like a doormat.'

'I won't judge you either, only if you get your history wrong. By the way was Jeremy in your 13th Century experience?'

She considered that. She was quite surprised to entertain the idea that the people in her life could have had parallels in Nest's time, but then Gwyn and Llewelyn did seem to be similar in their outlook on life.

'I suppose he could be; Ithel the bard was a poisonous toad and he hated Nest with a passion. Jeremy is too clever to be channelling Yestyn who was a raw young noble, what's more, he's probably too low a status in the nobility for Jeremy to channel.'

She told him about her life for the past year or two and when she was finished, his fists were clenched and his face pale.

'I've only met him once, but I could wring his neck for what he's done to you. If I'm honest I could wring his neck for just being himself. Everything the man said annoyed me intensely, and I'm easy going. I have to be; well, there're enough egos jiggling round in the media, TV especially, that my own over-inflated ego doesn't stand a chance. But you, Bea, you need to be more easy-going and relaxed about things, otherwise you'd have a breakdown every day.'

'But aren't you supposed to be the star, the presenter of the TV thing you do?' she said.

'*TV thing.* Right... Puts me in perspective. I'm the *presenter* of the facts, the historical facts. That's *all*, a facilitator not a TV personality. I won't do game shows and stuff like that.' He stopped and gave her a quizzical look. 'I'll tell you all about my life another time, hey? You can tell me about yours too, mind, not more of the Jeremy bits, except if you want to unburden, get it off your chest, y'know.'

'I thought you came over a little arrogantly when we met,' she told him thoughtfully.

'Don't remind me. What a prat I was - am.'

She shook her head, dismissing the idea but her expression was serious. 'How am I going to deal with him, Gwyn - get rid of him, finally?'

'That I don't know, not yet,' he told her.

He got up and walked over to her and bent down to take both her hands in his. He didn't pull her to her feet, just lifted each hand in turn to kiss.

'You need tea.'

'I'm awash with it,' she said, 'I need whisky, but I've got none.'

Chapter thirty-four

Distress

Be not afeard. This isle is full of noises…

Caliban - The Tempest

GWYN STAYED with Bea again that night because she was terrified of Jeremy returning in the dark. The question was, would he continue his now open harassment, or would he resort to more subtle means? For the first time since she'd returned, she slept in her old bed upstairs and Gwyn bedded down on the settle with cushions and brychans, so that he could keep watch over Stella and the 'kids'. Archie was taken up with Bea and lay next to her.

As she slipped between the cotton sheets of her bed, she felt a wave of nostalgia wash over her as well as blissful physical comfort, but she didn't sleep well. She dreamed about Jeremy following her endlessly round rocks on a bleak Winter beach, only to turn a corner and find herself in a dreary hospital corridor with swinging doors that lead to more and more stark white corridors. The tide was coming in and the corridors were filling rapidly with sea water that clutched at her legs. There were no other people in sight, yet Jeremy's voice was behind her, urging her onward, onward. Twice she found a door marked Exit, but each was locked, and each time she rattled the door and screamed only to have it open and a wave of sea water sweep her back.

Bea was woken at last by screeching gulls early in the morning. When she managed to focus her eyes, she felt a quiver of fear at the strangeness of the ceiling and the subdued light in the room. It was long agonising seconds before she plucked up the courage to turn her head. When she did and recognised that everything was happily familiar, she felt a rush of joy and propped herself up on her elbow to absorb the homely sights and sounds.

Eventually she climbed out of bed and shuffled slowly to the window, opening it wide to let in the cool air. It was a bright day at its beginning, she let her eyes wander to the far side of the river and the dunes awash with their undulating sea of grasses, painting the sky they touched cerulean blue.

'So tired,' she muttered and dragged herself back to bed where she fell on the top of the covers with the abandonment of a weary child.

Archie hadn't woken up. Bea couldn't move for exhaustion and she welcomed the physical sensation even as she felt her mind begin roaming on the journey to the distant past with the ease of a frequent traveller. Her eyes were closed and to all intents and purposes she was sleeping and as she did, she smiled.

Nest and the wolves were walking through a huge forest that edged the shore beyond the estuary. It was midday and the sun pierced the canopy in myriad shafts of light; arrows of gold shot by celestial archers. It was silent, the mixed leaves underfoot deadened sound and gave a spring to her step that she appreciated, now that her pregnancy weighed so heavily. She rested one hand on the edge of the scrip she carried and the other alternately rubbed her belly or curved round it in an attempt at support that was more comforting than practical. A little way from her, Mellt and Seren trotted along contentedly, snaking their way through the sparse undergrowth with ease, stopping now and then to sniff something or lift their noses into the streams of scent that were unknowable by humans.

She had been to visit Alis, a woman who lived alone in the forest since her husband died last Winter. Her children were grown and gone; her son, Gwilam, was the Prince's blacksmith and her daughter, Angharad, was that favourite maid of Joanna. She'd died some months ago in childbed; now Alis was suffering a great sadness.

Nest thought about the young woman as she walked homeward.

Sister of Air could do nothing for Angharad but ease the pain. Such a huge child to be breached and lodged so firmly in the birth passage. Poor Alis wanted Sister of Air to cut the girl's belly and free the child. Angharad was unconscious and Alis knew she would not live. All that blood she lost. Her husband was so fearful, would not allow it and so, lost both of them, as has Alis.

Of course, Nest's thoughts turned to her own forthcoming birth. Although she had seen her descendants in the swirling waters and in the flames and knew she was the first of a long line of women named Nest, she still dreaded anything amiss such as her own death or infirmity. The Sisters had hold of Ithel, yet there was Edith who hated her and had the ear of Joanna, who suspected her of adultery. And there was Yestyn, Yestyn who loathed her but still lusted after her.

Tis natural to fear when birth is coming so soon, she mused. *I must take tea of rosemary. It will ease my tensions and I will wash my hair with lavender flower soap to lighten my mind and soothe me. All will be well,* Nest told herself.

One of the laundresses in the llys told Nest that Alis had not been seen recently and they both agreed they were worried that she would be consumed by her sadness.

But she drank the rosemary tea I made for her. It is a good herb to soothe any sufferer and rosemary is for remembrance. How she cried when we spoke of poor Angharad; 'tis only to be expected, especially when she saw me with my child so soon to be born. But we must remember our sorrow and loss to feel present joy. Still, such sorrow is hard in the bearing. The oil of lavender I left will help her sleep too and it will ward off illness. It is too true that those who mourn often fall prey to common ailments.

She breathed deeply, relishing the mixed scents of the forest, the call of the birds and the hum of the insects. Here grew oak, hazel and birch and a smattering of pine, all with their own characters and habit. Nest loved them all.

I am glad to do what I can for Alis. Well, I have burned the sage branch and taken it all around her home. I love the scent and it will cleanse the place of all evil and purify the air. Maybe she will come and help me, as she said, after the babe is born, when my Nestie is born. The Sisters will welcome her.

She soon came to the ford in the river at Aberffraw.

In Bea's dream state she saw the river creeping out from the marshes and heading joyously for the sea, and on the far side she saw a huddle of huts and cottages round the Prince's llys. There was no stone bridge, of course, not until the early 1700s, she remembered.

'Come Mellt, come Seren!' Nest called as the wolves had lagged behind in the dunes. She heard Seren yip as they chased some prey and left them to their hunt.

I will visit Mother and Father, and leave these jewels on their graves, she told herself and fingered the beautiful shells in her scrip that she had found on the beach earlier.

Oh, I feel so weary now, but it is only that I carry a heavy nestling,' she thought, and rubbed vigorously at her swollen body while she walked.

She soon crested the little knoll where the church of St Beuno stood. There was a tiny field of wooden crosses, each marking the head of a burial mound and she walked slowly to one that rested near an ancient oak. They were both together there, her father first; his body had been washed into a cove up the coast; her mother was laid with him a few years later.

'There Mother, there Father,' she said and bending with difficulty, she set out the coloured shells around the base of the cross. 'May God keep and protect you. And in His mighty wake may all the old gods of the earth and air, the sea and the wind shower blessings upon you and your descendants and…' She laid a hand on her belly, '…may they pass easy into this world and kindly out of it.'

She straightened up slowly and was pressing her knuckles into her back to ease the tension when a voice arrested her mid-movement. It was the Princess Joanna and her maid, Edith, and it was she who stepped imperiously in front of her mistress and addressed Nest.

'You, woman! What do you here? Pagans must not come near God's house. Away with you, the Princess wishes to pass,' she told her.

Both she and her mistress stood unmoving on the path and glared at Nest; Joanna drew her skirts and her cloak closer, watched.

Nest replied, 'God welcomes all people to his house. I know this because I am a Christian.'

Edith flung up her hand in a scathing gesture. 'You? You do not worship here, ever. I'd as soon believe my Lady was a man,' she said, her voice full of scorn. 'Away with you.'

'Away with *you*, old woman,' Nest retorted. 'I was christened as a babe by the Augustinian Abbot, at the Monastery of Penmon, hard by St Seiriol's Well. But I need prove nothing to you. And I need not go to mass here. When do you worship with the common folk? I'll wager you hear mass in my Lord's chapel at the llys.'

Nest turned her back on the women and was about to move on, but the Princess spoke.

'All Christians must worship in church, Nest of the Shore. I wonder that you think otherwise. It is the law of the Church.'

Edith hissed triumphantly and folded her arms across her chest, a gesture of finality, but Nest turned to face the Princess and bowed her head respectfully. She contrived to look dignified as she cradled her heavy belly.

'Lady, pray forgive me. I know the law of the church, but I am excused from formal worship by Canon Yago because I have many sick people to help each day with my herbs and simples. I visit him each week to make my confession.'

Edith surged forward to glare into Nest's face then turning her head she spat on the ground at Nest's feet; her voice was laced with poison as she answered.

'You lie. You are a witch and the good Canon will have none of you in God's house. I wager he knows nothing of your potions and poisons. You dare not enter for fear of the flames of Hell or the flames of man, for you are a heretic. You! You dare to speak as a Christian?'

Nest shook her head in astonishment that the woman had voiced something so outrageous, yes, but also at the fury and loathing in the woman's voice. Her only answer was to raise her chin, say nothing and keep herself as upright as her condition allowed.

Bea, as she slept, felt the stab of fear that pierced Nest's heart.

But the Princess spun round.

'Edith!' she cried; her voice severe. 'Hold. Do not say such a thing. Hush, hush.' She was shocked and grasped the maid's arm, turning her roughly away, even as she crossed herself with the other hand. Edith's reaction was one of dismay to be treated so by her beloved mistress, and she staggered back several paces, her head bowed before the angry rebuke. Joanna wasn't finished.

'Go, Edith; return to the llys. I will speak to you later. I would not have another woman, any woman, so accused, whatever her wrongdoing. But to speak of that terrible punishment, that evil practice is a blight on God's Goodness and God's church. Ah, no, no talk of burnings!' She grasped the crucifix she wore always. 'Pray that no one has heard you utter such a thing. Go, I say!'

Her expression was furious as she flung her arm in the direction of the llys and did not look at her maid but crossed herself again. Edith was bereft, she uttered a single small cry and drawing her cloak round her body, she fled. Joanna turned to speak to Nest.

'I would talk with you, Nest of the Shore. I find I have need of something... something you may help me with.' She succeeded in being haughty yet hesitant. 'In here,' she said and gestured to the door of the church. 'Canon Yago will not begrudge you, indeed both of us, such use of this holy place for I am as tired as you look.'

Joanna lifted the iron latch, but she had to lean against the door to open it for it was made of good oak and was heavy. Llewelyn had given the people both stone and oak and they had built the small church themselves; it was on the site of the wattle and daub building that was their earlier place of worship. He had also endowed the Augustinian Abbey at Penmon. Christian worship was important to him. It was cool and dark inside the little church and smelled of herbs and the wax candles, so costly and precious, that had been sent by Joanna herself for feast days.

The Princess sat on a wooden bench near the door and indicated that Nest should share it with her. It was where the old and infirm might rest during worship, all others stood in the body of the church. As Nest lowered herself slowly, the two women looked at each other and it was the Princess who turned away first.

'It is difficult for me to find the words I wish to say to you, Nest of the Shore, and to ask you what I want to ask.' Joanna's expression was still unfriendly, and it was also guarded.

Nest recognised this and remained quiet, glad to sit and take the weight off her feet.

She has listened to the rumours about the Prince being unfaithful. Edith, oh noxious fiend, she must have nought save evil thoughts, for surely her actions are deadly and her words cause terror too. My babe – I must be so very careful.

She said, 'My Lady, perhaps it is best to give voice to what troubles your mind, for I can see you are sorely pressed by your thoughts.'

The Princess held her crucifix like a drowning person holds a log and raised it to her lips to kiss while her other hand held the edge of her plain brown robe and worried the fabric into creases.

Nest watched her. *Llewelyn can only do so much, mighty though he is. Even he is no match for an evil tongue that whips up self-righteous fury. She seems quite terrified.*

She eased her position on the bench and ventured to give the Princess a lead, if only to take her to a moral position where she and her unborn babe might be safer.

'My Lady, I also am anxious in my mind; I'm soon to be brought to childbed, as you see, and I am fearful. I have friends but no close family to take the babe if I die. Her father is in Ireland and knows nothing of his child,' she said.

'You speak to me of this babe, *your* babe?' Joanna's eyes flew to Nest's face, raked it furiously, searching for some dreaded meaning. Then she paused as Nest's words penetrated her confusion. 'In Ireland? How can that be?'

She was puzzled now and snatched at the crucifix with both hands. Her face was white.

Nest continued softly, 'Cormac the bard, he who came in the Spring. The Prince valued his music, as I think you did, my Lady. He has a rare gift from God to be able to make such beauty. It is he, Cormac, who is father to my child.'

As she explained Nest watched the Princess's expression move slowly from puzzlement to wariness.

'I have heard that it was another man,' she said and as she waited for Nest to reply her hands flew nervously to her face and she pushed a stray lock of hair under her wimple, adjusted her veil. Her hands fluttered over the already straight cloth of her brown surcoat as it draped over her knees; smoothing, smoothing, in repetitive rhythm.

Nest allowed the silence to grow.

She and I both love Llewelyn, but in different ways and with a different history. She is eaten up with jealousy fuelled by gossip. Her own shame weakens her. But I will not give credence to gossip by striving to proclaim my Lord innocent.

She watched Joanna as she said, 'Cormac will not be returning because he goes to study God's word and enrich his soul as an anchorite. He will live on the eastern coast, in a small chapel, he says. We parted as lovers who know they will not meet again in this world. I am content about him and wish him strength and joy.'

'But still, now you are alone,' Joanna ventured a cruel reminder and the very corner of her mouth twitched in the thought of a smile.

Nest was not deflated. 'I am a lone parent for my child, true. But I am never alone, my Lady. I have good friends. But I worry as every mother does, about the birth and whether my child will survive, whether I will. You know of these feelings, surely.'

Joanna ignored the unspoken plea of their common gender and fate. 'My Lord comes to visit you, does he not?' she asked. She kept her eyes on the floor as she waited for Nest to answer.

'He does, my Lady. He is as a brother to me. And he is a true friend.'

There was another silence which Nest was glad of because the babe was wriggling and her back ached. She also wished to relieve herself. At last Joanna turned to Nest. She hesitated again before speaking.

'I thought….I heard…' She shook her head, as if dismissing the idea she was about to voice.

Nest said, 'I know. Gossip. Such people who deal in it speak to be the centre of attention in their tiny world. They delight in the misery of others, especially if they are the first to bring news of a downfall or disaster, and even if that news is later found to be an evil or false report. They delight in their own fame as the news bringer and feel nothing for any pain they cause other than to relish the chance to repeat that too in another ear. Misery, tears and unbearable shock are their triumphs.'

Joanna's shoulders sagged.

'Yes,' was all she said.

So, Nest reached out her hand to the older woman, but when Joanna did not respond she let her hand fall on her skirt, but kept it open and after some silent minutes, Joanna put her own hand there.

Nest relaxed a little.

'He offers me protection in this world where a woman has few rights, especially a woman with an unborn babe,' she said. 'I prepare my medicines for his stomach and his headaches, so I can be useful to him in my own way.'

'Ah, yes. His headaches are a worry.'

They were silent, but when that lengthened, and Joanna still looked to Nest to be uncomfortable in her mind and increasingly in her body, she ventured a comment.

'Tis warm for the season, my Lady.'

Joanna released her hand and snatched away her wimple and veil, causing her pins to scatter on the floor. She dragged her hands through her plaited hair, loosening it a little, but keeping it in bonds.

'I find I am as hot as this even if there is frost on the glass in my chamber,' she muttered, distracted by her discomfort.

She pulled out the neck of her surcoat.

'Are you not warm too?' she asked Nest.

'I am with child and I am always warm, but I am not suffering what ails you, my Lady.'

'I know, I know. It is the time of my life that changes everything, my body, my mind, my marriage.'

Nest took out a small bunch of rosemary from her script.

'Let me make you more comfortable,' she said and gently bruising the leaves first in her hand, she fanned the Princess with the herb posy.

They sat in silence for a few minutes before Nest began to speak.

'I have been to visit Alis, the mother of Angharad, poor girl. The thought of her death adds to my own anxiety, but I have friends who are learned and careful midwives too. Sister of Air gave Angharad all the help she could when she laboured. Your maid spurned her and drove her away with violence.'

'Ah, Edith. She is angry, angry all the time,' Joanna told her, 'and little Angharad was a good girl and merry.' She took a deep breath. 'Ahhh, the rosemary is good. It clears the air and is calming and refreshing. I had forgotten about its powers.'

'Alis suffers still from the loss of her daughter and the unborn grandchild. She is also at the time when her woman's body is changing. But I gave her Yarrow, the oil of Yarrow to anoint her brow and a tea of the flowers to sooth her stomach and relieve the cramps. It helps the blood to move around the body so that it can heal and enliven. It is a blessed herb for women, steeped in magic, the magic of the natural world, made by God, not of the darkness,' Nest added as Joanna glanced suspiciously at her. 'It cleanses the body and mind and awakens spiritual forces to let in the benevolent power of the Good Lord.'

'Rosemary too?'

'Sage to burn and clean the air, to ward off infections, aye and rosemary to help you breathe purely. An infusion of rosemary in the water when you wash your hair will help it recover its maidenly brightness, my Lady.' She smiled.

'Nest, I confess I am reassured, by you, your words, and by the idea that I can be helped in my body's distress, and yes, the uncertainty of my heart too. Would you fetch your herbs to the llys for me?'

'I will, with pleasure.'

'I go soon to be in seclusion for a short time, to pray and to compose myself, so that I may help my Lord as a wife should when I return.'

'Go with God.'

Joanna smiled at her.

'I pray you and your babe will be well. It is a terrible yet blessed labour, childbirth. I know and my children thrive, but I have not forgotten the trial of it, nor the joy. Go with God, Nest of the Shore.'

When she had gone, Nest made her way as quickly as she could to the shelter of some bushes behind the church to relieve herself.

Chapter thirty-five

Cleansing

I had forgot that foul conspiracy…

Prospero - The Tempest

A SEA MIST drifted lazily around the church. Bea heard the latch of the door clang as Nest and Joanna closed it behind them and to her it had a doom-laden finality. She saw that Edith had not returned to the llys but had hidden herself around the corner of the building and near enough to the open door to have heard all that passed between the other two. Her expression was thunderous. As the Princess took her leave Edith quickly ran on before her, through the shelter of the mist and the trees and back to the llys.

Bea's sight followed her there. Beside her on the bed, the little terrier opened his eyes and watched her muttering and shifting as she slept.

Edith went straight to her own small chamber and, as she put out a hand to pull the thick curtain aside, she knew without doubt that there was someone in the room. She knew it was a man; there was a pungent smell of male sweat and horses; she knew who it was.

'Yestyn,' she whispered and in answer he stepped soundlessly from the recess and showed himself, drawing her into the room and dropping the curtain back in place.

'Your mistress, where is she?' he hissed, urgent, angry.

'She is coming back to the llys and will need my attendance. What do you want?' The dim light from her parchment-covered window was sufficient for her to see that he looked dishevelled as well as livid. 'Are you unwell? The wounds….?' She glanced down at his arm and lifted a hand to his cheek, still red and swollen from Nest's knife.

He slapped her hand away and began pacing the small room.

'She goes into seclusion, your mistress. Did you know? Into a priory and my Lord is sending me to lead her bodyguard.' He was furious. 'He is my commander, my Prince, yet this time I cannot obey him. Gruffyd has need of me; now, directly. I have had word that his force is mustering, and we are to begin raids on certain strongholds.' He kept his voice low.

'When, when?' She was shocked, began to gabble. 'But when will my Lady go? Strongholds? Belonging to the Prince? So, Gruffyd? You will follow Gruffyd then? When? When will my Lady go?'

'In the next two days.'

Edith interrupted. 'So soon? Two days? My Lady said nothing. I wonder does she know?'

Yestyn continued as if she hadn't spoken, seeming oblivious of her state. 'Yes, I must go to Gruffyd. He is the way forward for our people; he is the future of Gwynydd. But, here's the rub, if I leave now, today, my Lord Prince will realise that I am for Gruffyd and he will know that his son plans an insurrection. He will be warned. All will be crystal clear as the springs of Snowden. He said this very morning, we are to set out for the priory with the English bitch tomorrow...'

'Watch your mouth! My Lady deserves your respect, else you are nothing but a common traitor who plans to desert his Lord,' she told him, as she swung round to face him, her voice tight with fury.

He pushed her away with a hand on each shoulder, saying, as though to himself, 'I thought to begin the journey and slip away from the Princess's party in the dead of the night, to Gruffyd's camp. I will take a night watch and simply leave before the next man comes on duty. I can be thirty miles away by dawn.'

Edith gasped, took an outraged step back.

'You plan to abandon her to the common soldiery? Glad I am that I will be there to guard her, and with my own life if need rise. It is only because I wish her away from your dreadful land that I even listen to you and tend your wounds, that and my hatred of the whore, Nest.' She added ruefully, 'Would that you had harmed *her*! And for myself I regret the day my Lady wed this Welsh prince. I would that she was in England. All these years - a lifetime. I would that you Welsh would kill each other and then England will be all powerful again.' She spat the words at him, full of empty threat and futile triumph.

Yestyn continued his restless pacing and as Edith tried to catch his sleeve to stop him, he yanked it away, telling her, 'I am not sure you are to go with her. My Lord said nothing of any other women. She goes to be one of the sisters at the priory. The Prince said it is her wish.'

Edith snorted her contempt.

'My Lady will say the opposite. She could not do without me.'

'Please yourself. I am more concerned that I am being punished without being accused of any misdoing. Aye, it feels like a punishment for being wounded by that mad witch. I would take a man's punishment if I were not vital to Gruffyd's plans.'

Edith glared at him.

He said, 'I care not for your black looks, nor what you think. You tended my wounds – for your own ends. The Prince wants me as the woman's only noble escort, without my boon companions and friends of my own station, just the common solders. I am to stay there in attendance on her indefinitely, for as long as she stays. His manner told me he suspects where I got my injuries. His eyes raked my face and he was sorely troubled yet did not challenge me, and that gives me chance to leave quickly before he changes his mind and keeps me here. At least I can escape when we are off the island; a single night to wait.'

'Fool! The Prince is ever the diplomat. Why, your own family are powerful allies of his; they are on his side. They trade with many of the Saxon lords of The Marches.' Edith said.

He ignored her contempt. 'If only my father could see that we of Gwynedd should stay together to be powerful again. When he dies, and I would not wish him gone…'

Edith raised her eyebrows scornfully. He did not notice.

'…my brother and I share the inheritance and we are both for stopping trade, aye, and marriages with the Saxon and Norman scum. So, if I slip away from the party tomorrow, as we travel, it will be difficult to escape the eyes of the men and get away without losing too much time, or indeed my life. Thus, I am forced to wait for nightfall;

do you not see?'

She nodded curtly. 'Aye, aye, you make your plans well, do you not? And if you leave my Lady at the dead of night the Prince will send a hundred men to hunt you down and have you brought back and executed before everyone. If he does not, I will hunt you down myself and I will kill you. Then your family would be shamed. Remember I am Saxon and would be away from this harsh land of yours. And I am a gentlewoman, no scum.'

Yestyn paced the room.

'I know it.'

'You and I are on opposite sides, which is convenient for both of our plans. You will not harm my Lady...' she threatened.

'No, I will not let that happen. You have my word.' His voice was now calm, assured.

'What do you want from me then?' she asked, impatient now, hands on hips. Her Lady would soon call for her.

'You could persuade her to leave her departure for a few days then I might leave with my honour intact and give Gruffyd the time he needs to muster all his force.' Yestyn drew himself up. 'Then I can join him in good time.'

'In time? *Honour?* You would desert your Lord to join the opposite side in a war, for it will be war, and that keeps your *honour* intact does it? Is it more honourable to do that than protect a royal lady?' Edith asked, her voice incredulous.

'Yes, yes; If I abandon a woman, then yes, it is dishonourable.' He shrugged. 'But if I leave to fight with the opposition in a great cause, then win or lose, it is less dishonour. Indeed, if we win it is all honour.' But Yestyn was uncomfortable. 'There are casualties in war,' he offered as a small appeasement.'

'*Less dishonour*...I see, win, lose, whichever way the wind blows. Your Welsh loyalties are strangely flexible. You join son against father, yet I am glad, as it suits my ends.' She pursed her lips. 'I will speak to the Princess and try to change her mind, that is, once she is informed of the Prince's pleasure. I would have a more loyal escort for her than you, if she is intent on going.'

He looked a little easier, then a thought struck him. 'Ithel, he is hot for Gruffydd's cause. Where is he these past two days?'

She shook her head. 'I know not.'

Yestyn stopped his pacing to look at her, cupped his elbow in one hand and with the free one gently tugged at his moustache. He smiled. 'You hate him, do you not?'

She smiled in her turn. It was her answer.

He dropped his face to be at a level with hers and whispered, 'I will tell you something, Edith. Ithel wants me to kidnap the Princess Joanna, helped by some of Gruffyd's faithful followers, to hold her in ransom, against the Prince's co-operation. Gruffyd wants his own lands, he wants his sire to retire to the mountains and sit by a fire with a posset. He would prefer his half-brother Daffyd back in England with his other kin. He says Gwynedd is for the wholly Welsh, those Welsh in the prime of life too.'

'He plans that?' Her face was ashen suddenly; she was still as a rock. 'I will find him. I will find Ithel,' was what she said. 'Gruffyd plans kidnap then? Oh, my Lady's worthy stepson, whom none have harmed. This is your Welsh honour again, Yestyn.' Her tone was bitter.

She pushed him roughly from the chamber and they went separate ways.

Yestyn lifted his face to the cool air and walked away, his shoulders back, confident.

But Edith lost no time in going to wait on the Princess. An hour or so later she found a convenient errand that was needed and took that opportunity to search for Ithel. She was tense with anxiety and did not mention the proposed journey to the priory but waited to see how her beloved Princess would broach it. She did not. Nor did she mention her talk with Nest, though Edith had heard, of course. Gossip. It was dusk by the time Edith began her search for the bard. Ithel had a small chamber in the outer wall of the palace curtilage and had a boy to wait on him; a famous bard held residency and high status in the hierarchy of a royal household.

'Ho Ithel!' she called quietly at the wooden door. His boy opened it. He was hesitant.

'Your master? Is he within?' she asked but the boy shook his head firmly.

'He's not here, not for two days he's not, Mistress Edith,' he said, giving a courteous nod of the head and keeping his eyes down because Edith was known to cuff youngsters.

'Why are you here then?' she demanded.

'I wait for him, Mistress, I do. I keep the fire and the food ready. He likes it that way. I look after the harp too, but I do not touch it, no. No one else must touch it. That was my order from the master, that was,' he explained quietly.

'When did you last see him?'

'Morning, two days ago, Mistress. He was going out.'

'Where did he go?' She held the boy's eyes.

'He said he was going to the cove near where Nest of the Shore lives, round the cliff there. He said he must gather some shells of a special kind to grind into powder for cleaning his hands, keeping them dry for the harp. Well, I do that, the grinding of powder. I mean.' The boy ventured a shy smile, shuffled his feet.

'Open the door fully, boy,' Edith commanded but he held it firmly in place.

'Pardon, Mistress, but I don't dare,' he ventured.

She pushed past him and saw that the chamber was empty, no sign of activity save a cloth next to the harp which lay on the narrow pallet. The boy had been polishing it.

'Mistress,' the boy began. 'I only wanted to get the dust off it. I meant no harm. Please, my master will beat me…'

She ignored him and marched out and away without another word, out of the llys and towards the ford over the river. She was heading for the cottage where Nest lived by the far edge of the sea, but she was walking up the opposite bank of the river, the side which was mostly filled by the huge sand dunes held back by forest. She made her way in the shadow of the dunes and was well camouflaged by her dark cloak. The sand underfoot was rippled and hard, the tide far out and the river low. She made her way purposefully.

'I may see him if I climb to the top of the dunes. What is his purpose in going anywhere near Nest? What does he plan? Mind, it's two days ago,' she muttered as she walked.

The fishermen of the shore, Nest's neighbours, were all at sea and would be back with the tide, so the estuary and banks of the river held few boats. Their cottages were mostly lit by a faint yellow light cast by the tallow candles they used. There was no one on the beach. The families were indoors at this time. Edith tramped onward angrily.

'I see Ithel's hand in all this. He knew of the Prince's plans for my mistress, I'll be bound,' she said aloud, and had not gone more than ten more paces when a voice directly behind answered her.

'No, you are mistaken, woman. Ithel could not have known.'

Edith spun round, her breath caught in her throat, her hand flew to the small dagger she kept in the pocket of her cloak. When she saw who stood behind her she drew herself up to her full height and smiled, all her fear gone, evaporated, and she held out the dagger so that it could be seen.

'You,' she said, a scornful edge to her voice.

'Yes, it is I, Chwaer Awyr.'

Edith snorted her derision. 'You think to trip me up with your Welsh words? You are named **Sister of Air** – foul air, I say! You see I know you and I also know that you were told to begone, back to whatever disgusting hole you were spawned from.'

The only reply Sister of Air gave was a slow smile. Her long hair moved slightly in the breeze as though vipers stirring in the nest, waking to test the hazy air with their little black tongues. Behind her, from the water's edge, a lilac mist grew and spilled over, began to undulate across the sand towards them. She raised her hands in the air and formed her body into a graceful arc that was the beginning of a sinuous dance, a silent dance, a leisurely dance that encircled Edith.

'Your tricks will not unsettle me, hag,' Edith snarled, but she turned in concert to keep her eyes locked on those of the woman. Suddenly Edith had had enough. She simply strode away along the sand, heading for the open mouth of the estuary so that she could see if Ithel were anywhere near. She muttered disjointedly over her shoulder as she went.

'I'll have none of this…black arts …nonsense…my lady will hear of…I must find him…'

Two paces on and before she knew it, a cloak was thrown over her head and she was wound up in its folds, screaming, screaming, outraged. It was Sister of Air who had caught her, and she was dextrous and strong. She soon had a rope bound round the older woman's legs and threw her onto the sand where, beneath the rising mist, she looked nothing more than a boulder left by a strong high tide. Sister of Air climbed up into the dunes with practised ease and a little while later reappeared leading a mule.

She loaded Edith's squirming body onto the mule's back and secured her legs and arms with rope under its belly. Her muffled screams irritated the mule and he danced a little, but Sister of Air spoke gently, and it wasn't long before he settled down and allowed her to lead him away. They soon joined the path between the dunes, and made their way under the lowering sky, into the deeper darkness of the forest.

Chapter thirty-six

Choices

The fringed curtain of thine eye advance

And say, what thou seest yond…

Prospero - The Tempest

BEA TURNED OVER restlessly but felt nothing of the breeze that filled the room and made the curtains fly out like the wings of an albatross, nor did she hear the coarse shriek of the gulls as they were carried along on the air current.

'Yes, take her,' she muttered in her sleep. Her expression was fierce.

In her mind's eye she saw Sister of Air moving quickly through the dune paths, leading the mule behind her. Edith was strapped to the animal's back and she struggled, but she was firmly held, and the mule now seemed unbothered by the alien movement and followed his mistress. He also seemed unmoved by Edith's muted screams, once he had got used to the noise.

Bea murmured, 'Help *him* now…you must help Llewelyn…and Nest…Nest, it's her time…the babe…' She turned over impatiently. Tears began to course down her face.

A man's voice nudged at her consciousness.

'Time to wake up – come on, Bea, wakey wakey.'

It was Gwyn, holding a mug of tea, which he put by the bed. He shook her shoulder. Archie jumped off the bed and went downstairs.

'Come on. Nice day, bit breezy, bobbing clouds.'

She turned away from him.

'Bea, Bea, wake up there. Come on,' he told her firmly.

She mumbled a little and so he shoved his hands under her arms and hoisted her up into a sitting position, letting her fall back against the bedhead.

'There. Tea's next to you. Time to get up. I need to go to work for a few hours.' He waited and got no response, so he bawled her name, 'Bea!'

She was shocked wide awake and looked wildly around, felt the wet on her cheeks and wiped it on the back of her hand, her expression puzzled. Her head was swimming. Which time was she in?

'It's me, Gwyn. Remember? I stayed in case the bastard husband came creeping in the night. You were fast asleep, and talking,' he added. He stood looking down at her, hands on hips.

'Talking? Who to?' she muttered. 'Ahh. I remember.' She turned and saw the tea. 'Can't remember when I last had tea in bed.' It sounded wistful.

'Not so much of the 'in bed' more like on top of it and wrestling with the covers.'

'It was a dream. No, no. I was floating around inside my head, sure enough, but in the past. You need to go? Sorry, I'm holding you back, aren't I?' She picked up the tea and sipped, managed a weak smile.

He took out his phone and keyed in a contact.

'No, you're not. Hang on, just giving Thomas a call.' There was a pause and then he got through. 'Thomas? Gwyn here; with Bea… yes…' He gave a brief account of Jeremy's visit and several times held the phone away from his ear, wincing at the loud volume of Thomas's exclamations. 'Thing is, I need to go over to the university for a couple of hours, a meeting. So, I wondered if….'

'I don't need a bodyguard. I'll be fine, honestly.' She raised her voice, calling, 'I'm fine, Thomas! Don't worry.'

Gwyn put a finger to his lips as he listened to what Thomas was saying. 'Ahhh. Okay then, settled. Catch you later!' He disconnected. 'Some are born to greatness and some have greatness and bodyguards foisted upon them…Lorcan is on his way back to his place and said he will call in for a chat and to see the dogs and the kids. He'll be about twenty minutes, he said.'

'God, the whole village will know what an idiot I am. I was feeling a bit low yesterday but now I've had a good sleep I reckon I can handle Jeremy. I ought to be able to.'

'Maybe…but sleep's not restful if you've been rampaging round medieval minds,' he told her.

'It was strange, Gwyn.'

'Go on.'

'I feel as if I only just left them a minute ago. Weird sensation. It's as though they're real.'

Gwyn sat down on the edge of the bed.

'They are, were. If your theory of time being layered like an onion holds any weight, and events are being, have been, recorded in the rocks as though there is a gigantic computer chip under our feet, then they're alive now.'

Bea glared at him. 'Did I tell you that? It wasn't my idea though.'

'Erm, possibly. You've told me such a lot! But, you're right. It's an ancient belief held by many other cultures.' He grimaced impatiently and reached out to take the mug from her. 'You're spilling that! I'm waiting to hear what happened. It's as though I'm waiting for the next episode of this season's must-see TV prime-time drama, on every night for a week!'

She laughed and took the mug back from him.

'I couldn't believe it; Nest and Joanna met and talked. Nest actually helped her. But it's Edith, Joanna's wretched maid, she wants the Prince dead. His own son, Gruffydd, wants to take his crown and Yestyn's with him, about to defect. Joanna's going to a nunnery and Llewelyn doesn't want her to go. By the way did she actually do that, I mean according to history as you know it? Am I dreaming about the right history or am I fantasising completely?'

'The *right* history. Hmmm. You could debate that one! In fact, she did go to a nunnery, by all accounts I've seen. She did return home, we think. Some years later she died, and before Llewelyn too. He actually built and endowed a Franciscan Friary at Llanfaes, here on the island, in memory of her. 1237 that was. She was buried there, after she died…' He tried a wry grin to lighten her mood but was met with a blank stare. 'Ahh, just remembered, her coffin, actually a stone sarcophagus, richly carved, ended up in a cow pasture, here on the island, as a water trough.'

Bea was stunned. 'I think I heard that! Where's the body then?'

He shook his head. 'It happened around eight hundred years ago, Bea. Who knows what happened, where her body ended up. Even I, with a career in medieval history of the period, haven't been able to discover that. We don't know where Llewelyn's body is either. Mind you, they did find Richard III's body in that car park... But, the upside is...'

'What?' She sat up eagerly.

'When the coffin was discovered to be of such importance it was recovered and cleaned up. It's in the vestibule of St. Mary's Church in Beaumaris.' Gwyn smiled triumphantly.

'In the church porch, you mean? Now? But I think I saw that in my... visions, whatever they are. There were leaves and dust all around it. It was sad.'

'I always think so. The Princess Joanna, wife of Gwynedd's mightiest Prince. He ruled for forty years, or thereabout. Kept a rough peace, traded with the neighbours, economic détente; made Gwynedd a power to be reckoned with, and look where his wife's coffin ended up. Still, it's not her actual body, is it? Such are we all, eh? The detritus of history.'

Bea swung her legs off the bed, tried, unsuccessfully to straighten her old jogs and top which she'd slept in, but made herself more uncomfortable, by twisting everything the other way. She gave up. Her hair was loose and tumbled about her shoulders, her face flushed from the sleep and the talk. She looked at Gwyn.

'You are a bit of a pompous prat at times, aren't you?' she said, and yawned widely.

'History geek; comes with the territory,' he answered, unoffended.

Bea rubbed her face vigorously. 'I saw Nest looking in her scrying bowl. She saw this, she saw the coffin. How very weird to dream all this, Gwyn. Don't you think so?'

'*We are such stuff as dreams are made on, and our little life is rounded with a sleep,*' he murmured.

'Well, that was professor mode all right! The Tempest. Prospero. I'd forgotten that – almost. I read it a lot as a teenager; all the romance and magic appealed. This is a magical island after all.'

'Course it is, and we even have, across the Straits, the *cloud-capped mountains*, and here on the island there were *the gorgeous palaces, the solemn temples,* also Prospero. Shakespeare must have visited, I guess.'

Bea stood up. She dragged her hair away from her face. 'I think I'd like to catch up with Stella now. Archie's left me, I see,' she said as the dog, disappeared through the door.'

They smiled easily at each other for a second until the moment was ended by barking downstairs.

'See? They want me,' Bea said and headed for the door.

In the Post Office at this time, Thomas, Lorcan and Dana were gathered with heads together to look at Dana's photographs.

The evening before, when she met with Jeremy in Beaumaris, she was leaving the hotel and saw that his car was still in the car park. He'd said he was going to visit Bea at Nest's Point, 'the hovel', as he called it. In her police work, she had found that tiny openings in an ongoing series of events sometimes led to significant discoveries, so she took the chance and ran to her own car. It was parked just around the corner by the pier.

She decided that if she could get to her hide in the dunes before Jeremy arrived at the cottage, she might be able to judge something about his relationship with Bea from the quality of his reception, and then she could judge for herself how honest he was being with her. Up to then she'd seen no suggestion of an affair or any behaviour that smacked of mental illness in Bea.

Things went her way and she got herself up the long beach to her hide well before she spotted Jeremy striding along to the cottage. Bea had been standing at the cottage wall, looking out to sea and Dana had taken a long series of shots and some video footage of Jeremy's arrival. His actions all appeared normal and concerned, but she only had pictures and couldn't hear what was said. Then Gwyn had arrived and there had been the swift violence between the men, and she was left with a persistent unsettled feeling, that something was wrong with Jeremy's need for a private investigator.

When, the next day, she found Lorcan chatting to Thomas in the post office she decided to show them the shots and gauge their reaction too. It wasn't the right time to tell them of the real reason she was there in Anglesey. That, she kept to herself.

What she said was, 'I've got some shots here that you'll definitely want to see. I was over in my hide yesterday evening, y'know, in the dunes, and I saw this bloke with your friend, Bea at the cottage. She was at the end of the garden wall, looking out to sea and he sort of crept up on her. Well, I'm only guessing he crept up, because of her reaction which was totally shocked. It was her face and body posture, if you follow. Look...' She pointed to a series of shots. 'I was just using the viewfinder to see what was on the shore line over there and I didn't take any shots at first; suppose it was a bit nosy of me to carry on watching, but I thought the man got a bit pushy, even though he was smiling. Bea looked very worried.'

'Bastard,' Thomas muttered.

'And some...' Lorcan added. 'The husband?'

Thomas nodded grimly. 'After what Gwyn just told us on the phone and then to see these. Man, I'll kill him, I will.'

Dana held up a promissory finger. 'Look at this though...Gwyn turned up. Bea had used her phone by then, maybe to call him,' she suggested.

'Yes, Gwyn said the bugger had visited! Don't know how much Gwyn Roberts wants to be involved though,' Thomas muttered, but was taken aback when Dana showed them the shot of Gwyn punching Jeremy. 'Well, who'd have thought? Helped me too, when I was floored by the bastard the other night. I'm getting to like him, I really am!'

Dana had been in the shop when Gwyn phoned asking for someone to stay with Bea.

'I'm guessing my pictures back up what Gwyn said earlier on the phone?' she asked, and the men nodded. 'Anyway, look, that's all, folks.' Dana packed up her camera. 'I'll leave you two to make of it what you will. Not my business really. Actually, I'd better be going now; I need to visit a few of the smaller coves today, collect some data. I'll keep my eyes peeled for any more visits, shall I?'

'Do that, girl. Fancy him coming back like that and in broad daylight too.' Thomas thumped the counter, angry. 'Brazen I call it. Bloody brazen. If he comes near me, I'll swing for him, I will.'

Lorcan laughed. 'Sure you will, but better be able to stand up first, eh? Can't have you poking him with your walking stick. I'll get along there now myself, so that the hero of the hour can get to university, remember?'

Thomas smacked his head in frustration. 'What'm I thinking? Yes, get going, will you? I'm even more worried now. Here, take my girl some bread – today's...' he said and quickly dropped a small cob into a brown paper bag.'

Lorcan took the parcel. 'I'll go now. Dana, want some company on the walk up the beach?'

'Yeah, why not?'

They headed for the top path because the tide was coming in and made their way quite speedily, yet they didn't speak; it was a friendly silence. As they neared the church, Lorcan gently nudged the silence aside. He smiled as he spoke, stealing a quick glance at her.

'Y'know, Dana, I'm enjoying our chats, and I'm wondering if I could take you for a meal, or just a drink, or something? Spot of birdwatching, litter picking, dog sitting, y'know?'

Just then, the wind blew a strand of her hair from under her woolly hat and she used her left hand to catch it. Her wedding ring caught the light and his eye. She noticed and waggled her fingers a little, her expression guarded, vulnerable.

'Ah, I'm used to wearing it; had it some time, actually. I'm a widow, two years now. My husband was a firearms officer, Inspector, with Greater Manchester Police. He was shot and killed in a drugs raid one night.'

She flushed, realising it was one of the first genuine truths she'd allowed herself to voice since she'd come on this job.

But he was embarrassed. 'I'm that sorry, sure I am. I didn't twig it was a wedding ring. I wouldn't have asked, but…'

'Don't worry. It was his signet ring and we used it as our wedding ring.' She turned it round so that he could see the engraving on the front. 'And, yes, I'd love a drink…or some litter!' She smiled reassuringly. 'I'm not really over him yet, as they say, but I would like to make special friends now. Does that make sense?' It was another truthful comment and she realised she had turned a corner in her personal life just as she was close to making a decision about this job too.

'Oh, it does. I'm glad, I am – about the litter or whatever! Tonight?' he asked, and she agreed. Then she remembered that she hadn't got her food and flask, so she said she would go back to the pub to retrieve them and wave across the river at him from the dunes when she got to the hide.

'I'll be seeing you then. I can stay with Bea for an hour or two before I need to go.' He turned, about to walk on but paused thoughtfully. 'What I'd like to know is just what's going on with this husband of Bea's? What's he up to? She needs people with her at the moment, just in case he tries any more tricks. Sounds a basket case to me, sure. If I remember rightly, Nest never said anything good about the husband, but that was a sign that she didn't take to him, if I'm honest. And there's the dog and the pups to think of now, or she could go and stay with Thomas until things are clearer. I'll give my friend, Heather, the vet, a bell to see if she's on the island. Maybe she'd like to call and see the dogs.'

'That'd be a good idea, I think. See you later then!' Dana called, jogging back to the pub for her things.

Before long she was making her way back over the bridge, heading for the hide, when something caught her eye in the car park. It was Jeremy's distinctive car alongside Mairi's; they were parked nose to tail so that their open driver's windows were alongside. They leant towards each other as they talked. Dana's approach was shielded by a tourist information board and a van parked next to it. She crept behind it until, still hidden from view, she could hear them talking. She put her phone on record too.

'You'll have to make another arrangement then, chéri,' Mairi snapped. 'I really think that's just too fantastic to contemplate.'

Jeremy laughed softly. 'Scruples at this stage of play?'

'I do have one or two. I have a new business partnership and a bourgeoning reputation to foster. I can't afford a hint of gossip. I'm in the luxury trade as you know and people with pots of loot simply like squeaky clean. Besides, I am a doctor.'

He laughed outright. 'That's rich. What a time for you to remember.'

'Look, I don't quibble at persuasion; after all, it's stock in trade for a psychiatrist, but putting her out? I'd be struck off. I couldn't disguise it as a committal without the signature of another doctor, and not her husband, as you know. Physical coercion is a little infra dig, Jem. Really! It's practically gangster level.' Her voice was very serious, not the flippant tone Dana had heard previously.

'Darling…' he began.

'Darling? Really?' Her voice was toneless.

He sighed loudly. 'Haloperidol as a sedative is bona fide in your line of work. Admissions to psychiatric clinics are always tense, mostly due to patients claiming they're not ill. We need to get her in your car with a minimum of trauma.'

'A minimum of trauma for whom?' she snapped. 'Do you think I can't get her in my car without drugs and trauma? Give me some credit.'

'I seriously doubt it, especially now she seems to have a Welsh rugby prop minding her.'

'I can get Bea to my clinic. Simply trust me, won't you?' There was a hard edge to Mairi's voice. 'All right. I have a mild sedative with me in my bag in any case. It'll have to be tomorrow.'

Dana sensed the conversation was reaching its conclusion. She knew she must make a move before he drove away and perhaps saw her near the car park, but she was desperate to hear everything.

Jeremy said, 'Give me your hand, my angel, my very wicked angel.' There was a slight noise that Dana knew was a kiss. She pictured him in the lower car, as if he were on bended knee, kissing Mairi's outstretched hand.

'That's all very pretty, chéri, but will I get my share of the money when you cash in or inherit or whatever mechanism you employ? I guess you'll need a fair packet to pay off those little gambling notes, won't you? Otherwise the bad boys will come to collect. You see, I read crime novels and the bad boys always collect. And do remember, if you want me, you're going to need another pile to spend on me. Au revoir. Later then?'

'Later,' he answered, his voice now relaxed and warm.

Dana suddenly realised the engines had started and there was no chance of walking past to the beach, so she ran to the stone bridge and down the side of the bank to crouch under there until the cars had both gone. She needed to decide what to do next; what on Earth to do next.

Chapter thirty-seven

Threat

If thou neglect'st or dost unwillingly what I command, I'll rack thee with old cramps, fill all thy bones with aches, make thee roar...

Prospero – The Tempest

IT TOOK THIRTY SECONDS for Dana to come to her senses.

'Why am I even asking the question? How long have you been a police officer?' she muttered to herself. At the very least there was a conspiracy to commit fraud, the intention to kidnap and commit an assault, but she had no solid evidence of a crime that would stand up. She had a couple of recorded conversations which were done without proof of identity, but more would be needed. After all nothing had happened to Bea yet; nothing that Dana knew of. All she knew for sure was that Jeremy had used her just to keep an eye on his wife for his own ends rather than for her safety.

It was clear that if she believed everything he'd told her about Bea she would be naïve at the very least, especially as she'd seen how the woman behaved and had heard background and many first hand witness accounts from three other people. Dana felt it was time to adjust her moral compass and to make a decision about her own future too. Did she really feel fulfilled carrying out surveillance and minor investigations? She used to investigate very serious crimes and had a whole team to command. She needed to do some serious thinking, that was for sure.

She waited about five minutes before ambling casually from her hiding place, head bent as if searching the river edge. You never knew who would be looking out of a window in the little cottages across the river and it wouldn't do to have people assuming she was behaving furtively. She made her way along the river bank a little way. The tide had turned, and the breeze had stiffened, light clouds scudded across the blue of the sky. A couple of men were loading a small day boat moored in the channel, ready to take the tide. They were fishermen, judging from the collection of rods and boxes they were hefting on board. Both waved, and she returned the greeting; she'd seen them in the pub when she was with Lorcan and Gwyn. Everyone was very friendly here.

Dana made her way down the beach to her hide and promised herself she'd get over the river to Bea's side if she saw anything suspicious, but she'd have to watch the tide. High on the dunes she had a better view of the whole beach from the village, as well as the approach paths to the cottage from the high ground behind it. This would be the best look-out. Dana shook her head, wondering how she could be so taken in by Jeremy. Her point of view had changed completely; now she was watching out for Bea, not reporting on her movements. She settled down, adjusted her cameras, took out a chocolate bar and waited. She had decided to tell Lorcan what she had overheard when they met later that night, come clean about her involvement and ask if she could help along with Gwyn and Thomas.

She'd no sooner finished her snack when she spotted Lorcan heading down the beach towards Nest's Point. She stood up and they exchanged a wave.

He was about to knock on the door when the dogs sounded a loud warning, and almost at once the door was flung open by Gwyn.

'Hey, only me!' Lorcan bent to greet the dogs. 'You could keep an army at bay, I'd say for sure.' He laughed said to Stella, 'How're the kids?'

Gwyn laughed too. 'Tickles me, that! Kids! They're fine, I think.'

Bea joined them. 'Come in, come in. Don't stand on ceremony,' she said.

'You've brightened up,' Lorcan said.

'I've had a night's sleep. Makes a difference,' she replied and added hastily, 'Gwyn did the babysitting down here.'

'Slept like a log, *down here,*' Gwyn added with a grin.

There was a tiny noise from near the hearth and Stella suddenly trotted back to the pups. They all watched her, puzzled, but it was Bea who said, 'It's that puppy.'

'Something up?' Lorcan muttered as the two men joined Bea and the dogs.

'It's the littlest one, the one born last, Gwyn.'

'Ahh, my favourite. Bit of white on his back paw.'

Stella curled herself around the whole litter but was furiously licking the smallest, who now and then gave a tiny whimper. Archie came over and pushed his nose into Stella's fur on her back and he raised his muzzle over the puppies, sniffing delicately. Stella gazed at him for a second or two then recommenced her cleaning. The communication between them was clear for the humans to understand. It was a worried enquiry then a reassurance, between friends. Archie returned to his sheepskin nest in the fire nook.

Lorcan took out his phone. 'Will I give Heather a bell, Bea? The others are snoring. He's upset though, restless.'

She and Gwyn exchanged a worried glance. 'I think so. Would you mind?' Bea said.

He made the call; Heather was in the area, at a riding stables, doing a routine job. She told them she'd be along as soon as she could and to keep the pup warm and with Stella. Gwyn looked at his watch, ran a frustrated hand over his hair, then said he really need to be gone and to keep him updated. Before he rushed off, he looked over his shoulder at Bea, who was crouched next to the dog bed.

His expression was puzzled yet wondering and as though she felt the intensity of his gaze, Bea turned quickly and met his eye. In that moment they both felt a powerful jolt of recognition; he saw Nest, the birth approaching, and she saw the Prince, anxious on her behalf.

It lasted only a second or two because the puppy mewed feebly, and Bea turned back to it. Gwyn rushed off to his appointment. Lorcan had been watching the dogs and had missed the exchange, but there had been an atmosphere of calm about the cottage that wasn't present last time he'd seen them together and he had noticed that when he came in.

He said, 'Y'know, this little one's just that – *little*. Maybe the other fatties are pushing him off her teats, or maybe he's not one to thrive quickly, might take a day or two to get over the shock of the birth.' He laughed gently. 'Listen to me! Me making out like a vet an'all. Maybe Heather's rubbing off on me, all that chat about births every five minutes. She seems to spend a lot of time at farms, helping with births of one kind and another. Apparently, it's all down to the plumbing, biological plumbing I mean.'

'It is in your line of work then,' Bea replied, and he laughed.

They watched Stella nuzzling the smallest pup. He whimpered a little as she stopped cleaning him with her tongue but nudged him towards her belly. The others made tiny piglet noises and rolled helplessly away as she adjusted her position; Bea righted them and helped the littlest to the teat. Stella touched the pup gently with her nose, then glanced quickly at Bea, flicked her ears back, a smile.

'She's in love with you, sure she is,' Lorcan murmured.

'Mutual feelings,' Bea answered. 'Will Heather be long, d'you think?' Stella was nosing the pup again. It wasn't feeding as vigorously as the others did and it kept up a feeble crying.

'She said it was only routine vaccinations, so she'll be along fairly soon.' Lorcan watched her stroke the dog. 'You and Mr. History getting on better then?' he asked, and she smiled.

'I guess we are actually. I really needed help and he was there. Well, Thomas would have been but for Jeremy pushing him over. I would never have imagined he'd do anything like that, but it turns out I've been quite wrong about him. He pushed Gwyn too, you know.'

Lorcan paused and looked into the fire.

'What is it?' Bea asked, a tiny shard of foreboding touching her heart.

So, he told her about the photographs Dana had shown him and Thomas earlier, but was shocked when he saw how affected she was. In fact, she was mortified, but she couldn't decide whether it was because people had witnessed Jeremy bullying her, or because someone had taken the shots without her knowledge. Everything felt wrong.

'He looked pleasant enough in the shots; his body language was all caring, but you looked as though you were trying to fend him off. It was the bust-up at the end that shocked me, sure it did. I've led a sheltered life I think, even with the penguins and killer whales.'

Bea realised that what made her burn with the sheer injustice of it was that Jeremy always did look pleasant even when he was saying the most vile and obscene things to her.

'There's no sound, is there?' You couldn't hear what he was saying, so I guess someone could imagine he was being solicitous. It's one of the things he does. Believe me he was being cruel, just plain cruel. No one but me heard of course and as usual. What did Dana say, the birdwatching woman, right? The one who popped over here?'

'Yes, she is, the birdwatcher, and I think she's okay, don't worry yourself. I've a feeling she's discreet. The thing is, she was disturbed by the scrap at the end. She was looking at some rare terns, Roseate terns, over here and then saw him arrive and shock you. You did look scared, Bea. She thought you might need help,' he said, hoping it would reassure her rather than make her feel spied upon.

Bea let her messy plaits fall over her shoulder to hide her face. She felt ashamed, not spied upon, ashamed that finally someone had seen her behaviour.

'Look,' he began, 'I believe you; I've met characters like him, plenty of times. Why don't you go and stay with Thomas for a while? You could take Stella and the kids.' He glanced over at them. 'The littlest is having a steadier drink now. That's better.'

She shook her head. 'No, I'm staying here. I need to get a solicitor. I'll go to Beaumaris when the littlest's okay. I don't want to leave any of them just now. Stella's been through a lot.' She stroked Stella. *What would I do without her? I've only known her a couple of days but it's like we were meant to be together. The puppy's got to be okay. How will she bear it if he's ill or dies?*

Just then the other pups began to wake up and shuffle closer to Stella's belly. Lorcan watched, torn between studying Bea's face and trying to judge how the littlest pup was doing, when his phone rang. When he saw the caller ID he answered it with resignation.

'Don't tell me!' he began. He held the phone away from his ear as the caller replied. 'Sure I will, Harry. Yep. I'll be seein' you,' he finished and to Bea he said, 'My goats've escaped the embarrassment of a fence and are chomping the neighbour's dahlias like two kids in a sweetie factory.'

'Goats?'

'Little devils, they are. I'll have to go, Bea. Will you be okay? I can give Dana a bell and ask her to pop over from the dunes. She's there now and I'm sure she'll not mind. She was worried about you yesterday. Maybe she could just set up her hide and be outside, be around if y'man comes again. I'll not be long.' Lorcan knew he was gabbling but the dahlias and his neighbour's wrath were bad enough, but Bea's expression and complete bodily stillness was making him very feel uneasy.

She said, 'No, I'll be fine. Don't disturb her, please. I'm fine. Come back when you can, though.'

He hurried to the door, saying, 'Heather'll be here in a jiff. See you soon, then.'

He jogged up the lane until he was on a level with the roof of the cottage and he turned to the dunes opposite, searching for any sign of Dana as he dialled her number on his phone. He knew he needed help, Dana's help, whatever Bea said; better to be safe than sorry and events were flying along on the wings of a storm. Dana answered at the first ring and told him she had him in her viewfinder. He waved, and she stood to return the greeting. He explained quickly what he had to do and apart from laughing at the idea of chomping goats, she agreed to keep her eyes peeled until he came back.

When Lorcan left, Bea locked the door behind him and went back to the dogs, sat herself by the hearth. The three bigger puppies had finished feeding and were being cleaned up by Stella, so Bea gently retrieved the littlest to prevent him from rolling into harm's way as his mother moved energetically about her task.

'Poor littlest one,' she crooned as she held him close, gently smoothing his new-born fur. 'Soon have you bossing the plumpies. The vet's on her way, don't worry, Littlest. Good name for you now, but I bet you'll grow big,' she told him. He waved a fat tiny paw in his sleep and gave a wheezy little sneeze. 'Not got fluid on your lungs, I hope.'

Stella threw her a glance at the note of worry in her voice but settled when the puppy squirmed contentedly in Bea's lap. He soon fell into a doze.

Bea was far from settled; her mind was filled with a coil of motives, fears, shame, sickness, death and all these people determined to help her.

It's not that I don't need help, I do really. It's just that I think I'm going to have to sort things out for myself otherwise I'll just be weakened beyond what I am now. What would Auntie Nest have said, or Mum? They'd both say I had to face things and make my own decisions, act for myself. It's the only way to grow, go forward. I'm hardly a child. One thing's for sure, I'm definitely getting divorced and the other is I'm staying here. It's where I belong, and I've got Stella and Archie, of course. I need to think of them as well as the puppies.

Littlest stirred uncomfortably and sneezed again. *Oh, where's the vet? I can't lose this little one.* The puppy's closed eyes and soft new fur tugged at her heart. 'I can't lose him, can't lose him,' she murmured. Her eyes own closed.

The fire crackled in the hearth, but it was a fire of sea coal that sent its coil of smoke through the chimney hole. Bea could smell the rosemary and marjoram in the pottage bubbling gently in the big pot over the fire. There were scents too of leeks, barley and beans. But then she felt the babe stir, gasped in pain, gripped the stirring spoon she had been using, almost snapping it.

'Oooo, that was sharp. You can't be wanting to come into the world yet? I'm not ready, cariad,' Bea whispered to herself and knew she was feeling Nest's pain, and all her unease about the birth and survival settled on her shoulders too.

The flames danced beneath the pot and when Bea looked away, she found that the scene before her had changed and was happening in the depths of the forest, across the river. There was a trivet over the fire there too; a brace of rabbit stewed slowly with thyme. Around the fire sat the four Sisters, all in comfortable poses, relaxing as they cooked their food and talked pleasantly. The light faded away from the amber and lemon circle of the flames, melting softly into the shadows of the forest. Beyond the trees the sun was a dusky apricot line melting into the horizon as twilight blanketed the island.

Bea's eyes found two separate paler shadows among the outer grey leaves and branches, and as she focused, she saw that they were figures, people, people she had seen before. Ithel and Edith. They were both sitting on the ground with their backs against a tree, both had their arms bound behind them around the trunk and their feet were tied together too. Both were silent and their expressions furious; Edith's hair had broken free of her coif and lay lank and dishevelled over her shoulders. Ithel's robe was ripped, exposing his bony chest, white in the shadows. But neither could speak because they were gagged. Bea felt their rage and shivered. Evil intent swam around them on the breeze.

Suddenly Sister of Air lifted her head.

'I hear them calling,' she murmured to the others around the fire. 'Nest has need of us, Sisters.

They stood and prepared quickly, dousing the fire, lifting the pot off the trivet and covering the food. They would take it with them.

'Listen!' whispered Sister of Earth. The wind carried a clear ribbon of sound, the rounded howl of a wolf.

Before they left, they threw old brychans over the two captives and checked their bonds were secure.

Sister of Earth told them, 'We have those who watch for us and see you. You will stay here, and we will return. Be assured.'

Bea's vision changed, and she was in the cottage, the wolves at her side. She felt her belly cramp once more and hugged her stomach, gasping with discomfort.

'I'm fine,' she said and reached out a hand to rest it on Mellt's back, closed her eyes a moment, smiled. 'At last,' she murmured. 'Wonderful.'

The feeling was suddenly shattered when there came a knock on the door. Bea opened her eyes to see, as she knew she would, that she was back in her own present.

Someone at the door. Who?

Chapter thirty-eight

Peril

Art thou afeard?...

Caliban - The Tempest

ARCHIE LEAPED UP and ran to the door barking, Stella was quickly beside her when Bea stood with the puppy in her arms. The dog was anxious and trotted around Bea, gave a short whine, stretching her nose up to the pup. Archie kept up a steady bark.

'Don't worry, dogs, it'll be Heather,' she said and opened the door wide, only to fall back a step when she saw who it was.

'Mairi.' She swallowed, moved her hand around the puppy. 'What do you want?' Archie dived outside and ran sniffing about her legs.

'Charming.' Mairi gave one of her tinkling laughs, smiled. 'What do I want? I'm here to help you, of course. Jeremy said you were happy to come along to my clinic where I can really give you the care you need. Would that be alright? You do need a good rest and then you'll be right as rain.' She pushed a strand of hair purposefully behind her ears and tucked her thick plait into the collar of her coat, checked her zip.

Stella began growling and the little terrier joined her as soon as Mairi spoke; they pushed past her, circled, nudged her continuously. Mairi took a step back, tried to push the bigger dog away with her hand and all the while, Bea was silent, shocked into immobility for a moment. Then she felt the puppy move against her and her heart felt lighter than it had for a long time.

'Thanks, Mairi, but no. I'm going nowhere. I did tell Jeremy, but he ignored me.'

Mairi put her hand in her pocket.

'I've brought the car up to the very door, as you see,' she said and stood back a little so that Bea could see the white Range Rover on the edge of the river. The tide was turning.

Mairi continued, 'No need for you to walk. Look, you can bring the little creature with you if that will make you comfortable. It's important to you, I see that now. We'll get someone to look after these dogs, don't worry.

Over on the dunes, Dana had watched with disbelief as the Range Rover drove up the beach. She had almost persuaded herself they wouldn't go through with it but the second she saw, through her lens, Mairi's hand go into her pocket and saw also the unmistakable syringe half-exposed. She leapt from her hide and pressed the speed-dial for Lorcan's number even as she plunged down the side of the dune and raced across the beach. The phone was turned off.

Bea saw something moving fast across the river behind Mairi and as she shifted her eyes to focus, Mairi took her hand out of her pocket, the syringe held down with her thumb on the plunger and stepped lightly forward. Dana raced towards the river, and when she plunged in, each step caused huge explosions of water and enough noise to divert anyone's attention, except Mairi. She was intent on her purpose, her eyes blazing with resolve and was in the act of lifting her hand to strike when Dana yelled to her to stop. Bea heard, saw Dana running towards them, and in that last instant, she turned to see Mairi's hand lifted to plunge the weapon down at her neck. Bea stumbled back and fell against the door, her arms covering the sleeping puppy.

But Stella was quicker than Mairi. She hadn't taken her eyes off the woman and as she moved to strike, the dog leapt up, growling deep in her throat and grabbed the arm in her jaws. Mairi screamed. She was pulled forwards and down by the dog, dropped the syringe on the path and tried to hit Stella with her free hand, still screaming high-pitched angry cries. As it was Stella let go of the arm and putting herself in between Bea and Mairi she didn't let up her furious noise. Archie danced hysterically round everyone's legs, snatching at Mairi's trousers, snarling.

When Bea saw the syringe fall from Mairi's hand she froze.

'Mairi, what are you doing with that?'

'What do you think I'm doing, you stupid bitch? I'm trying to help you,' she said and clamped a hand over her injured arm. 'Oh, my arm. It's probably broken, scarred at the very least. I'll sue you, don't think I won't. And you can pay plenty. I know that. Ah, my God it hurts too.'

It was then that Dana reached the cottage and, jumping over the garden wall, she took hold of Mairi's arms from behind, immobilising her.

Mairi shrieked again. 'Ahh. Let go! Who the hell are you? I'm injured. Get off me! Oh, my arm, my arm. What are you doing? Let go. Let go, I said.'

'You were going to stab Bea with that. You're going to stay still while we get the police,' Dana told her as she held her with ease against her body.

'Yes, go on. Get the police. We'll see who's taken away then. That dog attacked me. Yes, call the police, I'll start with that dog, vicious bloody animal and that stupid old one too. They'll both have to be put down. Both uncontrollable.'

She tried to kick backwards at Dana's legs; some damage might have been done as Mairi wore heavy walking boots, but she was no match for the other woman who seemed to know every move she could think of. Mairi's squirming and struggling had no effect on Dana's grip.

'Do that again and I'll just drop you to the ground. Stand still,' Dana told her, calmly. 'I saw what happened and I've got proof of your actions on my camera. It's still running. Keep quiet anyway. In fact, shut the hell up. You're giving the dog a headache.'

'And you are holding me against my will. Let go!' Mairi shrieked as loudly as she could.

'I said, stand still then we can talk,' Dana told her.

Stella hadn't stopped barking but stayed on guard in front of Bea and it was into this scene that Heather arrived, driving quickly up the rocky side of the beach in her Landrover. She grabbed a bag from the seat next to her, jumped out and ran towards them. She hadn't been expecting more than a sick puppy.

'What's all this blether?' she shouted above the barking.

'Heather! Thank God!' Bea cried. 'It's the vet for the puppy. He's not well.'

Dana nodded at Heather, telling her, 'I'll explain in a minute. We met briefly the other day. But this one's no friend of Bea's' She nodded her head at the struggling Mairi, who was still screaming at the same volume as the barking dogs.

Dana signalled with her head at the syringe on the path and continued, 'Will you pick that up carefully please? Put it in your bag for now, if you don't mind, preferably in a container of some kind; careful of the prints for evidence purposes. I don't want this one to get hold of it again.'

Heather gaped in disbelief. 'What the …?' but she quickly bent and retrieved the syringe.

'Yep. She was going for Bea with it. It's probably got a strong sedative in it, at a guess.'

Mairi screeched furiously, 'Let me go. There's nothing of the kind in that syringe. How dare you?'

Heather said, 'Haud yer wheesht. No one's bothering what ye say.' Then she turned back to Bea. 'Shall we go and see to this wee chap? I think we can safely leave this one to your friend. She seems capable.' She raised a questioning eyebrow at Bea then to Dana she said, 'Yes, you're Dana, you called the other day. And would you be the lassie Lorcan's been nattering about?' she asked, and Dana nodded.

'How would you know?'

'I'm by way of being family.' She gestured to Mairi with her bag. 'Yon's a right chancer, from what I've heard.'

'You could say that. I'm alright here; more than fine. I'll deal with things. You go and see to your patient'

Heather nodded and took Bea with her into the cottage, along with the reluctant dogs. They closed the door.

'Just you and me,' Dana told Mairi as she let go of her arms. Dana stood with her legs braced.

Mairi wheeled round to face her. 'How dare you? That's common assault, I think you'll find, and holding me against my will!' She gripped her injured arm dramatically.

'I think you may find it's against the law to stab someone with a syringe against their will.'

Mairi was smaller than Dana but she lifted her chin defiantly as she snapped, 'Not if you are her psychiatrist and she is in the middle of a psychotic episode – I think you'll find…' She turned to her car.

'If you wanted to commit her to a mental health unit as a practising psychiatrist, you wouldn't be acting solo, *I think you'll find*. Anyway, off you go! I'll be seeing you…count on it. Go on, sod off.'

'Typical of Bea to have someone as uncouth as you for a little chum. Maybe you're more than that? She has been ignoring her husband lately.' Mairi cradled her injured arm. 'I'll be getting that dog dealt with, by the way. That's a firm promise.'

'Just go, before you really annoy me.' Dana's face was expressionless, she folded her arms and watched silently while Mairi stalked to her car. She turned it with difficulty as the tide was rising under her wheels, then she sped away, causing a huge wake to arc on either side of the car. She would just make it to the end of the beach.

Dana knew she'd find her again, no problem at all. She watched the Range Rover until it disappeared round the bend into the village, then finally turned to knock on the door, calling that Mairi had gone. It was Bea who answered, and she drew her rescuer indoors and thanked her. She was shaken by the attack and Dana offered to stay when Heather went but Bea asked her to watch from her hide until Gwyn returned, as he'd promised, and to phone if she saw either Mairi or Jeremy.

'Thanks, thanks more than I can say, really. Gwyn said he'd only be a couple of hours. Should be back fairly soon.' Her voice was weak now. She still held the littlest pup, watched by Stella who had returned to the others. Heather guided her to the settle.

'The mad woman? What's her game? She assaulted you!'

'I don't know what's going on with Mairi. I hardly know the woman. She and her husband are friends of my husband's. She usually ignores me but now it's as though she's stalking me; keeps turning up. I've no idea why she'd attack me like that.' Her voice was flat with shock.

Heather was decisive. 'I'll get the contents of that syringe checked out. I think it'll be important.'

Dana agreed. 'She said she was your psychiatrist. Why would she do that?' She looked steadily at Bea, who answered firmly.

'I haven't got one. I don't need one. This is what's more disturbing. I am not ill.'

'Look, Bea,' Heather said, 'We know it. The problem is, why did she say it? Is she the one who's ill?'

'She's actually a psychiatrist herself; that's no safeguard against mental illness though, is it?'

Heather nodded. 'No indeed.'

Dana laid a hand on Bea's arm. 'I'm going to check out some things I've seen while I've been down here. I won't say anything yet, but I think I may be able to find out what she's doing. I'll just say that for now. Can you trust me?'

Bea was intrigued, had mixed feelings that anyone could fathom out Mairi or Jeremy, especially Jeremy. She agreed to trust and wait; after all the woman had saved her, hadn't she?

It was Heather who spoke up next. 'More importantly, the wee chap who's offside? The littlest pup, Lorcan tells me. This is the one, I take it?'

She examined him carefully. 'He's just not been getting enough of his mum's attention. There's nothing wrong with him; clear lungs and a good heart, normal temp, don't worry, Bea. Just make sure he has his fill at feed time, move the others out of his way and keep him warm; no chills and rolling off the bed. Okay? I'll call back tomorrow to check on him. I'm on the end of the phone, remember?'

Dana and Heather tried again to get Bea to allow one of them stay a while, but she was adamant that the cottage was impregnable, and she'd lock up. Dana borrowed wellies to get back over the rising river and Heather took her rucksack and bags with most of her equipment and said she would walk to Lorcan's.

'It's only half a mile and I'm a fit old bird. It's handy that I'm off duty in an hour. Half day. I've all my big gear and plenty of drugs in the Landrover, all well secured in the safe boxes. In any case the tide'll stop the druggies. They'll drown before they get anything. Keep it safe enough. I'll call in the morning. I'm an early riser, by the way.'

The two women left, and Bea went to lie down by the fire again.

Getting to be a habit, all this lying down!

She laughed to herself and felt strangely calm considering the events of the last hour or so.

Now, that's not normal. Very weird. Mairi and Jeremy? I wonder.

Her eyes were heavy, and she lay down her head and listened to the sound of the rising wind and the sea as the tide came in. In her mind's eye the sea roared so loudly that it filled her mind, and black waves tumbled towards her, breaking into glaring icy cascades.

Outside Dana went back to her hide and kept watch. She tried Lorcan's phone again, got through and told him everything. The appearance of the syringe had sealed it for her.

Chapter thirty-nine

Decision

*Thou most lying slave, Whom stripes may move,
not kindness! I have us'd thee, filth that thou art,
with human care...*

Prospero - The Tempest

IT WAS DARK as the sisters headed across the river to Nest's cottage and found a welcome but no urgent need for their help; the sharp pains that made Nest cry out had stopped and her wolves were now relaxed. Although her labour had started, they all felt it would be many hours yet before the babe was born. It was a comfortable, happy meeting and Mellt and Seren lay dozing by the fire as the women chatted and sang.

The sisters slept by the fire with Nest and only woke as the late dawn of the Autumn day began to gild the outgoing tide and the oystercatchers raced along the river, whistling and carolling. The women broke their fast with small oaten cakes made freshly by Chwaer y Ddaear and the mead that was made from the honey of Nest's own bees.

Nest stretched and ran her hands over her tight belly and told the others, 'Sisters, my pains are only a little closer. I think baby will tarry more hours yet before she comes to greet us. Did you not say you have a task that needs doing?'

So, after Chwaer y Ddaear had examined her and agreed about the baby and about the task, the others rose and were making ready to leave when Sister of Water put a kindly hand on her sister's arm, saying:

'Chwaer y Ddaear, I think we three alone should take our prisoners to the llys, as we decided. Once the good Prince hears what they have to say for themsleves he will surely treat them as they deserve and we will return before the new little sister arrives to greet the midday sun. I would be more content if one of us, you, stayed with Nest. Babes can be contrairy.'

And Nest was glad because childbirth was frightening. Mellt and Seren followed the others across the river and into the edge of the forest and then took their leave with happy yips before loping home along the shore.

A gentle wind soughed through the branches and the Sisters made little noise as they walked below them and along the track through the trees. All the wild forest creatures were used to the women and went about their morning business. The sun rose brightly, thrusting shafts of gold through the canopy to light first a glade of flaming leaves, then another of shining toadstools poking through the forest litter, or yet the dancing diamond stream threading its way to the river. The air was sharp with the scent of changing leaves, pine sap and salt and the Sisters breathed deeply of the rich perfumes as they moved briskly to their camp.

As expected, the prisoners were as they had been left the night before and fear and fury mingled in the baleful looks they threw at their captors. Both struggled angrily to show their feelings and grunted behind the restraint of their gags.

Sister of Water laughed at their efforts as she stood easily before then, hands on hips, looking down at the dishevelled figures tied to the tree.

'**Chwaer Tân, you are Sister of Fire**, put fresh kindling under our pot and raise bright flames. Our prisoners must be hungry,' she said, smiling.

'Sister, they stink. They are more in need of cleansing than food. I will waste none of our food on them.' Her voice was heavy with sarcasm. 'You are **Chwaer Dŵr**, so do you give them a drink lest they faint on the way and you might douse them with what's left over to wash off some of their filth.' She tossed her long ropes of red hair behind her shoulders as she bent to feed the kindling and blow on the tiny embers and set their cauldron on the trivet. It would cook slowly.

'Not I!' **Chwaer Dŵr** turned to her third sister. '**Chwaer Awyr**, you have a fondness for this woman,' she said and grinned. 'What would you...?'

'I would spurn her, kick her as she did me, I would call *her* hag and fling her wailing into the empty night of friendlessness. But I will not. We should do nothing but what we have planned, and for that I am impatient and then we will return to welcome our friend. Indeed the hearts of this pair need more cleansing than their wrinkled bodies, but we cannot do that; tis far too great a task.'

The three women clapped their hands high above their heads and began a wild whooping dance around the tree where Edith and Ithel were tied. The captives threw their heads to left and right trying to see what went on, their eyes bulging in fear. But as soon as the dance had begun it was over and the Sisters stood before them with knives in their hands.

The gags were yanked from their mouths and after coughing and retching the captives soon found their voices and hurled abuse.

'Foul witches. I'll see you roasting in the Holy flames for this. My Lady will avenge me!' Edith screeched, spittle flecking her mouth. 'Why do you hold us here? What harm have we done you, hags?' The skirt of her gown, which was heavily mired with mud, had rucked up round her legs and she had lost a leather shoe and she beat her heels on the ground in a frenzy of frustration.

Chwaer Awyr said, 'Your foul mouths do harm daily. You are a shrew and a gossip, woman, and you,' she nodded at Ithel, 'are a traitor to my Lord Prince and also, you have harmed our friend, Nest, who is equally dear to our hearts. You lusted after her and tried to do her great damage.'

In reply, Ithel was no less vicious and cursed them by the old gods, promising them they would be, 'Locked in the eternal darkness of the earth, buried alive together with all the frenzied creatures of the soil to feast on their cringing flesh.'

The Sisters ignored them, but for a sardonic curve of the lips or a raised eyebrow, and even a grin of amusement. Instead they cut through the bonds that held them to the tree and then those that tied their legs and forced them to walk up and down the clearing until they could stagger moderately well; a difficult task after their days of captivity. A gleam of hope and of malice lit the eyes of both Edith and Ithel. When they had loosened their limbs sufficiently, the Sisters, having not spoken a word, undid their hand bonds then fastened the two people together with stout leather thongs, side by side. Edith's left hand was fixed to Ithgel's right in front of their bodies, and his left to her right behind their bodies, much in the form of a dancing couple in the simple country romps of the ordinary people.

Then the Sisters used their sharp knives to cut away the clothes they wore until they were both naked. When they realised the intention of the Sisters, the captives screamed and struggled mightily, but **Sister of Air** stopped this quickly by the simple method of holding a knife to each throat, just under the the point of their jaws.

'Are you ready?' **Sister of Water** asked them but both were puzzled.

Ithel said, 'Kill us if you mean to, instead of shaming us here, fiend.' He stood up as srtraight as bodily discomfort allowed him.

'Feel no shame before our eyes, Ithel ap Deykin. We have no good opinion of you that can be destroyed by the sight of your mealy, sagging and all too naked flesh joined with this woman, fresh from your lusts,' **Sister of Air** explained, her voice kindly, her expression bright with revenge and amusement.

There was an outraged shriek from Edith. 'What lust, you heathen harpie? What game is this?'

The Sisters did not deign to answer as **Sister of Fire** tied a long leather thong to each of their necks and tugged it.

'Come,' she urged them, 'We are taking you home to the llys, together. People will think what they will think. It is the way of the world. Are you not glad to return after all these days? The Prince may wonder where his bard is, and the Princess will surely miss her servant.'

'I am no servant, I am gentle born and a Lady in Waiting, you witch. My Lady will puni...' Edith began but stumbled and finished her speech on a screaming note when one of the Sisters pushed her from behind.

'Walk on apace,' cried **Sister of Fire** and yanked the thongs again until they both began to move.

The captive pair were dragged on through the forest. Brambles snatched at their bare skin, stones and sharp-thorned branches pierced their tender, unshod feet. The sisters walked in silence and so did their captives but the quality of the silence was very different. The Sisters were fulfilled and purposeful whereas, Edith and Ithel were brooding and fearful, humiliated and trying to stay afoot. They were cold too, and hungry. It was a crisp day, and bright, but clouds gathered in the West. Edith tried to shield her body from Ithel's view by turning her shoulder but he pulled her back as he stumbled then when her arm touched his bare torso, she winced and yanked him the other way. It was an uncomfortable walk.

The first leaves were beginning to fall from the birch and oak and floated sedately to the cushioned forest floor. As the party moved onward, the captives made more noise than the Sisters because of their hampered gait and their fury, and this disturbed the birds in their wake. A murder of crows flapped loudly from their nests in the canopy and swooped around the group, raucous and testy. A blackbird shrilled a warning; robin, thrush and wren gave voice to the cry too. Over the forest canopy, a flight of geese chattered and grumbled on their journey.

They were soon at the edge of the dunes and then the beach with no trees to shield their progress. The Sisters kept up a steady pace and where the river Ffraw burst out from the marshes, they crossed the pebbled shallows and both captives stumbled and screeched. As they climbed the slope to the llys, Edith hung her head, trying to shield her face with the curtain of thin greasy hair and her breasts with her arm, but Ithel continually pulled her arm down with his, his expression disdainful, his head held high, defiantly so. She tripped often and then he laughed at her. People were about their daily business but in no time at all the strange procession was seen and there were stares and then shouts and finally lewd calls and laughs. Neither of the captives was well liked.

The Sisters stopped when they were at the gates to the llys and

Sister of Fire spoke to them in the hearing of the small crowd who followed. Everyone knew of the Sisters and revered their skills and their strangeness, and despite it being a Christian community, it was generally felt that women such as they were favoured by the old gods and must be treated with care and respect.

'You must await the pleasure of the Prince,' **Sister of Air** told the captives. 'His is the right to ensure justice in his land.'

The people stood respectfully back to let the Sisters pass, then continued their jeering and laughter, and this was soon joined by missiles; animal droppings, wet seaweed, clods of earth, more manure and the crowd laughed and booed the shrinking pair; dogs barked, children shrieked. Edith and Ithel stood before the gates, she cowed and ashamed, he defiant, berating her, calling her a Norman whore.

It was not long before the spectacle caught the attention of those at the llys, indeed some of the Prince's Teula had been at the gate laughing too. The Prince's household steward, Owain, came to the gate to discover the cause of the disturbance and was soon in possession of the information he needed. However he did not release either of them from their bonds because both had done him much diservice over the years. Instead he left them standing there to suffer their shaming and went to the Prince to discover his wishes.

He had not been gone many minutes when an angry voice was heard approaching and a young man appeared. It was Gwilam, the blacksmith, husband to the dead maid, Angharad who died in childbirth. He had long regretted that he had not allowed the still living babe to be taken from its dead mother's womb and knew his cowardice to be born of his deep fear of losing his Angharad. So, when she did die he fled, fled to the forest and was gone, alone and grieving for days. Even in the midst of this grief he had not lost his trust and respect for the Sisters, so when he heard how Edith had treated **Sister of Air** when she was tending Yestyn, he vowed to atone by helping the Sister if he could.

Gwilam pushed through the crowd and strode up to the naked captives. He was red in the face and sweating, fresh from the heat of his forge.

'You, woman, you accused **Sister of Air** of letting my Angharad die. You are a liar, woman; **it was my own fear that would not let her help when all was near lost.** And you are a traitor to the Prince. I've heard that you plot against him!' he shouted in her face, standing close.

Edith was shocked. 'No, no – you lie. I do not plot against the Prince, 'tis him!' she stuttered and tried to lift her left arm to point at Ithel, but tied as they were he resisted and yanked her bonds. She stumbled and was pulled against him, causing them both to fall to the ground.

The crowd cheered and shouted and amidst the pair trying to right themselves, Gwilam stepped in and lifted both by the hair until they were upright. He kept the hold and propelled them towards the gate of the llys.

'Then you can tell this to my Lord. It is his right to hear what you say,' he told them through his teeth. He was a big man and easily moved them before him, protesting loudly as they stumbled.

'Wait, wait,' cried Edith. 'I am as old as your mother, would you have my Lord see me shamed like this? Have pity, give me some cover.'

'You are not one to show pity, woman. Everyone knows your evil tongue; you are a scold, and the children know the feel of your hand for certain. My Lord Prince will not be moved by your condition; I warrant he's seen worse corpses on the battlefield.'

Ithel restrained himself and kept silent.

Gwilam marched them to the hall where Llewelyn sat on his great chair on the dais, listening to Owain the steward.

The Prince watched them approach, his face unreadable by all present. Gwilam inclined his head respectfully and pushed the captives to the floor where they knelt with heads bowed. Edith began to cry soundlessly and her tears splashed onto the rushes.

'Gwilam, what's this?' the Prince asked quietly.

'My Lord Prince, two traitors brought here in shame by the Sisters.'

'Shamed indeed. Yet two people of some import in my household.

I see Ithel ap Deykin, my bard, a post of honour. And I see a woman of the royal retinue, the favoured Lady-in-Waiting to the Princess Joanna. Why are they shamed thus, Gwilam? What are their crimes or wrongdoings?' His voice was calm, moderate.

Gwilam was about to speak when Edith interrupted, her voice strong, despite her tears.

'Hear me, my Lord, this man, your bard, is the traitor, not I.'

Ithel tried to push her over and stop her speaking, all the while his voice a snarling growl of fury as he berrated her, calling her deranged, out of her wits, a liar, a Norman whore.'

It took only a moment for the Prince to silence him by a signal to one of his household knights. The man stepped forward and put his dagger to Ithel's throat, telling him quietly to, 'Hold your noise.' Another instruction was given, this time to Owain, who took a brychan from a stool near the high table and went down into the hall to cut both captives' bonds and then covered Edith. Llewelyn saw that Ithel stood defiantly when accused of a dire crime, and so left him without.

Llewelyn adressed Edith first. 'Speak, tell what you know, not what you suspect.'

So, she told him how Ithel plotted with Yestyn to kidnap Joanna on her way to the nunnery and Ithel's idea to ransom her; she told of Yestyn's alliegence to Gruffydd and how he wanted to usurp his father, the Prince. She relished the telling of Ithel's hatred of Joanna and his wish for a break with England, but she had hardly finished reciting his treachery when **Sister of Air** appeared at the foot of the dais. She gazed urgently at the Prince until he motioned for her to approach, and as she whispered her information in his ear, his face darkened. She had told him of Ithel's attack on Nest. She also told him that Nest was in labour.

Llewelyn acted swiftly and decisively.

He ordered that Ithel's harp was to be brought from his chamber now, and broken into a thousand pieces before him.

'You will play no more before princes or commons,' Llewelyn told him. 'You will be chained by Gwilam here and taken this day to the castle at Caer yn Arfon and there put in the dungeon until further notice. You will also go naked to your imprisonment.'

On hearing the fate he was to suffer, Ithel held his head higher, but those close by him saw tears run down his face when his harp was mentioned.

The Princess had heard of the commotion and joined the throng in the hall. She was shocked when she saw Edith and then devastated to hear what plots Edith had become involved with. She had been her confidante and body servant since her childhood, but she stood back as Llewelyn decided her fate. Her **allegiance** must be to the Prince, yet she was not unmoved as he said Edith was to be sent home alone to England, because that was clearly where her heart lay. Joanna could not argue in Edith's defence as this was true. The punishment was for her involvement in these plots as well as her abiding and poorly hidden hatred of the Welsh. She was to be allowed only one set of clothes and a cloak and would be taken to one of the Marcher lords, who Llewelyn called a friend, and set to work. Edith gripped the brychan around her body and did not then disguise the expression of contempt and hatred that she showed to the Prince.

Yestyn was found next and brought before his Lord, pushed to his knees. His injuries were unhealed and he trembled with pain, yet he too showed a defiant face to Llewelyn.

'You, one of my Uchelwr, one of my favoured band of knights, that noble and **chivalrous** band of brothers; you are now unworthy of that brotherhood and also of my trust. You were placed here to be in my service and thus bring honour to your own house as its heir and to your noble father who loves and **reveres** you; but not for much longer, I wager. You are to be sent home to him in shame and in chains as a traitor. He will welcome the responsibility of punishing you himself for the sake of his house.'

Yestyn was dragged away, shouting his fury, by two of his former brotherhood. Then Edith and Ithel were taken away separately to begin their own punishments. Ithel remained scornful and silent, but Edith cried out most piteously to Joanna and the Princess's heart was sore as she turned away her head.

Then it was that Llewelyn addressed his wife.

'My love, my wife and Royal Princess of all my lands, I myself will give you escort on your journey into seclusion, I and all of my Uchelwr, for your safety and honour. I find myself at fault for not doing this before now and I ask your pardon.' He looked into her eyes.'I also ask pardon for ever doubting you in any way.'

'You have it always, my Lord,' she answered and saw he was was comforted by her words and she knew by that he was truly contrite.

He continued, 'Furthermore I will leave a large guard outside the nunnery for your protection for as long as you wish to remain, and I will long for your return.' He reached out his hand for hers, which she gave quickly. He kissed it gently.

He then dispatched a messenger to bring his son Gruffydd from his own castle. His father wished to speak to him on a matter of utmost importance.

Still holding Joanna's hand, he pulled her to his side and told her of the message about Nest being in labour.

'My lord,' she said, 'I have come to know Nest better and I too wish for her safe delivery. Can we send a messenger now to see how she does? I would that you also send gifts for the child, but later will do for that.'

'Wife, it will be done. It is also my wish.'

So, he sent for **Sister of Air telling her** to return to Nest's cottage and discover how she fared. His page, Ralph, was to go and accompany her as his trusted messenger, and return to his Prince with the news himself.

Llewelyn rose from his chair and, offering Joanna his hand, he escorted her from the hall.

Chapter forty

Unmasked

I am right glad he is so out of hope...

Antonio - The Tempest

IT WAS LUNCH TIME by the time Gwyn set off for the cottage; the weather was still bright and crisp, and the tide had just turned. It ushered in a lively offshore wind which made the marram grass on the dunes lie flat and neatly combed. It also sent a hazy sheet of sand skimming the beach, so Gwyn pulled up his hood and bent into the wind, enjoying the buffeting. As he neared the end of the dunes where Dana had her hide, he caught the flash of a camera and stopped to scan the tops. He smiled when he saw her stand, and they waved at each other.

It took a while to rouse Bea from sleep. Gwyn could see her in front of the fire and once she saw his face at the window, her eyes first registered alarm and then, quickly, relief.

'Thank God it's you!' she said, opening the door, drawing him in. 'I should have asked Dana or Heather to stay; they did offer after she'd gone, Mairi, I mean. She was here, Gwyn! She tried to stab me with a syringe, probably full of sedative. Stella saved me; got hold of her hand just as she was about to do it. She bit her, leapt up and bit her, and held on too! She saved me, Gwyn. Then Dana appeared from nowhere and grabbed hold of Mairi from behind and Heather arrived then. God, it was awful. I think she wants me *dead,* her and Jeremy between them. They must be in this together. Now that *is* paranoid, so maybe Jeremy's right. I know it's dramatic but it's real, real and frightening, Gwyn,' she gabbled.

He took hold of her hands that were clawing at the ends of her plaits.

'Shhhh, Bea. It's okay. Let's go inside, hey? Look, Archie's waiting.' He nodded pointedly down at the little dog who sat pressed against her side, looking up at her.

She stooped, picked him up, tucked him under her arm. There was a tiny noise from further inside.

'Oh, Littlest is crying. Heather said his health's okay; has to be kept warm and fed, no rolling out of bed.' She pushed Archie into Gwyn's arms then rushed over to the dog nest and found Stella busily nuzzling all the pups, but Littlest was being trodden on by the others. Bea rescued him, tucked him under a fold of the blanket and put him onto a teat.

'Whoa!' Gwyn said. 'Hungry little piglet when he gets going.' He returned Archie to Bea. 'He doesn't mind being treated like a monarch, does he?'

She managed a smile. He chatted about nonsense and soon she began to relax a little with the dogs; then he offered to get them both some lunch, if she was okay with that. She was. While they were eating cheese on toast by the fire, he told her his news.

'It's a bit disquieting as a matter of fact. I'd just arrived home and was on my way into the house when who should I see in the car park on the other side of the river? Only that woman, Mairi. I spotted the flashy car first, got my binoculars out just as she was joined by a bloke in a dark red E-type Jag. Your husband. I'd spot that pillock without binoculars. So, basically you're not wrong about them being in it together.'

Bea stopped eating; her face blanched almost instantly. 'They were actually meeting *here?* So close. Is that what you're saying?'

He nodded, watching her, his eyes searching her face to gauge her reaction. 'Yes, they were, Bea. Got it in one. You okay?'

She nodded.

'They were standing very close and arguing into each other's faces, quite intimately, I thought. She was cradling her arm and when he grabbed it, I guess to examine it more closely, she slapped him hard and then stormed off, got in the car, locked the doors. He left then; went to his own car and drove off and I think it was the top road to towards Rhosneigr.'

She said, 'He could have just turned into the village, not gone on to

Rhosneigr. He could park up and be heading here on the top path.'

'No, I didn't see his car go that way and I was watching for a few more minutes.'

She rushed to the window, scanned the beach and the dunes opposite.

'Bea, I'm here now. I can handle him. I'd like to handle him, believe me.'

She felt the hairs on the back of her neck prickling and turned to look at him. Gwyn stood in a pose of furious readiness, and he wore a dark blue woollen cloak with a big gold brooch at the shoulder, brown calf skin boots and a heavy leather belt around his red cote. His sword was sheathed in its jewelled scabbard and his hand rested on the hilt. His knuckles were white as he gripped it and his face was dark with fury.

'Gwyn, Gwyn?' Bea whispered. 'Are you…? You look…' she faltered and grasped the window sill to steady herself, but before she could fall, he was with her and caught her round the waist.

'Hey, whoa! I can handle him, honestly. You look weird though. Better sit down again.' He guided her back to the fire. 'I seem to say that every time I see you.'

'It's just…you looked like the Prince for a minute. It's dark in here.'

'No, it's light in here. Sit down, go on. So, you imagined me as Llewelyn?' He grinned. 'You actually saw me? I didn't feel any different. D'you think I should?'

'Look, Gwyn, yes, I saw you… *him*. I don't know how you should feel, do I?

'I just thought…'

'Yes, for a second or two, you *were* Llewelyn, or he was here, a slip in time, you know, as I explained. I'm beginning to think these layers of time are quite loosely stacked. I'm slipping between them as though I'm darting behind trees in the forest.'

He grinned. 'What I wouldn't give for an hour in Llewelyn's shoes, boots probably. Back in this time though, I saw something else happen in the car park.'

She tensed. The puppies snuffled in their sleep, Littlest tucked under Stella's chin.

'There was another bloke in the car park. He was in a van, looked like a builder's van. When The Arse had zoomed off in his E-type, and Mairi was left brooding in her car, he got out, went straight over to her, knocked on the window. She did jump then, and with what happened next, I'm guessing she unlocked it in shock. Anyway, he then wrenched it open and dragged her out, actually pushed her back against her car and tried to throttle her, hands round her throat, the full works.'

'What? What happened then?'

'She kicked him, pushed him away then stalked forward like a bloody panther. He backed off but kept shouting.'

'Sounds like her, but who was he?'

'No idea. Didn't look like a builder. But they were obviously very familiar with each other. She pushed him away and tried to slam the door, but he bawled at her and you could tell she was equally furious with him. It wasn't some random attack. They knew each other very well indeed. I guess you'd have to ,to throttle someone but then stop in the middle, as it were and carry on yelling.'

'What did the man look like?' Bea's mind was racing ahead to make sense of the scene.

Gwyn rubbed his chin, stared at the ceiling trying to picture the man. 'Stocky, dark hair in a buzz cut, fortyish, about your height, casual clothes, good stuff at a guess. Why?'

'Could be her husband. Could be,' she said. 'But in a builder's van? He's a consultant, orthopaedic trauma.'

'Well, into construction then. Maybe he was in hiding, surveillance, y'know. Maybe he borrowed the van. Wouldn't be the first time a bloke followed his erring wife, would it?''

'I think I heard something about a house extension and a clinic or something. So are you saying he suspects her of meeting Jeremy on the quiet?' Bea was ridiculously cheered by the idea and she flashed a grin. It felt strange; her face muscles were unused to such spontaneous action.

'It does look that way and would explain the throttling.'

'Mmmm. Is that what you think about a marriage? What happened then?'

'I know nothing of marriage - as yet. For grown up stuff like that, I am but a child, I'll admit. Anyway, he stalked off to the van but still shouting what looked like threats over his shoulder, lots of gesticulating. She drove off, no I don't know which way, a neighbour knocked on my door and I missed it. You can hardly keep binoculars in front of your eyes when someone is talking about their gutters.'

Bea suddenly craned her neck to look through the window.

'Look Gwyn, it's Dana. She's come across from her hide. She saved me you know—well, her and Stella. Everything is so ridiculous. I never thought I'd be saying a phrase like that and meaning 'saved my life'. I'm supposed to do that; I'm a doctor. It's strange, really.'

Gwyn took a single stride to open the door. 'Hello there!' he said and, arm extended in welcome, stood back to allow Dana in.

'Okay if I pop in, Bea?' Dana called before she stepped over the threshold.

Gwyn made a dramatic gesture of smacking himself on the forehead. 'Here I go again, presumption in cart loads. Bea, it's Dana, okay?''

Dana waited on the threshold, out of sight of Bea.

Bea hadn't heard and continued to stare out of the window intently.

'They're here! By Our Lady, 'tis not too soon!' she muttered quietly to herself, then she stepped back and clutched her stomach. Gwyn heard her groan and turned to catch her just as she took a faltering step, doubled up and sank to her knees.

'I've got you, don't worry,' he said. 'Bloody hell, you okay?'

Dana stepped into the room. 'What's up?'

Bea shook her head, slowly raised herself. 'Bit of a stomach ache, not to worry.' She patted Gwyn's arm and he moved it from round her waist. 'I reckon it's all the stress of the past few days.'

Gwyn nodded. 'I saw The Arse in the car park this morning. So, he's back. Mairi's here too and apparently her husband has joined the party.'

'That's weird,' Dana said. 'Mairi's husband. Bea told you about the attack, the syringe?'

'Yes, just. Most things are, if you overthink them, Dana, but why would Mairi's husband being here sound weird to you?'

Dana made a wry face. 'I have something I need to explain to you two.'

Bea and Gwyn looked at each other.

'Come in. Sit. Tell!' Gwyn said.

Dana told them her tale. When she'd finished Gwyn took a deep, considering breath.

'As I said, I saw him, Jeremy - just saying his name makes me want to beat him to a pulp – saw him earlier in the village car park talking to Mairi,' he said.

Dana said, 'Mairi, mmm. We've had words. She's vicious, determined.'

'Of course, the syringe. You saved Bea then. What if you'd not been here? And you're a bit of an athlete by all accounts. Can handle yourself too.'

Dana shrugged. 'Goes with the job.'

Gwyn had his hands on his hips, head bent, thinking. 'I think he went left out of the dunes car park, so he may be tracking round here the back way, over the top fields. Could you stay a while down here, with Bea and the dogs? I'm going to get up behind the cottage and see if I can spot him.'

Dana agreed readily but Bea said, 'Hey, I am here you know. And grateful as I am for all your care, both of you and everyone, I may have seen the light at long last. He had me followed, so there is a plot and I'm not psychotic. It's as though a veil has fallen away from my eyes, and I feel a whole lot better about myself and everything. But I am a bit confused about you, Dana. I can't think straight. It's odd that someone comes and tells you they've been spying on you for money and then saves your life, well probably saved it.'

Dana was used to this sort of ambivalence and challenge in the way people felt about her job, her mindset, her entire moral compass, her reliability as a friend.

She said, 'I'm sorry, Bea. I understand completely and if it's any comfort, he had me fooled for a while and I've cracked some tough nuts when I was in GMP. It was meeting you and other people who know you that made me doubt what he said.'

'Bea, you should tell her what he did to you. Go on, just briefly. It was him in the wrong, so much in the wrong; makes my blood boil. I guess Dana knows his worth by now, but just tell her how evil he's been.'

Bea took a breath. 'I don't know if I can, not just now.' She hid her face in her hands.

'Don't then,' Dana said. 'It'll keep. I think I may have heard a fair bit.' She told them about the conversations she'd overheard. 'So I know. You've been through a lot. I'm really sorry.'

Bea listened, shivered. 'Haloperidol? That makes sense now; the way I felt, the weight gain. It's colourless, odourless, tasteless. The sleeping draught. Why did I allow him to…? I must have been out of it alright.' She wiped her eyes, looked straight at Dana. 'I feel I ought to be outraged and throw you out, but honestly, I'm just relieved I know where you're coming from now. Now you've cleared some things up for me, I do actually feel better about myself. What happens now, for you?'

'As it happens, I've decided to change my slant on life, close down my agency. I think I've had enough, and I need something more fulfilling. I've always been into photography and the sea so I'm going to apply to do a degree in Marine Biology at Bangor. I think Lorcan might help. But I'm not leaving just yet because Mr. Fitzmartin needs to be put right about one or two things. I hate loose ends and he needs tying up! And that wasn't meant to be funny.'

Bea and Gwyn both nodded and she said, 'So, Gwyn, you're going out the back way?'

He took hold of both Bea's hands and said, 'Okay, yes, I'm off to do a bit of stalking, see if there's anyone prowling, and I'll be back anon. Let Dana stay in case Jeremy comes with men in white coats. An ex-police officer, an inspector, no less, is a good ally whatever the situation. I'll not be long. Just stay put you two, okay?'

Gwyn hurried to zip his jacket, caught the fabric in the zip's teeth and swore, 'God's Blood!'

'Bit medieval isn't it?' Dana raised her eyebrows. 'And I might be offended.' Her eyes twinkled..

'That's me all right – medieval,' he said. 'Look, I'm sorry if you are offended. As it happens, it was a very bad medieval oath. Just slipped out.' He picked up Nest's oak cudgel, which was by the door, adding as he left, 'Might be useful in a purely medieval manner.'

When he'd gone and they were alone, Dana offered to make tea and Bea nodded.

'Tea, yes thanks.' She moved across to Stella's bed to see her and the pups.

When Dana came back into the main room five minutes later, Bea was nowhere to be seen and the front door was unlatched and ajar.

'Now, where is she?' Dana wondered aloud. She walked out onto the path and looked up and down the beach. She wasn't in sight. There was spray on the air and the wind chased it along the empty beach. 'I'd better stay here. After all, y'never know, Jeremy is off his head and we don't want anything going down with these dogs.'

Just as she turned to go back indoors, she heard a faint bark coming from behind the cottage. She ran around the seaward side and saw Archie's tiny form disappearing over the horizon.

'Oh no! Where's he going? I didn't know he could still run. Pretty fast for an oldie. Bloody dogs; give me cats any day.'

She knew there was no point trying to catch him, and Stella and the litter were indoors. She just hoped nothing bad would happen to the old dog.

Bea had reached the top of the high field by the time Dana returned indoors. She scanned the fields but could see no one, not even Gwyn, who had gone up there before her. She was exhausted and leaned forward, hands on knees, to catch her breath. The wind was noisy, and it wasn't until the little dog jumped up at her leg and barked wheezily that she realised Archie had somehow got out and followed her. She gathered him in her arms, and he licked her face earnestly, then lapsed into coughing for a few seconds.

'Okay now?' she asked him when the fit was done. 'I didn't know you could walk this far, you little sausage. You always make me pick you up.' She ruffled his head affectionately and turned slowly around, searching for any sign of people.

'No one,' she told the dog. 'Doesn't mean they're not there. Goodness; I'll have to sit down a minute, I'm puffed.'

Chapter forty one

Joy

By providence divine…

Prospero – The Tempest

SHE MADE HER WAY to the lee of a broken stone wall, once part of a cottage, and sat down on the seaward side; she pushed Archie under the edge of her coat, but he poked out his head before resting it on the folds of the padding.

'So tired, so tired. Why is it such hard work?' she muttered, and Archie licked his lips, his ears laid back showing his anxiety. He whined and pressed closer to Bea as she fell into the arms of the distant past.

'It is well, Nest,' murmured Chwaer y Ddaear. 'I can see the babe's head. She will soon be in your arms. Take heart.'

Chwaer Dŵr wiped Nest's brow with a cloth soaked in warm water infused with oil of lavender. 'Breath deeply and slowly between the pains, then pant like a dog when they come,' she said and held out her hand for Nest to grip.

Mellt and Seren lay by the fire with their heads on their paws, ears erect and swivelling this way and that, listening intently. They kept their eyes on Nest as she knelt in front of the settle, her forearms rested on the seat, her head hung down on her hands. Chwaer y Ddaear knelt on the floor next to her and rubbed her back as she tensed for another of the pains.

Outside the wind whistled in delight as it raced into the estuary, snatching grass, leaves, sea debris and birds high above the ground to whirl in a mad dance. Chwaer Awyr stood by the open door, her hand on the edge of the frame as she turned to watch Nest.

'The wind is crying your news loud for all to hear, Nest,' she called, laughing. She had been for water to the Faery Well on the top field.

Nest usually drew her water from the stream behind the cottage, but the Sisters wanted spring water to bathe the new little one when she came. It was then that the fishing boats returned on the incoming tide with their catch, so she closed the door for privacy, just catching the happy greetings and busy shouts of instruction as the men moored their boats. Still smiling, Chwaer Awyr poured the water from the bucket into the clean cauldron to warm it.

'How goes it?' she asked the others.

'Tis dreadful hard, Sister,' Nest gasped and stretched her face in a grimace of pain, arched her back away from the heavy pressure that she felt was bearing down on her. 'Surely my belly will rip if the babe doesn't burst out soon?' Nest cried. 'By Our Lady; have I not heard other women say just that many a time,' she said and laughed a little at herself and the others smiled.

Chwaer Tân was sitting on the settle next to Nest and she reached over and drew Nest's long hair away from her neck and plaited it loosely so that she would feel a little cool air.

She said, 'I can see nought from here. How goes it?'

'The babe is impatient to leave the womb. There! A crown of thick hair. It has the tinge of Autumn leaves upon it, wet though it is, Sisters. Nest, do you hear?'

'No!' Nest screamed between her clenched teeth, then after panting heavily she added, 'How can I hear when I am screeching like a gull?'

'Your screams are whispers compared to some. Are you in pain though?' Chwaer Tân asked her. She took the cloth from her sister and wiped her forehead.

Nest couldn't answer. She flailed with her hands, trying to grasp something then as they were offered she took Chwaer Tân's hands and held on until the other woman yelped in pain. 'Is the babe coming?' she asked the others who were able to see.

'Yes, she comes,' they all cried together.

The wolves sat up, cocked their heads, licked their lips as they watched.

Nest gave a mighty groan after the baby's head had appeared and then took in great gulps of air. 'Is she all out then? Is she born yet?'

she gasped.

'Another push, my dear, another great push and she is!' cried Chwiorydd aer. 'Take breath!'

Nest did and in one long rushing movement, the baby slipped from her mother into the waiting arms of **Chwaer y Ddaear** and a warmed cloth.

Later, Nest lay propped on the floor on a pallet heaped with soft pillows and brychans, in front of the fire. The newly bathed child lay swaddled in her arms, the wolves each lay there too with their heads on her legs; she said, 'My babe, Nestie. She has Cormac's colouring. I am glad.'

'She is beautiful, Nest. Look, the sun is at its height,' **Chwaer y Ddaear** said softly. 'She was born to be always in the light,' she added and the others nodded.

There was a knock at the door. The wolves were silent, alert, so the women knew there was no danger and when the door was opened they saw it was the Prince who asked to be allowed in.

When he saw the baby he said, 'Nest could only be more beautiful if there were two of her, and this is how the good God allows such magic. What will she be called?' he asked.

'Nest,' he was told and he nodded, smiling.

Bea smiled too. She felt an insistent movement at her side and laughed when she remembered Archie. He was struggling to extricate himself from the folds of her coat and when she helped him, he tilted his nose to the air and began to growl softly. She lifted him out and set him on the grass so that she could get up herself.

Here I am time travelling again and I only came up here to see if Jeremy was around. Hopefully not. But God, it feels wonderful, really wonderful to have seen that, been there. Bea tugged her coat into shape to make it more comfortable. *What is Archie yelling for?*

He was standing next to her barking insistently, his rough little voice giving way to a cough every few beats. She bent to pick him up again then as she straightened, she scanned the fields. What she saw made her secure the old dog under her arm with the coat tucked under him, holding him in place.

Jeremy was walking towards her across the headland.

Chapter forty-two

'Tis time

Our revels now are ended...

Prospero – The Tempest

'RUNNING AWAY AGAIN?' he called when he got within hailing distance. He looked pleased. The sunlight was in his face and his blond fringe swept roughly across his forehead by the wind. He was dressed for walking and he looked younger, tough.

No one who saw him waving like that, would suspect what hell he can create, just what damage he can do, Bea thought.

She took a couple of paces forward, to face him head on. That felt right. Archie continued to bark. Bea wondered where Gwyn was. She was surprised she wasn't as frightened of Jeremy as she thought she might be, because she had something else on her mind. Although she had just woken up in one sense or returned from the past, as she now thought of her visions, her mind felt wonderfully clear. It was as though her entire being was suffused with joy. Nest had had her baby. And she, Bea had been given the gift of her experiences.

Jeremy shook his head in theatrical disbelief as he came within speaking distance, calling pleasantly, 'Well, there you are, Beatrix. I must say it's increasingly difficult to meet you without the minders. Where's your Welsh lout? Local rugby team practice? Do they use a sheep's head or a brick?'

Bea watched him approach, looked him in the eye. She felt a confidence that she'd forgotten, so when she spoke, she sounded quite different from her recent self.

'I know about Dana, the private detective you hired to follow me. And you are having an affair with Mairi. I don't know why I didn't suspect before.' She viewed him dispassionately, the blindfold gone.

He smiled again, his easy confident smile and he appeared to her to be completely undaunted by her newly acquired knowledge.

'Mmmm, Mrs Smythe, Dana. Yes, well worth the money, not that I've paid her yet and perhaps I shan't as she's spilled the beans, so to speak. Yes, I have been kept up to date on all your little adventures. As I told you, Beatrix, I do need to protect my investment and you're very valuable indeed. I think I've already explained to you. Do keep up, darling. So, no divorce. We're married and it's for better or for worse, well, worse for you obviously. Sounds corny? Maybe, but I care not.' He stood with his hands in his pockets and when his phone rang, he kept his eyes locked on hers as he answered.

'Mairi, my angel?... Yes?... I'm with her now as it happens... On the cliff...Yes, pop up why don't you?' There was a long pause as he listened to Mairi and even with the wind, Bea could hear the tone of her voice, though not the words. She was shrill and furious. Jeremy finished the call by saying, 'Don't let it bother you too much, my sweet. It will all be sorted out. Just come on up here, to the top of the cliff.'

Archie had kept up a steady rumbling growl and as the phone rang, he began to bark furiously, so much so that he kept scrabbling to hold his position wrapped in Bea's coat, only his head showing. She hoisted him up and tightened her grip. She didn't try to stop him barking because she knew how irritating Jeremy found it. She didn't try to move her her own position either, didn't try to run from him, go back to the cottage. She simply stood and watched him.

When he'd finished his call he said, 'If you don't stop that dog, I'll take him from you and throw him off the cliff. I should have done that a long time ago.' His voice was cold and his speech precise.

'No Jeremy, you won't touch him,' Bea said.

'Ah! What's this? An attempt at rebellion?' He laughed heartily. 'Where do you get your ideas from? Is it the locals, or are you invigorated by the sea air?'

Archie quietened his protest to a persistent growl and Bea was able to speak at a more normal pitch. She said, 'I think it's that I'm no longer drugged with – what did you use? Haloperidol? Was that it? I've realised that all my feelings of ill health were side effects, of course they were, each and every one of them. I'm only making a guess at the drug of choice because that's undetectable in a drink, colourless, tasteless. I am a doctor, remember. That's how you've been able to give it to me, isn't it? Was it in the insipid cocoa you forced me to drink? And it's only now I've been here without you for a few days that I've begun to feel my mind and body clear of the sluggishness, the muzzy head, the tremors, the kaleidoscope of anxieties.'

Jeremy smirked and began a slow hand clap applause.

Bea continued, 'Mairi tried to stab me with a syringe full of something; at a guess, more Haloperidol. Am I right?'

'There you go again,' he drawled. 'Paranoia. She wasn't stabbing you; she was injecting you, silly girl. You're ill and she's your psychiatrist.' He laughed lightly, without humour, slightly irritated and impatient. 'Classic denial of illness and need. Beatrix, we're going to get you in Mairi's clinic...' He turned to scan the fields and the beach, and his expression became one of complete satisfaction and he folded his arms across his chest. He had seen Mairi approaching. 'You'll be needing a long-term confinement, probably committal – danger to yourself and the public and all that crap.' He glanced over his shoulder. 'Ah, the lovely Mairi, sylph-like, supple, creative, enthusiastic...' he grinned.

Bea scanned the fields, didn't see any sign of Gwyn, only a smiling Mairi. The sky darkened with heavy iron grey clouds that raced in from the West.

'Hello!' Mairi cried as she came striding along the rough track. 'Am I in time for the entertainment?' She exuded an air of brisk enjoyment, although, as she got closer, Bea saw that the expression in her eyes was one of fury.

Bea watched Mairi and Jeremy together with a strange sense of detachment. There was an air of intimacy about them, certainly, but it wasn't just sexual, it was an intimacy of evil and it was Mairi who looked the more intense of the pair in this respect. Strange not to have noticed it before.

And Bea felt a growing sense of horror as she remembered Jeremy's treatment of her and instantly understood what they were planning now. She shuddered. She was certainly frightened, but it was different from the fear she had usually felt when Jeremy was goading her or hurting her. This time it felt primeval, as though she were faced with predators and she had to fight for her life. She tightened her hold on Archie. He was quivering and kept his eyes on Jeremy.

Still no sign of Gwyn.

Mairi sidled up to Jeremy and linked her arm through his. She shook her head at Bea. 'Bea, you have to face reality. It's time you got what you deserve, which is a lovely psychiatric clinic where you can languish for the rest of your days in a drug induced haze, that or the instant alternative.' She flicked her eyes to the cliff edge.

The sound of the rising waves roared in Bea's ears. In front of her a race of gulls was highlighted vividly against the darkening clouds.

Jeremy patted Mairi's hand. 'My dear, I'm afraid your patient is being difficult,' he told her.

She pouted. 'Now now, Bea, Jeremy needs your money to pay off his gambling debts and I need a big pile of it because I simply adore money.' She caught a lock of hair that escaped from underneath her fur hat and tucked it back. 'Gosh, getting quite wild up here,' she remarked.

Still no Gwyn.

Bea was shocked. 'Gambling? You gamble?' she asked him. It was difficult to image him losing control, being pushed beyond reason, being desperate.

He shrugged. 'Always have. It's exciting, makes me feel alive, and God knows I need to feel something. You're enough to dampen any man's fires, darling. Once I have taken care of you – yes, that is a neat pun – then I shall be on a winning streak again. All will go my way.'

'So that's why you were so evil when you came home from those late-night black-tie events? You said it was the Lodge, some Masonic thing, but you were off gambling, and I expect you lost and just took it out on me?'

'Of course I did. Why shouldn't I? You were simply there for the taking, asking to be punished. Bizarre.' He shrugged.

Bea took a couple of steps forward, further away from the edge of the cliff, about five metres in. She was suddenly sharply aware of the scene she had witnessed when Ithel attacked Nest, probably in this very place. But Jeremy and Mairi moved to block Bea's path.

'Don't leave the party yet, we've only just begun the entertainment.' He pushed her back roughly and she almost lost her footing but hands on her back pushed her gently upright. Bea swung round. It was Mairi standing behind her and before she could turn and escape, she felt her arms gripped.

'Steady on there,' Mairi murmured, smiling. 'Can't have you falling, can we?'

Bea felt a stab of the familiar fear she had whenever Jeremy was close to her, and as she pulled herself out of Mairi's grip she wrapped her arms tightly round Archie which made him wriggle so much that, to her horror she dropped him. He yelped loudly in fear and skittered away from the forest of moving feet.

'Oh, Archie!' she screamed, ran after him, arms outstretched. Mairi began to shriek with laughter and as Bea bent down to encourage the dog to come to her, she put out her foot and tripped her up. Bea crashed down, landed heavily on rough ground, banging her head and cutting her mouth on a rock.

Archie's barks increased in pitch and volume but could only be heard in snatches as the rising wind drowned them out. He was desperate to run to Bea. She was on her hands and knees trying to regain her balance, her head swimming. Archie darted round Jeremy's legs to get to her, but he kicked the dog out of the way. Archie yelped loudly again, this time in pain.

'Archie!' She screamed. 'Stop it! How could you do that? You're a bastard, Jeremy, you know that!' Bea yelled, trying to stand. A sob filled her throat, but the emotion she felt was fury.

'Archie! Archie!' she called, but her voice was snatched by a ferocious blast of wind.

The same gust suddenly snatched Mairi's hat and whirled it off inland and she screeched with laughter. With her hair free she looked a wild figure, the bright mass of it writhing around her head. The dog ignored the tumbling fur globe that was the hat, where normally he would have chased anything bounding past him like that; instead he held up his hind leg, which was hurt. He tried to get near Bea once more, still barking, hysterical.

She was struggling to get her legs under herself. She heard Archie and called again to him, tried to stretch out her hand, but Jeremy kicked that too, with the same power-driven swing a footballer would have used, and Bea cried out in pain, drew her hand to her body. Then, when she was almost on her feet, both Jeremy and Mairi took hold of an arm each and hoisted her up roughly.

'Let go! Get off me!' Bea screamed. 'Let go. What are you doing?' Anger, not fear coursed through her.

'Helping! We're helping!' Mairi shrieked and laughed, all the while pulling at Bea's arm.

'Stop it!' Bea yelled, and threw her body weight sideways at Mairi, only to have her head yanked backwards when Jeremy got hold of her hair. It had been in a loose plait, but the wind had freed it. He wound it round his fist and using that to direct her, he turned her body towards the cliff edge, now four metres away and began to push her. But when Bea pushed her, Mairi had been forced to let go of her arm to avoid falling, so the struggle was momentarily between Bea and Jeremy.

The next second he roared with fury. 'What's that...?' he began and then screamed again. Archie had taken hold of his lower calf, had bitten deeply and was holding on, snarling. 'Get it off, Mairi! Mairi!' he shouted, as he tried to shake his foot from the dog's grip.

But he didn't let go of Bea's hair, rather used it as a lever to pull against and she was dragged and hauled about. She stumbled and tried grabbing his jacket to stop herself falling.

By then the ferocity of the wind and the sea was building. Bea thought she saw a figure moving in the distance, but it was difficult for her to focus clearly because of the position she was in and the fact that the wind was drenching the cliff top with spray as the sea grew tenfold in as many seconds, a giant expanding, filling its lungs.

'I'm coming, I'm coming.' Mairi called.

She managed to push some of her flying hair into her jacket and at the same time frantically searching round for something she could hit the dog with. It wasn't long before her hand landed on a half brick, smoothed by age and she grabbed it. Then, eyes alight with excitement, she crouched like a wrestler, arms out and whipped this way and that, trying to get near enough to the moving mass of figures to hit the dog, who still hung onto Jeremy's leg.

He shouted obscenities and wrenched Bea around unmercifully, all the while trying to loosen the dog's hold, get it off his leg. Archie held on to the top of Jeremy's boot, one of his fangs embedded in the exposed skin, blood drawn by the wind and movement running down his white muzzle. Bea screamed too but the one sound that drowned out all other was the sea and the wind. She managed to get her hands behind her head to grasp Jeremy's ear with one and rake his face with the nails of the other. He roared with pain and anger and yanked her hair viciously until she cried herself.

A huge squall had sprung up and the sky was seal-grey streaked with indigo, shot with flashes of white as the clouds, lit by sheet lightning, careered across the brown horizon. The sea had grown monstrous, colossal waves rolling in, each one higher than the last until at the end of each sequence the biggest wave of all smashed into the cliffs and sent a deluge of spray ten metres inland.

Bea and her attackers were drenched, and little Archie finally let go of Jeremy's leg, stumbling a few paces before falling down, exhausted. His white coat stood out in sharp contrast against the blackened and soaked ground. The shock of the last wave had separated the three people and it was Bea who found her purpose first and half crawled and ran to reach her dog. Mairi was on her before she did, and they grappled ineffectively, neither getting the upper hand.

It was then Bea caught sight of a figure running towards them through the murk.

'Gwyn! Gwyn!' she shouted, and it was that lapse of attention that allowed Mairi to push her to the ground. She slapped her hard across the face and before Bea could react, she straddled her, kneeling on her forearms, all the while struggling to get something from her jacket pocket. Bea screamed and screamed, thrashed her body this way and that, regardless of the pain in her face and head, tried to thump Mairi's back with her knees, to lift her feet up high enough to kick her. It was no use though.

Jeremy had been hit by an enormous wave that crested the top of the little cliff and knocked to his knees. It took him some effort to struggle to his feet and he stumbled, but before the next wave hit, he regained his balance and was up. He pushed Mairi away.

He yanked Bea onto her feet, dragged her towards the edge of the cliff. Once more the waves were building and the wind bellowed, the air was full of water and devils. Bea pulled and fought with all her strength but found she was losing ground. She glanced frantically behind and saw Gwyn fall as he raced towards them. Her heart sank.

She hit Jeremy with her uninjured hand, the other felt useless after she'd raked her nails down his face. She kicked him and even managed to bite his arm, but still, roaring maniacally, his features contorted beyond any recognition, he pulled her on.

Bea was at the last of her strength when Gwyn crashed into them. She heard him yelling incoherently and furiously, no words, just noise then she fell backwards and crawled away from the edge, frantic to get away and to get Archie.

Gwyn and Jeremy fought, locked together, pushing, snatching, pummelling; their faces were masks of horror. They were on the very edge of the cliff on a patch of slick turf when another wave hit them. It separated them for a second and there followed a moment of timelessness when the eyes of the two men locked, both suspended in the middle of their movements, neither knowing which direction death lay.

And then Jeremy was gone.

Gwyn fell back onto the gritty land and the spray pounded his still body.

The next he knew his head was cradled on Bea's lap and she was trying to bend and kiss him, sobbing and crying as she did. She'd got Archie and she could feel him shaking and when she opened her coat, she caught the faint sound of him whimpering.

'Oh, don't cry, Archie, don't cry. You're safe now.'

The first thing Gwyn said was, 'I'm not crying, I'm not…Bea, Bea! Are you all right? Is he gone?'

Bea's laugh was a sob. 'I was talking to Archie and yes, he's gone! He's gone, Gwyn.'

'That woman?'

'Ran away!'

Chapter forty-three

That instant

Of the very instant that I saw you,

Did my heart fly at your service

Ferdinand - The Tempest

NEST GAVE THE BOWL a half turn and set the waters swirling gracefully around. She rested her hands on the rim and took a soft breath to compose her mind, then looked deep into the water mirror. At first, her own face was reflected faithfully and clearly, and she saw her fatigue in the too shadowed eyes, paler cheeks and the long tendrils of hair that escaped her usual neat coronet of plaits. But she smiled at herself.

'All is well. 'Tis the exhaustion of a new mother and I am overjoyed to feel it. I, a mother, the mother of Nestie. She is but one day old and she glows with beauty, everyone says so. Every mother says so of her own too!'

She glanced down at the crib next to her, where, on a new fleece, lay her baby. Her friend Madoc, the netmaker, had woven the rush crib specially for her and Joanna herself had sent the fleece and swaddling clothes from the royal nursery, and a tiny silver bracelet. Joy and contentment eddied around her as the waters in the bowl moved and she searched the glossy wavelets for sight of someone she had come to value very much.

'Is she there? Is she content now, as I am?' she asked the waters and saw the picture coming together, searched into the future, even as she considered events that had gone before.

I have not often travelled thus, onward in time's layered halls. Chwaer y Ddaear, it was, helped me open my inner eyes to see time unfold. What a wonder. Once I saw a distant daughter, with her own

Nestie and the hens and I felt blessed by the good God. They were outside this very cottage with a small white dog, such as she, Beatrix, has. And it is Beatrix, Bea, I seek now. Where is she? I must concentrate. She is of my line, one of my decendents and she was sore troubled and belittled by deceit. Oh, how my heart feared when I saw her enemies plotting and a foul death waiting. Chwaer y Ddaear, blessed friend, watched over her then with the Sisters, even as Bea watched me, and we saw her courage grow, saw her tormenters vanquished, even as in a battle.

But now, now she rests and gathers herself for a new challenge. She found friends, true ones, and she allowed them to help her. Now I see her on the very brink of something entirely new. But what am I thinking? She knows love already, not the blindness of infatuation, but the great love she bore her parents, and Nest of that time, the selfless love she has for her animals. Love comes in many forms and she is offered this new one.

Nest reached down to where her wolves lay pressed against the crib. She sank her fingers into the soft fur of their great necks and both gazed up at her, licked their lips in deference and love.

'Mellt, Seren, my great ones, we have Nestie to care for now,' she murmured and they both lay their heads down again, contentedly.

Nest turned her focus to the waters once more.

'Ah, the dunes and their dancing grasses, there in the path of the salt laden wind. And the man, Gwyn, who looks like a son of Llewelyn, strong, dark, menacing – except when teased.' She smiled. 'There she is...' Nest murmured and looked deep into the vision.

Bea sat on the very top of the dunes, gazing out to sea and muffled to the ears with a scarf and new coat. Thomas had bought it from a local market, a thick ski jacket in sea blue. It was a gift and he took away her old padded one to dispose of because he said it would be like wrapping herself in a bad memory, because she'd worn it on the cliff that awful day. She sat cross-legged and rested her chin on her hands and Archie sat between her legs, perched on her woolly hat. She was thinking about Jeremy.

He was my husband and I am glad with all my heart that he's dead. I can't feel anything but that. And I'm okay with the thought and it sounds bad, even if you say it to yourself. That's how I feel just now…. He was evil, and he was going to kill me. He sure as hell hurt Arch. That's another thing to wrestle with, the fact that someone hates you so much they actually plan to kill you, not kill you in a fit of passionate rage, but plan it coldly. He almost managed it. If it hadn't been for Gwyn… and Archie – he slowed Jeremy down, gave Gwyn time to get there. And Stella; she saved me from Mairi.

'Here you go. Tea,' Gwyn said, handing her a mug he had filled from a flask. 'Penny for the thoughts then?' he added and sat down next to her.

'I'm glad Mairi's dead too,' she said.

'Ah, yes. So that's what's on your mind. She didn't get far, did she, after she ran off? Apparently didn't even look left as she pulled out onto the main road. The artic bent its front bumper, but the Range Rover was a write-off, I hear. Waste of a brand-new car!'

'She tried to kill me, Gwyn.'

'I guess it's hard to come to terms with, something like that.' He became serious, took her hand. 'But she died instead. Rolled over several times, thrown out of the car and landed with her face in that pool. Death by drowning, they said at the inquest. Ironic after they tried to throw you in the sea. No blame attached to the lorry driver, not speeding; witnesses said she pulled out. She was running from the scene of an attempted murder, don't forget. I'd say she got what was coming to her. I don't want to gloat over a death like that, but she wanted to well and truly profit from yours. Stark raving bonkers? Was she? Or was it pure evil? I think it was that. And The Arse, death by misadventure. Weird description. It sounds like the adventure didn't work out the way you wanted, which I suppose his adventure didn't.'

She looked at her hands, as they stroked Archie. 'Don was inconsolable and so shocked. He'd had no idea about her and Jeremy until just recently. That was when he followed her to the car park, and you saw them. I think he believed me that I didn't know anything either. Do you think so?' She searched his face for the truth.

'Definitely. I had a chat to him. Nice bloke. And the police attached no blame to us for Jeremy's death. No other witnesses. No one would have believed a tale of him trying to throw you off the cliff anyway. There was a storm and he fell. What was more awful was what he did to you all that time.'

She was quiet, trying not to remember.

'It's only been a fortnight, Bea. Are you feeling a little more in this world yet? By the way, great up here, isn't it?'

She stroked Archie. 'Yes, it is, and yes a little. I think Arch is too. I can't forget him screaming when he saw Jeremy, but animals can live for the moment and he's happy now. He's dropped ten years since we've been here.'

'Must be the influence of a good woman.'

'You mean Stella and the kids, the ready-made family, now he's been promoted to step-dad and no longer just uncle.'

Gwyn laughed. 'I meant you, Bea – the good woman.'

She laughed too. 'Aww – sweet.' She glanced over her shoulder at him and saw the expression on his face. 'Oops. You're serious.'

'Indeed. But as you are determined to be flighty, I have to tell you that I can go off people.' He raised his mug to take a drink. 'You know how to squash an ego, my girl.'

She became serious in a second. 'I'm an emotional wreck, Gwyn. I really feel like I'm going to take a long time to recover. Don't get me wrong. I'm not wallowing in self pity here. I know I've gone off medicine, at least hospital practice, for now. Maybe I'll return to a different branch when I feel more together. For now, I've resigned. I've paid off all Jeremy's debts and put the house up for sale. I'm not even going back. I've sent my mum's solicitor, family friend, to sort all the official papers and he's getting a firm to clear the contents. But all that's worn me out.'

'Money? What about money to live on?'

'Mum was famous. I'll tell you details another time. I've got money, don't worry. And I've got this lovely place to live and all the dogs now. What worries me is how long will it be before I feel like moving on with my life, not looking over my shoulder, not hearing his voice in my head telling me I'm fat, disgusting and inadequate, but with big words?'

She gave him a faint smile. 'How long before I feel better? A month? A year? Hey?'

'Maybe a lifetime. Things are bound to come back to you, but in time they will be less acute. I'm guessing. They're part of your past, but the important thing is you handled it. You fought back, escaped, stood up to him here. He didn't take your soul. He hurt you, sure. But you've got friends and you have love - the animals I mean,' he added hastily. 'And you've had, or still have that gift of seeing the past, the distant past. That's beyond wonderful. Maybe the huge emotional turmoil opened up your other senses.'

'I hadn't realised how emotionally mature you are.' She looked taken aback.

'Me neither, if I'm honest. So, I'll do what emotionally mature people do and change the subject.' He pushed his dark hair from his face. 'So, are you going to become a medical herbalist or something, like Nest – our Nest I mean? Didn't you say she had a book of all her cures and recipes?'

'I don't know yet, Gwyn. I've read through her book. And that's another thing I'll always be grateful for; I had Auntie Nest in my life; we were very close. I learned more about caring for people from her and Mum than anyone else. That's an important part of being a good doctor, having that instinct for people, a sensitivity, empathy. Well, that and everything else, the scientific side. That's what I noticed about Auntie Nest's Herbal, all the recipes were very precise, loads of notes about adverse reactions and side effects.'

'I'd like to have a look at that.'

'Sure. Oh, and there's something else you'd be interested in; she had a little book of prayers somewhere; it'd be quite old; I guess more in your line of work. All gold and hand painted. She called it a psalter.'

Gwyn had spluttered suddenly into his beaker of tea.

'Do you know about those things? Gwyn? Gwyn? You all right?'

He was taken with a fit of coughing and the tea in his beaker sloshed out as he shook. He managed to clear his throat and took hold of Bea's arms to look into her face.

'Let's get this straight. Nest, your Nest, had a psalter; you have it, an illuminated, handwritten psalter?' His voice was quiet.

'Somewhere. I haven't come across it yet though. And I seem to remember that Llewelyn's Nest was given one by the Abbot at Penmon – which would make it…'

Nest bent her face close to the water mirror, 'Yes, yes, it is mine!'

'A 13th century illuminate psalter. My, my, my; that'd be a turn up for the books, probably worth hundreds of thousands of pounds…'

'If we find it. And I'd probably want to keep it; after all, if it did belong to the first Nest, it's lived in the cottage a long time.'

He looked at her a long time, smiling. 'You're right, and "Her worth is far above rubies…" Nest, I mean. And you.'

Bea smiled. The wind was strong and offshore as the tide turned.

'Now I'm going to show my emotional maturity again; must be careful not to wear it out - Lorcan and Dana? Yeah?' he gave a suggestive grin.

'What?'

'Y'know…seeing each other.' He tried a theatrical wink. 'She's applying to Bangor as a mature student doing a BSc in Marine Biology, as per what she said. Oh, and she's going to sell her wildlife photos, which are spectacular; I'm buying one of the oystercatchers winging it past my cottage; having it blown up and on a giant canvas. And Lorcan's going to be around to help her with her studies; he's doing home-based research for the government, litter and stuff. Heather's delighted; Thomas told me everything; so all's well with the world.'

'And he's better now. I love Thomas like a second dad really.'

'Everybody's loved up. Heather loves minding the pups, as does Archie. She's only given us an hour for this breath of fresh air, then she has to do some calls, I believe; cows and TB tests or flying llamas or something.'

Bea stared at him. 'Are you growing a moustache?'

'I might be. Why?'

When you turned then, you looked just like Llewelyn, a young Llewelyn.'

'Really? Great. My hero. Speaking of which. Is Lorcan having the littlest pup?'

'Yes, he's to be called Cormac, a fine Irish handle. He's shot up though. Heather is having the one with the ginger bit on her tail; Alis, she is. Dana is having the one with the white bit on his chest, Bill. And that leaves me and Archie, and Stella with the little bitch. I'm calling her Sky. All accounted for.'

'They've only just opened their eyes; two and a bit weeks old. What a time that was! Remember?'

'How could I forget? You came over to be my minder.'

'Llewelyn looked after Nest, didn't he?' He stared at her pointedly, but she gazed at the distant lilac horizon.

'Tide's going out fast.'

'Okay, child, change the subject,' he muttered and sighed. 'What are you going to do with your time whilst you recover or whatever; before you start your career as an apothecary? Anything? Maybe veg-out on the beach?'

'Cheeky. What's wrong with beachcombing? You have an easy time of it strolling about in front of a camera, chatting about medieval remains. That can't be hard. No need to pretend you are outraged. Anyway, I'm going to write an historical romance, based in 13th century Anglesey. It's all in my head; a love story about Llewelyn Fawr and Nest of the Shore. I can write, Mum always said I could, and I've got her typewriter and it's guaranteed to produce a best seller for me!'

Gwyn moved closer to Bea, took Archie from his place and put him on his own knee. 'A love story? You said I look like him and you know you look like Nest, Llewelyn's Nest, and all the others…'

'And…?' Bea pulled her hair from her face, not without a fight as the wind had suddenly snatched it up.

'From the minute I saw…The first time…No, that won't do at all….' He smiled at her. '"Of the very instant that I saw you, did my heart fly at your service".'

'Ferdinand to Miranda. *The Tempest*.' Bea smiled at him. 'And I think the same could be said by Llewelyn to Nest.'

'It was, it was,' Nest whispered to the water mirror.

'Can the same be said by you to me?' Gwyn turned to face Bea. Archie got off his knee with a grunt and went to sniff at some sea pinks.

'Yes, it can,' Nest whispered. 'It can.'

'Llewelyn's going to say it to Nest in my story. I'm going to make it later in his life, when his wife has died, and Nest needs him once more.'

'Can she see into my own future time?' Nest wondered. Her hands gripped the bowl. It was very quiet in the cottage save for the gentle, steady breathing of the wolves and the babe. The fire crackled on the hearth and small creatures rustled amongst the roof turf; homely sounds of contentment.

Gwyn put out his hand and turned Bea's face towards him.
'Don't avoid the question. Can it?'
He bent and kissed her gently on the lips.
'Yes,' Bea said. 'I think so, Gwyn.'
He kissed her again and she said, 'Yes, I can.'
'What are you going to call your book?'
She answered without hesitation. 'Llewelyn and Nest.'

Nest herself sat back contented. She touched a finger to the water to still it. *May they be blessed with love and a child, as am I.*

Outside the oystercatchers trilled in the evening air and baby Nestie stirred in her crib.

Gwyn got up, offered his hand to help Bea up, and when she stood, he kissed her again.

'Is this a beginning then?' he asked.

'It's the beginning of our story, I think. I hope,' she said.

After a time, they turned to make their way slowly back through the dunes to the river when suddenly they both stopped, arrested by the sight of two figures, faint in the light and moving before them.

A man and a woman. They walked close together, the man's arm round the woman's waist. The wind took their cloaks and her unbound hair and made them banners in the sunlight.

Gwyn was awed. 'Llewelyn and Nest. Can you see them? Tell me you can,' he whispered.

'Oh, yes, I can see them, Gwyn.' Bea said. 'They are together.'

*****

Author's note

Anglesey is not my home, but is second only to that home. It's a place of dreams, a magical isle where the spirit expands and the heart is light. For many years my family and I stayed in a holiday cottage on the beach at Aberffraw, and it was there that I imagined this story, imagined a life for that cottage where the tide comes in almost to the garden wall.

The estuary at Aberffraw, the surrounding land and the village are as I have described them, but I have taken creative licence to add a bigger rise to the land and a cliff where, in the story, so much happens.

The cottage stands at the mouth of the estuary and when the tide comes in and the river meets the sea, the water spreads out as far as the dunes opposite. At other times, the river is a crystal streamlet running away from the village. Stand by the cottage wall with your back to Aberffraw and look out to sea, and the view before you has probably not changed for a thousand years or more. Yes, the dunes are regularly sculpted by the wind and the waves change the river's path a little each year; the marram grass grows and the gorse is always bright yellow .

But I wondered about the people who saw this view a thousand years ago and then I discovered that Wales' greatest Prince, Llewelyn Fawr, had his favourite court, right here - just eight hundred years ago.

Nothing remains of this llys, this court, but I was hooked on his story. There are many excellent history books that present the facts and I've faithfully used only those recorded facts: his long reign, his family, his relationship with England, the culture, commerce and politics of medieval Britain at the time, both inside a royal court and for the ordinary people.

Llewelyn's wife, the Princess Joanna, did have a relationship with an English noble and he was indeed executed by the Prince. Llewelyn outlived his wife, and a carved stone sarcophagus, considered to be hers was found in a pasture on the island. It had been used as a water trough, but is now secure in the porch of St Mary and St Nicholas Church in Beaumaris.

Beaumaris and its unfinished castle did not exist in Llewelyn's time but Llanfaes did. In those days it was an important medieval port town and the Prince endowed the Friary there in Joanna's memory. The site remains, as does the church of St Seiriol at Penmon and part of Penmon Priory's buildings, along with all the names of the rivers, mountains and the land itself. So today, it's possible to visit all of the places in this story and envision the vibrant life there eight hundred years ago.

I had read the recorded history of Llewelyn the Great, and decided to write a story with him as one of the main characters, and of course, I had to imagine what the man was like. I also wondered who might have lived in a cottage by the sea in Aberffraw in the 13th century. What would the cottage have been like, if it was there at all? Would the Prince have known the person who lived there?

Christianity was well established in Llewelyn's time, and I visited the church that was built then, St. Beuno's in Aberffraw. But there is much folk law evidence to say that people still regarded the old gods and the religion of a thousand years before that when the Romans came and drove out the Druids. The natural world was an important part of medieval life, and although all medicines relied on the use of herbs, minerals and other natural products, many people believed that such cures were made more potent with the addition of spells and magic.

This research led me to the very person I needed to live in the cottage by the sea; she would be a wise woman, practised in healing and one who was sensitive and skilled with the supernatural gifts. I called her Nest, a popular Welsh name then, and imagined her as one of Prince Llewelyn's loves.

For the modern day characters I remembered the peace to be had in that cottage. Then I found someone who would run there when she needed a refuge. I imagined Bea, and her reasons for escape. She's a doctor, intelligent, independent and modern, but that didn't prevent someone significant in her life abusing her.

As for the concept of a time slip, I've long been interested in the idea that time exists in overlapping layers and that past events may be recorded in the very rocks and buildings where they took place.

Einstein said, '...the distinction between past, present and future is only a stubbornly persistent illusion.' I believe that too.

Shakespeare believed in magic, or at least the power it can hold over people. In *The Tempest* he imagined a magical isle and although it's thought Prospero's isle was off the coast of Italy, near Naples, I always wonder whether Shakespeare ever visited Anglesey and made this his magical isle.

And, like Shakespeare, maybe each of us has a special magical place, even if it is solely in our own imagination.

*****